Philip Boast is the author of *London's Child*,
*London's Milli*_____ ___ _____ ____
is also the auth___
saga, and *Prid*____
Australia. He li____
and their three ____

Also by Philip Boast

London's Child
London's Millionaire
London's Daughter

Watersmeet
Pride
City

Gloria

Philip Boast

HEADLINE

First published in 1994
by HEADLINE BOOK PUBLISHING

First published in paperback in 1994
by HEADLINE BOOK PUBLISHING

10 9 8 7 6 5 4 3 2 1

ISBN 0 7472 4555 X

Typeset by Keyboard Services, Luton, Beds

Printed and bound in Great Britain by
Cox & Wyman Ltd, Reading, Berks

HEADLINE BOOK PUBLISHING
A division of Hodder Headline PLC
338 Euston Road
London NW1 3BH

For my mother-in-law,
Joan

PART I

The Face of an Angel

Chapter One

Friday, 6 July 1900

It was evening in London after the fifth blazing hot day in a row, so that even the shadows felt hot by now, and through the open door Gloria watched the locomotives roaring and lumbering like dinosaurs beside the airless platforms. Above their shimmering green flanks the glass roof of Marylebone Station, newly built and kept proud and shining by teams of Great Central Railway workmen, glared like the sea with the last rays of the sun, casting a shifting illumination on the steaming, smoking scene below.

It was the same old London story, she saw; the end of another day. The commuters had fled the heat like a shoal of minnows, top hats into First Class, bowlers to Second, billycocks in Third – the workmen's trains departed later, and would return earlier. In the shop, the suffocating gaslights flared and glimmered, and Gloria's broom swept the door shut behind the last customer. With luck, she thought, any more'll think the place is closed. Slipping to the shop window, she peered out again, as she always did when her duties would permit –

when she thought she could get away with it, in other words.

'It must be nearly time ter go 'ome, fer God's sake!' she said.

'Yer know wot 'appens ter people wot take His name in vain,' said Doris behind the counter.

'It can't be worse than this,' Gloria said, glancing back, and the sun flashed a brassy nimbus in her blonde hair. She was slim and strong-featured, with a lively and direct blue gaze that caught you straight in the eye.

Gloria Simmonds was taller by a head than Doris – she was taller, for that matter, than her own father, who was a drayman for the Railway – but she'd inherited his high cheekbones, and their strength looked lovely on a tall girl in the first flush of adulthood, giving the corners of those wide-open, innocent eyes a bewitching slant. Her eyebrows were almost black, sweeping firmly into the bright curls on her forehead. Her mother's height, her father's stubbornness, and his temper too – you could see it rise in her colour, everyone said that. For now her breasts were flattened by the dowdy Great Central Railway dress, and frumpish petticoats brushing the floor hid her long legs, but they were easy to imagine from the way she moved. Most men thought that was all there was to her.

Gloria was seventeen years old, and she had been standing up for the last fourteen hours. She stared longingly from the shop window, her right hand still by habit working the broom for the soothing *swish, swish* noise so that the old bastard, Mr Samson Hullabye – who was at least forty years old – wouldn't come bristling from the back office.

Through the ripply shop glass the shadowed concourse under its lid of sunlight seemed a strange, pressurised, underwater place to her eyes, the long-distance railway travellers moving in slow motion through the heat as if half walking and half swimming. They were of the class that dressed up for travel: mothers in overcoats and hats dripping flowers, wilting nannies towing toddlers who wore skirts whatever their sex, their breeched elder brothers strolling in tweeds just like Papa's. The sight of the children filled Gloria with pity: their lives were as privileged as her own had been, as organised, as lucky, and as empty; and most of them would grow up to realise it as little as Doris Mabb.

'Lend us yer finger on the string 'ere,' Doris said. 'Ta.'

Incredibly, Gloria marvelled, Doris was still tying granny knots around stock to be returned, as she had been all day between customers and fawning on Hullabye. She was dull as dishwater, without vitality or wonder but always busy as a bee, her thin pallid face framed by lifeless mousy hair which smelt of carbolic soap. They were exactly the same age and their mums were friends: Mrs Mabb and Mrs Simmonds were always calling up and down stairs and popping round for a chat, making up for the life they didn't have with their husbands. Little Doris seemed to have been born with an invisible sucker, and would attach herself like a barnacle to a chosen object, never to let go. Whenever Gloria came around the corner, Doris seemed to be there.

If Gloria were alone sleepily flicking pebbles into the Regent's Canal one afternoon and someone sat down behind her, it would be Doris. And when Gloria started at the Railway shop just before Christmas last year, Doris's smile greeted her from behind the counter.

''Allo, stranger!' Doris had waved.

You couldn't complain. Doris was what she was: a pain in the neck.

Gloria went back to the window and Doris followed her with her eyes. 'Wot're yer looking fer?'

Gloria didn't reply.

Doris copied Gloria when they were children, modelled herself on Gloria as they grew up, made girl friends she would never have made but for Gloria who knew *everyone*, silently envied Gloria who lived a charmed life with three brothers and a sister in one of the best four-bedroom flats the Gardens could offer – which was fine indeed. Gloria's father obviously adored her and she had a mum who kept her peace (Doris's mum was an indomitable scold who had driven her dad to the bottle). Gloria was everything that Doris, in her adolescence, dreamed of being, Gloria hared through life: golden-hearted Gloria with the face of an angel.

Without brothers or sisters, alone in her bedroom with her thoughts, Doris had dreamed of Gloria's face in her mirror, imagining those gorgeous slanted eyes were her own. Sometimes Doris actually distorted her features with her hands and fingers, as if Gloria's face lay beneath her own dry skin and would break through like the sun – she stared at herself until her mother called through the door,

'Wot the blooming 'eck yer getting up ter in there!' It was obvious to everyone that Gloria would make a success of her life, she was so at the centre of things. Doris's circle of friends, good solid girls such as Sally Kean and Molly Flitch and all the like-minded young ladies of the Wharncliffe Gardens Railway Settlement, had great expectations. A girl had to get on in the world, and Gloria, everyone agreed, was just the girl to do it. Success meant a husband, a family, and a Wharncliffe Gardens flat with at least three bedrooms: one for Mum and Dad, one for sons, and one for daughters. Wharncliffe Gardens girls married Wharncliffe Gardens boys, a place for everyone and everyone in their place.

But no one had warned them that their innocent adolescent bodies would betray them with frightening drops of blood, or that at the same time as they became attractive to men they would become ugly to themselves. *By their rags ye shall know them*: these were words straight from the pulpit, they must be true. They were the children of Eve.

But Gloria had laughed – as she laughed at everything – at Doris Mabb's guilt, and at Doris's awareness of sin flourishing in the dirty festering sidestreets surrounding Marylebone Station and Wharncliffe Gardens. To Gloria everything was a lark, she was friendly with everyone – too friendly, Doris decided. Nothing touched that girl, Doris realised with secret resentment, Gloria was all bubble and no brain. And Gloria's laugh was much too loud. The other girls might have decided that Gloria was born to make a fine wife to a fine husband, but Doris held her tongue, demurring from their gossip in the most effective way, with silence. Excited, they wondered what she knew that they didn't, and the less Doris said, the more they read into her words.

Doris had started at the Railway shop six months earlier than Gloria, who was stuck at home nursing her poorly little brother. For the first time Doris began to feel herself Gloria's superior. Doris had a pay packet, she gave it all to her mum, she paid her way: Gloria didn't. By the time Gloria joined, Doris knew that the race of life is won by the tortoise, not the hare. All the things that once had counted in Gloria's favour, her lovely face and her kindness, her sense of life and her vivacity, counted against her here. Here, in the Railway's world of iron schedules, kindness was called softness, vivacity was unladylike, laughter an affront. Their friendship didn't work so well now the boot was on the other foot, but Doris wasn't about to give up her advantage after all those years in Gloria's shadow.

'There's more dirt in the corner,' she pointed out. Gloria gave her a look, but she was the one with the broom. 'Don't be like that!' Doris said busily, enjoying herself, impregnable behind the closed counter-flap, 'yer'd rather it was I wot told yer than Mr 'Ullabye, now wouldn't yer? Fings 'ave got ter be done proper. I dunno know what yer find to look at frough that window.'

But Gloria continued to stare out. Beyond the glass was the real London, she knew: the mysterious, romantic city of coming-and-goings and hither-and-thither, of teeming life, passing them by. Grimy-faced porters plodded the tarry concourse, weary as donkeys in their green GCR jackets and baggy trousers that didn't show the dirt, yawning and scratching their elbows while they waited for the last big departure of the day, all of them like uncles to her. By the barriers, watchful passenger guards circled in their tailored green uniforms with gilt buttons, GCR woven in gold thread on their green caps. The initials GCR were wrought into the iron of every green-painted railing, GCR embossed on every carriage and seat-cover, even branded into the handle of her broom. There has to be more to being alive than this, she thought.

In the shop the quivering gaslights hissed like snakes.

'Phew,' Gloria swore, pulling at her green woollen dress stamped with GCR on her left breast. 'If it gets any 'otter in 'ere, I'll melt. I can feel the sweat running down me legs, Dor.'

'Don't talk ugly,' Doris said. 'Yer can't shock me, I know yer too well.'

'Do yer?'

'I know that demon in yer smile.' But Doris didn't sound nervous. She sounded self-satisfied and in control.

Gloria squashed her nose against the glass, making a flattened expression that delighted one of the toddlers; no one else noticed her. She squinted through one eye to get the angle on the station clock hanging high above the shop. *GCR* was gilded elegantly across its face as though the Great Central Railway owned time itself. It showed three minutes to eight.

With a grin she held up three fingers to Doris, but the

swish, swish of the broom in her other hand never changed its rhythm.

'Gawping out that window when there's work ter be done!' groused Doris. 'Wot yer playing at? Yer like a cat on 'ot bricks terday, *and* yer were late ter work again, but I didn't say a word ter a soul, did I?' She could keep up this toneless grumble for hours, and she did, like a weary old horse plodding in front of a cart. Everything she had once admired in Gloria she now held against her. 'Because of me yer get away wiv everyfink. I wish *I* did. Why can't yer be yer age like everyone else? If Mr 'Ullabye told yer Dad 'ow yer always a thousand miles away out that window, 'e'd throw seven fits—'

'Me Dad wouldn't 'ear a word against 'is little girl!' Gloria said.

'Sssh.' Doris threw a speaking look at the back room that served as Mr Hullabye's office. Through the quarter-open door they saw the roll-top desk with the bottle of stout on it, which hardly left room for his chair or the waste-basket with the whisky bottle in it – the poor man hadn't been the same since his wife died, Doris knew; his tippling wasn't his fault. And all men drank, it was expected of them. Doris worried all the time about what Mr Hullabye, who had so many troubles, would think of her if he came out and caught them chattering, so that even his absence dominated her. Her fingers fretted the *Strand* magazine into a neat stack, just as he liked it, to please him when he appeared.

'Do yer fink 'e misses 'er terribly?' she whispered.

''E didn't miss 'er much when she was alive,' Gloria

sighed. 'Yer don't make it any better fer 'im wearing yer long face, make 'im weep ter look at yer I should fink. Be cheerful, cheer 'im up.'

'Yer got ter treat grief wiv respect.'

''E never looks that miserable ter me.'

'Yer left yer nosy mark on that window!' Doris hissed, as though it was the end of the world. Gloria grinned, then wiped a cloth on the glass with the same rhythm she used for the broom.

'Two minutes,' she said. The Railway organised their lives to the second, and that was the way most people liked it.

'Yer shouldn't look forward ter stopping work,' Doris said, bossy because Gloria had disagreed with her about Mr Hullabye, when Doris knew she understood him better than anyone.

Behind Gloria there sounded a piercing, superheated scream, then smoke came churning from one of the huge old MS & L locomotives, newly repainted and gleaming in its Great Central Railway livery. The 7.59 p.m. was about to depart on its hundred-mile journey to Leicester, signalling almost the end of the day, and Gloria held up her thumb irreverently, counting down.

Oblivious to the busy hubbub on the concourse, the dark figure of a man waited without moving by one of the pillars. He ignored the row of large Bibles fastened on chains for the use of passengers waiting for their trains; his face was buried in a newspaper. He did not turn the pages, absorbed in his reading of the tiny print. A well-dressed woman, late for her train, strode past him chivvying a crying child. The

11

guard's whistle blew, carriage doors slammed. The man was still there, navy blue working jacket, heavy serge trousers. Gloria's counting faltered as she watched him. His hands were blistered, the knuckles skinned. There was clay on his boots.

The train departed and silence fell.

When the steam cleared he was no longer there. The concourse was almost empty.

Gloria raced her broom up the aisle, gave it a final swish, then ticked off the last seconds to eight o'clock on her fingers.

'It's eight, Mr 'Ullabye!' she called, breaking the rules, but only a grunt came in response from the tiny office. He'd keep them in deliberately now.

'Yer blooming idiot! Wot's yer 'urry, Gloria?' Doris asked, then her eyes glinted suspiciously. 'Yer 'aven't got anyone tucked away we don't know about, do yer?'

But that was unthinkable. Wharncliffe Gardens families kept themselves to themselves, an island of Anglican prosperity in the Roman Catholic sea of Lisson Grove.

'Yer a one ter talk,' Gloria shot back. 'I saw Brewer's boy walked yer 'ome last night.'

Doris preened. He had fallen into step beside her, Mr Brewer's cock-of-the-walk son with his clean fingernails – her, Doris Mabb! Probably he was at a loose end (she had been honest enough to admit to her pillow), because he could choose any girl he wanted, (and did), and he was just a dream, but with each footstep Doris had swelled with pride, and now she was thrilled to talk about him. 'Do yer fink 'e really likes me?'

'Wot's important is wot do yer fink of 'im,' Gloria said. 'That Charlie's got an 'igher opinion of 'imself than I 'ave, I reckon.'

'Just because 'e 'asn't asked *you* out!' Doris pouted. ''E's got prospects, I know that much, 'is Dad's a foreman, 'e don't work wiv 'is own 'ands. Wot do yer know about men anyway? Yer too clever by 'alf, Gloria Simmonds. Well, yer not too good fer me.'

'All right, the sun shines out of Charlie Brewer's ear'oles, if that's the way yer want it!'

'Yer'd do better if yer buckled down,' Doris advised triumphantly. 'Yer won't be young long and there's bad types around. Only a good reliable woman gets what she deserves, remember.'

Gloria sighed, knowing what good, reliable women got: they got wedding bells, babies, and no more life for themselves. The thought of marrying someone with a life like her dad's filled her with dread. But even at the Emmanuel Girls' School, a dutiful little mouse sitting at the desk behind Gloria's own, Doris had had wedding bells on the brain. It had been Doris who got hit by most of the books thrown at Gloria by Miss Miller.

'A good, reliable woman deserves a good, reliable *husband*.' Doris pronounced the divine word with an aitch, just like the Reverend Vezey-Mason did. To Doris, anything muttered in an upper-class Oxford accent from the pulpit of the Emmanuel Anglican was tantamount to being a pronouncement from the mouth of God. 'Husband, father, breadwinner.'

Gloria knew Doris was right, but before she could admit it Mr Hullabye came out of the back office. 'Late in, so you'll be late out!' he said, tapping his fob-watch. He was an angular, sour-faced man with black hair strapped across the top of his head, and he wore a black suit to show he was a manager employed by the Railway, not a common tradesman. 'I know you girls backwards! Two minutes late this morning, one of you, and you tried to keep it secret between yourselves, but don't think I don't know everything.' He was clipping his words to show he hadn't been drinking.

'Yes, Mr 'Ullabye,' Doris said when she should have kept her trap shut. She couldn't help drawing attention to herself. He stood beside her *Strand* magazines without noticing them, then brushed against her as he lifted the counter-flap.

Doris knew his roving hands and hated their slyness, but she told herself it was her fault for being in his way all the time: his fingers couldn't help brushing against her dress when he squeezed past her behind the counter – it was so cramped that she couldn't blame him. In a way, being a widower, he was an excellent prospect, and at least he had noticed her as a woman. Whenever stock had to be lifted on to the top shelf Doris was ashamed of her raised arms revealing the curve of her bosoms to his gaze, so she usually asked Gloria to stand in for her, pretending she felt giddy or had a headache. Gloria could fall in a mud puddle and come up smelling of roses, Doris knew, and *she* chatted to Hullabye without a care in the world. But Doris couldn't lift a finger without provoking the older man's attention that she secretly desired, and now her cheeks wore a flush and she fell silent.

'Another day, another day's pay,' Gloria yawned, closing her eyes. She put up her arms and ran her hands through her hair. Sam Hullabye stood close to her, drawing in the scent of her, and Doris looked up under her lashes. He had eyes only for Gloria, Doris realised with a jolt, not for her.

Doris stared at Gloria, shocked.

After the burning day the deserted concourse stank strongly enough of tar and steam and coal-smoke to constitute a medical remedy. 'Two minutes late for work,' Gloria mimicked loudly, pinning on her straw cap with a single jab as she came out of the shop, 'so yer can't leave till two minutes late! 'Ow blooming trady can yer get?' Doris, following, said nothing, so Gloria faced her. 'Wot's up?'

'Cat can look at a queen,' Doris said.

There was no sign of the man who had so stood out among the smart passengers with his blistered hands and clay-stained boots. 'Thanks fer covering fer me when I was late this morning,' Gloria said.

Oversleeping was a dismissal offence. 'That's wot we're 'ere fer, Gloria,' Doris said heavily, 'so yer can get yer beauty sleep.'

'Look!' Gloria pointed at Hullabye shutting up shop. ''Ere we go again, 'im and 'is daily routine. What a funny bloke 'e is.'

''E used ter be a soldier,' Doris murmured, 'I should've

thought 'e'd 'ave told *you* that by now: 'e's used ter 'aving everything just so . . . I s'pose 'e's going to walk yer 'ome an' yer want me out of yer way.'

'Why should 'e!' Gloria laughed. ''E lodges away along the New Road somewhere, don't 'e?' But Doris kept her silence while Hullabye shut up shop, alone with her own thoughts. 'Ta anyway fer keeping yer mouth shut, Dor, yer a real pal,' Gloria said, giving her shoulder a warm hug. 'I want ter see that old smile on yer face, the way fings used ter be wiv us. Keep yer chin up, wot?'

'Nuffink gets through to yer,' Doris burst out. 'It's all water off a duck's back to yer, Gloria,' she said fiercely, averting her face.

What's that all about? Gloria wondered, but she let it go, waiting impatiently by the redbrick arch for Hullabye's daily performance to end. He was a proud, pathetic little man, shooting his threadbare cuffs and pulling down the rattling metal shutter with a flourish. Finally he padlocked it, then pocketed the key almost with sadness, as if he wished it was his own. Doris stared at her feet.

'There's no 'arm in 'im really, I don't suppose,' Gloria said reassuringly, trying to be kind.

'Yer always give everybody the benefit of the doubt, as though nuffink really mattered,' said Doris with a tremble. 'Yer don't 'ave the faintest idea wot I put up wiv. I don't suppose that matters ter yer, neither.'

Off duty, Hullabye's voice lost its edge and he tried to sound kind to them. 'Mind now, you young ladies go straight home. The streets are a dangerous place for you pretty things.' He smiled at Gloria. 'Make sure you are in

16

attendance here tomorrow at six o'clock on the dot. I'll take no excuses. Miss Mabb—' Doris looked at him, flushing – 'you're not to cover for Miss Simmonds if she's late, as I know you have done in the past. Your loyalty is to the Railway, you know, before your friends.'

Both girls knew how true this was. *Look after the Railway*, ran the motto, *and the Railway will look after you.* The Railway owned them to the minute, but in return gave them a fine life. The expense of building Marylebone Station had almost bankrupted the Great Central, but no employee of standing or responsibility was let go. Rather than employ Londoners, many old trusted hands were brought down from the north: Gloria's Dad, Bert, still carried a trace of Lancashire in the back of his throat. When the army of Irish navvies descended to break down the stinking, rat-infested slums covering the site, thousands of filthy itinerant families – far more than anyone believed could have squeezed themselves into so small and squalid a space – were flushed like germs into the light of day. These homeless ne'er-do-wells were left to find somewhere else to go, and the fine yellow-brick mansion blocks went up for the Railway's folk. The tenants of Wharncliffe Gardens, looking down on shabby sidestreets taken over by the dirt-poor Irish communities, never forgot how far they had risen, and how much they deserved it: God helps those who help themselves, after all. Even the Wharncliffe Gardens children stuck together, singing as they streamed home from the Capland Street schools to the Railway Settlement playgrounds behind their tall railings. '*We all go the same way home, in the same direction – Oh what a collection! We all cling together like the ivy on the old garden wall!'*

The Gardens was proud of this community spirit. The residents hardly saw as human the poorest of the poor, the Irish who swarmed and multiplied under their noses in the shanties of Skid Row that festered along the banks of the Regent's Canal. But Gloria saw.

'You may get on home now,' Hullabye said. Gloria almost ran, but even so Doris caught her up, and in the entranceway Gloria turned with resignation.

'I'm frightened,' Doris admitted. Away from Railway territory she lost her self-confidence. 'Let me walk wiv yer tonight.'

'Blooming 'eck, there's nuffink ter be frightened of round 'ere!'

'Yes there is,' Doris said.

Gloria sighed. Together they walked into the soft evening light that filled the warren of turnings outside the station, skirting the piles of rubbish behind the Hôtel Grand Central with its fine Maple's furnishings, imperious commissionaires and gleaming chandeliers visible through the rows of windows. Then poor lodgings closed in, clustering so tightly around them on each side that Gloria brushed the walls with her outstretched hands. Doris hurried behind her, clasping her bag and worriedly looking over her shoulder.

'There's someone following us,' she said.

Gloria looked.

'Remember Jack the Ripper,' said Doris, but Gloria only laughed. The narrow hovels trapped between them a fug of beer, sweat and boiled Irish apricots – the potatoes they lived on. Every window hanging open laid bare people's lives in the grim rooms behind: the clink of plates, dark figures moving, a baby crying itself to sleep, Dad grousing, the splash of dishwater into the gutter.

'Gloria,' Doris said, ''old me 'and. I 'ate this, and there *is*.'

Behind them, hobnail boots tocked along the stones of the central gutter.

Gloria squeezed the dry fingers. She walked with her long stride, Doris tripping busily beside her. They turned right, then left, then right again.

In the bright glimpses between the pub alleys, stables, and rows of terraced dwellings, Gloria saw that the traffic was still packed solidly along the New Road despite the lateness of the hour: a stalled jumble of drays, with a battered Stephenson tramcar standing incongruously tall among them, stretched back past Chapel Street and the queue for the baths, to the Edgware Road. The horses, old campaigners where London traffic was concerned, all looked asleep, so she knew Dad would be late home unless he'd seen ahead and cut down one of the back-doubles he always seemed to know, showing off that a sharp foreigner from Manchester could know London better than Londoners. In fact Grandad Arthur had been a Londoner and Dad had been born here, but Dad never gave away for nothing anything that might make him swell in the eyes of other men.

Gloria looked over the top of Doris's bobbing head, fascinated by the people she saw around them. 'Irish,'

Doris whispered. Everyone who had hidden from the heat of the day was coming out. At the mews, Pat Ryan the farrier shaped a glowing horseshoe on his anvil, his leather apron salted with streaks of sweat, summer dust scuffing about his shoes as he worked. 'Evenin' to ye, Gloria girl!' he called, pushing up his leather cap with his thumb in salutation, 'warm enough for ye, is it now?'

'Can't wait fer me day off, Pat, that's the truth,' Gloria called cheerfully. On a couple of Sundays or a Bank Holiday each year, Dad in his shirtsleeves had taken the Simmonds family on a day-trip to Brighton, its highlight a fixed-price London Ordinary slap-up, eaten on the beach among all the thousands of other Londoners. Gloria remembered being allowed to buy an Italian ice from a tiny shop lodged in an iron tower on the Chain Pier. Once, most wonderfully of all, the family had put up for three blissful days at a tiny bed-and-breakfast on a Kemp Town alleyway, with a view of the glittering sea from the attic she shared with her sister Annie, the view Gloria held behind her eyelids when her head touched the pillow during the dark winter months: remembering a piece of heaven. Last year Dad took only young Albert and Bill and left the girls behind; not that he didn't love them, but what with them being only girls... And one day there would be a good, reliable husband for Gloria, and nothing would change.

'Come on, don't let 'im stop us,' Doris said, tugging Gloria's hand, 'wot yer stopping fer?'

But Gloria watched the powerful farrier straddle the horse's foreleg and clamp it between his knees, using tongs to size the hot metal to the hoof, disappearing in a billow of acrid smoke. His hands appeared and whacked a few long, soft nails into the horn with a paddy-hammer, not too many because it was a shoddy job done down to a price. Gloria moved her eyes without turning her head. The man in the dirty boots watched them from the corner, his face hidden by the brim of his cloth cap, one among a hundred others, except that he had the newspaper tucked under his arm. When she looked again he was not to be seen. Suddenly the farrier's face loomed out of the smoke at them, dirty and running with sweat, making Doris squeak.

'I'd be wishing for a day off meself,' the Irishman grinned at the girls, taking a deep breath, then spat through his yellowed teeth, 'but it's a hard life, paid by the shoe.'

'Pat gets his 'oliday picking 'ops in Kent,' Gloria said as they walked on. ''Is whole family trails along wiv 'im, even the littl'un.'

'Yer got no business talking ter them,' Doris whispered, 'what wiv it's Friday yer can smell the fish on their breath.'

'Do yer really fink it matters?'

'Yer can see wot they're like.' These people frightened Doris. Not because they were poor, but because they were different. They lived in chaos, whole families in a single room – and so many children! The street was lined with musclebound, sunburnt navvies in stinking shirts, stone pitchers of ale hanging from their fingers, their elbows employed to swing it into their mouths. And the women were huge, with what Mr Mabb called Irish Arms – their legs growing thicker towards the ankle. Their faces were so red and merry that even the women, it seemed, drank here! 'I'm not interested in types like them even if yer are,' Doris spat, 'I stick to me own sort, wot's worth knowing.'

She flinched as a little dark-haired girl wearing nothing but a determined frown weaved between them, pushing a wooden pram obviously cobbled up by a loving dad. Inside crouched a nervous-looking Jack Russell dog, her baby. The girl stopped to tuck him in, then scampered on through the evening crowd milling along the middle of the road.

'See wot I mean?' Doris said, incredulous at Gloria's smile. 'I dunno wot the world's coming ter round 'ere, I can't stand it. A girl don't feel safe on the streets now. Let's get 'ome.'

Gloria heard her sigh with relief as they came to the broad, safe highway of Lisson Grove, lined with poplars and plane trees stretching into the distance. The horse-dung from the endless traffic had been matted and dried by the sun, muffling the clop of horse-hooves and rumble of cartwheels so that the calls of the cats'-meat man around the back of the Portman Street cold-store rang out oddly loud. When he appeared, the cats entwined themselves around his shuffling ankles, gazing up implacably at the dark red cubes of horsemeat he held on dripping skewers. ''Allo me darlings!' he said.

''S'all right,' Gloria whispered to Doris, ''e's talking to 'is moggies, 'e don't care about yer.' But the cats'-meat man waved to Gloria before walking on – she was friends even with him, obviously!

Then Doris pointed back along the pavement. 'That's

the one I'm worried about. 'E's after us, Gloria.'

But seeing the pointing finger, the man quickly crossed the road and disappeared into Church Street.

'Not now 'e ain't,' Gloria shrugged.

'Maybe 'e knows where we're going.'

They walked on, the high spiked wall on their right hiding the locomotives in the Railway goods yard, though smoke billowed over the spikes from time to time, and then the ground began to shake to the slow rhythm of a coal train across the points.

'I want ter be married,' Doris said in a low voice as the noise subsided. 'I want ter 'ave a family so I don't 'ave ter work out 'ere; so I can stay in me own place all day an' only see me friends.'

'I don't never want ter be old,' Gloria said. She called out a cheery hallo to someone else she recognised.

'Oh, stop it,' Doris said.

They climbed the slope where the Regent's Canal disappeared into a tunnel beneath their feet, journeying underground to somewhere beyond the Edgware Road. Gloria leaned over the parapet on tiptoe – it was built so high to stop urchins throwing things down on barges sliding from the tunnel's mouth – and saw her father among a group of men on the towpath. Bert Simmonds always looked the same, short but somehow lifting himself almost as tall as the other men, pot-belly sucked in, white shirt with the sleeves rolled up tight and the clips on his black braces shining against the twilight. Coppery flashes flew from the men's hands into the black water: they were throwing penny pieces.

'They're at it again,' Gloria said in disgust. Doris ran to the steps to see. Along the far bank a tribe of skinny, unwashed Irish oicks from Lisson Grove's slums had gathered to dive for the coins, their naked bodies disappearing underwater for a heart-stopping length of time, trawling the broken prams and bicycles and old cookers of the canal bed for coins that often as not turned out to be worthless washers, coming up to the jeering laughter of the men on the Wharncliffe side. God help those Irish lads if Slove the bobby caught them breaking the byelaw: Gloria knew it wasn't against the law to throw money in the canal, but it was to go swimming. There was no running water in their jerrybuilt community, so cleanliness was proof of their guilt: the Irish boys rolled in the towpath ash to dirty themselves if they saw Slove's bristling Kitchener moustache and police issue boots approaching, and the bog-drum word spread along the towpath: '*Watchit, here comes Sluv!*' Slove vainly pronounced his name Slove as in Clove, a vanity young Wharncliffians, peering through the playground railings to watch the events thirty-five feet below, respected and understood, and the Irish guttersnipes mocked.

Bert looked up and saw his daughter. 'Be up, angel!' he called, waving her away, 'I'll be up when we've finished!'

'It's those poor boys in the water I feel fer,' Gloria told Doris as they crossed the bridge.

'They're Irish,' Doris said.

Ahead of them, built partly over the tunnel, the six brand-new mansion blocks of Wharncliffe Gardens were

laid out as neatly as pats of butter. Rising five storeys into
the evening sky, here was another world above the canal.
Clean washing lined the flat roofs like flags, being taken in
now before the dew came down. Smoke wafted from the
tall chimneys as the wives cooked supper: many husbands
ate meat twice a day within these walls, and then jam roly-
poly for pudding too. Women appeared in the high
doorways and leaned over the balcony railings, holding out
thick jam sandwiches, and the courtyards echoed with calls
summoning children to bed. The youngsters wanted to stay
and play bus-horses again, but coveted the jam sandwiches
more, so got nabbed and steered inside. Older boys hung
back as the East Street fire engine rocked past on rumbling
wheels, brass gleaming and white horses stamping, called
no doubt to one of the spate of fires brought on by the hot
weather. The firemen, who had no bell, cried out 'Hi-ya-
hi!' to clear the way. Doris paused by the railing-gate to
watch them go.

Behind the engine, Charlie Brewer came into view with
Sally Kean on his arm. She was wearing her pretty lavender
dress with the white lace, her chestnut hair falling on her
freckled arms. She turned half away, but knew poor Doris
had seen her. 'Oh 'allo there, Glo,' Charlie said, pretending to like her, hardly glancing at all at Doris. 'Weather's
keeping nice.'

Doris watched them go, then turned on Gloria almost
with savagery. 'There! I wish I'd never told yer about 'im
now!'

'I'm sorry, Dor.'

'She deserves 'im,' Doris said, talking nearly to herself.

Gloria banged the railing-gate closed behind them and they crossed the compound. No broken windows here, every door was painted and every landing swept, the fortunate children played safely in the playground provided by the Railway. There came the sound of someone getting smacked for being late to bed. Young girls ran inside, jostling in the lobby doorways in their smocks and broad-brimmed straw hats with fluttering ribbons. The boys complained, but followed obediently. Their dads, respectable Railway employees, sat behind the railings on the landings above, cleaning their workboots ready for tomorrow, their wives quietly setting thick white mugs of tea beside them. Drawing lungfuls of smoke from clay pipes, these watchful men were busy even off-duty, wearing waistcoats despite the heat, some repairing their children's toys – the lead soldiers that always needed attention, or dolls that had been too loved. Everyone had a smile for Gloria, even the engine drivers, on the top rung of the social ladder, returning from far parts of the country, wearing suits to walk home.

'Good evening, Gloria,' they said, and Gloria thought, *We all cling together like the ivy on the old garden wall*. The sons grew up to be their fathers, the daughters to be their mothers. She could look at any of the older women here and see herself in thirty years' time. She waved at a couple of the mums chatting and they waved, then turned their backs.

'Aren't yer coming up?' Doris said.

Gloria looked over her shoulder.

The man sauntered up the road as though the carts and

carriages didn't exist, hands in his pockets, very at his ease, thank you, but completely out of place here with his dirty boots and torn cloth cap. He had tucked the newspaper under his other arm. For a moment his eyes met Gloria's through the railing that separated them, then he turned down the steps towards the canal.

'It was 'im!' Doris said in a terrified voice. ''E looked right at yer, bold as brass! 'E knows fer certain where yer live now. I'm gonner tell me dad if 'e ain't down the boozer. Nah,' she decided, 'I'll tell me mum.'

Gloria watched her go. Probably the only man Doris had believed anything good of was Charlie Brewer, though sometimes she seemed to set her cap at old Sam Hullabye in the Railway shop, who could probably bring her nothing but unhappiness – and Gloria was sure Doris knew that. To be fair Doris didn't trust women much either, least of all herself. Gloria paused in the lobby's wide entrance, listening to Doris's buttoned-up boots tap upstairs, echoing in the concrete stairwell to the third floor.

Her heart was beating fast. But by the bridge her father was crossing the road now, short steps, holding up one arm to stop the traffic, his red face as always making him look angry. Then, with a whirr of bicycle wheels, Gloria's brother Bill came around the corner of the building, legs splayed and his face lighting up to see her. Five years younger than she, he'd been christened William, but everyone except Vezey-Mason and Dad called him Bill. At this time in the evening he was surely coming back from Vezey-Mason's confirmation class. He was clutching a bag of butter to his chest; Mum must have asked him to stop off on his way home and pick it up fresh from Bert Grimes's in North Street. For Gloria's benefit he scuffed his shoes along the gravel to lose speed – the machine he was so proud of had no brakes – then twist-skidded to show off. Marks were awarded by the amount of dust that erupted from the back wheel. 'Ten out of ten!' young Bill exclaimed, his face shining for her approval.

'If Dad sees yer doing that 'e'll 'ave your skin,' Gloria said. 'Cocky little blighter.'

'Don't look pleased ter see me, then.' Bill stuck out his tongue. ''E won't—'

''E's right behind yer,' Gloria said. 'Quick, chum, get inside!' She caught the butter and Bill raced his bike into the lobby, locked it in the cupboard under the stairs, then they ran up the four floors together, Bill determined not to be beaten by a girl, but Gloria outstripped him easily at the end. She hated to lose just as much as he did.

'Yer cheated,' puffed Bill as they went inside, ungracious as ever in defeat. Gloria saw that Mum had left the household rubbish by the karsy door instead of putting it out. Little Jack must have been ill and taken up all her time today.

'Yer cheated, yer cheated,' Gloria parodied Bill's whining voice. 'Young Bill, yer know, yer sound just like yer dad,' she said, putting the rubbish on the landing to take down. Dad hated it cluttering up the flat.

'Wot's wrong wiv that, Gloria?' Bill demanded, astonished.

'Shut that noise, both of yer,' Mum said. The wooden spoon was in her fist and she was boiling a bit of something at the Horseferry cooker for Dad's supper. She skimmed the froth off the top with the spoon while grabbing the butter for the crock with the other hand. Everything had to be ready for Dad. 'Where yer bin? Jack's asleep, if yer wake 'im it'll be your fault. I can't stand any more of 'is crying.' She'd nursed Bill until milk came from his ears not to have another, but Jack happened nevertheless: the 'mistake', the cry-baby who let them all down.

'Yer dad'll be 'ere in a minute,' she said, handing Gloria the breadknife and the loaf. 'That man works 'is 'eart out all day: our poor Mr Simmonds shouldn't 'ave ter come 'ome to all this fuss, should 'e?' In her home she protected Dad from everything, calling him Mr Simmonds although they'd been married almost eighteen years, and Dad wore her respect like armour. 'Where yer been, Gloria? I'm fed up wiv yer skiving off these days.'

'All right, I'll 'elp yer, as usual,' Gloria said, 'since yer put it so nice.'

Mum stopped. 'Yer not too big ter feel this spoon round yer 'ead,' she said.

She was as tall as Gloria, but her shoulders were rounded to make her as low as possible – Dad's word for tall was fat: he was clever about it, always on at her, so by now she believed him. She never thought of him as too short, only herself as too big. Mum had been a beauty when she was younger – she was hardly past forty now, though her grey, dragged-back hair and stiffened features made fifty-five of her. Statuesque, Dad had said, a real lady. Mum'd been an MS & L buffet waitress, but Dad, boosting himself, liked to invent a perfect world for his children to believe in: a real lady. Mrs Simmonds struggled hard to make his family live up to him, but Dad didn't hide it that Jack was *her* failure. Albert, his eldest boy, was steady enough to make engine driver one day: 'He's got his father's head on his shoulders!' Bill was lazy, but there was hope for him; Annie, who was fourteen, was just a girl.

But as for Gloria, she was what her mother had once been to her father – the apple of his eye.

'Put out the white cloth, Gloria, and lay the table, *and* the cutlery,' Mrs Simmonds ordered, as though they lived at a rate of a hundred pounds a year and the children ate meat for supper. Mr Simmonds, at least, deserved the best. As he came through the door, slamming it behind him, she stooped.

The smile Bert Simmonds had worn earlier, in the company of men, was gone. Here he was home, and impatience filled him, his face red with blood and sun, the king in his castle. 'Supper's not ready then!'

'The children couldn't eat earlier wot wiv the 'ot day,' Mrs Simmonds said, not apologetic but in a tight voice, blaming herself because she'd let him down. Dad was always right; at home he had the monopoly on it. 'I 'aven't even 'ad a moment ter take the gash out—' She sounded exhausted by looking after Jack.

'*I* been out driving in the sun all day,' Bert said, then his anger evaporated, or he pretended it did. 'Hallo, angel,' he greeted Gloria, giving her a squeeze, and maybe a kiss too but she turned her face away. She was a card, his girl, you never knew what she was thinking. He sat down in his chair – the only one with arms on – at the head of the table. Mum slid his plate in front of him, but he ignored it, looking up at Gloria. 'I'm a lucky man. They work my little girl too hard at that Railway shop.'

'We need the money,' Gloria said.

Her father's face darkened as though she was criticising him, the anger that never left the inside of him showing through. There was only one place for Dad in the family, and that was on top. 'Don't I do enough fer all of yer, is that it?'

'Eat yer commons, Dad.' Mum sounded Lancashire for the first time, and Gloria knew that meant she was nervous. 'That's Mr 'Umphrey's best tripe wiv yer onions, don't let it get cold.'

'I bin burning me 'eart out all day. And I come 'ome ter get nagged at,' Bert said, starting up the familiar complaint, 'nagged at, niggled at—' A complainant got better service, it was a simple fact of life. When Gloria laughed he glared, but she could get away with anything: his little girl knew better than Mrs Simmonds did when he was putting it on. His wife, when you came down to it, was just someone chosen from the crowd, but his daughter was his own flesh and blood.

'I don't like yer working, Gloria. I'm ashamed of it, ter tell the truth,' Bert admitted. 'A man 'as 'is standards.' But a drayman for the Railway wasn't really his own man – he was a man paid a wage. Once Bert had been a cabbie with his own cab, he had been his own man. The recession of ten years ago broke him and he'd taken it harder than he showed. There'd been nothing Mrs Simmonds could do to comfort him, her efforts to be loving only drove a wedge between them. A woman couldn't know what he felt: his inability to feed his family was an assault on his manhood. Only little Jack had been born after that, and for the baby's sake Bert took work with the Railway – it was all Jack's fault really.

And now even Gloria had to work, adding to his humiliation. He had to keep his face up with the other men, chucking away his money in the canal or down at the pub with them, but the fact was he could barely feed his family on a drayman's wage.

The window was open but Bert felt he was stifling. It wasn't the heat, it was fear, and he wanted to roar with rage, looking at the smooth, uncaring faces of his children unaware of what *he* felt, thinking only of themselves, stuffing bread and jam into their mouths as though there was no tomorrow, without a thought about where it came from, the fruit of his hard toil. Gloria's few bob a week was a joke, no one understood how hard life was for a man, how heavy his burden was: ten, twelve hours a day on the hard wooden seat of that dray between Marylebone and Waterloo, no shelter from the burning sun in summer, or the icy winds and hail in winter, and none of them came up to him and said simply *Thank you, Dad. We need you. We appreciate what you go through. We do understand.*

Bert knew how hard life was in London, how far you could fall. He protected his family from it, and blamed them for not knowing. Suppose he lost his job? It could happen. Waterloo Station was being knocked down and rebuilt, and he'd heard talk that the new station would lose the link with the South Eastern Railway, the source of most of his work. But he didn't burden his family with these worries. Dad was in control.

Gloria watched him. Bert put his hands on his knife and fork, then looked at her with that false wink of amusement in his eye. Something had changed between them in the last six months or so – especially that wink. There was something knowing in it, so out of place with them sitting around the table, young Bill quietly savouring a jam doorstep with butter on it too, because it was Friday, and Albert reading a six-shilling novel from the circulating library. No one talked. They listened to Dad eating. Father was in his home, and nothing wicked was in the world.

'Put that book down,' Bert said. 'We don't read at table in this family.'

Mum was washing up, Annie drying the plates, and Gloria found Dad napping in the sitting room beside his telescope, which was still pointed in the direction of Lord's cricket ground, even though it was dark. She turned down the lamp and night rushed through the windows, the lights of Hampstead Hill glowing in the distance behind Dad's head, and in the other direction, between his feet propped on the windowsill, lay St Paul's Cathedral and the glare of the Crystal Palace. Gloria went back to the kitchen.

'Dad asked me ter take down the rubbish,' she said, her heart in her mouth.

'Wouldn't 'e let yer leave the gash till morning?' Mum groaned, finishing up, patting her hands dry on Annie's cloth. 'Gash' was Mum's word for the rubbish: her father was a sailor and these nautical words had always stuck with her, treasured symbols of his rare and violent visits home. The kitchen was a galley and the cook was a lolly-banger who lit the gas with 10-A non-safety matches.

'Yer know what Dad's like,' Gloria said, hiding her trembling hands behind her back. She had to go through with what she'd started now.

'I don't know what's got into Bert lately,' muttered Mum, rubbing a piece of carrot over her hands to keep them supple. ''E don't listen ter a word *I* say, I know that.' She was trying to get the children on her side. Under Mum's wing everything was safe, a homely world of washing-up and dirty washing, to be grumbled about but immensely reassuring. Dad, who talked about family feeling more than anyone, made it seem artificial when he was there. No man could ever deserve Gloria unless Dad chose him – preferably a husband mostly absent at work. Mum wished her children would never grow up.

'Take the gash down then, if that's wot 'e wants!' Mum said, and Gloria whisked herself off with a sigh of relief. The stairwells, empty and silent, were lit by electricity. Gloria carried the gash-sack down into the darkened courtyard and emptied it into a dustbin by touch.

Instead of going back up, she stuffed the empty sack quickly behind the dustbin, where she could pick it up later, then stayed where she was for a moment as her eyes adjusted to the dark.

The sky was a faint sapphire blue, smoke from the generating station spoiling it. She crossed the playground towards the gaslights that illuminated the street.

Nothing moved on Lisson Grove. Hitching up her skirts,

she ran across the road. Here were the steps leading down from the far side of the bridge. Finding her way by her hand on the rusty iron railing, she dropped down into the darkness of Skid Row.

On the towpath a dark figure moved.

He came towards her, his boots crunching loudly on the ash.

Then he took Gloria in his arms and covered her face with kisses.

Chapter Two

'I thought ye were never coming down, mavourneen,' Jamie whispered, pulling Gloria to him in the dark, plunging his hands in her hair. The brassy strands tickled his mouth; she didn't know what she did to him, he thought, filling him with feeling just to hold her tight. 'I thought ye'd leave me all alone with meself. I'd kill meself if ye didn't let me kiss ye!'

Passionately he kissed Gloria full on the lips, all the pain and worry of his day evaporating with the softness and innocence of her mouth against his own. She tugged at him, then relaxed.

They parted, staggering apart in the dark. Gloria recovered her breath.

'Jamie Reilly!' she said, scandalised, delighted.

'We're much more than friends,' came his voice. 'Ye stole me heart, an' I'm never sorry for it.'

'Yer'd be much more than sorry if anyone saw us now!'

Both of them looked up involuntarily at the bridge streetlamps, but they were too far down for the light to reveal them.

'Suppose someone saw us even if we *were* just friends,'

Jamie said sadly. 'We'd never be safe, mavourneen, me being who I am. *What* I am.' She heard his Irish navvy's work-boots crunch on the ash and cinders that were spread across the towpath so that the barge-horses should not slip in their weary labour; then her arms were gently taken in his hands. 'Even if I didn't feel the way I do for ye. 'Tis no game between us, Gloria. Certain it never was for me.'

She touched his tatty jacket, not secondhand but completely worn out, the stitching that repaired it feeling as thick and coarse as string. It probably *was* string: Jamie could never look after himself properly.

'Was?' she said.

Jamie Reilly was no taller than her, but with a whipcord slimness that made her want to feed him up. The Wharncliffe Gardens lights shimmering in the canal outlined his profile, a lovely nobbly nose that was too long and too thin like the rest of him. His teeth gleamed in a mouth as generous as Gloria's own. His eyes were a deep, gentle brown, with long black lashes. From under the cloth cap his fine black hair – cut straight as a knife – fell into his eyes: he was always pushing it back with his hand when he was nervous, like now.

'I saw ye the first day ye started work, Gloria,' he remembered, 'nearly Christmas 'twas, an' ice on the roofs. I saw ye walk by Pat Ryan's stable, head held high, watching everything with eyes wide open; but ye didn't see the way I stared at ye. I couldn't see anyone else but ye. Me soul had gone out to ye.'

'Yer were spouting yer 'ead off about Marx!' she laughed.

'Aye, but the opposite message to what Marx intended, perhaps.'

'Get on in the world! Get Capital! Yer always 'ad ter be different.' She nudged him. 'Yer sounded like a banker.'

'I wasn't like those other men. I wanted ye to know that from me first word, Gloria.'

'I fell fer Karl Marx. Wasn't sure about yer, though.'

'He wanted a world better than anything that has ever existed.'

'Yer 'ad 'ungry eyes, but soft 'ands. I thought yer was rich.'

'Words were all I had, mavourneen,' he said sadly. 'I'd never been strong like me big brothers, Fergus an' Declan.'

'I was sure yer was soft in the 'ead! No one ever talked to me like that before, knowing I'd understand.'

'I'm a stranger to meself when I'm with ye. Everything changes for me because of ye.'

'Yer full of blarney,' Gloria told him fondly, knowing every wonderful word he said was true, because she knew she was in love with him. 'Yer still got yer storybook in there, I bet.' She tapped the hard pocket of his donkey-jacket with her knuckles, making a hollow rapping sound against the cover of the book within.

'Now, that's never a story!' he exclaimed, ''tis a gentleman named d'Holbach.'

'Yer funny ideas,' she said fondly, putting the hair out of his eyes with the back of her hand, just as he did; but her doing it was different, and he smiled. 'Wot is it this week, Jamie?'

'Mr d'Holbach believes that men are unhappy because they're ignorant of nature, of the real world.'

'Poor men.'

'Women too. He says we're all in the same boat, mavourneen.'

'I never met anyone wiv ideas before. Not like yours. Yer ought ter live wiv us, Jamie, not down 'ere. Dad clouting yer because you got yer nose buried in yer books, it's no life fer yer.'

Jamie was silent. 'But the man's right,' he said at last. 'Think what I owe him, ill as I was with Scarlet Fever, bringing him in no wages, only costing him.' He hesitated. 'Ye don't believe anyone could be happy without ye, Gloria, but maybe they could.'

'Not yer,' she said.

''Tis not up to us, mavourneen.' He caressed the glow of her hair in the dark, all he saw of her. Every muscle in his body ached for her, his sun-blistered shoulders and torn hands felt on fire for her.

It was the first time he had been in love. He had never dared kiss her with all his heart until now. Now, when he must lose her. 'Me Gloria,' he said tenderly, wondering how he could tell her.

'I love yer voice,' she said, 'it's all lilty and musical, like yer speaking a song, yer know?' His fingertip found her ear and traced its shape among the whorls and creases, making her shiver. 'It's serious fer me too, Jamie,' she told him.

'I know,' he said, 'that's the sadness of what I've decided. Ye're young, mavourneen, there's so much ye don't know about the way things really work.' He was nineteen. 'If ye

Dad knew about me, sweet Jesus, an Irish boy with his precious daughter—'

'I'm not his property,' she laughed.

'That's a lie,' Jamie said. 'Ye're so full of yeself, Gloria – oh, and 'tis what I love about ye – but ye can't escape what ye are.' His voice rose. 'Bert Simmonds's daughter, Gloria Simmonds of Wharncliffe Gardens. Have ye seen the way that girl walked? Like she owned the stones themselves.' He squeezed her arms lightly with his long fingers. 'Then she fell for a poor Irish boy,' he whispered, 'an' he ruined her.'

'Yer never would—'

'I will hurt ye, if I stay here, Gloria. Because ye are popular. But have ye never heard of envy, mavourneen? The higher ye ride, the harder ye fall.'

'Come off it. We're ordinary folk, nuffink fancy.'

'Ye are compared to some people.'

'Such as?'

He let her go and swept out his arm, a deeper shadow across the darkness of Skid Row behind them, hardly a light showing. *Us, the Irish. Poorest of the poor, lowest of the low.* 'Thy folk have jobs, an' standards, an' they're English, an' they never would forgive ye, Gloria, if they knew of ye an' me.'

'They don't know wot yer really like,' Gloria said.

'No more do ye.'

'But that's the thing about yer, Jamie!' she explained. She was starting to sound frightened, knowing there was something he was not saying. 'Yer not like people think yer are. Wot d'yer mean, not stay?'

'Ye can't change the world, Gloria. Everyone's got to have someone to look down on in this country.' He shook his head, then knocked back his hair angrily. 'Them ratepayers of St John's Wood, they look down their noses at Wharncliffe Gardens folk, d'ye see? So thy folk look down on us in turn. That's all that matters. That'll never change. Well, we've had enough of it!'

'Love,' she said suddenly. 'Yer said *love*.'

'I knew ye weren't listening to me. I love ye an' that's a fact, an' I always will.'

'Oh Jamie,' she said numbly. He squeezed her hand. With her own work-roughened hands, she felt his fingers, covered by blisters that had burst, forming hard scabs.

'Yer bin out labourin' wiv yer Dad!'

'I'm well enough now to pull me weight. Father's right.'

''E's never. 'E doesn't want yer ter 'ave time ter think! Yer can't think in the Stone Yard! The dust'll get in yer lungs,' she said miserably.

'Ye sound just like the priest, though ye voice is higher than Father O'Hanley's, to be sure. Gloria, ye can't look after me like ye do ye little brother, Jack. Ye can't be everywhere. Even if ye were a saint, which ye are not. An' there's more to life than thinking, mavourneen. Food on the plate, a roof over ye head, all ye an' yours take for granted. An' pride.'

He led her to a bench. During the day, the bargees laid their harnesses across it when the barge-horses were taken off for the tunnel nearby. They heard the water lapping its smooth concrete walls. 'Sit down quietly now, beside me.'

'No, I've got ter get back quick . . .'

'Why?' he said quietly, and Gloria was lost for an answer. He pulled her down lightly beside him. 'Ye want more than what we at present get from life, Gloria, just as I do. Yes, just as I do, an' in this world, Gloria, not the next. But—'

She pulled off that silly baggy cloth cap he wore, touching her fingers into his long hair. 'Wot yer want is an 'aircut,' she said.

His left arm was warm against her right side. They were silent for a moment, then he reached up and took her hand from his hair, kissed her fingers. 'God Almighty, what a tangle we've got in between us, girl. It was never fun . . . I mean every word.'

'Yer do always.'

'I waited at the station tonight, as I arranged, but ye wouldn't look at me. I followed ye all the way to the Gardens but ye wouldn't turn round. I had to speak to ye.'

'Trailing me like that – I was sure Doris would cotton on about us!'

'Sure an' I'm a fool, but a clever fool—'

'Too clever by 'alf, reading yer newspaper whenever I looked, when yer should've been thinking about me – I thought eight o'clock would never come.'

'Listen to me.'

'I am listening.'

'Gloria, be silent for one moment. Until I met you I was anything I wanted to be, because I've an imagination and a head on my shoulders. A priest, maybe, joined the seminary – that was Father O'Hanley's plan for me. But my own father won that battle. A man's work it is with a pickaxe in the Stone Yard. Hard labour that I owe my folk, mavourneen. Not ideas, not dreams. A hard day's pay for a hard day's labour, and coming home like me brothers, with real coins jingling in me pocket.'

He pulled the d'Holbach book out of his jacket pocket and, before Gloria realised what he was doing, sent it splashing into the canal.

'Oh my God,' Gloria said. 'Yer going ter do wot yer told. Yer going ter marry an Irish girl.'

'Sure an' they're pretty enough,' he said. 'But they're not Gloria. Not the one.' He touched her lips. 'The one.' Gloria felt the blood rush into her hands and toes. It was plain what he was saying.

'I love you!' she said. They'd run away together like in a penny broadsheet.

But there was something else in his voice. She trembled, then hung on to his shoulders. 'Wot's wrong?'

'Father's going north. Mother's going with him. A new life.'

Gloria shook her head.

'Ye know I have to go with them, mavourneen,' Jamie said gently.

'Yer said yer . . . wot yer felt fer me.'

'An' I always will love ye.' He tousled her hair, trying to be brave. 'Father's got it red-hot on his mind, an' the man's right. Fergus an' Declan see it too. A place where we are men, not Irish this an' Irish that, not looked down on by people like . . .' he nodded his head at the lights of Wharncliffe Gardens. 'All the people who are no worse than us an' no better, just think they are.'

'I don't.'

'They'll never let us marry. There's no life for us here, Gloria.'

'Take me wiv yer.'

'Chasing the pot of gold at the end of the rainbow? Upping sticks, carrying all we have on our backs, Mother in the handcart with her cough, a piece of tarpaulin for shelter from the rain? Begging for work, living on our muscles? Is that the life ye deserve?'

'Yes, if I'm with *you*.'

'Gloria, Gloria. It cannot be.'

'If we was married.'

He caught his breath. 'Your father would never permit it, for one thing, and for another, neither would mine.'

'*Your* father wouldn't!' Gloria said, outraged. All her anger boiled over – and she *was* angry, very angry. She felt like the sea in a storm inside.

'Ye don't suppose for a single moment, now,' Jamie said mildly, 'that me father admires the English for despising him?'

'I'll talk ter 'im. We're not all like that.'

'I'm trying to spare ye this,' Jamie said patiently. He'd worked it all out beforehand, in his mind. Probably he'd been over it a hundred times. 'I didn't want it to be like this. *I've decided that I have to go.*'

They fell silent as a group of men straggling home from the public crossed the bridge above them. With their heads and shoulders silhouetted against the streetlamps, they leaned on the parapet and shouted insults to the darkness of Skid Row. One, drunker than the others, teetered on the edge and urinated into the water below. The urine made a heavy bubbling sound close by Gloria and Jamie. 'Yer—' Gloria said.

'Ssh.' Jamie gripped her arm. A bottle tossed from the bridge crashed among the ragged rooftops by the canal. The men cheered the noise of sliding tiles, barking dogs, the crying of babies. Their manhood proved, they staggered on their way. Their bodies, and finally their heads, dropped from sight behind the parapet. The railing-gate clanged.

'Wharncliffe Gardens,' Gloria whispered. 'Me own folk.'

'Now ye know.'

'Will yer at least let me come down after church on Sunday?'

'Jesus,' he said, 'but ye're a marvellous woman. Ye fill me heart with love and sorrow.'

'Oh my God!' Gloria clapped her hands to her face. 'Wot's 'appened ter the time? I was only putting out the gash!'

Kneeling on her single bed in her white linen nightdress, Doris kept watch from her bedroom window. Her knees had cramped but she didn't move. Just after the Emmanuel Church had chimed ten o'clock, the figure of a girl in a green dress had hurried across the road. Doris, folding her petticoats, had seen her only from above and behind, a difficult angle. The girl walked like Gloria, those long strides that Doris envied, and she had Gloria's hair.

Doris had combed her hair with one eye on the window, waiting.

It was full night. Still the girl had not returned, and Doris's knees ached from her vigil. Below, the roadway stretched in pools of light from St John's Wood on her left, crossed the darkness of the canal and Skid Row in front of her, then bordered the enormous Railway goods' yard away to her right. Further in that direction lay the brilliant sprinkling of pub gaslights, hard and implacable as stars, that her father knew so well.

A party of men gathered on the bridge and there came the crash of a bottle – harmless Friday night fun. Her father left them; she recognised him clearly in his black suit with its considerable belly, the chain of his fob-watch gleaming as he crossed beneath the streetlight. He got the railing-gate open on the second go, then turned with dignity and waved goodnight to his pals. A couple of minutes later the sitting-room door creaked loudly but there was no other sound, as always he'd taken his shoes off. Doris waited for the loud click of the latch closing, which he always forgot. When it came she backed off the bed, keeping her eye on the window, and rubbed the blood back into her knees. Nothing would happen while the men were still kicking it up on the bridge.

In the sitting-room she found her father passed out on the sofa, with his empty shoes clasped to his belly as usual, and she unpopped the wings of his collar as quickly and efficiently as if they were married. It took only a moment to unbutton the fob-watch from his waistcoat; Mum often claimed it for safekeeping anyway, in case he lost it or gambled it away to Captain Criterion's racing sharps.

Leaving her bedroom door open an inch, Doris held the fob-watch into the bar of light from the sitting-room: eighteen minutes past ten. The men had left the bridge. She watched with pursed lips as less than a minute later Gloria appeared, alone, at the top of the steps. Gloria adjusted the shoulder-strap of her dress, looked around her, waved back at someone below, then hurried under the streetlamps back to Wharncliffe Gardens.

Nineteen minutes. The bedrooms had thin walls, and Doris had heard what a girl could lose in nineteen minutes.

Snatching the sack she had stashed behind the dustbins, Gloria ran upstairs. Mum was coming out of the karsy with her hair in a net. 'Where yer bin? I said do the gash—'

'I bumped into Doris and stopped fer a chit-chat.' If Mum ever checked up, which was unlikely, Doris would cover for Gloria. She always did.

'That's all very well, but yer Dad's woke up and gone ter bed,' grumbled Mum, 'an' Jack's been bawling. Go and see ter 'im before I clip 'im one fer the sake of me 'eart, would yer?'

'All right.' Gloria paused with her hand on the door to Jack's room.

'If yer up before me,' Mum said, as if it almost never happened – in fact she was a hopeless lie-a-bed – 'yer might get yer Dad's brekkie on the go fer me.'

'As well as work in the shop all day?'

'Yer growing up,' Mum sighed from her bedroom door. 'Time was yer'd do anythink I asked yer to. Now yer too full of yerself. All me friends says so too, even Mrs Mabb. I preferred fings the way they were.' Her wave goodnight was almost a gesture of dismissal.

Gloria went into Jack's room. It was dark, and she found the bed by touch. A hot little hand gripped hers, and there was an excited whisper.

'Did yer see 'im?'

Chapter Three

Jack put the light on and at once Gloria touched her hand to the bulb. 'Ouch!' He'd obviously had it on before: it was still hot enough to make her suck her fingers. 'Yer twit,' she scolded him, 'yer know wot Dad'd do if 'e caught yer wasting the electric.'

'Yer bin kissing.' Jack, returning to bed, hugged himself with his thin arms at the accuracy of his deduction. He got Sherlock Holmes' stories from Dad's old *Strand* magazines.

'Yer too young ter know about kissing,' Gloria said, sitting on the side of the bed.

'Colour in yer cheeks,' Jack said, then giggled when she flicked his nose. 'Ouch!' She couldn't hide her grin for him.

Her youngest brother, the mistake, was eight years old and knew more of Gloria than anyone: she was the centre of Jack's tiny world, he knew everything through her. She looked at him with a fond sigh. His pyjamas were much too big for his skinny arms and legs which were lost in the baggy folds, and he sat propped by plumped-up pillows. Dad would have tanned Jack's scrawny arse about the light, Gloria knew, then there would have been crying all night again, and the more Dad shouted that he had to *work* tomorrow, the more helpless the crying became. So often out of school and confined to his sickbed, Jack led hardly any life of his own.

He lived through Gloria, seeing through her eyes: most evenings she sat with him after work, cheerfully passing the time in the company of the little boy with the face of a thirteen-year-old. Jack probably knew much more than the adults everything that went on at the Railway shop, and all the things Gloria saw and felt: she never could keep a lock on her tongue. Sam Hullabye's drinking, the way he accidentally-on-purpose brushed against Doris behind the counter, even that he never had the nerve to try on that sort of stuff with Gloria. 'I'd give 'im wot for,' Gloria had bragged, 'yer wouldn't catch me putting up wiv that sort of nonsense like Doris does.'

'P'raps she's afraid ter do anything about it,' Jack had said. 'Or p'raps Sam wants ter be 'er friend, and she wants him ter be, but they don't neither of them know 'ow ter say it or show it.'

That was Jack for you: he was just a kid, but he could put his finger bang on it. The doctor in North Street didn't know what was the matter with the weakly child any more than his parents did, and had given up on him much as they had. The baby had been born delicate, with an enormous pale head, and almost died; every year they thought winter would carry him off. The family had grown used to the thought of Jack's death, and though nobody said so, deep down in their souls they wished it was over. Jack's face was dragged down as no child's should be by his struggle, but his large eyes were calm and had a way of looking transparently into you, as though nothing was hidden from him in his short life. And he could say, like that, something you'd never even thought of, which left you shaken and thinking about Doris in such a different way.

'Yeah, 'course I saw Jamie Reilly,' Gloria said.

'Knew yer would.'

'An' I kissed 'im!'

'Kiss me too,' the little boy said.

'A splonker fer yer.' Gloria kissed his cheek – his pale skin felt so smooth that she looked at him sadly. 'I dunno wot I feel,' she confessed, 'I'm all at sixes and sevens. Jamie's the most interesting man I've ever imagined. 'E's too thoughtful an' too sensitive and 'e's lovely. 'Is 'air falls in 'is eyes like this.'

Jack watched her lift the back of her hand across her eyes.

'Are yer meeting 'im 'cause Dad would go through the roof?'

Gloria turned out the light. 'I fink Dad knows about 'im,' she said in a low voice. 'Yer know 'ow word gets about. I don't fink 'e believes it yet. 'E wouldn't believe 'is golden girl could do anyfink wrong.' She smoothed the wrinkled sheets, then tucked them in by touch.

'I'm not sleepy. I was asleep all day. Dreaming.'

'Jack, would yer be upset, terrible-like, if I went?'

She heard him sit up and the light clicked on. He looked at her seriously. 'Yer out of yer tiny,' he said irreverently, then gave an exultant chuckle. 'Through the roof – I'd say 'e would!' He lay back with a sigh. 'It wouldn't be the same wivout yer, Glo. But nuffink would change, yer know. Not Mum or Dad or anyfink.'

'See, tonight Jamie Reilly almost asked me to marry 'im.'

'I dreamt yer went,' Jack said. His voice was small and trembling but his eyes looked enormous. 'There was only me left.'

'I can't see 'ow 'is dad could turn me down,' Gloria muttered to herself. ''E knows Jamie could prob'ly never do better than me. It's all pretty straightforward really. I love 'im, and 'e loves me, an' nuffink else matters.'

'Yer don't suppose they'll ever let an Irish face into the Gardens, except ter clean the drains?'

'All I know is, I'm not going ter be another Doris Mabb, or like Sally Kean, breaking me 'eart over a lump like Charlie Brewer. Jamie's got more brains in 'is little finger—'

'Yer got a little devil in yer somewhere, 'aven't yer, Gloria?'

'Yeah,' Gloria said. 'A little devil called love.'

'I'd do anything ter be seventeen,' Jack said with terrible longing. 'Yer don't know 'ow lucky yer are.'

Because the heatwave made manual labour almost impossible around the middle of the day, the awful *clank* of the Stone Yard bell summoned workers an hour earlier than usual, at six, in return for a longer lunch-hour. Gloria fought her way up from sleep. 'Shut it,' groaned Annie, rolling on the other side of the bed and clutching her hair over her head. She would be leaving school at the end of next month, perhaps to go into domestic service in St

John's Wood, as only a piss-kitchen at first but all-found, bringing in Dad no extra money but ridding him of a mouth to feed. And Aunt Maggie had risen from a piss-kitchen maid to be Lord Faversham's head cook in Belgravia. The bell continued its flat clanking summons as Gloria dressed, her fingers scampering on her buttons, already late for work at the Railway shop.

Bill and Albert, queueing at the karsy door, glared at her. They were going to spend their lives working for the Railway, Gloria knew. Albert already did weekend work in the yard, and like all boys they wanted to be engine drivers.

'Yer late,' they said accusingly.

'Yer gonner be clocks in yer next life, yer know that?' Gloria banged the frying-pan on to the stove and set Dad's bacon sizzling.

'An' yer gonner be *late*!' they said. Both wore white shirts with the sleeves rolled up. Albert carried a razor proudly, just like Dad's.

'Where is 'e?' Gloria put on the kettle for his tea.

They pointed at the karsy door.

The milk had gone off overnight but she slopped some in Dad's mug; he'd never notice. As she put the loaf on the board he came out doing up his trousers – corduroys, despite the coming heat – and tucked in his white shirt with the rolled-up sleeves. He had a pot-belly starting, which was why his belt was so tight, and moved slowly until the veins in his legs eased up. The boys slammed the karsy door behind them.

Alone, Dad's eyes followed Gloria around the kitchen as she worked. He kept his silence, letting her know she was late with his breakfast and he was strict about it, then sat at the table to pull on his boots. Then he looked at her with a grin that was both possessive and doting. 'Wot, no kiss fer yer old dad this morning?'

She kissed his forehead as she went past. He tied on his leather gaiters, still watching her. 'Yer my girl,' he said, 'I still can't believe 'ow clever I am.'

He saw in Gloria only what he wanted to see. She put his bacon on the plate and slid it in front of him, but he didn't eat.

'Sit down,' he said, 'we'll 'ave a chat while we're alone.'

'I'm late fer work.' She filled his mug with tea, but he held her fingers and for a moment his face changed.

'Sit down an' don't give me none of yer chat, Gloria.'

She sat.

'Now then.' His voice lost its edge. 'There was fings I didn't like ter say last night, not in front of everyone. Let's keep it friendly, shall we?'

Gloria helped herself to some tea and drank it quickly.

'I know girls,' Bert said as though he was talking to himself. 'I know wot yer like. We got ter look after yer, 'aven't we? Some of me pals playing Pitch'n'Toss by the canal last night 'ad a word in me ear.'

'Yeah, I saw yer wiv 'em.'

'Natch, I didn't believe a single word wot I was told.'

'Wot about?'

'Yer know right enough.' He chewed his bacon, gulped his tea and made a face, but didn't lose that horrid lying grin of his – she knew he was taking his time. 'There's a boy bin bothering yer,' he said pedantically, 'an' yer 'aven't told yer dad, wot would do somefink about it. I was embarrassed ter 'ear it from other folk. Yer dragging our family name through the mud.'

'I never am, Dad!'

''Ow did I get to 'ear about it then? I don't say yer mean to, just that yer don't know wot yer doing. I 'eard 'e was Irish, one of them street Arabs, but I didn't believe it.' He looked at her directly.

'It's nuffink ter do wiv yer!' Gloria snapped.

'Yer seventeen years old and yer my daughter and everyfink's ter do wiv me.'

'But—'

'Don't yer forget it neither! They don't wear underpants, yer know. They sell 'em, they're naked beneath. They're disgusting.'

'Dad—'

Bert smiled kindly, too kindly. 'Yer won't let 'im see yer again. And that's all there is ter it.' He emptied his mug, plonked his billycock hat on his head, departed for work, and that was that. Then he poked his head back through the doorway and gave her a bussing kiss which she was too surprised to avoid. 'Only the best for my Gloria, right?' he asserted.

She stared after him down the stairwell, her hand pressed to the greasy mark on her cheek. He hadn't given her a chance to explain herself, he'd just ruled everything out. Only the best for her – but to him that meant, *do as you're told*. Gloria felt her colour rise and flung herself back into the flat. She threw his plate in the sink, not caring if it broke, and his mug after it. Bill came out of the karsy and stared at her. Wearing his white shirt like that he could not have looked more like his father.

'Shut it, Bill,' she said. 'Aren't yer just so pleased wiv yerself? Like 'im ter the life, yer are.'

'Wot did I say?' Bill complained.

'Yer like 'im ter the life, Bill!'

None of them knew the frustration she felt, Gloria thought, except perhaps Mum. She snatched her bag from her bedroom and ran downstairs, the hard soles of her buttoned-up boots clapping the steep concrete steps, and she almost turned her ankle, grabbed for the railing. If a girl went wrong here, there was a favourite Wharncliffe Gardens saying: *Did she fall, or was she pushed?* Gloria would not have been the first to fall from the Gardens' high standards.

Doris was long gone from the lobby. Outside the youngsters, all in dresses, were playing bus-horses as always, as though they wouldn't spend the rest of their lives performing such tasks: for the moment they were tied together with harnesses made only of wool, and the driver flicked his giggling teams with a harmless woollen whip. Gloria was terribly late and today responded to their cries to join in with a distracted shake of her head. Older children in breeches were playing Cut-a-Lump and Four Ways to London, but the eldest boys, in sulky, yawning groups, pretended to ignore Gloria, then followed her with their eyes. She let the railing-gate bang loudly behind her and dodged through the traffic along Lisson Grove, unusually heavy as the drivers – one or two of whom called out to her by name – worked to make the most of the cool, early morning air. The sun was already hot on the left side of her face, streaming down Lodge Road where Dad would be harnessing up the poor nags at the Railway's stables. She knew it was going to be another scorching sunny day and that she'd never see it.

It seemed dark in the shop, though the walls hissed with gaslights. Doris came furiously down the aisle. 'I've 'ad it up to 'ere wiv yer!' she said. 'I bin 'aving kittens 'ere all alone.'

Gloria gave a sigh of relief. So the manager was out.

'I thought I'd get the blame, Gloria. Yer don't know 'ow lucky yer are, the early editions 'aven't come in, the ganger's off sick, but the street-sellers 'ave got 'em from somewhere – Mr 'Ullabye's 'ad to rush off—'

'That's all right then,' Gloria said, slipping her bag under the counter. 'What 'e don't know won't 'urt 'im.' She turned at once to serve some customers and it was several minutes before she was free. She came back with a smile.

''Ow can yer smile?' Doris said. She backed away before Gloria could touch her. Her eyes were dry, which was a bad sign; a tearful Doris could always be brought round. 'I used ter fink yer could do anyfink, Gloria, but yer just a smile. Yer could smile if yer were crying, yer could.'

'Wot's got into yer?'

'I know where yer went last night.'

Gloria stopped. 'Yer like the rest of them, sticking yer nose into other people's business.'

'Yer not other people, yer one of us.'

'Someone split ter me Dad's pals. Now I know 'oo it was, Doris. I thought yer were me friend.'

'I thought yer were mine,' Doris said unresponsively. 'I saw yer cross under the streetlight wiv me own eyes.' She shrugged Gloria's hands from her shoulders. 'Yer went down ter the canal.'

'Wot if I did?'

'Well, everyone knows wot that means.'

'Oh, do they!'

'I know wot yer did. It's that yer *don't* look guilty wot gets me, yer just stand there wiv yer bright smile an' yer bright eyes, as if butter wouldn't melt in yer mouth. But we know, we all know wot goes on down there! Nineteen minutes.'

'Yer spy on yer friends, do yer?'

'It's more than just letting yerself down,' Doris justified herself. 'It's letting all of us down I mind about.'

A customer came in and Doris turned away. Gloria served him and gave him the wrong change – not too little, too much, and he was gone before she could stop him. She rested her hand on the door-jamb and stood looking at the smoking, steaming cacophony, and commuters barging their way along the platforms, then closed her eyes.

'It was Sam, wasn't it?' Doris said.

'Sam? Sam *'Ullabye*?' Gloria turned, shocked. Sam as a possible suitor had never crossed her mind. 'But 'e's *old*.'

'I saw the way the poor man looked at yer last night.'

''E looks that way at anyfink in skirts since 'is wife died! Yer can 'ave 'im all ter yerself, my dear.'

'Sam's not old, 'e's mature.' Doris's relief was so obvious, now that Charlie Brewer was spoken for, that Gloria almost laughed. 'Yer played up ter 'im,' Doris told herself, 'but then, yer so full of yerself yer play up to anyone. It wasn't Sam's fault.' She met Gloria's eyes. ''E's too good fer yer.'

'If that's the way yer want it. Listen, Dor, can't yer show Sam wot yer feel, some'ow?'

''Oo was it yer was wiv then?'

'No one yer know.' Gloria advanced on Doris. 'An' we didn't do anyfink wrong, unlike yer would've, that's if yer 'ad the guts ter fall in love.'

'I never would've done nuffink wrong,' Doris said, but she looked away.

'Thinking wrong of others is half-way ter doing it yerself,' Gloria said.

'Sam's not ter blame. It's all me, it's all my fault,' Doris said, tearful at last. Gloria hugged her with a sigh.

''Is name's Jamie Reilly,' she confessed. 'Believe me, Dor, that's all that 'appened.'

But Doris pulled back laughing, appalled. The forgiving wetness in her eyes evaporated at once. 'Yer mean yer just sat there an' talked to an *Irish*?'

Chapter Four

Once Gloria caught hold of something, she couldn't let go. The more she was opposed, the more her determination rose. Doris was jealous because Gloria's guilt didn't show, but Gloria knew she had nothing to feel guilty about: Doris peeping from her bedroom window should be ashamed, not her. Gloria was angry enough to prove them all wrong, and a dozen times during the day, in her imagination, Jamie came into the shop and asked her to marry him. A customer holding out his money seemed to turn into Jamie, and she could not answer the simplest question about train times. She supposed she would have to become a Roman Catholic, and imagined the angry face of Vezey-Mason at the Anglican church when he heard; but being religious he'd have to forgive her. As soon as they understood her feelings, Mum and Dad would forgive her too ... but Gloria would long remember that look on Doris's face, that dried-up spitefulness.

She knew that, for a while at least, she'd have to go. She didn't know where; all that was vague. Once, in a youthful fit of rebellion against his father – after a beating for stealing some strawberries from the Church Street market, though he bleated he hadn't stolen them – her young brother Bill had tearfully packed his worldly goods into his pillowcase, including a cheese which Dad gave him, tied it on a stick and left home for ever. Boys were expected to run away from home, it was part of how men grew up, but for girls it was different. But that was what Gloria wanted: they would have to take her seriously, on her own terms. Young Bill had crept home as soon as his cheese ran out, none the worse for the overnight experience, and accepted his beatings thereafter. But Gloria would not be home in a week, or even a month. They'd be sorry.

That night she dreamt of walking across the fields with Jamie. His parents were in a brightly painted gypsy caravan behind a hedgerow somewhere, visible only by the smoke winding from the funny cranked stovepipe as his mum boiled the kettle for tea on their journey, and his jolly-faced dad whittled some repair to the axle with his knife. There was nothing in the slightest romantic for Gloria about this picture. Her emotion was of freedom. All the trees had shadows, grass-pollen stuck irritatingly to the hem of her skirt after the recent rain, and she sneezed as they came to the hayrick. She and Jamie sat amid the crumbling yellow bales swinging their legs, and Jamie talked of Jamie-things pressing his d'Holbach book in his hands. She took it from him and threw it into the grass, making him laugh, and she filled his eyes. He stood up to his father these days, and got better work. The muscles were hard on his shoulders.

'Soon,' Gloria whispered, 'we'll come back to London and show them all how happy we are, because we've made so much money, and we don't need them . . . we don't need them . . .'

She awoke terribly overheated. Harsh sunlight already blazed through the window. Her sheets were crumpled and sweaty, and Annie was sitting on the foot of the bed combing her hair for lice. She had a large mole on her left shoulder-blade that moved as she combed. In the kitchen there was the queue for the karsy as usual. Dad, his neck already chafing his stiff Sunday collar, flicked the boys a penny to run down Lodge Road to hay and water the nags, and be sharp about it. His black jacket for best was getting awfully tight around his aggressive pot-belly, and the armpits radiated creases, but his shoes were immaculate mirrors. If you didn't wear the same shoes every day, they lasted for ever, and Bert would tell that to anyone who listened; he was proud of the age of his clothes. Mum was fussing in her usual battleship dress of bottle-green velvet, but she'd found a fringed parasol for a different effect, to be excused by the heat of the sun. 'She's gonner boil like a cod in that velvet,' Annie said without sympathy, showing the first hint of rebelliousness as she followed Gloria into adulthood. Annie would spend an hour at least putting on her dress, also green.

Gloria would rather have died than wear Great Central Railway green on Sunday as well as every day. After breakfast she put on her best skirt, purchased with her own earned money. It came not from the market but from a proper shop, and was the lovely deep wine colour called maroon. Its style did not require too many petticoats, and flowed with her legs as she walked. She wore her cream blouse with silky flounced wrists and a high flower neck almost to her chin, secured at the throat by a cameo of her grandmother, Elsie. The stunning effect was completed by a matching maroon jacket, full in the bust and nipped tight at the waist, kept in order by as many maroon buttons as could be fitted down the front of it.

'Yer look like a bell 'op,' Bill said.

'Yer look like a big jacket wearing a little boy,' Gloria shot back, and Bill flushed bright red – he was vainer about clothes than either of the girls, but Mum always bought him two sizes too large to make them last. Gloria went into Jack's room, knowing he was well enough to come today. Jack loved church, loved looking at the people in their best. She tied his laces and with a lickety-spit parted his hair exactly down the centre, the way Mum liked it. He looked so frail and sweet, and Mum'd get an *ah* from the other mums. Dad checked his family off at the door, organising their departure to the minute: they always walked to church as one. Some Roman Catholics came past them along Lisson Grove towards their own church on the corner of Lodge Road.

Like Marylebone Station, the Emmanuel Anglican Church was new, specially built for Railway employees. Doris, wedged between her mum and dad, ignored Gloria. The pews creaked as the church filled, the employees and their families claiming their places in front, and girls from the Female Orphanage who had lost married parents sat facing the centre near the chancel. Just as the service was about to commence, the destitute children from the workhouse were filed in to be seated at the very back. They were not allowed the dignity of underclothes beneath their dirty linen shifts, not even the girls, and there was much competition among the smartly dressed Wharncliffe Gardens boys to peep back under the pretence of prayer.

The service seemed to go on for ever. When the collection box was passed round, the Wharncliffe Gardens families all demonstrated the powerful flick of the finger they had perfected which propelled a penny into the box as loudly as half a crown.

Jack looked up at Gloria and squeezed her hand.

The families came outside into the heat of the sun and broke up at once, the children racing home for their bikes, the men loosening their collars and turning to their pals, off to the public. Dad unbuttoned his jacket and thrust his hands in his pockets, bobbing like a little sparrow beside the slower, rambling bulk of Mr Mabb. The women clumped together under their parasols, not wanting to get started on Sunday lunch. Gloria found herself stuck with Mrs Mabb, who was in fine flood complaining about her husband. 'Not that I'm saying a word against 'im, mind, if only 'e'd stand up for 'imself . . .' She wasn't content to rule the roost, Gloria knew, she was one of those embittered souls who are happiest being unhappy. Gloria looked anxiously up the road, thinking she'd never get away.

Suddenly Jack keeled over in a faint – there were shouts that it must be the heat, and Gloria rushed forward with the others, then caught his wink. 'Undo 'is choker!' shouted someone. 'Give 'im air!' shouted another, and someone propped Jack's head on their foot. Gloria backed away in the confusion, then turned and ran along Lisson Grove. She began to giggle. She couldn't help herself. The most wonderful feeling ran through her that everything was going to be all right. She forced herself to walk, covering her mouth with her hands to make herself calm. Excitement at meeting Jamie made her run again, and she thought of the look in his eyes when he saw her maroon dress – not that awful Great Central Railway mound, the ghastly clashing green that made her hair look like cheap brass. Gloria in her own dress, herself. She thought only of herself.

She stopped as half a dozen men appeared, lifting a handcart up the steps from the canal, Constable Slove giving the orders. The men put down the hand-wheeled ambulance on the pavement and took off their hats. Youngsters gathered curiously. A little pair of clean white feet stuck out from under the dripping tarpaulin. Slove, with a drooping moustache, pushed the drowning-cart away down Grove Road. He was followed by a trail of frightened, fascinated, neatly turned-out Wharncliffe children, until their scolding mothers called them in. The men scratched their elbows and shook their heads, dispersing.

Gloria ran down the steps to the deserted towpath.

'I don't recognise ye in that skirt,' Jamie said behind her.

'D'yer like me in it, then!'

'I never thought ye'd truly come. Not for one single moment.'

'Yer know me better than that. Yer should 'ave a 'igher opinion of yerself, Jamie Reilly.' But he didn't kiss her.

Gloria nodded at the wet footprints by the canal. 'Wot 'appened?'

He put back his cap with his thumb. 'Ye see what yer folk did well enough, Gloria.'

'I'm sorry.'

'So are we, mavourneen.'

'It's not *my* fault.'

'That's just it. Ye don't know anything. Ye just refuse to admit what's staring ye in the face. It's a kind of murder.' At last he took her hand. 'Ye'll attract a devil of mind, dressed like that.'

'Cheer up, mate!' she said, and straightened his cap.

He led her down into the warren of shanties where she had never gone before, and Gloria's smile faded. Following a winding path of beaten dust – mud, she supposed, when it rained – she looked around her. Skid Row was choc-a-bloc with people, hundreds of people everywhere you looked, lurking in the shadows; thousands of people made homeless by the building of the Railway. These people were so poor that their lives were unrecorded: they could not be helped by the law that guaranteed working men tuppenny fares from the bright new suburbs of Tottenham and Walthamstow. They could not help themselves: too old, too young, too sick, with no hope of work, they had fallen from sight and settled here like sediment. 'Why don't the authorities do somefink?' Gloria breathed through her mouth at their smell. Nobody watched her go by, no children followed her. Flies settled on her lips. 'I never knew,' Gloria said. 'I never even knew this was 'ere.'

'Welcome home, mavourneen,' Jamie said gently. 'Here

I spent a year of me life on a straw bed, and learnt to read books, a poor immigrant in the wealthiest country in the world.'

Here, between the canal and the marshalling-yards, were the Irish. Their encampment was a jungle of odd, sometimes brightly painted sheds, sometimes raggedy tents, like the half-uprooted shreds of a travelling circus. Splintered planks, paper and mouldy plaster were cobbled together at any opportunity to make a home. Dogs lurched on chains, snarling, jealously guarding bits of old sacking, or a broken chair leant against a table. The path they followed wandered in a sort of circle that seemed to trap the heat and smell within it. From the centre of the conglomeration rose the roof and dormer windows of an older house, its brick walls almost hidden by the slanting roofs of shanties piled like outhouses against the first two storeys. The poor donkey tethered there had aligned himself to the only angle of shade, hanging his head and swishing his tail. Gloria, brushing the insects from her face, thought how appalling conditions must be in the rain.

Jamie stopped.

'This is it?' she said in surprise.

'Sweet home.' Jamie patted the donkey then stuck his head round a plank door. 'Yoo-hoo!'

'Come in, Jamie,' said a voice, 'and shut the door.'

'Let me do the talking,' Jamie whispered, and they held hands tight. 'Ye keep ye mouth buttoned, Gloria, I know ye. Agreed?'

'Jamie—'

'An' hope to die,' he whispered.

She laughed and brushed her knuckle affectionately over his lips, but his eyes were serious.

The room he pulled Gloria into was all furniture, not a spare inch around the prize table in the middle: she was hemmed in by an organised chaos of chairs, beds, a cracked iron stove with 'Bodley' cast across it in raised letters, iron saucepans of every size, a broken donkey harness, painted plates, knick-knacks and trophies. A stolen sign, hung like a picture, proclaimed PRIVATE PROPERTY. Blankets hung around the walls: whether they were for decoration, to keep out draughts, or because there was no room to keep them folded, Gloria could not tell . . . all three, probably. It was a homely and defiant place.

Four figures watched them and she forgot Jamie's stricture. ''Allo, 'ow are yer?' Gloria said brightly, her irresistible smile spreading. 'Nice to meet yer. 'Ot enough, ain't it.'

There was an uncomfortable silence.

Jamie cleared his throat. 'Mother. Fergus and Declan ye know.'

In the corner sat a woman with a cotton scarf over her head, quiet but formal. It was only with a shock, after looking at that lined, petulant face for a few seconds, that Gloria realised this must be Jamie's mother and not his grandmother as she had first thought. Her eyes were like bruises above a puckered, bitter mouth. Her small frame was overshadowed right and left by her elder sons, Fergus and Declan, each of whom seemed as tall as a cliff. Gloria smiled her greeting – she had seen them many times through the Stone Yard gate, their long straight hair swaying around their bare, sun-blackened shoulders as they team-worked with chisel and sledgehammer. But there was no banter now, and they were motionless. She turned away from their stare that was so protective of their mother.

'Father,' Jamie said, nodding in a different direction.

The man at the table was dressed in a dark suit, but his shirt was collarless and open at the neck. His hair was iron grey, rather frizzy as if soaked too often in salt sweat, and to Gloria his lumpy yellow hands seemed made of horn, not flesh. Yet though he was as heavily built as his other sons, his face was Jamie's: the same nose, though blunter, the same alert eyes, not unkind. But age and authority had added weight to his features and robbed him of his smile. He looked straight at Gloria.

'Seen enough? I told him not to bring ye. His own father, an' he disobeyed me for ye. Now send her home to her mother's apron-strings, Jamie!' He looked at Gloria with contempt. 'We don't need thy pity, English girl. We're not dirt, we've nothing to be ashamed of.'

'Mr Reilly, it's not like that at all,' Gloria said, but he talked over her voice, not listening to her. '. . . Seen us,' he finished, 'satisfied, are ye?'

Gloria felt her cheeks burn at his injustice. But when she tried to reply his voice rose, drowning her out.

'Me sons are everything in the world to me, girl. I conceived them, they're mine, I brought them into the world with me own hands.' Gloria glanced at his wife, whose face was now half-hidden by her scarf as though 'nowledging how small was her part in this business.

'Everything they have was mine. I broke me back to feed them. When they were sick an' crying I stole medicines to make them well. When the bogyman came I comforted them. Me three sons,' he said proudly, 'now grown into men just as I am.'

'I'm not trying ter come between yer,' murmured Gloria, acutely conscious of the sun, shining through a gap in the boards, slanting into her eyes and hair. She must be by far the brightest object in the room.

'Father,' Jamie said. 'Ye of all people must understand what I'm feeling.'

'So this is the fine fancy woman ye wanted to show off, Jamie,' the woman cried as though she could bear no more. ''Tis Seamus's blood coming out in ye!' She looked vindictively at her husband. 'I waited for this to happen. 'Tis the punishment for ye.'

''Twas long ago, Noreen,' Seamus said firmly, 'an' all forgotten.'

'Forgot!' Noreen exclaimed, then something buried inside her broke, and she screamed at her husband. 'I know *she's* forgot ye! She's dead, by thy own careless hand, and God's justice, but that's better than ye or she deserved.' She pushed herself back in her chair with the force of her emotions, she wouldn't look at Gloria, and Gloria could tell she hated everything about her. Jamie was very pale.

'Look at him,' Noreen muttered, 'he has his father's blood, does Jamie. When his father was young he never could look at a skirt without putting his hand up it, could ye Seamus? That's what brought us low, him an' his sluttish Protestant whore—'

'Jamie and me never done nuffink wrong,' Gloria protested hotly when Jamie said nothing. 'Yer take that back!'

'She means me father,' Jamie whispered. ''Tis nothing to do with us.'

'Everything between ye, too, is wrong.' Noreen merely glanced at Gloria. 'I know where ye live, young 'un, an' I know the church ye go to. I've seen ye together – Jamie's easy to follow with those noisy boots of his, did ye not know? I've watched ye in the shop, girl. Ye're no worker: ye never would serve him well.'

'Best to say nothing,' Jamie whispered, his breath tickling Gloria's ear, ''tis not the time.'

'Yes, I know what Jamie feels,' Seamus said quietly. 'There's such a thing as love, I know. He is growing to be a full man, and we men are prisoners of our balls, God knows it, but sometimes there is more. Love can exist, like a flower, for a day or a month, before it dies. An' the more beautiful it is the more its dying hurts.'

Gloria realised Seamus must be thinking of the Protestant woman Noreen had spoken of so bitterly; she saw how deeply he must have loved that other woman. And clearly Noreen had not forgotten her, or forgiven him for loving her.

'I'm sorry . . .' Gloria said, 'I thought – I didn't know—'

'Girls like ye are always trouble,' Declan, the biggest brother, said. He clenched his fists. 'Ye come in here and cause nothing but harm and open old wounds.'

'She's turned Jamie's head,' Fergus added seamlessly.

'Have her and forget her, Jamie lad. Get her out of ye.'

'I love her,' Jamie said.

Fergus and Declan roared with laughter. Gloria thought this was the most horrid place on earth.

Seamus raised his hands. 'That's it now. Stop it now, both of ye, that's enough.' He looked them in the eye until they stepped back, then turned to Gloria. 'Girl, I'll speak to ye straight. We didn't ask ye here, ye have brought yeself on a misunderstanding. This isn't thy place. Ye're a pretty young thing, but ye're not of ours. Make a good marriage with a good fellow of thy own sort and take me blessings. 'Tween ye and Jamie, though, is a different race, a different country, a different God. Jamie owes me, d'ye understand? We're a family, an' he owes *us*.'

'It's true,' Jamie admitted, pulling away from her. 'Don't ye see, Gloria?'

'There's a small – 'tis very small – inheritance of capital come to us up north, an uncle of Noreen's.' Seamus spread his hands. ''Tis my chance to make amends to Noreen. Not the life we have here, living like strangers—'

'Underdogs,' Fergus said.

'To be our own men,' said Declan passionately.

'We'll be walking into the unknown,' Noreen said, squeezing Declan's hands, 'but a friendlier unknown than what we have come to know here.'

'Money and property,' Jamie said. 'A proper home. A house with walls.'

Fergus looked at Gloria. 'All that *she* has already.'

Gloria remembered Jamie's words. 'Get on, yer said. Get *Capital*, get money. But what about *our* future? A world better than anything that has ever existed,' she reminded him. 'Why shouldn't there be room in it fer me wiv yer?'

'A woman,' Fergus sneered, then gave his mother's shoulder a comforting pat.

'An Englishwoman,' shuddered Declan.

'Yer minds are made up,' Gloria said furiously, 'yer just as bigoted and sanctimonious as my lot is. I thought yer was free. Aren't there no women in yer pie in the sky? Few brood mares, maybe, but it don't seem to me there's any room fer love – 'cept maybe a woman's love for her children, the poor cow!'

'Ssh,' Jamie said angrily.

'An' a father's love for his son,' Seamus said. 'Jamie knows who his family is.'

'It's a man's world an' that's that,' Gloria screamed, 'an' the rest of us keep yer mouths shut!'

'Easy now,' Jamie said with a fierce look in his eye for her. 'Ye're letting us down. Ye an' me, Gloria. Ye're not helping us.'

'She's had more than her say,' Seamus told him.

Gloria appealed directly to Jamie. 'It's like a kangaroo court, their minds are closed. But yer an' me aren't their prisoners. We aren't.' She squeezed his hands, but he would not respond.

'A woman wouldn't be ordering me about like that,' said Fergus.

'Never an Englishwoman, that's a certainty,' drawled Declan.

Jamie took Gloria's elbow. 'I think we've all said

enough.' He drew her towards the door, swung it open with his foot. 'Come on, Gloria.'

'Let her go, boy!' Seamus said, but the look in his eye was for Noreen. He was proving something to his wife: exorcising the ghost of the Protestant girl he had loved so many years ago, perhaps. And perhaps still loved. 'Leave her be, boy,' he said tiredly. 'Let her go.'

But Jamie pulled Gloria out and slammed the door behind them. 'Come on, quickly.' He led her round the side of the building. The sun had reached the donkey now, which shook its long ears in the sun, flies clustered like bubbling tar in the corners of its eyes.

'I've never known Father so angry,' Jamie muttered over his shoulder, leading her through a gap between the sheds, 'there'll be hell to pay.'

'Wot, about me?' Gloria let herself be dragged after him, panting, the dust scuffing around her knees. 'Oh, don't worry.'

'Best to get ye quickly home. Ye're in danger here.'

She swept back her hair with her wrist. 'From yer?'

'From Fergus an' Declan maybe.'

'Slow down, Jamie.'

'Hurry! I wish ye'd never met me. I'd do anything but let harm come to ye. Got to get ye back quick and quiet.' He tugged her half running along the rough, rubbish-strewn ground between the Railway tracks curving in on their right, the canal curving on their left to cut them off, then ducked through a gap in the wire. They scrambled up to the tracks crossing the canal, dirtying their hands and knees, then Jamie pulled her beneath the Lodge Road bridge and they leaned back, panting, against the smutty bricks.

'Get yer 'ands off me!' Gloria said. He let go of her hand at once. 'I thought yer loved me,' she said tearfully, slipping her sooty fingers back between his. 'Yer wouldn't back me up. Yer just stood there agreeing wiv everyfink 'e said.'

'Even ye could see how much Father needs me.'

'Yer running away from me. Yer frightened of feeling anythink fer me like wot I feel fer yer. I *do*, Jamie.'

He put his arms around her and hugged her so tight he cut off her breath. 'For the first time in her life Noreen has power, don't ye understand?' he said through clenched teeth. 'See things how they are, Gloria. The inheritance is in her name, an' after all these years that she has lived meekly in *his* shadow an' put up with *him*, Father's big opportunity depends on *her*. She'll squeeze him to the last bitter drop, believe me.'

'Surely she wouldn't.'

'Surely she will,' Jamie said. 'Don't ye comprehend at all how people are?' He buried his face in Gloria's hair. 'I've made a terrible mess of ye.' Then he kissed her lips with tenderness. 'Ye're not like anyone else.'

'Neither are yer, Jamie.'

With a quick motion he opened his shirt and took something from inside, lifting it over his neck. For a moment she thought it was a cross, but then saw it was only a dull silver coin, cheap-looking but almost as large as her palm, as though made to fit the human hand. The thin circle was mounted in a copper claw to protect it, black with years of ingrained dirt and verdigris, only the knuckles shining coppery where they had brushed his skin. Not even a silver chain to hang it by, just a loop of hairy string.

'Where'd yer nick it from?' she asked cruelly, knowing he was going to go and there was nothing whatever she could do to stop him.

'Because I love ye,' he said inexorably, 'this will bring ye luck.'

'Oh, the string, is that?' she cried. 'Luck o' the Irish?'

He hung it round her neck. 'Make of it what ye will.'

'Oh, Jamie.'

'Listen,' he said fiercely, ''twas my mother's. Not Noreen's. 'Twas my *mother's*, 'twas Tilly O'Neill's. She was Irish, not English, but her Protestant birth put her beyond the pale to so many of her class – d'ye understand me now, Gloria?'

'Don't go, that's all I understand.'

'Me father took this from around her neck. She didn't give it to him, he took it. She was dead . . . 'twas a lodging-room in London – Southwark, I believe – she were a barmaid at the Tabard Inn, a poor place where they were in love. It wasn't in his gift, so he gave it to her child. To the child of the woman he loved, poor Tilly O'Neill's baby. To me.'

Now she saw why Jamie could not free himself from his father. She should not blame him, but she did. 'I don't care where yer come from, only where yer going. If it's not wiv me, give it ter yer own children one day, Jamie. Or yer wife. Not ter me.' She said miserably, 'If yer father gave it ter yer, seeing where it comes from an' all . . . it must mean everythink ter yer.'

'I know what it means,' he said.

She made to lift it over her head, returning his gift, but he stopped her.

'Now ye understand what ye mean to me, Gloria, an' always will . . .'

A goods train rumbled slowly past them, the wheels clanking *tickety-bang* across the points, echoing up from the canal bridge below them and down from the road bridge above them. His mouth moved silently. With a deafening roar of smoke and sparks the shunting engine passed them by, then quietness fell again.

'Gloria, goodbye.'

'Wait.' She dabbed soot and smuts from his face, and he still held her, but they were standing like brother and sister in their misery, not lovers. He let her hang on to him, trying to be kind instead of quick in pulling himself away, his kindness making it worse for both of them. 'Wait!' she said.

He kissed her, but she turned her face away.

He pressed her handkerchief to his lips, then broke away from her.

'I'll forget yer an' never think of yer,' she said coldly.

He walked, then ran until he was gone from her sight. Gloria put her hands in her hair. She ran along the railway tracks after him until she turned her shoe on the cinders. He was gone. She pulled off the thing he had given her, breaking the string, and threw it as hard as she could.

'Jamie!' she shrieked, but he did not come back.

A stone kicked up a puff of ash a few feet from her. Gloria turned, frightened that she would see Fergus and

Declan, but she seemed to be alone, nothing but steel rails and cinders. Then she saw that a row of children's faces had appeared along the parapet of the Lodge Road bridge above her.

'We know wot yer bin doing,' chanted the children delightedly. 'We know!'

Seamus Reilly's face flushed dark red with exertion. The old donkey would never pull all this on the cart, never; the table was upside down on top of the junk-pile with its legs stuck in the air like a dead elephant's. Fergus and Declan had finished tying off the ropes and, without a wave, were already pushing the handcart along the track towards Lisson Grove, their bodies bent over the handles and the afternoon sun slanting in their eyes, Mother walking beside them in her loose black dress and shawl. Seamus had decreed they must all be out of London before dark, following the old Roman road which would be fastest and busiest: no one would remember them, poor Irish. They'd camp under the hedgerows at Willesden Paddocks, maybe, perhaps even getting as far as the asylum at Colindale if the handcart lasted . . .

Seamus looked around him without sorrow, at the empty shack with its earth floor, the sunlight starring the wooden walls where the rain came in when it rained and the wind blew in when it blew. For three years and eleven months they had passed their lives in this sad place, the Railway having wooed them with the promise of construction work that had now almost stopped. Noreen and he had lived apart within this twelve-foot by eight-foot hovel – that was the state their marriage had come to, Fergus and Declan siding with their mother, but not daring to stand up to their father's fists. Seamus sighed, scuffing the dirt with his boots. Jamie had been ill here and almost died, but Seamus had lost him anyway, lost the son who was most precious to him – first to the books, second almost to Father O'Hanley and a celibate life, but now and most of all to that bit of skirt. The worst thing was that Seamus could understand him: Jamie was his very own blood, the side of himself Seamus tried to deny. He rolled his tongue in his mouth and spat. For him there were no regrets at leaving here, no nostalgia. This had never been their place.

The donkey nodded amid the flies that buzzed around his head. Jamie had cut holes in an old straw hat; Seamus found it in the cart and fitted it over the beast's ears, knowing that was what Jamie would have wanted. He stood flapping the flies from his own face with his hat. Still the boy had not returned. In the distance, through the buzzing, swarming air came the tolling of the Emmanuel Church bell for three o'clock. He didn't dare leave the cart; thirty seconds and it would be stripped bare. One of the kids wandered too close and Seamus boxed his ear as a hint to the others.

Jamie came into sight along the towpath. Christ, but his face was dirty, smuts all over him, grime and brickdust streaked his jacket. Plain as a pikestaff what the boy's been up to! Seamus thought with rising spirits; Jamie's a man at last. 'Got her out of ye, then!' he called.

Jamie stopped in front of him. 'No,' he said. 'Let's go.'

'I see ye finished it right!' Seamus put his arm round

82

Jamie's shoulder and chuckled man-to-man.

'I never touched her,' Jamie said in a voice without emotion. 'I said goodbye. I'll never forget her.'

'Ah, tomorrow's another day, an' there's plenty of fish in the sea.'

But Jamie was almost crying, the tears sliding clean runnels down his dirty face, and Seamus looked at him with impatience then contempt.

'Ye'll get over her. An' there's another matter.'

He beckoned with his eyes and Jamie slouched after him into the hut. Seamus turned without taking off his jacket. He bunched his enormous fists and struck Jamie flush hits on the face, left cheek then right, blooding him, then pummelled him with heavy thudding blows to the body, dropping him. Jamie writhed in the dust, winded, then sprawled motionless, looking up at his father.

'I told ye not to bring her here,' Seamus panted. 'Shaming us. Bringing her here and shaming us.'

Jamie didn't understand. 'But ye said we had nothing to be ashamed of.'

'Look at me! Blind, are ye?' Seamus swept his fists around the bare walls, then dragged Jamie out by his collar and pushed him against the ridiculous donkey-cart piled with worthless stuff. 'This is all I am. *Of course I'm ashamed of meself!*'

Jamie stared at his father who was choking on his rage and shame. Then he put his arms around the old man, hugging him tight.

'Oh, Father,' Jamie whispered, 'I'm sorry. I am so sorry.'

* * *

'Geroff wiv yer!' The sun boiled down on Gloria's head. 'Shove off, why don't yer?' She found a few lumps of cinder to chuck at the children, who ducked from sight as one, but they soon realised that Gloria couldn't throw them hard enough to hit, the lumps falling harmlessly short into the brickwork, so of course they made a game out of her despair, dodging and taunting. 'Yer little 'orrors,' Gloria muttered, 'wait till I tell yer mums. Yer won't 'alf get a tanning.'

She'd lost her handkerchief to Jamie, so she walked along the tracks sniffing through her nose and wiping her face with the back of her hand, remembering how he wiped the hair out of his eyes. Her sobs increased. Joyful cries erupted behind her as the kids found a way down, dirtying their Sunday-best clothes, smudging with soot and grime their faces polished for church, and followed her along the tracks. Some of the older girls stayed behind to look after their baby sisters. One toddler slipped down and started crying, but the bigger boys took no notice. Gloria wondered what had changed. They were coming after her like a pack of dogs, noisy and mindless and out for a bit of fun, their minds set on the chase.

She felt the first touch of fear.

The heat reflecting from the rails and ash was tremendous, and Gloria searched for a way out. Ahead of her, stretched towards her like fingers, pointed the platforms of Marylebone Station, the exact opposite view from her usual one – the window of the Railway shop was hidden somewhere in the shadows. On the right the Lisson Grove wall looked easy to scale at this distance, shimmering as though made of air, but she walked along the other side of it every day and knew its bricks were formidably solid, spiked along the top. She turned the other way, picking up her dress and hopping clumsily across the rails towards the Park Road side of the yard. The children pushed close as she climbed the wire, laying bets. She could break a leg here. The top strand was barbed but anything seemed worth it to get away from these little monsters. She couldn't think what had come over them. Gloria's knees, spread wide, stuck out of her skirt as she straddled the top wire. Her jacket had come undone.

'Go 'ome before a train comes!' she called in a wobbly voice.

'We know wot yer bin doing!' they yelled.

Gloria jumped down on the far side, hearing a wicked tearing noise just before she hit the ground. Her skirt was torn, only an inch, but a flash of white petticoat showed. She held the sides of the tear together, too upset to shout back at the children behind the wire. She was in a mews turning, horses were nodding their heads at her over stable doors, and at the far end she saw the traffic – smart carriages mostly – passing along Park Road. With a gesture behind her, grateful to get away from the Railway, she walked slowly up to the road doing up her jacket and turned left, finding herself in a busy, anonymous place. The gentlemen striding along the pavements paid her no notice whatsoever, and the ladies appeared not to see her.

The children stared after her through the wire.

'Come on,' cried the leader, a pimply boy of thirteen whose mum had charged him faithfully to look after the others, 'we can get round at 'er back the same way! Yer young 'uns,' he added over his shoulder, 'mind yer don't rick yer ankles, and mind the trains.' His friends chased one another back across the rails the way they had come. The younger children followed behind in a group, holding hands, the girls helping the littlest over the rails.

Gloria came to Lodge Road and stopped. On the bridge the girls who had stayed to look after the little ones looked at her and seemed frightened, as if they saw in Gloria what they might themselves come down to. What a sight she must look, Gloria realised, touching her hair: it was tangled all over the place, and when she put her fingers to her face they came away smudged. She went on doing up all those jacket buttons, her fingers working busily, but she couldn't take her eyes off the girls watching her. Below the parapet the other children streamed back across the tracks, climbing up the slope, wriggling under the wire. There'd be hell to pay with their mothers, but their shining faces said it would be worth it. When Gloria walked, they followed curiously. When she looked back, they stopped. But each time she looked they were closer.

''Aven't yer got anyfink better ter do?' she screamed at them, and it felt like everyone in the street looked round at her. She caught her reflection in a pub window, her cheeks black as a navvy's, her clothes ruined by soot from the train she'd hardly noticed when she was with Jamie.

A couple of lads repairing a garden wall laughed, Gloria supposed at her, but she couldn't raise her usual cheery backchat. Her tongue seemed stuck to the roof of her mouth. 'Look wot the cat's brought 'ome!' they chuckled, dirtier than her, but when she remained silent, the warmth of their friendliness evaporated, and their faces became fixed. 'Bugger off,' one swore suddenly, with a jerk of his trowel, looking back at his house as though he expected to see his wife keeping an eye on him there, and Gloria really thought they would do her violence. No one had ever spoken to her in this tone before, or looked at her with the loathing, and yet desire, she saw in their eyes.

She found herself hurrying, almost running, followed by the excited children and the cold, knowing stares of the men. Ahead of her stretched Lisson Grove and the mansion blocks of Wharncliffe Gardens. From familiar doorways older women watched her pass with stony faces, letting her know exactly what they thought of her, though not a word was spoken.

''Allo, Mrs Flitch, 'ow are yer!' Gloria called, catching up a woman in white gloves walking ahead of her. She tried to sound cheerful, but was horrified at how frantic and ingratiating her voice sounded. Mrs Flitch peered from under her parasol; it had a tasselled fringe, trying to steal a step of fashion on the other Wharncliffe Gardens mums.

'Gloria?' she chirped, giving a delighted clap of her elbows to her sides. Her eyes were bright as a bird's, but she was rather shortsighted. ''Aven't seen my Molly, 'ave yer? I sent 'er out for the milk wiv Doris Mabb.' The two of them together for safety: Mrs Flitch knew you couldn't be too careful these days, you heard such stories. Mind you, it was often as not the girl asking for it, in her opinion, given what young people were like nowadays. Take Gloria, dressed up like a dog's breakfast like that, asking for trouble. In *her* day, Dad would have given them all a good smacked bottom for even thinking about dressing like that . . . her squinting eyes ran over Gloria's disarranged clothes from her toes to her head. 'Gloria, wot *ever* 'ave yer bin up ter!'

Gloria tried to smile. 'Me? Nuffink . . . why?'

It was obviously a lie. Look at those clothes. Nothing! Mrs Flitch was insulted by such brazenness.

'We know wot she's bin up ter!' chanted the children. Out of the mouths of babes and little children, thought Mrs Flitch, her worst fears confirmed.

'I wasn't born yesterday, my girl.' She puffed herself up on her short legs, feeling the unusual pleasure of domination, knowing the standards she lived by – her father's standards – to be both betrayed and justified by this girl. It was the parents one felt sorry for in such cases, she thought without any direct experience of such matters, the Simmondses were honest folk and it was impossible not to sympathise with them. In a flash Mrs Flitch saw through everything she had liked about Gloria, how she had used her prettiness and vivacity to deceive them, her humour and warmth as a false front. The girl had always been too popular. Suddenly Mrs Flitch realised that Gloria Simmonds's breezy, friendly manner had in fact been demanding and intrusive. And that irritating way she looked you straight in the eye as though she was almost as good as you were, though you were twice her age. You couldn't trust a girl who smiled all over her face, and Mrs Flitch wished she had said so before.

So the rumours about a man were true. Edna Flitch forgot where she had first heard them, whispering like

flames in dry grass; from one of her daughter's friends –
Doris perhaps – but Mrs Flitch was quite certain that this
tangled, messed-up girl she now saw in front of her was the
real Gloria. ''Ow could yer do this ter yer mum and dad,'
Mrs Flitch demanded with tears in her eyes, though
showing no inclination to wipe them on her white gloves.
''Ow yer ever going ter face them?'

'But, Mrs Flitch—'

'Don't yer "but" me, Miss Simmonds,' the older woman
said very quietly. 'Yer keep away from my girl. She's a
good girl, Molly is, and I don't want ter see yer wiv 'er, do
yer understand?'

'Yeah, I understand.' Gloria's voice trembled. 'But, Mrs
Flitch—'

Mrs Flitch raised herself on her toes, sensing weakness.
Weakness was guilt, every policeman knew that: Mrs
Slove, the constable's wife, had once assured Mrs Flitch of
that fact personally over the washing. Constable Slove
could tell a bad 'un just by looking at them. Mrs Flitch
leaned forward. Just listen to the girl's voice; her protesta-
tions of innocence simply confirmed her guilt, and she was
shaking all over.

Mrs Flitch licked her lips. 'Better tell me all about 'im!'
she exclaimed officiously.

Gloria heard a warning bell ring in her brain as loudly as
the East Street fire alarm. 'I got ter go . . .'

'Yer can't go 'ome like that,' Mrs Flitch said implacably.
She didn't offer the use of her bath or even a place to sit
down for ten minutes.

'I 'aven't done anyfink wrong.'

Mrs Flitch let her silence speak for itself.

Gloria pushed past her.

'Yer'll 'ave ter face us one day,' Mrs Flitch called with a distinct sensation of pleasure. Without standards a girl was nobody, and Mrs Flitch's pleasure turned almost to excitement as she saw Mrs Kean along the road, and crossed to tell her something that would raise that lady's eyebrows . . .

Gloria looked back. She knew the old gossip's news would be the talk of the neighbourhood in half an hour. Perhaps she could get home and clean up in time to deny everything . . . ride out the storm. Or do penance; that would satisfy them. They didn't stone sinners below the walls of Jerusalem nowadays, did they? No, not if the sheep returned to the fold. *How I hate them*, she thought with amazement.

For a moment the most wonderful feeling of freedom washed over her.

As she came around the corner of the Roman Catholic church, she bumped into two girls carrying milk-pitchers. They stared at her.

'Gloria?' Molly Flitch giggled. 'Is it really?'

'I told yer,' Doris said, not looking at Molly. 'She's bin wiv 'im, 'er Irish bog-man.'

'Wot if I 'ave?' Gloria said. She put one hand on her hip, pushed back her hair with her wrist. 'Wot of it?'

'*Gloria!*' chirped Molly, sounding just like her mother.

But Doris advanced a step. She was very serious. 'Yer know somefink, Gloria? Yer *ugly*.'

'Yuss, I'm just like yer!' Gloria shouted.

'She's in an awful state,' Molly said.

'Gloria,' smirked Doris, 'I'll let yer in on somefink. 'E did yer jacket up on the wrong buttons afterwards.'

Gloria's hands flew to her front. What Doris said was true; somehow she'd fiddled them up topsy-turvy. Doris's smirk infuriated her. She felt the muscles in her face harden as though she had reached a decision. Because Mrs Flitch and Molly and Doris were right, she realised, astonished. Because if something really had happened between her and Jamie, she would have wanted it to. Gloria, the golden-hearted girl who'd always done everything she was supposed to, really had let them down. Had wanted to.

'Yer bloody hypocrites,' she said, 'I don't care wot yer fink.'

'Yes yer do,' Doris smirked. 'Yer one of us, Gloria, and yer always will be.'

Gloria pushed past them. The milk slopped white splashes across the paving. 'Leave 'er,' Doris said, resting her hand on Molly's arm, 'she'll come crawling 'ome. I don't know wot we ever saw in 'er.'

Now that she had made up her mind, Gloria ran like the wind along the Lisson Grove bridge, over the canal, then down the steps to the towpath where Jamie had kissed her on Friday night. That kiss had been so serious for her, and so innocent, that she couldn't bear to hesitate here or remember being as happy as she had been, but instead ran as fast as she could along the path into Skid Row. She was very hot. A stitch began to jab her beneath her lowest rib. *Ye'll attract a devil of mind, dressed like that.* She was afraid of turning her ankle again. Without Jamie to protect her, several men shouted at her, and dogs lunged at their chains. At least she couldn't get lost, the roof of the Rat's Castle showing above the shanties guided her in the direction of Jamie's door. But when she knocked on the door the rotten boards fell open.

'It's me – Gloria!'

Strange faces turned towards her in the gloom; no one moved. A woman lay on the earth floor with babies suckling at her breasts, other women were bent over in the act of arranging sacks to make beds, children clinging to their skirts with suddenly frightened faces. They had no furniture, none, and she could smell the women's fear, their passive desperation.

'I'm sorry!' Gloria cried.

She backed out, shaking her head, then ran with the sun in her eyes back the way she had come, her face burning. Sobs choked her throat; she was growing tired now. With all her strength Gloria ran up the steps, pushing on her legs, then ran along the top of the tunnel, along Aberdeen Place, with the walls of Wharncliffe Gardens falling away behind her, until she came towards the Edgware Road.

They were long gone.

Busy traffic stretched as far as her eye could see from Marble Arch to Maida Vale. As she stood in the middle of the road, vehicles curled around both sides of her, thinking she was crossing. Gloria fell back to the pavement.

They could be anywhere. In fact, no doubt of it: Mr Reilly would have made sure that they could not easily be followed.

Gloria walked slowly back towards Wharncliffe Gardens. She did not even look up at the proud mansion block where she had lived. She was alone with her thoughts, and she knew exactly where she was going. Without Jamie, she would find what she was looking for in the cinders and ash of the Railway yard.

She imagined what Dad would say when he heard of her disgrace: he would simply be unable to believe anything bad of his little girl. Worse for Gloria was her feeling that, by growing up, she'd let Mum down.

I do have a choice, she thought. I can lie down and let it roll all over me, or I can stand up and fight. I needn't accept drudgery, I can make my own rules. She heard Jamie's voice as real as though he was still with her. *Get on. Get Capital.*

'A girl's got ter get on in the world,' shouted Gloria defiantly from the bridge, 'even if the world don't like it!'

Chapter Five

On Monday morning Doris walked to work alone, crossing Lisson Grove Road at the cobbled junction with Rossmore Road so as not to dirty her buttoned-up boots with manure – the cobbles were washed every weekend; otherwise, despite the efforts of the crossing-sweepers, the junctions became as slippery as Prince's skating rink with the first rain, and the poor horses fell and broke their knees. A small tear trickled from her eye at the thought. She was overwrought, having slept hardly a wink last night, filled with pity and shame at what had happened so suddenly and so completely to her childhood idol. Gloria had ruined herself; it was nobody else's fault – the girl must always have had that weakness inside her, gnawing away at her. And what had Gloria thrown everything away for? For nothing.

Doris was sure Gloria wouldn't come crawling back to the people who had exposed her guilt. Doris wouldn't have.

But suppose she did?

Doris found her handkerchief and dabbed her eyes, rubbed her swollen lips. The day was going to be another scorcher, the sun was already hot on her shoulders as she entered Marylebone Station. She hurried across the concourse to the shop. Mr Hullabye – slicked hair, thin domineering mouth, and that cheap black suit – was just reeling up the clattering shutter. The key still in his hand, he stared at her face. 'What, Miss Mabb, is something the matter?'

''Ow could there be!' Doris cried, and the childless widower looked after her in surprise as she brushed disrespectfully past him. This plain girl, he told himself, could not possibly realise how the simple feminine curve of her hip recalled poignantly within him, in his loneliness, sexual memories of his wife. She was young enough to be his daughter; he felt no love for her, none, though he desired her as a piece of soft machinery, the way a man desired any woman. Not intimidated by her as he was by the other girl who worked here, he allowed his arm to touch her shoulder as he took down the Bryant & May matches from the shelf. She flushed as usual, and he hid his amusement behind his frown, but then she turned to face him from the counter, her lips slightly parted. She showed fine, small teeth like a cornered animal, not at all unattractive like this, showing a bit of spirit, but not too much.

'What is the matter, Doris?' he asked in a kindly, paternal voice. 'Is there anything I can do to help?'

When she didn't reply he lit the gas-mantles, shook out the chuckaway match between his fingers, then dropped the counter flap closed behind him. In a few minutes he must fetch the newspapers from the ganger, who was not permitted to drive his wagon with its harsh iron rims on to the macadam concourse. 'Where is our Miss Simmonds?' he murmured.

'Why don't yer call 'er Gloria?' Doris couldn't halt her blurting tongue, and Hullabye realised she saw into him more explicitly than he'd believed she could. 'She's all yer care about, why don't yer call her by the name yer thinking of 'er wiv?'

'Then I should be obliged to call you Doris.'

'No, I don't want yer ter,' she said, looking him in the eye. 'Get away from me.'

'Where's Gloria, Miss Mabb?'

So easily did this silly child accept second-best. He watched her face struggle as though another person were concealed behind her flesh.

'Gloria's fell in love,' Doris Mabb cried.

'I see.' Sam Hullabye put his arm around her shoulders to comfort her. 'Is there such a thing?'

'Yes, oh yes.'

'You would believe that at your age,' he said sadly.

'Yer was married, wasn't yer?'

'It seems so long ago now.'

'A girl can't 'elp feeling deeply,' Doris told him earnestly.

'Then what you feel must be right.'

'I thought – from the way yer looked at 'er – at Miss Simmonds—'

'Come into the office. We can't have people seeing you like this, Doris.' He led her through and sat her in his chair. Doris fumbled out her lace handkerchief and held it to her eyes. He closed the door with his foot, watching her. Sunlight glowed in the single grimy window, striking not a single highlight from Doris's straight hair.

'For months I've bin lying ter yer, Mr 'Ullabye,' she snivelled tearfully. Doris knew that nothing moves men more quickly and truly than crying eyes: she'd got that wrinkle from the Woman's Realm page of the *Daily Mail*, and long ago that was how her mother had inveigled herself into Mr Mabb's sentimental heart – with the help of a lick of strong onion smeared on her handkerchief. 'Yer see, Mr 'Ullabye—' she blubbered.

'Sam,' he insisted. The papers would have to go rot this morning.

'Sam, I've bin a fool! I know yer can't never forgive me. Gloria's bin late every morning.'

'Then she is dismissed forthwith. She knows the rules. I shall tell her the moment she comes in.'

'But I bin covering fer her. That makes me guilty too, don't it?'

Sam touched her eyelids with his finger, then set his hand roving on her hair, and this time she did not flinch away. 'Then, Doris,' he said, 'I like you guilty.'

'I don't believe a word anyone said about Gloria last night, not till I 'ear it fall from 'er own lips,' Mrs Simmonds insisted, resting her chubby white hand on her broad hip. She wore a housecoat and a hairnet to look shipshape and Bristol-fashion for when she saw the other mums later, as though everything behind her front door was unchanged. 'Wot yer mean, not bin slept in?'

'Where's me bloody breakfast then?' Bert Simmonds said, snapping his braces and yawning as he came to the table. Bloody Monday morning. He put his finger to young Bill's head like a pistol and Bill scrambled out of Dad's top seat. 'Call this tea 'ot, Mrs Simmonds?' Bert demanded when she paid him not enough notice.

'Annie says Gloria's side of the bed's still made up.'

'Glo's sulking, Dad,' young Bill said confidently. 'She wants ter get our attention. Yer know wot girls is like.' Young Bill in shirtsleeves hadn't forgiven Gloria for saying he looked just like Dad; even if he did, there was nothing wrong with that, in his opinion. He couldn't hook the nasty way she'd said it out of his mind, that was all.

'Yer don't know nuffink about wot we feel, young Bill,' Annie said, not daring to criticise Dad directly, cutting the bread a touch ragged so she wouldn't be dragooned into any more of Gloria's tasks. Dad pulled a face and poured his tea down the sink. 'That's more than sulking – not bin slept in!' Annie repeated. 'I'm in there too, aren't I? The sheet's not creased on 'er side and 'er pillow's got no dent in it. I always know when she gets in 'cos she's got cold feet: she slaps 'em on me deliberate.'

'Yer wouldn't know, yer sleep like a pig!' young Bill said.

'That's enough of that talk,' Dad warned him.

'Well, it's true,' grumbled Bill as Annie stuck her tongue out at him, making a face back at her.

'I don't care if it's true or not, young Bill,' Bert said, not noticing what was going on behind his back, 'keep yer big mouth shut.'

'But Glo's a quiet sleeper,' Mum went on, 'remember as

a baby she slept quiet as a mouse? It's Annie wot snuffles ter raise the roof.'

'I would've seen if something was wrong wiv Glo,' Bert laid down the law. 'There's not much passes yer dad by. No secrets in our family.'

The children fell silent, reassured, then looked at one another as Jack came out of the karsy. The little boy was still dressed in pyjamas because he wouldn't go to the Capland Street school today; the headmaster, Tommy Summers, was enthusiastic about thrashing the public school spirit into his pupils and Jack's tears embarrassed everybody.

'Gawd, young'un, yer got black bags under yer peepers,' Mum said, 'yer look like wot I feel, yer do.' So Mum knew something was very wrong after all. 'Wash yer face and wipe yer backside, did yer?'

'Not at table, missus,' Dad said.

'Well, 'e's got ter be told.'

The little boy rubbed his eyes. 'I'm sorry, I didn't sleep very well.' He held out his hands.

'Clean enough,' Mum said grudgingly.

Albert came in. 'Still no Glo?' he asked brightly. 'She's really done it this time.'

'That's wot I said,' said young Bill, glancing at Dad.

Dad poured himself a mug of proper tea at the sink. 'Shut it, all of yer. Yer want to know wot I fink.' He waited until all their attention hung on him. 'Right,' he said, sitting down, 'it's only a matter of deduction, get it? She was upset by whatever 'appened to 'er yesterday, and I reckon she was attacked – yer know wot fings is coming ter round 'ere.

The streets of London are not a safe place, my lads and lasses.'

'All I know is,' Mum said, 'I felt my face go red as a beetroot when Mrs Flitch and Mrs Kean told me wot they'd seen, and then Mrs Mabb joined in too. I've never been so embarrassed in my life, and all the time it wasn't wot they were saying wot was worst, it was wot they was *not* saying. And all the while they was going on about 'ow sorry fer me they were, the old biddies.'

'Imagine wot it was like fer Gloria,' Bert said. 'That's right, she was upset by people's dirty, wagging, malicious tongues and cleared off fer a good cry. Makes sense, don't it?' He simply refused, Mrs Simmonds knew, to believe anything but his own picture of his darling girl. Men were hypocrites about their women; Bert never could credit that his daughter was the same sluttish gender as the buffet waitress of the same age, Mrs Simmonds remembered with some pleasure, with whom he had fornicated as dirtily as could be behind the old MS & L engine sheds. 'Let's wait until we 'ear Gloria's side of the story,' Bert said wisely. 'There'll be a perfectly innocent explanation, mark my words.'

'She was covered in smuts,' young Bill said fastidiously, 'an' 'er buttons was—'

Albert mentioned the unmentionable. 'They say she went with a man,' he said, shrugging. 'That's wot they say.'

'I won't 'ear no more of that talk in this family!' Bert shouted. 'Fer 'eaven's sake, Mrs Simmonds, where's me egg? Yer 'olding that spoon just fer decoration or wot? C'mere, Annie, yer call these slices?'

'I did me best,' Annie sulked.

'I can't wait till yer off me 'ands, girl, that's all I can say.'

'Gloria's yer favourite, isn't she, Dad?' Annie said clearly. 'Wotever Glo does 'as ter be right; wotever the rest of us do must be wrong.'

'Impressed wiv yerself, Annie? Yer can keep yer slices fer yer St John's Wood toffs if these are the best yer can do.'

'Don't be like that wiv 'er, Dad,' Mum begged, dredging his egg from the boiling water without looking at it, so routine was the task. 'I'll need 'er at 'ome till this blows over.'

'But Mum!' Annie said.

'*If* it blows over,' said young Bill gloomily. 'Didn't Glo fink of us at all?'

Mum wasn't having it. 'Even more reason ter stick together as a family. It's no good just saying it. Every time some little fing 'appens it's like we're going ter break up an' I can't stand it any more.'

'That's not my fault,' Bert roared. 'I'd be a rich man if it weren't fer feeding the lot of yer!'

'Now, stop it, Dad,' Mum said firmly. 'We got ter pull together ter get over this, 'aven't we?' There was a cunning light in her eye, as though she had sensed an opportunity.

'Get over wot?' Bert demanded, not really seeing her, the way a husband didn't look at his wife when they'd been married for eighteen years. 'Nuffink's 'appened! Yer'd fink it was the end of the world the way yer lot go on! Gloria 'asn't done nuffink wrong, she wouldn't. My little girl probably slept on the bedroom floor, that's all, so she could get off ter work early! Fer once,' he added.

'Yer can't deny it any more,' Mum said. 'Yer know somefink's 'appened. I'm not worried about Gloria, she's old enough and ugly enough ter look after 'erself. That girl always falls butter side up anyway. It's *us* I'm finking of.' She was looking at her children, not at Dad.

'Look, all right,' Dad said. 'I'll 'ave a word with various people.' The children glanced at one another. Various People was one of Dad's favourite phrases. A Word in the Ear of Various People was what he did when anything needed to be sorted out, like when young Bill's bike went missing. 'Storm in a teacup,' he grumbled.

Albert tilted back his chair on two legs. 'Some of me pals said Glo was into deep water an' 'ad been fer a long time, an' we never knew. She lied to us.'

'Not my Gloria,' Bert said firmly.

'Deep water with an Irish.' The word hung in the air.

Bert decapitated his egg with one chip of his knife. 'I'm not listening ter any of yer. There'll be a perfectly innocent explanation, mark my words. We'll 'ear Gloria's side of it.'

Jack cleared his throat. 'Dad.'

'Me boy.'

'Yer know she's gone, don't yer, Dad?'

Bert pointed his knife. 'Off ter yer room.'

'I 'eard yer talk ter 'er on Saturday morning. Yer knew more than yer saying.'

'That does it. Out, right now.'

'Did yer, Dad?' Mum said.

'That's my business.' Bert ate his egg in silence. Jack watched him with his enormous eyes.

'We all knew Gloria 'ad it coming!' Annie said. Her lips trembled. 'I fink she really 'as gone. There was footprints on the kitchen lino this morning, an' ash where 'er skirt touched the floor.'

'I don't see nuffink,' Bert said.

'I mopped it.'

Bert jabbed his teaspoon into his empty eggshell to break it up, as he always did. Nothing annoyed Mum more than picking out the bits of shell from the cup.

'Gloria came 'ome last night,' Jack confessed. 'I saw 'er.'

'Yer never did,' Bert said offhandedly.

'When she thought we was all asleep,' Jack whispered. 'She came back ter see me.'

'Yer!' Dad laughed, so Albert and Bill laughed too. 'Yer so special, yer pipsqueak!'

'Listen ter 'im, can't yer,' Annie said.

'I'm always awake,' Jack whispered. 'I felt the air move. The door creaked. She came back fer 'er clean dress, the yellowy one wiv the blue bows wot goes wiv 'er 'air and 'er eyes.'

'Yeah, Jack, I know it,' Annie said. For the first time in months she held his hands, frightened he'd stop.

'The one wot the shoulder-strap broke on just after she got it from the Church Street market,' Jack said, 'an' she sewed it up, remember? An' she took 'er coat.'

'In this weather!' Bert scoffed, looking at his boots, but you could tell he was taking in every word.

'An' she took 'er comb an' a little mirror, all that girly stuff, everyfink she could get in 'er bag.'

'An' all of us slept through this, I suppose?'

'I didn't,' Jack said.

'Shines out 'is backside,' Dad muttered.

'She didn't *want* yer ter 'ear 'er. She was crying; she didn't make a sound but yer could feel it all through yer.'

'That's all she came fer, was it? Quick sniffle an' clear out 'er fings an' buzz off?'

'She came ter say goodbye,' Jack said. 'It was the last time I'll see 'er.'

The others all looked at Bert. 'Oh, Dad,' Mum said, putting her arms around him. 'It'll be all right, Dad.'

'I'm not paying that little scamp no mind, 'e's got 'is 'ead in the clouds worse than Gloria,' Bert said. 'Yer was dreaming, Jack.'

'She came ter say goodbye.' Jack went to his bedroom door. 'It's last night. See it? Night, just a bit of streetlight through the window behind me.' He stood in the open doorway with his eyes closed, his pale face turned towards them: his bare feet were flat on the lino, his arms and legs sticking half out of his pyjamas, looking so frail that he might blow away in a puff of wind. 'She moved as quiet as a shadow. Backed out of 'er bedroom there, laid 'er bag down, dead quiet, by the table where yer watching me now. Yer could 'ear Annie snoring, that was all. Gloria shrugged on 'er coat, then 'er straw 'at, yer know the one, wiv a pin. She saw me an' stopped wiv her hands still up on 'er 'at, yer could see the 'atpin gleaming.'

'Wot did she say?' Annie asked, her eyes round. She was living it through Jack's thin, sad voice.

'She didn't say a word, just looked at me. She knew I'd be there. None of yer ever looked. I told 'er, *Yer running away*. I knew she was. She slipped across ter me, an' then she dropped down on 'er knees, right 'ere in front of me, an' gave me an 'ug so tight it hurt. *I'm gone*, she said. She kissed me straight on the lips, yer know the way she does. That was all. Then she went. I waited and waited. Then I closed the door.'

'She didn't come an' say goodbye ter me,' Annie said, trembling.

''Oo would?' young Bill stuck in. 'Couldn't get away from yer fast enough, I 'spect.'

'There's one way ter clear this up,' Albert said sensibly, 'check the girls' room an' see if 'er fings are missing, like Jack says.'

'Sit down!' Bert said.

'But Dad.'

'No.'

'Just a quick look. It's better to know, isn't it?'

Bert tightened his fists. 'Yer bloody dare, boy.'

'Now, Dad, we don't want that gutter language in our 'ome, do we?' Mum said. The two elder boys looked on, discomfited by her interference.

'Dad doesn't want ter know,' Jack said, going up to him, and they realised that he was the only one of them who was not afraid of Dad.

'It can't be 'appening,' Bert muttered. 'She's always 'ad the best of everyfink, top of the milk, remember, Mum?'

'Yer couldn't've done more,' Mrs Simmonds comforted him. 'It's 'er I blame. I don't say I believe a word of wot people said about 'er, once they found out about 'er, but it's a proven fact there's no smoke wivout fire.'

'She don't care wot people say,' Jack cried. 'She *hates* yer – don't yer understand?'

All the children looked at Mum and Dad. Mum beckoned them. 'All of us together,' she said, holding out her arms. 'My family.' Jack ran back but the boys pushed him away.

'It's our fault, isn't it,' Annie said quietly.

'Annie, yer'll do the washing-up,' Mum warned. 'It doesn't matter wot *she* said, I wouldn't believe a word of it now. I always knew this would 'appen. I always said that big smile of 'er's would get 'er into trouble one day, didn't I? She'll come crawling back an' won't I give her wot-for, I'll tell yer! An' Dad'll give her a larruping wiv 'is belt, won't yer, Dad.'

'I 'aven't got time fer this chit-chat,' Bert said, taking down his drayman's leather apron from the hook and slapping his billycock hat on his head, 'I still don't believe a word yer saying, but I got ter get ter work.'

'Listen ter me!' Mum said, but he stormed out and slammed the front door. 'Poor Dad,' she said, ''e did look up ter Grandma Elsie, and 'e didn't 'alf take it 'ard when 'is cab business went bust and took 'er money wiv it. I never bin able ter make it up ter 'im.' But there was a calculating light in her eye, and she didn't look too upset about it.

Jack slipped into the girls' bedroom and they heard him chucking out Gloria's remaining clothes from the wardrobe in a sudden frenzy, her old shoes that Annie hadn't grown into yet, sending them rolling and clattering across the floor. 'Gone!' he shouted. '*I'm gone!*'

'Wot am I going ter tell me pals?' young Bill said.

'Gloria's dumped our family in it,' said Albert.

'She meant to,' Annie said in a small, dull voice.

'I won't miss 'er!' Bill claimed suddenly. 'She was 'orrid ter me! 'Ow *could* she do this ter our dad?' He sounded on the point of tears in defence of his father.

'It's not the end of the world,' Mum said. It was the first time they had heard Mum even hint that her marriage to Dad was less than perfectly happy, and the children could hardly get over the shock. They had thought every family was like them, and now they realised how much they had needed Gloria. Mrs Simmonds licked her lips. 'Yer got yer Mum. Listen, kids, we've got *us*, 'aven't we? We'll show 'em – we'll stick together better than before, won't we! Yes,' she promised, 'we will.'

'Wot's going ter 'appen wivout Gloria ter boss us about?' Annie asked tearfully.

'She only bossed us because she cared about us,' Jack cried.

'We got us,' Mum said, gathering them into her arms. 'She had ter fly the nest sooner or later, that one.' Mum hugged her children tight, as though to mould them into one big new child to make up her loss. 'It's not our fault, she was that sort of girl. A girl shouldn't 'ave a strong personality, it's not ladylike. I always said she made too many friends, and people wot make friends make enemies too, it's a fact of life. She's got wot was coming ter 'er, an' learned 'er lesson. She'll be back.'

The children edged looks at one another, then at Gloria's clothes and shoes they could see scattered by Jack across the bedroom floor. Gloria wouldn't be back, and Mum knew it. She was counting on it. There was a sort of awful silence as the children realised the truth.

'We'll look after yer, Mum,' Albert said loyally.

'I told Gloria, *Yer running away*,' Jack said in a voice muffled by his mother's bosom. She was pulling him so tight that he could hardly move. Who would look after him now? Mum would. Mum would look after all of them. He murmured: 'An' I understood.'

PART II

A Working Woman

Chapter Six

Gloria woke with a shout. She was late for work! Doris would be walking down Lisson Grove without her. Quick, get up – her father would be staring at the cold Horseferry cooker, his fists planted on his hips in the way he had, roaring to anyone who'd listen, 'Where's me breakfast?' And Mum coming in all of a fluster, half asleep herself and bumping around helplessly, 'Sorry Dad, wot's all this about?' And then they'd both roar for her: '*Gloria!*'

But Gloria wasn't there.

She rolled over uncomfortably, groaning and muttering at the hard wooden slats digging into her back and hips, her head feeling as though it was propped against a piece of iron. But when she opened her eyes she saw only the dark, comforting inside of her straw hat which had slipped over her face.

She knew that her parents wouldn't realise at first how their cruelty had driven her away from home, and perhaps they never would. Their gossiping friends at Wharncliffe Gardens would rally round to support them; Mrs Mabb with tea and sympathy for Mum, digging up the dirt on the side, and Mum sharing her experiences tearfully, 'Yer better learn from wot's 'appened ter us. Keep a tight grip on that young Doris of yers, they grow up so fast, they go wrong so easy . . .' And later the other housewives nattering around Mum as they hung out their washing, the one social event, except church, impossible to avoid in their community: their sunlit windy haven from the darker, man's world of the streets below, the women gathering up there on the flat, asphalted roofs amongst their fluttering linen where they could speak their minds, pegs in their mouths and wicker clothes-baskets canted on their hips, lying the babies inside when the work was done, their mouths set free and chattering nineteen to the dozen. ''Ear wot that Gloria Simmonds did to 'er mum and dad, wot couldn't do enough fer 'er? Ran away from 'ome! Not *their* fault. That girl was bound to fall in with a bad set, when yer fink back about it, no respect fer 'er own social class wot would've looked after 'er. She fooled us, and now she's got wot she deserves. She never was one of us . . .'

Not one of us.

Gloria stared at the inside of her hat. Sunlight was speckling through the straw weave. She didn't know where she was. Silence, only birdsong. Wharncliffe Gardens was gone, swallowed up by London as though it had never been.

She heard heavy footsteps marching on the gravel. They stopped beside her. 'All right, ducks,' came a man's loud, deep voice, 'on yer plates.'

The tip of a truncheon appeared under Gloria's hat-brim and flicked it off her head. Brilliant sunlight lanced into her eyes and she cried out.

She did not recognise where she was – pale green tree-trunks, shaved green grass bordered by crotch-high dark green iron hoops to ensure that promenaders kept to the paths. Sheep grazed in the distance. Where the sky should have been, a policeman's broad red face and ginger whiskers came close, leaning over her. Another constable stood close by, slit-eyed.

'Wakey-wakey.' The first crusher put his face so close that she could smell the fried bread on his breath. 'You got feet, madam. Use 'em.'

Gloria was lying on a park bench. She swung her legs over the edge, her coat sticking uncomfortably to the dew-beaded slats. 'Wot yer on about?' she demanded, snatching up her hat. Her joints ached; she must have achieved a couple of hours' sleep. An ornamental fountain had commenced splashing nearby, and she realised how thirsty she was. 'I got the same rights 'ere as anyone else, 'aven't I?'

'On yer way,' said the second flattie impatiently. 'Boozed up?'

Ginger-whiskers shook his head, and Gloria realised he had been sniffing her breath for drink, as though she was a down-and-out. Her colour rose. 'I can stay 'ere as long as I like – it's a free country!' she complained, tousling her hair and yawning.

'Ho, free country, is it!' Ginger-whiskers stood straight, his hands behind his back, swinging his truncheon by its strap. This seemed strange to Gloria, as she knew that a constable was allowed to draw his truncheon only by necessity, except amongst the Irish; but she could clearly see it twitching back and forth like a pendulum between his legs. She felt confused and intimidated by his impatient, worldly manner. All Wharncliffe Gardens children were taught that the police were their friends, to be asked the time or for their help across the road, and Constable Slove even lived among them on the second floor. But this policeman was not treating her as a friend or even a citizen, but as a criminal, just for sleeping on a park bench, when in fact the Simmonds family sometimes crossed to Regent's Park and spent all Sunday afternoon lying in the sun, Dad catching up on sleep, his hands clamped over his belly and his chin nodding on his chest, the girls setting out a picnic maybe, and taking up two whole park benches if they so wished.

Suddenly tears filled Gloria's eyes as she remembered the family she had left behind. 'A free country, now?' ginger-whiskers said tolerantly. 'Show us yer bob and it is.'

'Wot d'yer mean?' Gloria asked, baffled.

The constables glanced at one another. 'If yer can show me yer got one shilling in yer possession, yer can do what yer like,' ginger-whiskers explained. ''Owever, yer must not loiter or sit about without some reasonable means of existence, which is one shilling. If yer can't produce anything more than that pretty smile, yer will be moved on or compelled to enter a Workhouse.'

Gloria searched her purse. Only a few copper coins. 'I was paid on Friday morning,' she said, astonished when he did not believe a word of it, 'but I . . .' she could not repress a hitch in her voice as sadness welled up inside her, 'I gave it ter me mum.'

'No waterworks, now,' warned ginger-whiskers. 'Only doing my job.'

The second policeman ambled to the next bench and, with a practised jerk of his truncheon, levered its ragged incumbent on to the gravel. The figure scrambled up, cursing, then saw who it was and kept her mouth shut.

'A shilling makes yer respectable,' ginger-whiskers told Gloria, 'ninepence brings yer under the suspicion of the law. The sergeant'll be along any minute, so out of it wiv yer. The gates are open now, yer can leave the proper way. How'd yer manage ter sneak in past the railings?'

Gloria picked up her bag. 'There's a gap by the tree over there.'

'Bloody idjit!' shouted the ragged figure by the next bench, hopping angrily from one foot to the other, 'bloody spy!' she screamed at Gloria, 'now 'e'll 'ave it sealed up. I lost the best bed in London 'cos of yer – I'll spit in yer eye an' choke yer!'

'Now then, enough of that,' ginger-whiskers said in the deeper voice he could use when he wanted. 'Stick clear of that one,' he advised Gloria, 'I can see yer a good girl at 'eart and I don't want yer ter get into no trouble. Run away from 'ome?' he said sympathetically. 'Run straight back to it.' He touched his truncheon to the brim of his helmet, setting her on her way.

Gloria plonked her hat on her head with all the dignity she could muster. When she looked round, he was still watching her, and she waited until she saw the two policemen continue their rounds before cutting back to the fountain. Kneeling, she held back her hair to her shoulders, put her face to the water and drank. Something moved upward between her breasts with a heavy, sliding weight, then before she could stop it tumbled out of the top of her dress and splashed into the pool. She grabbed for the sparkling circle before it was gone, missing as it changed shape with the refraction of the water, wetting her arm to the elbow. But it was not gone after all: flashing, it hung from the string around her neck as if mocking her efforts to catch it.

'Yer *thing*,' she scowled. 'I don't want ter remember yer, yer bastard.' She pulled it up by the string and cradled it in her palm, wiping the glittering moisture from its dull surface, gazing into it. A man's cruel face; on the other side, a thing like a candlestick.

Jamie Reilly had hung the coin around her neck beneath the bridge. She'd broken the string chucking his worthless gift after him in a temper, then been ashamed of herself because it must have meant so much to him, and *that*, not him, (she told herself) was what she couldn't get out of her mind. '*'Twas my own mother's, 'twas Tilly O'Neill's, d'ye understand me now, Gloria?*' Given his talisman to her, then run away in his father's shadow like a faithful dog, the coward. She didn't love Jamie Reilly, not at all. She'd spent three hours yesterday evening searching for the useless thing in the cinders of the Railway yard, finding it in the end by a sudden gleam in the last of the sun, wedged between the rail and a sleeper in almost the exact place she'd started. Having given up hope, she'd stared at it lying on its necklace of broken string for almost a minute before snatching it up. She'd repaired the string with a granny knot, but it was still too long, and she had been aware, as she walked the streets looking for a place to sleep last night, of that heavy weight swinging between her breasts, as if polishing itself. It wasn't a necklace; it was something else.

'Sell it,' whispered the old woman, and Gloria glanced at the ragged creature who had been turfed off the bench and had crept up behind her. She was encrusted with dirt and smell, poorer than the Irish.

'Why'd yer follow me?' Gloria demanded.

'Look at yer!' the old woman cackled. 'Clean clothes, nice 'air – couldn't resist yer!' With a grimy hand she reached out to Gloria's blonde tresses escaping beneath her hat, then did not touch them. 'Tragedy Tib 'ad 'air like that once. Over me shoulders, it was.' The crone wriggled sadly beneath her rotten clothes as though remembering the feel of it, then brightened. 'And ninepence too, did I 'ear? Luvverly girl. From somewheres, are yer?'

'Wharncliffe Gardens.'

'Never 'eard of it! Bin sleeping under the 'edgerows? Show us wot yer got!' Her exhausted eyes fixed on the coin Gloria held in her palm. 'Take Tragedy Tib's advice and sell it,' the woman repeated, nodding. On her bent head the thin yellow-white hair was held back by a rubber band, and she held out her hand for the coin with fingers that were bent like claws.

Gloria clutched it tight, backing away. 'It can't be worth anyfink, it was given ter me by someone poorer than me.'

'Everyfink's worth somefink!' cackled Tragedy Tib, revealing teeth like splinters thrust into her gums. 'There's poor and poor. That's worth a bob, capital sum, see, keep the flatties off yer back, then they can't touch yer – and that's worth a fortune, I'll tell yer! Oh, 'eaven it would be.' She closed her eyes, dreaming.

Gloria pushed the coin down the front of her dress.

'Yer'll 'ave ter sell that dress too,' the old woman said, opening one sly peep of her eye, 'and that coat, or yer won't last five minutes wiv people like us. Ordinary people. I s'pose yer 'ere in Town ter fall in love wiv a gentleman, and 'e'll sweep yer off yer feet.' She swept out her arm in a big, dramatic gesture, then clamped it to her flat chest. 'And it'll be 'appy ever after.'

Gloria wasn't about to be put down by this horrible creature. 'Why not!' she said, with a smile.

'That's wot they all says. All wiv a smile like that. Young 'opefuls. Well, I'm a working woman: see these teeth 'ere?' Tragedy Tib opened her mouth wide, as though she was screaming, showing two particular gaps where her incisor teeth had been. 'Sold 'em! Cold winter, that was.'

Gloria was so appalled that she didn't know whether to believe her. 'Is that why they call yer Tragedy Tib?'

The old woman sucked her tongue through the holes. 'Tib's me name, Tragedy's me trade, darling. I'm no beggar, I give value fer money.' The flesh seemed to shrink from her features, the left side collapsing as though she had suffered an apoplexy, a face of terrible hardship and misery. Her eye fixed on Gloria, very respectful, but unwinking. Tragedy reached out her hand, knuckles up, as if in dominion rather than beggary. Then she turned her hand over and opened her palm. In it lay a tiny sprig of leaf. 'Penny a sprig,' she said, 'lavender perfume.'

But that wasn't the end of it. She didn't drop her hand or look away, until finally Gloria took a penny from her purse and dropped it into the outstretched hand. 'Only a penny ter yer, but it's a bun ter me,' said the old woman cheerfully. 'Now yer got eightpence left. But yer got that fing round yer neck. Sell it. Yer want ter be like me? Yer can give away almost everyfink of yerself, but yer can't kill yer will ter live. I knows a billy-fencing shop wot'll give yer ten bob fer that. Sell it!'

Gloria shook her head.

'Oh yer poor darlin',' Tib said, and tears started in her flat, dark eyes, 'yer frightened. Yer frightened out of yer mind, aren't yer? Oh, me poor dear. I'm so sorry fer yer. Once I was just like yer.'

Chapter Seven

Gloria secretly hugged herself as they walked in the early morning sunlight, congratulating herself on her good fortune in finding what she most needed, a friend, so quickly. The dry sprig of lavender already crumbling in her buttonhole was well worth a penny, she told herself, for the old woman's friendship. Tragedy Tib, with her stooped walk and rolling shoulders, obviously knew the ropes; and what she knew she could teach Gloria – the best area to rent a room cheaply, where to find a job, cleaning perhaps, or sewing, or as a shopgirl in one of the big department stores that now permitted female employees. With this knowledgeable friend to help her, Gloria knew something was bound to turn up.

'Wot yer looking so cheerful fer?' Tib demanded, disgruntled.

'It feels—' Gloria tried to explain her sense of freedom. 'Somefink's bin lifted off me shoulders, that's all! Look at me! Me mum would 'ave me guts fer garters fer wearing me shoes dusty like this, or fer wearing me 'at so jaunty. But 'ere I am!' She stuck out her hand. 'Gloria, by the bye.'

'Yer young, Gloria,' grumbled Tib, 'yer make me feel old just ter look at yer.'

Behind the two women stretched parkland to the horizon, and in front of them, beyond the fountain and a wide road, rose the fine façades of grand houses adorned with statues, and private walled gardens showing the tops of trees. 'The Duke of Westminster's place,' Tib groused. 'Not a good area that, yer get moved on in no time at all, but there's a drinking fountain in Grosvenor Square wot goes *whoosh* into yer mouth just nice. Yer shouldn't've drunk the water from the pool back there, yer'll get stomach ache.' She glanced at Gloria. 'This is called Lover's Walk. Don't look so pleased wiv yerself! Now yer got over the shock and the sniffles yer fink yer got London in the cup of yer 'and.' She sighed. 'I seen yer before – all the girls like yer, stepping off the train sometimes, wot spent all their money on the ticket, bright faces an' wide eyes, an' nowhere ter go.'

Gloria seized the opportunity to talk of practical matters. 'Where do they get rooms?'

'A room! Wot, yer? Wiv only eightpence fer deposit? Never-never land, I should fink!'

'But surely there's lots of people'd let me stay till I could pay 'em back . . .'

'Born yesterday, yer was! There's doss-houses an' public shelters, an' the crypt of St Martin's will take yer fer nothing, but not twice, an' yer got ter keep yer shoes on. Sell it,' she repeated.

Gloria touched the hard place between her breasts.

'Forget 'im,' Tragedy Tib said. 'None of 'em's worth it.

I've forty or fifty years under me belt an' I got me pride, but I never 'ad a man fer love and I don't miss it.'

''E never laid a finger on me,' Gloria protested.

'Didn't love yer then,' Tib said shatteringly, then held out her arm to stop Gloria as they came to a busy corner. 'Stick wiv me, I'll see yer all right,' she tossed over her shoulder as she set off between the traffic, palming a red apple from the back of a passing cart without a break in her hobbling stride. Gloria ran after her. 'Look,' Tib explained, wiping apple-juice from her chin, 'it's too grand fer us round 'ere; that wall's 'Er Majesty's back garden. Yer want a gentleman ter fall in love wiv yer—'

Gloria stopped. 'I won't do nuffink wrong, Tib.'

'That's wot they all say, an' of course they don't do nuffink wrong, 'cause nuffink's wrong wiv love,' Tib reassured her gently. ''Ere, want 'alf? Oh, I dunno wot's right,' she groaned as they walked on. 'I know being 'ungry's not right. I envy yer, ter be frank, yer got everyfink on yer side; yer young, yer got looks, a girl's got ter make the best of 'erself while she can . . .' They followed the trees of a broad thoroughfare being watered and swept for some parade or other, then Tib cut through a backstreet to the river. 'I wish I was yer, Gloria,' she called back longingly, lifting her face to the muddy-smelling breeze, 'God, I wish I was!'

'Don't be silly, Tib,' Gloria tried to comfort the old woman.

'Yer a good girl,' Tib snivelled, 'I'll 'elp yer. Breakfast comes first – a real tightner, wot? I knows the very place!' A tram carrying civil servants to work rattled past them as Tib led Gloria along the Embankment, the soupy Thames swirling upstream on their right, seagulls forsaking the dwindling mudbanks to perch on the buoys and mastheads of the fishing-luggers and oyster-boats moored three deep along the wharves beyond London Bridge. 'Ye-o-o, 'ere's yer fine Yarmouth bloaters,' carried the fishermen's cries. 'Fine cock-cock-cock crabs all alive-O! Had-had-haddick!' As they entered the crowd, fisherwives barged them aside, fishtails swinging from their aprons, their brawny forearms glittering with scales. A boy slept curled like an eel in a basket and porters shoved around him, trembling with the weight of fish-trays on their heads, their shirts wet with sweat and ice. Stiff yellow triangles of haddock were heaped on the stones, the smell of fish growing very strong with the power of the sun. Gloria saw spalpeen boys, exhausted by their labours in the early hours, ducking their heads under the water-pump outside Rodway's Coffee House. 'Come on!' cried Tib, cheerful again, thrusting through the little girls clustered around the door, who at once set on to Gloria, begging her to buy their matting-bags of whitebait, or smelts, or herrings on sticks – one little waif in particular, with enormous soulful eyes, was irresistible, but as Gloria reached into her purse Tib snatched the penny from her hand. 'Don't deserve me, yer don't,' said Tib furiously, hustling Gloria inside, and the door sprang abruptly closed on the babble outside.

Inside the coffee house were rows of full tables, a sea of busy elbows working and heads nodding on to loaded forks, mouths chomping almost in silence but for the echoes of digestion. Tib spied a couple of vacant places and bustled over, plumped herself on the bench and dropped her elbows on the table with a sigh of luxury. 'Bring us yer full tightner, twice!' she instructed the huge man who came slouching past them in a blotched white apron, 'an' don't 'ang back!'

'Show us yer necessary,' he growled.

'Show 'im!' Tib nudged Gloria pertly, and Gloria flashed tuppence between her fingers.

She was almost trembling with hunger and realised she had not eaten properly for twenty-four hours. Both were silent and impatient until the food came, stacked swimming in grease on tin plates with a couple of pewter tankards of hot coffee to wash it down; then they were too busy to speak until they had gobbled every last mouthful, Gloria copying the way Tib ran her slice of bread and butter around the plate to mop up the last greasy smear. 'Shiny plate, saves on the washing-up, see.' Her eyes softened and Gloria wondered what sort of family life the poor woman was remembering. Fetched back to the present, Tib kept up the show, sucking her filthy fingers luxuriously, then held out one arm like an opera singer while the other pressed her belly for a sonorous belch. 'That's 'it the spot! Now, listen,' she said seriously. 'Yer never know yer luck. I'll tell yer this. Yer got ter go where respectable gentlemen go while yer still look respectable, girl. The British Empire Club, maybe, yer gets lots of young gentlemen from abroad there.'

'So wot?'

'Cor, Glo, I don't know wot yer'd do wivout me! A man's

got ter 'ave a wife fer the sake of 'is social face, the Balls, an' the Races, an' Polo, an' Tea-Time, if nuffink else. Unmarried they are, just stepped off the P&O; lonely, single, luvverly bachelors with six weeks home, on the lookout fer an English rose ter take back wiv 'em on their elbows. A man's got 'is natural juices, and wot yer fink they do fer a wife out there, go native? No bloody fear. Like as not yer'll end up in India, seeing the world an' talking posh, sipping tea on the lawn showing yer stiff little finger. An' all them servants!' The waiter glowered at them. 'Pay the man, that's right, fourpence won't kill yer. Good girl!'

She tugged Gloria into the sun which burnt hazily down, London smelling like the inside of a fish and the river leaden and stagnant, high tide lapping the deserted quays. The boats and stalls had vanished as though they had never been. Above the warehouses St Paul's Cathedral hung shimmering in the boiling air. Tib sniffed. 'It's breaking,' she said. 'Gonner rain. Come on. Got a way ter go.'

'Tib,' Gloria said as they walked.

Tib eyed two young scamps asleep in front of a shut-up shop window.

'Tib, it's just that I don't want ter get married yet.'

'Shut up, shut up!' Tib turned furiously. 'I'm fed up wiv yer, yer ungrateful bitch!' *God knows where we are*, Gloria realised anxiously, staring around the narrow street as the angry woman ranted. 'Yer always say wot yer don't want!' Tib screamed. 'Yer driving me up the bloody wall! Wot choice yer got about anyfink, anyway? Yer fink life owes yer a living or somefink? Look at them two.' She pointed back at the sleeping youngsters. 'Asleep me foot. They're

128

breaking in, walls is thin beneath shop winders, didn't yer know?'

'I'm sorry I got yer back up, Tib.'

'Yer frightened yer going ter see yer dad, are yer?' Tib's voice softened. 'There's millyuns and millyuns of people in London, an' lots o' diff'rent Londons, as many as there are people. Most of us never see one another. Yer ever seen anyone twice in a diff'rent place? Not less'n yer wanted ter. An' I'll tell yer this, Gloria. Yer never see yerself, 'cept in every window. Yer safe, if yer want ter be.' Her anger collapsed and she added tearfully: 'In a year 'e wouldn't recognise yer, anyway. Me dear, my advice is ter go 'ome, right now. I mean it! They'll take yer back if yer crawl.'

'I won't go 'ome,' Gloria said, 'not if that's wot 'ome's like.'

Tib squeezed her arm, understanding, then brightened. 'Gloria an' Tib, firm friends, wot? Let's 'ave some 'okey-pokey ter celebrate!' she crowed, spying a white and gold Assenheim's ice-cream barrow, a black dog sitting beside it wearing a white ruff and, like all dogs since the new law, a muzzle. 'Two 'okey-pokeys, Jack,' Tib ordered the Italian with the wooden spoon, and he scraped dabs of the watery stuff into cornets. Gloria hesitated before handing over her tuppence. 'I only got tuppence left,' she said. 'There's a luxury!' crowed Tib.

As they went on she pointed at a shabby doorway. 'Why d'yer fink I brought yer 'ere? Gloria, face it.' She touched the string around Gloria's neck, lifting part of the coin above her dress like a crescent moon. 'The melting-pot'll give yer fifteen bob fer it, maybe.'

'I don't know,' Gloria said uncertainly, 'I suppose yer right, but—'

'Remember the way lover-boy treated yer,' Tib said cunningly. 'Ran away from yer, didn't 'e? An' 'cause 'e ran away, yer ran away too. There's men fer yer, wot? Sell it, love.'

Gloria remembered Jamie Reilly running away, and how much she had wanted to hurt him because he didn't have the guts to take her. She flushed as she recalled her taunts to try and keep him. But he had been so gentle . . . she knew he really had felt deeply for her, because actions spoke louder than words. *Because I love ye, this will bring ye luck.* Hanging it around her neck. *Make of it what ye will.*

'No, it's mine, it's all fer me,' Gloria said, clutching his gift tight.

'A girl can't always say no to everyfink,' Tib explained to her, 'yer'll 'ave ter learn ter say *yes*.'

'Yes!' Gloria laughed, but Tib wasn't amused.

'Stop it, yer fine madam,' she glowered, lowering her head.

'Yes!' laughed Gloria. 'Yes, yes!'

'*Stop it*,' Tib said, but Gloria danced around her, arms outstretched, hair and coat and dress flying. 'Stop it, yer firkytoodle!' Tib swore, putting her hands over her head, then started swearing with really dreadful words, the sort that men exchange before blows outside the pub at closing-time, that dripped from a woman's lips like poison.

Gloria stopped, panting, then walked off.

'Don't run away!' Tib cried, her eyes losing their baleful glare.

'Yes!' shouted Gloria.

'Me dear! Me sweet!' Tib ran after her, wheedling. 'I'll show yer wot ter do, where ter go, yer need yer old Tib.'

'Yes?'

'Yer the girl wot always says yes!' Tib grinned until her gums were white. 'All right, yer win. I'll show yer where the British Empire Club is.'

The broad thoroughfare of the Strand was shadowless, breathless in the noonday glare. The crowds along the pavements were a motionless blur beneath the haze, while above them the buildings shimmered and quivered with heat, as though in London, brick and Portland stone were less enduring than human flesh. Gloria passed her hand dizzily across her forehead.

Tib looked back. 'Wot's up?'

'I'm tired out, it must be the 'eat.'

'Poor lamb, yer've not 'ad an easy time of it, an' not much sleep last night neither, I bet.' She slipped her hand into Gloria's. 'Come on, lamb, I knows a place yer can always rest yer 'ead.'

Tib turned along narrow sidestreets for the shade and Gloria traipsed after her past mounds of putrefying vegetables, breathing through her mouth to avoid the smell, yawning. Tib's callused grip led her across a further broad street. 'There's Leicester Square, my lamb, no unescorted ladies here . . .' The sun struck in their faces along Jermyn Street. Tib nodded down a turning to her left. 'Any number of useful places down there, Windham House Club, but they mostly know one another and can't get away wiv anyfink. There's the Nimrod an' the Sports . . . an' the British Empire.'

Tib knocked open a railing-gate and went down the steps into a graveyard. Plonking herself on the grass by a headstone with a luxurious sigh, she rested her back against a tree. 'Put yer 'ead down 'ere,' she murmured, patting her lap, 'get forty winks, poor lamb. There's time enough. I'll look out fer yer.'

Gloria lay down. 'I'm not going ter sleep . . .' she muttered.

She woke feeling that her spine and legs were stuck hard to the ground. Her neck was stiff, one arm bent uncomfortably under her. Her straw hat had been removed, but her face no longer needed its shadow: the sun was gone, its place taken by billows of cloud so dark that the sooty spike of the church spire seemed pale against them. Tib's huge, seamed fingers appeared, lightly pinching Gloria's purse between them with an almost delicate gesture, swallowing it as if by magic into the ragged sleeve. The fingers, creased and engrained with grime, reappeared and the stink of the old woman enveloped Gloria. Something tugged lightly at the front of her dress, and the string necklace began to slide upwards.

'Lie still, yer bitch,' Tib said, her rags now incongruously topped off with Gloria's smart straw hat. 'Don't move, or I'll bloody yer nose an' finish yer.'

With a cry Gloria clamped her hands over Tib's wrist, but it was greasy with congealed sweat and slid from her grasp. The old woman twisted away, dragging at the string with all her strength, for a moment pulling Gloria by her neck like a dog on a leash, Gloria scrambling on knees and knuckles after her, afraid the string would break again. She missed Tib's ankles but jumped up and the two of them bumped against the railings, fighting and wriggling. Tib gave up at once.

'I told yer ter sell it,' she murmured tearfully. 'Look wot yer made me do.' Backing around the railing, suddenly she hobbled up the steps with surprising speed. 'I got yer 'at!' Tib laughed from the road, tipping the brim with a flourish, then flicked a coppery flash into the air with her thumbnail: the last penny from Gloria's purse. 'An' me supper too!'

She dodged behind a cart, giggling victoriously, and was gone.

The silver coin hung from between Gloria's opened buttons, rotating in the grasp of its dirty claw, its dull reflections seeming to mock her face in the stormy light.

Stuffing it back inside her dress, Gloria buttoned up, then buttoned her coat too, shivering.

She looked around her. The pavements were empty beneath the dark clouds. She was utterly alone.

Chapter Eight

Gloria sat on the steps. A warm, stormy breeze was getting up, whirling scraps of paper in the corners of the churchyard, sending tickling strands of her hair flying across her face. A piece of paper fluttered in front of her, an old Order of Service from some wedding or other, and she snatched it and tore it up. Her bag was opened, the purse gone, but the theft of the hat was worse: a girl felt naked without a hat. The wind flapped the hem of her yellow dress, showing her ankles, her shoes half-off to ease her swollen, aching feet: she felt each toe with its own blister from the day's unaccustomed walking, Tib's callous merry-go-round from Hyde Park to Billingsgate and the Strand to St James's. Gloria was determined not to feel sorry for herself. She put her hands on her forehead to stop the hair flying in her eyes, which had made them water.

'Face it, girl,' she told herself, 'yer was royally fleeced. Yer can't blame Tib, it's yer own fault. Yer asked fer exactly wot yer got, yer ninny.'

A verger came out of the church holding down his hat, a long key in his other hand. 'Not 'ere,' he said, swinging the railing-gate half shut behind her, 'closing time.' There was no sympathy in his averted, impatient face; in a way, Gloria realised, he had not seen her. He was thinking of his tea which his wife would have laid out ready.

'I need somewhere to sleep,' she told him.

'Not 'ere.' He closed the gate another inch.

London was a country, a place of customs and rules which she must obey. 'Then where can I go?'

'Not 'ere.'

'That's all?' Gloria sparked.

'That's enough, young woman.'

He made her squeeze past him, then slammed the gate and locked it angrily, staring after her. Gloria crossed the street. A costerwoman wearing large gold earrings dumped a mess of cherries and plums from her basket rather than carry them home. Gloria waited, looking around, feeling dirty and unglamorous, then snatched one guiltily. It tasted fine.

'I'm gonner prove yer all wrong,' she told herself. 'I'm never gonner crawl back 'ome so yer can praise yerselves ter the 'eavens saying, *We was right all along, an' this proves it: Gloria's crawled back ter us.*' Vindication, being right, showing that she had done nothing wrong so that everyone could see it, was now much more important to her than money or pride. She wanted people to look at her, really look at her, and she thought of Jamie Reilly without love. What a lovely young man, and she had really thought he could change the world. Him standing by Pat Ryan's stable looking at her with his soul in his eyes. Taking her in his arms, covering her face with kisses. She'd believed in him.

She dashed her hand across her face, brushing away

Jamie and everything that had been between them. But remembering his voice. His plans, his ideas.

Get on! Get Capital!

That was man's talk. There was only one way for a woman to Get Capital, she must marry it. Tib was right after all: to find a fine young gentleman, a girl made ambitious by circumstances must go where the fine young gentlemen go. And Tib had pointed out St James's Square, the heart of Clubland, just three or four hundred feet away down York Street.

''Ere I am, an' 'ere I go,' Gloria told herself. 'Fight, an' fight, an' never surrender, girl. Fings always turn up fer the brightest after they've been blackest.' There was a pub opposite the churchyard and she gave her face a spit and polish with her handkerchief in front of herself in the frosted glass, then started brushing her hair. She found two more pubs in the first few yards of York Street, and by the time she passed the third, her reflection walked with style and a swing. Gloria had made up her mind to look good and nothing was going to stop her, but there were no quickwitted Irish to chi-hike with here. An old boy in an impressive tailored suit passed her going the other way, and she gave him an impressed smile, the sort that over the counter of the Railway shop made younger men buy a book they didn't want, but this old bird hurried on, though he kept looking back over his shoulder. He didn't say anything and neither did she. But anything was better than being ignored, and Gloria was elated. By the time she reached the square, by willpower alone she was feeling on top of the world.

An hour later all that had changed. St James's was nothing like the crowded backstreets of Marylebone or Lisson Grove, with families spilling out on to the pavement and children playing. These neat pavements encircling the railed park, with only a statue of someone on horseback in the middle, were a desert. The silence of it gave her a headache. The imposing residences hid any life like a secret inside them, as thick curtains were dragged by flunkeys across the windows. When someone did arrive or depart, it was usually by private carriage or hansom cab. No one noticed her. With dusk there was more coming and going: men in evening dress disembarking for the East India United Service Club, mahogany-faced sea-captains hobnobbing with colonial administrators, groups of younger men on leave coming out hailing hackneys with glowing cigars and well-fed laughter. All of them ignored Gloria as though she did not exist.

The lamplighter came running round, reaching up under the glass globes with a long bull's-eye pole tipped with flame, and his spotty dog barked at her.

She stood miserably in her shadow under the white glow.

Finally a uniformed commissionaire descended some steps. 'Shove it, child,' he grunted, not looking her in the eye. 'Yer giving me the snake, it's making me nervous.' He pointed. 'Hoof it ter the north side fer a try,' he suggested cunningly, keeping his side of the square clear.

'But I'm not doing nuffink wrong,' she said.

'I know wot yer doing,' he said, watching her go.

Almost at once she struck gold. The toff sauntering down

the steps of the British Empire Club was about thirty years old, with a black moustache and square jaw, and as he glanced at her his appreciative smile revealed firm white teeth. Gloria's heart thudded. He held white gloves in one hand and a silver-topped stick in the other. For a moment he paused between the steps and his carriage, watching her, then bounded inside. She heard the double knock of his stick on the roof and the driver cracked his whip along York Street. Gloria stared after the vehicle, at the lamplights sweeping over the black paint and flickering in the long spokes of the wheels.

At the top of the street the carriage suddenly turned, as if returning, but then stopped at the kerb, deliberately it seemed, in the pool of darkness between two streetlights, as though waiting for her. The blinkered mare snorted and shook her mane, then was still. The muffled driver sat like a statue, the whip in his immobile hand gently swinging its lash in the wind.

Gloria waved and ran along the road. She made herself slow down for a more dignified entrance.

The door was swung open by pressure from the silver-topped cane. She glimpsed buttoned red leather illuminated by a slant of lamplight, but the rest of the interior was dark. His shadow moved.

'Jump up then!' came his voice.

Gloria drew back.

Suddenly she knew what would happen. She would get in and Doris Mabb's worst nightmares would come true. She would be seized by Jack the Ripper and unspeakable things would happen while the horse clopped patiently ahead of the carriage through the streets of London, whilst from the outside nothing would seem to be wrong. A lady would be safe with such a man, but not the kind of girl Gloria might appear to be, the lapels of her overcoat huddled to her neck and the wind tangling her hair.

'Haven't got all night, don't you know,' his voice came.

''Oo are yer?' she demanded.

'Ho, we don't even say our aitches, what? I thought you were a better sort than that.'

Gloria said: 'Let me see yer face.'

'Your price is too high.' She heard his stick bang the roof. 'Drive on!'

The carriage turned, circling her, and drove off towards Jermyn Street.

'I'm just as good as yer are.' Gloria, enraged, walked at first, then ran after the disappearing vehicle. 'D'yer 'ear me?' she shouted, 'yer no better than me, yer aren't! Yer no better!'

As she came running up to Piccadilly through Church Place, she didn't notice the round-shouldered, ragged figure, complete with straw hat, hobbling across the narrow shadowed entrance behind her. Tragedy Tib's eyes were fixed on the empty churchyard, and as soon as she saw the gate was locked, she turned and hobbled down towards St James's Square and the British Empire Club.

Amazed to find herself in a jostling mass of women and men sliding like a river along the elegant glass windows of darkened shops, Gloria was swept into a broad thoroughfare so crowded with dogs and barrows and carts that she

140

did not know which way to turn. Horses' heads tossed among the women's extraordinary feathered hats and their colourful dresses and umbrellas, so that it took her a few moments to recognise the curved Quadrant, familiar from a hundred fashion prints of ladies modelling glorious trousseaux and princess bonnets. She was in Regent Street.

But these women she now saw were every shape and size, with faces of every sort, just as nature made them: cheeks round and red as apples or flat as flounders, eyes black or blue or green starred by gaslights, noses demurely retroussé or aquiline as witches' beaks. Above the garish skirts of every hue, only one thing was the same. Each pair of lips was stretched into a smile.

The men, of course, were drunk. They hid it because that's what men are best at, but Gloria remembered the Railway clerks pissing from the canal bridge to assert their superiority over the slums below. Their thumbs stuck in their waistcoat pockets, the arms of giggling girls clamped in the crooks of their elbows, these Blackford swells in their hired suits swaggered cockily from pub to pub with their prey in tow and that odd blue pallor stealing into their faces, gaslight and too much gin. The girls let themselves be stalked and pulled along, each mouth wearing that terrible grin, and suddenly Gloria understood who was the hunter, and who the hunted. Not many men would make it home to their wives with money in their pockets.

Faces turned up to the sky, which curved like a black road above the gaunt gaslit façades, each windowsill trailing its spike of shadow upwards. The first drops of rain fell. For the moment there was a breathless silence, then the heavens opened and every hackney was instantly booked, the enormous crowd seeming to melt away like the floodwater which slid down the gutters and drains. Within minutes only a few dregs were left, girls in shawls calling to one another by name, companions in misery staring glumly from the shelter of the Quadrant's façade at the empty roadway that shone like beaten silver.

'Coming down in bucketsful, and well set in,' muttered one of them. 'That's it for tonight, gels.' Peering between the shop-pillars, her ginger hair was plastered to her shoulders by a mixture of suet and rainwater, and the drops clustered along each coarse strand as big as beads. 'You off home to bye-byes, Whitey?' she called to another doorway.

'Glizzard'd kill me if'n I came 'ome alone,' Whitey said, running in, shaking out her umbrella over Gloria with a fierce look in her eye. She was a short, plump crumb of a girl in an orange and black dress, a black fishnet shawl strung across her stocky shoulders, her hair boot-blacked and her eyes stark with kohl. The rest of her face, apart from startling crimson lips, was thickly pancaked with white lead. 'I fink we got a dolly-mop 'ere, Lady Abigail,' she said to her companion, tossing her head at Gloria.

'No I'm not!' Gloria said.

'What does it matter tonight?' the ginger-haired Lady Abigail said. 'There's bugger-all for any of us.'

'It's the principle of the fing,' Whitey said, fighting her corner. 'It's us an' them.'

'That's wot people like yer always say.' Gloria wasn't going to be put down.

'The dolly-mop speaks,' Whitey sneered.

'Yer can't talk – yer wearing enough icing-sugar ter stick yer on a cake!'

Lady Abigail laughed, but Whitey glowered so fiercely that it seemed her face might crack. 'That's fighting talk, that is.'

'No, no, Whitey, you never learn.' Lady Abigail touched Gloria's arm and grinned with ochre-yellow teeth. 'Whitey's a fool! – always picks on someone bigger than herself. You're new, my sweet, aren't you?'

'No!' Gloria had learnt that lesson: never show weakness. 'Me name's Gloria.' On an instinct she gave her mother's maiden name. 'Paz. Gloria Paz.'

'From Gloria in the George Bernard Shaw play? That's how Whitey started on the streets, by the steps of the slaney. The theatre crowd's such good trade.'

'I blooming never!' Whitey exclaimed. 'I might be over the 'ill, but I'm not *twice* as old as wot she is.'

'Gloria's me Mum's name, too,' Gloria said with a tremble in her voice, 'it's supposed ter go back. Foreign, Spanish maybe.'

'Bleeding dolly-mop amateurs,' Whitey said, 'I'm fed up wiv it. It waters the pot an' there's less fer us perfeshnals.'

'You've been listening to Willy,' Lady Abigail tick-tocked her finger reprovingly.

'*An*' she's a foreigner.'

Gloria looked around her: the stone façades were dark and dribbling with wet, the wind was blowing the rain up the road. Yes, London was like a foreign country.

'You'll pick up when the publics close,' Lady Abigail reassured Whitey, and Gloria realised that Whitey was so hostile because she was very frightened. Without a customer, there would be no pillow for Whitey's head tonight.

'This blasted bloody wevver,' Whitey confessed miserably, 'they'll stick in their cabs ter the Supper Clubs, then it'll be after midnight till they're out.'

'I'm going to try on one of the cock and hens clubs,' Lady Abigail decided.

'Yer go yer barket,' a third girl sniffed, her voice distorted by a streaming cold. She hawked her nose on the pavement with a satisfied sigh. 'Know yer market, I mean. Is me dose red?'

'Off 'ome wiv yer, Miz,' Whitey addressed her jealously, 'yer still a good earner. Willy'll tick yer fer a room.'

''Luck, Whitey.'

''Luck, Miz. 'Ope the brat ain't bawling.'

'Let's see, the Red Beer's got a canopy,' Lady Abigail decided cheerfully, flicking her fingers at the rain, then turned without a second glance at Whitey and Gloria and left them standing alone, her down-at-heel shoes clapping out of hearing along a sidestreet.

Whitey looked at Gloria, waiting until the last echoes died; only the rush of the rain remained. She raised her voice. ''Oo yer wiv?'

Gloria shook her head.

'Everyone's got someone. Miz an' me, we got Willy Glizzard. 'E's all right, the bastard. Come on, luv, can't stay 'ere, the Vine Street nick's just round the corner.' She touched Gloria beneath the eye. 'No blubbing, now. Don't show that side to London, only the best 'ere. Stick under

me umberella!' She snatched Gloria's hand and ran her
across the drenching road to the shelter of a doorway
beneath an ornate lantern. 'Cording's, this is – can't do
much better than this – Waterproof Garments, by Royal
Appointment ter 'Er Majesty the Queen.' All the time she
was eyeing Gloria as a man would, summing her up. 'Yer
need an 'ot cup o' tea, I fink, once yer stop feelin' sorry fer
yerself an' pull yerself together, an' no mistake. An' I'm
not seeing yer quite at yer very best. Come on!' She tugged
her past the shop fronts then tucked them both into the
broad entrance of the International Fur Store, its windows
shadowy with beautifully dressed wicker mannequins,
ladies' heads swathed in hats of baby leopard-skin, fox
stoles showing their claws. Whitey bent solemnly forward
so that the water trickled in a stream from the broad brim of
her hat on to the marble, but she didn't take her eyes from
Gloria. 'This is me pitch,' she said. 'It's all mine, by right.
Bin 'ere donkey's years.'

''Ow long they called yer Whitey?'

'Since it's bin me name.' The prostitute pulled out her
collar with one finger to show her skin beneath, raddled
with syphilitic sores. A gentleman strolled past beneath an
umbrella. 'What they don't know won't 'urt 'em,' she
nodded contemptuously. The man stopped to look in a
shop window.

''E's just looking,' Gloria said.

'Yuss, an' I know wot 'e's looking fer,' Whitey said
comfortably. 'Men don't look in shop winders, goes against
their nature. 'E'll be back, I might get some remedy
ternight after all.'

On the far side of the street there was an outburst of shouting and catcalls as a huddle of girls spilled from a doorway. After some angry pushing and shoving the ones who had lost their place in the shelter struck across the street in a group, walking cockily though they were barefooted, bottles swinging from their hands. One had a baby asleep on her back, its head bobbing from the sacking. The mother bumped into a lamp-post but her expression, fixed on Whitey, didn't change.

'No shelter 'ere,' Whitey said. 'No room at the inn fer yer 'ere, Janey, nor you Maisie . . .' The others gathered round.

''Oo's the new girl?' they asked, picking at Gloria's clothes.

'Shove off,' Whitey said, 'this is my place.'

'Yer past it,' slurred the one with the baby, sliding her shoulder along the glass like a cat. 'Yer past it, Whitey, an' yer know it. Why don't yer give up?'

'Why don't yer give yer baby some milk?' Whitey demanded aggressively, not giving an inch.

It was horrible looking at the baby, asleep or dead, and Gloria drew back through the crowd to cleaner air. Drops of rain pattered on her shoulders. The man's voice spoke behind her.

'How much?'

Gloria flushed bright red, but of course in the dark he could not see. 'Hey!' Whitey shouted, 'wot yer up to?' She pushed Gloria angrily aside. 'Don't mind 'er. Do yer now, sir?' she asked willingly.

The man beneath the umbrella pointed his manicured finger at Gloria. 'Her.'

'No, sir, not that one, sir, not ternight.'

'Saving 'er fer yerself, Whitey?' jeered the girl with the baby.

'Shut yer 'ole!' shrieked Whitey. A cunning note entered her voice. 'No, I'm saving 'er fer Mr Glizzard. Yuss, that's wot I'm doing, then it don't matter if I don't work ternight. Clear off, all of yer!'

The man grabbed Gloria's arm. The girl with the baby made a drunken swing at Whitey with her bottle, missed, and Whitey kicked her smartly on the ankle. The man tugged at Gloria and a couple of the other girls caught her round the waist, dragging her the other way in a confusion of arms and legs. The man, his face close to Gloria's, stuck out his lower teeth in determination and deliberately twisted her arm, hurting her to make her go with him, to make her cry out to the others to let her go.

'Stop,' said a quiet, sharp voice. Looking ashamed of themselves, the girls parted to let a wiry, nondescript-looking man through. Among them, it seemed, his word was law. His face was like a blade, as cleanshaven as though the barber shops were still open. He looked round the girls, the rain pouring down on them. He wore a gleaming Cording waterproof, beautifully tailored, though perhaps for a form more substantial than his own; his head was kept dry by a soft felt trilby. The girls' skirts were heavy with rainwater, splashed with filth from the roadway, but his shoes were shining patent-leather Walk-Over pumps. His narrowed eyes stopped on Gloria.

The man with the umbrella hoisted himself to his full

height and recovered his dignity. 'Dirt!' he said of her. 'Scum!'

The newcomer glanced at him. 'Run fer yer life,' he said, calm, but in a voice as sharp as steel.

The man backed, then ran. A couple of the girls shouted curses after him, then turned their hard, flat eyes back to the man in the soft felt hat, hanging on his every word.

Whitey pushed Gloria forward. 'Permit me ter interdooce yer, Gloria,' she said. 'Mr William Glizzard, of Savile Row.'

Chapter Nine

'Get off the earth,' he told the girls. 'E-vap-o-rate.'

He pushed Gloria beneath the lantern of the International Fur Store, his fingers on her jaw, examining her features with quick flicks of his eyes.

'I was going ter bring 'er ter yer, Mr Glizzard,' called Whitey from the rain, where her solitary figure remained, watching them heedless of the downpour. Her hand was pressed to her left cheek.

He spared her a glance. 'Wot's up wiv yer phiz, Whitey?'

She took her hand away, revealing three deep vertical scratches. 'Janey caught me one. I'll be chipper in a week—'

'Yer finished,' Willy Glizzard said, running his fingertips along Gloria's high cheekbones, plunging his hands beneath her hair to check her earlobes for jewellery, staring into her eyes.

'I brought yer the girl, Willy, an' she's worth it, ain't she?' griped Whitey. 'Look 'ow she 'olds 'erself, the way she stands. An' maybe she's got choosing-money.'

'That's all!' Willy said impatiently. 'All right, Whitey, I'll see yer in Reen's shoes first thing. It's a monarcher a week

149

fer yer, on a good week.' He flicked her a small silver coin without turning. 'Find yerself somewhere fer ternight. Now get out me air!' he shouted, 'I want ter breathe.'

Alone, he studied Gloria quietly.

'Gloria,' he said, rolling the name around his mouth like a sweet.

'Don't touch me,' she warned him, when his hands dropped to her shoulders.

'I never touch the merchandise,' he said. 'That's the first law a pimp lives by, didn't yer know?' He pushed back his hat with his thumb, but didn't take his face out of hers. 'Yer really are wot yer seem ter be, ain't yer?'

Her mouth moved. She shrugged.

'Real tears,' he whispered. 'I've never seen a woman cry.' He reached up, but she flinched away. 'Tears are weakness, my luv.'

'I'm not afraid of yer, Mr Glizzard.'

'That strong, are yer? Whoops!' He held her up before she fell down. She pushed him away with the palms of her hands, then pressed them dizzily to her head.

''Ere only the strong survive,' he whispered, sticking to her again. 'But yer got it.' He eyed her figure appreciatively. 'Yer got it in spades. Yer don't mind me looking at yer, really, do yer. No, I can see yer don't. Yer want me ter look at yer, don't yer! Yer want ter be pretty an' nicely turned out. Yes, yer do, whether yer admit it or not, all yer girls do, bless yer 'earts. Yer safe wiv me,' he decided, taking her elbow. 'That's wot we're fer, after all.'

But she wouldn't move.

'Yer can't stay 'ere all night,' he said gently. 'Yer exhausted, an' yer don't look a 'undred per cent. Yer got a pounding 'eadache, I can tell just by looking at yer, yer poor thing. I'll advance yer shelter an' a place ter lay yer 'ead, no questions asked. Come on now, my luv. Quick-march! Filthy night!'

This time he took her by the hand, leading her a few doors down then turning into Burlington Street, not hurrying her, but all his senses attentive. 'Yer stood up fer yerself back there,' he muttered as they walked, 'but when it comes down ter it, a girl 'as ter make sensible decisions.'

'Where are we?'

'Nice 'ouses! One of the finest parts of London, though I do say so meself.' He squeezed her hand reassuringly. 'Of course my part of it's not quite so nice.' He wanted her to understand. 'It's an 'ard life, this, living at the bottom of the sea. Look, 'ere's Savile Row, yer see a few bob along 'ere, rock-solid middle-class dwellings, I calls 'em. An' just on t'other side of them rooftops, wot yer got but Bond Street an' Berkeley Square fer the real spondulicks. Love is love, believe me,' he said sadly, 'an' a customer's a customer, only the size of the wallet differs. The dregs come falling down, an' down, an' Willy Glizzard feeds on 'em.'

He stopped her on the corner, a terrible look in his eyes. 'Yer lovely,' he said. 'Wot yer done ter me?'

He turned right along Savile Row, going only a few paces before the street ended in miserable ramshacks: a ragged school, some tumbledown stables leaking wet straw into the coachyard; over this a tangle of steep roofs canted this way and that, and garret windows stared from mouldy plaster gables. Willy put his head down, hurrying, tugging her after him through a covered archway, past sleeping shapes covered with stolen straw, into a winding court open to the rain. The overhanging confines smelt sewery, and in one place a bulging wall was shored up with mossy battens. There was even a tiny James Smith umbrella shop, less than four feet deep with all the stock packed into a single bow window: 'By appointment to Mr Gladstone', claimed a handwritten sign. At the far end, beyond a mess of windows and doors that were all at different levels above and below ground and had steps up and down to them, an archway led into some other thoroughfare. To Gloria's ears the sound of falling rain echoed very loudly here, trapped between the walls. Willy tugged her up some steps and gave a special knock on a peeling door. After a pause it began to open and he thrust it aside. Gloria found herself pulled into a narrow passage.

On the hoop-backed chair placed within reach of the door sat a very old lady, blinking sleepily. Her face was a map of wrinkles and she was dressed in black lace, with red boots. Beside her was a pile of dirty sheets, neatly folded. 'I wasn't!' she cackled.

'Yer was sleeping it off,' Willy cursed her over his shoulder, climbing the stairs, 'yer out, Reen. Whitey's taking yer place. Out on yer neck tomorrer morning.'

'Yer mind me dignity, young Glizzard!' she shrieked after him, 'I knew yer ma, that's all!'

'Don't mind 'er,' Willy muttered, 'she got no class.'

Footsteps thudded to an open door on the landing and

Gloria shied back, her heart thudding in her head at the sight of the man who appeared. He wore a pink striped jersey, once red no doubt but faded. His eyes did not move; he turned his whole head to examine her, and his face was peppered with scars as if from birdshot. 'Meet me pal Strawberry,' grunted Willy, ''e's the bully wot settles any trouble.' He pulled Gloria past him, starting another flight of stairs. 'She's coming in an' she's not going out,' he called down. 'Say it.'

'She's not going out, guv'nor.'

'Right, Strawberry.'

'Right, guv'nor,' Strawberry said, and crossed his arms.

When the steps rose no further, Willy paused to unlock with a brass key the hardwood door in front of him, the lock turning with a heavy, well-oiled click, then lit a candle and climbed a further staircase into a room that made Gloria look around her in wonder.

'I'm not like them,' Willy said.

The bare boards were covered by a sumptuous maroon rug, no doubt from some exotic country, woven with a dark yellow design that teased the eye with its pattern, half-seen by golden candlelight. The carpet was turned slightly up the skirtings, as if made for a room bigger than this, but paintings lined the walls in rich gilt frames, though they were mostly hung very low down, as if to be admired while lying on the four-poster bed. Everything must have been ferried up in sections: above the artwork the walls angled inwards with the pitch of the roof, barely clearing the bed-drapes, meeting at an apex over their heads. At the foot of the bed stood a beautifully polished dresser with a fine porcelain pitcher and bowl; in the corner behind the stairs she saw a roll-top desk, closed up, and a swivel chair. Rain pattered down the single window. Willy followed her around with the candle.

'This is ever so kind of yer,' she said. The bed looked so soft and comfortable that Gloria's heart went out to it, and she longed to flop down and sleep for a week. 'I'll clean up fer yer in the morning, I promise I will.'

She turned, and he grabbed her elbows and kissed her.

He recoiled angrily, as though *she* had done it, then took off his hat and threw it in the corner. 'Fer God's sake get out of 'ere,' he said, shaking his head dismally. 'It's all nicked, there's nothing 'ere wot's mine. It's nice as a ha'porth of silver spoons – shine, that's all, just shine. Yer look so beautiful standin' there.' He clenched his fist so angrily round the candle that she thought the stem would snap. 'Wot yer fink yer was doing out there?' he shouted. 'Go 'ome!'

Wax dripped on his hand and he found a candlestick, shoved the candle in it, then lowered it carefully on to the frayed lace covering the dresser-top. He wouldn't meet her eye. 'Wot yer looking at me like that fer?' he muttered. He went into the corner and shrugged off his raincoat with angry jerks of his shoulders, but then hung it up neatly. A terrible cry came up from the street below and they both listened. There was only the sound of the rain.

'Don't put me out,' she said. 'I couldn't face it.'

Without his posh raincoat he looked such a funny little man, she thought, watching him struggle with himself about whether to let her stay or not. He thought he was so tough, but she could see him deciding first one way, then the other, looking at her with almost an appealing expression. He was no taller than her and much skinnier, wearing a tight suit, the jacket buttons undone to reveal a stylish, peacock-coloured waistcoat.

'Yer don't know wot yer doing ter me,' he said, staring at her angrily, then contradicted himself. 'No, yer do, yer all the same!' he swore. He took off his soaking shoes and socks and wrung them out, but he kept his trousers on. The socks, she noticed with sleepy admiration, matched his waistcoat.

He pointed at the bed. 'All right. My side over there on the left. Yer side over there on the right. Fair?'

It was a very broad bed, and Gloria was used to sharing, but still she said doubtfully, 'I don't know.'

'Trust me.'

He took her coat, then blew out the candle and lay apart from her in the dark. Gloria yawned sleepily.

Cheating with his deep, slow breaths, he waited until he was sure she was asleep.

Willy Glizzard rolled over, feeling her damp heat beneath the sheet, and to him it was erotic. 'I lied,' he whispered, sending his hand stealing into the folds of her skirt.

The softness of her made him feel harder than ever; his mouth filled with saliva, thick and slippery with desire, as he hoisted himself over her, lifting her skirt carefully so as not to awaken her. Parting her bare knees with his own knees, he freed his trousers with a quick jerk of his belt and sank down on her, then covered her mouth as he pushed, hard. Her eyes flickered open beneath him as she woke. 'It's all right,' he groaned, 'don't worry.' He took his pumping weight on both hands, covering her mouth with kisses instead. Her head turned from side to side but she was trapped beneath him, and he laughed excitedly. She seemed unable to resist or to stop the pleasure her body was giving him, and the more he pushed into her the more of a man he felt himself become. Her struggles were caresses to him, her scratches heightened his excitement. 'Don't stop,' he hissed, 'I can't 'elp meself.' Then he cried out, shoving with all his strength, as he lost himself in her. 'Oh God, I can't 'elp it. I don't know 'ow ter keep a girl, I love yer, I must be crazy!' He shouted out her name, and again how much he loved her. Then abruptly his strength left him and he flopped on her. For a moment he felt as though he had come to the summit of a tremendous hill and owned the whole new landscape below.

'There, that wasn't so bad, was it?' he whispered in his self-congratulation, then sadness washed over him to hear her weeping. 'I can't even trust myself,' he muttered. 'I didn't really mean ter do it. I must be out of me mind, spoiling the merchandise! I dunno wot came over me ... she's only a girl ...'

Gloria could not answer him. The wet smell of her dress seemed to be growing more powerful until it filled her mind, she could think of nothing else. As a sick feeling rose up her throat, she could not swallow it down. Her head thumped and she gulped. 'I think I've eaten something,' she mumbled.

'Wot's the matter?' Willy demanded suspiciously, then

jumped to his knees. 'Not in 'ere! No, not on me carpet! There's a pot under the bed—' She erupted with a terrific gagging noise. Willy backed to the far side of the room, clutching the sheets around him like a maiden as he listened to her retching.

'Oh my God,' he said. 'It's cholera.'

'It's not cholera, yer bloomin' coward,' Whitey said. She looked down at the sleeping girl covered by the sheet. 'It's exhaustion. She was tired and worried frantic last night, that's all. Gave yer a proper scare, though, I bet!' she added with relish. Willy stood there in his shirtsleeves looking both dangerous and ridiculous, the way men did without their breeches. Hard muscles moved under that handsome, wicked face of his in the sunlight pouring through the window, and Whitey didn't push him too far. She searched in the night-pot, opening the window to get rid of the smell of the vomit, then chucked the contents down the roof. 'Nothing worse than gone-over cherries and plums, I'd wager, or drinking stale water. Yer safe, Willy.' She touched the 'gooseberry' sheet, stolen off someone's washing line, which covered the girl. 'Don't yer 'ave *anyfink* of yer own, not even in yer own bedroom? Yer mean ter a fault, Willy, really yer is. Got choosing-money ter buy 'erself in, 'as she?'

'I dunno.'

'That's not like yer, Willy! A beauty like that don't need it, maybe.' She peeled back the sheet, then tightened her lips at what she saw. 'Yer couldn't keep yer 'ands off her, could yer! Yer a real bastard, Willy Glizzard.'

Willy was both cocky and defensive. 'It's not my fault. Look at 'er, she's lovely. 'Ow was I ter know she 'adn't been around?'

'Well, she 'as now,' said Whitey, scratching the three long scabs down her cheek, which were starting to itch. 'Wot's got inter yer, Willy, yer lost yer sense? A stunner like 'er would've bin good fer fifty quid intact, if yer'd 'andled 'er right. Instead yer go an' ruin 'er yerself. An' fer wot?'

'Because she makes me feel like a real man, that's wot.' Willy's voice rose. 'That's the first time I've 'ad a girl an' felt more of a man after than I did before, an' she's mine.'

'Yer a fool,' Whitey sighed. 'Yer don't 'ave a monopoly on it, I recall I was a fool fer yer once.'

'Well, I wasn't fer yer, yer old whore.'

'Yer was this time,' Whitey said, looking down at the sleeping girl. 'A royal fool.'

'Yer go on about it,' Willy said dangerously, 'I'll change yer face. I mean it.'

'I know yer mean it, yer never say anyfink yer don't mean.' Whitey nodded at the stairwell. 'Stop ogling 'er bubs an' start behaving like a proper pimp, why don't yer? Get out of 'ere awhile an' do somefink useful. Hey, Willy,' she called, 'don't ferget yer trousers. And ask Reen ter step up, will yer?' she added insolently, 'I 'ate changing sheets. I'm not yer bleeding maid.'

She listened to his footsteps fade downstairs, then turned back to the bed. 'Yer can stop pretending an' open yer peepers now,' she said with rough tenderness. 'Welcome ter the slippery slope.'

Gloria's eyes opened. 'Oh Whitey, I did try ter make 'im stop.'

''Course yer did,' Whitey said in an unconvinced voice, checking her makeup in the mirror.

'I felt so ill, an' I just wanted ter forget about 'im. But he – he—' She choked back a sob.

'I know wot yer did, luv.'

'Yer aren't blaming *me*?' Gloria tried to reach out to the older woman. 'Wotever I did made 'im worse.'

'Nah, better,' Whitey said, with a wink in the mirror.

'It wasn't like that – it was awful!'

'Willy didn't fink so,' Whitey pointed out sensibly. 'Yer scored quite a bullseye there, in my opinion, yer clever girl. Don't expect no sympathy from me.'

'But I just wanted ter sleep.'

'What's new about that wiv men?' Whitey turned wearily. 'That's usually when they takes advantage of yer, when yer not feeling yer best, or when yer've 'ad one or two too many. Don't be ashamed, we live an' learn. Still, yer as big a fool as wot Willy is, because, my dear, yer did feel a little bit fer 'im, didn't yer?'

Gloria sat up and tried to fiddle the straps of her dress over her shoulders. 'I think I did. It sort of 'appened.' She saw her bare knees were showing beneath the hem and tried to pull it down.

'Never mind playing the outraged virgin any more, yer won't need that dowdy old thing again. Face up to it. I'll get Reen to wash that, we can use it downstairs.' Whitey shook her head at the foolishness of youngsters. 'It's called innocence. Stupid, in other words. Yer thought, 'e's not so bad, an' 'e's bin kind. Yer gave it away fer nothing,' she said with contempt. She studied Gloria's dry-eyed face. 'No waterworks terday, huh? Yer learned somefink last night. Next yer'll learn ter turn 'em on an' off, I daresay – those luvverly slanty eyes yer got. Cheer up! Yer'll be one of us in no time.'

Gloria shook her head. 'Willy said 'e loved me.'

'Bless yer, luv,' said Whitey cheerfully, drawing the dress over Gloria's shoulders, 'they all say that.'

'But 'e *showed* me 'e did.' Gloria hugged her camisole and petticoats around her.

'Reen!' bellowed Whitey, chucking the dress down the stairwell, 'where the bleedin' 'eck are yer, yer old tart?'

'I need a bath,' Gloria appealed to her.

'Wot, yer fink we got running water or somefink! I'm going ter carry bathwater up four floors like a milkmaid, am I? There's the bowl an' pitcher, use it. Reen's bringing some rags.'

There was a scuttling sound and Reen came up the stairs, black lace and red boots even at this hour. ''E's in a terrible mood,' she grinned toothlessly in Gloria's face, but she was speaking to Whitey. ''E knows 'e's bin a naughty boy, does Glizzard. 'E's being defiant, got 'is ma's temper. Gimme yer petticoats,' she hissed at Gloria, 'legs in the air, gel.'

'Go on, Glo,' Whitey said tiredly, 'I've done it fer worse folk than Reen, I can tell yer.' She slopped water from the pitcher into the bowl. ''Ere yer are.' She stood close beside Gloria as she washed herself, then touched the smooth pale skin with a sigh of loss. 'Ruined.'

'She could still fake it,' Reen said.

Gloria looked at her in the mirror. 'Wot, pretend I liked—'

'Not fake pleasure, yer idjit,' Reen cackled. 'Pain.'

'They don't want yer ter enjoy it,' Whitey explained, combing out Gloria's shining hair with brisk businesslike strokes, 'they just want yer ter be clean. Oh!' she cried, affecting a girlish tone and sobbing dramatically, 'stop, stop, yer 'urting me! Yer'll get ten times the price,' she finished in her usual flat voice. 'We'll even give yer a little tube of the red stuff. Not going too fast fer yer, am I?'

'Somefink disgusting about the thought of enjoying it,' Reen grumbled. 'An' wot man'd ever want yer ter? 'E'd 'ave ter fink of yer, not of 'imself. Why, yer couldn't charge nuffink.'

Whitey found something. 'Wot's this!' She used the teeth of the comb to pull up the string around Gloria's neck. 'Oy-oy-oy, somefink religious?'

Gloria tried to hide it behind her palm. 'Yuss, it's worthless.'

Whitey prised away her fingers with amazing strength and Reen put her sharp chin on Gloria's collar-bone, peering over her shoulder. 'Choosing-money?' she said, with an exhalation of rummy breath.

'It doesn't mean a fing,' Gloria told Whitey urgently, shrugging Reen away.

'If yer say it don't, then it do,' said Whitey slowly. 'It means a whole lot ter yer.' She turned it over in her hands. Gloria grabbed it back.

'Mr Glizzard, sir!' yelled Reen, 'a little somefink fer yer up 'ere!'

Willy came up. 'Get away from 'er, yer 'orrid crones,' he said when he saw what they were doing. 'Leave 'er alone.'

'Look at this!' Reen said. 'She says it's just religious, that's all.'

Willy ignored her, taking Gloria in his arms, and putting his face close to hers. 'I bin finking about wot I did last night, an' I'm truly sorry,' he told her with that irrepressible, saucy grin she couldn't help liking him for. She could see he wasn't really sorry, and he was looking at her in that way again.

'Don't give me none of that soft soap,' she said coyly.

'There's something I do mean, Gloria Paz,' Willy said sincerely. 'Will yer ever forgive me? Say yer'll forgive me.' He searched her anxious blue eyes with a brown, steady gaze whose honesty she could not doubt.

'No, don't,' Whitey said. 'Never trust 'em.'

'Yes!' Gloria told him, 'I might forgive yer,' and he hugged her.

'As a personal favour ter yer, Glo,' Willy Glizzard said, and with one hand he flicked the string over her head, palming the coin effortlessly into his breeches pocket, 'I'll 'ave this put on somefink better'n a bit of lousy string, wot? An' I'll keep it safe fer yer, just in case yer change yer mind about anyfink. 'Cause I can see it *does* mean somefink ter yer.' He grinned, kissing her mouth and giving her a smack on the bottom at the same time. 'But not more than me, right?'

Chapter Ten

The hot spell broke and the weather turned unsettled just as harvest-time began to empty the streets of London: one day it would be raining, the next the air shone as sharp as a pin. Gloria looked from her window down the jagged rooftops dwindling to the gleam of the Thames, the dark stain of Southwark beyond, the river's loops to Greenwich and the vivid hills rising behind: the countryside which overlooked London like a mute green witness.

Whitey brought meals up to her on a silver tray stamped *Hôtel Cecil*. 'Congratulations,' she said ironically, looking enviously around Willy's room and Gloria in it, 'yer made it over the top over all of us wiv one bound.'

'Wot yer talking about?' Gloria said.

Whitey braced her hands on her hips, unimpressed. 'Only career that starts at the top and ends at the bottom: prostitution.'

'But I'm not,' Gloria said. 'Listen, Whitey, I'm glad yer cuts 'ave mended,' she called after the disappearing figure, but Whitey, plodding downstairs, just grunted at this attempt at friendship, and shut the door behind her. It was the first time Gloria had heard the lock click closed, her senses becoming attuned to Willy's place, and she couldn't get it out of her mind all afternoon. She was as much a prisoner here as she had been working in the Railway shop, or at Wharncliffe Gardens.

'Why are yer keeping me locked in?' she demanded angrily when Whitey at last returned.

'Sorry I frightened yer. Sir's orders,' grunted the prostitute, putting down the tray on the bed. This hotel served only two mealtimes, lunch and supper; breakfast did not exist because Willy slept till noon after his night's activities. Whitey shook her head to see Gloria's freshly washed face. 'Waiting fer 'im ter get back already? I'll never get the 'ang of yer young girls. Yer infatuated wiv 'im, aren't yer.'

''Ow could I be, after wot 'e's done?'

'That settles it,' Whitey sighed. 'Yer a little bit soft on 'im, yer are. Yer angry wiv 'im, an' frightened of 'im, an' excited by 'im. Gawd save us.'

'Does 'e talk about me?'

Whitey gave a single barking laugh. 'Yer the princess in the tower, yer is, Gloria. A prisoner of Mr Willy Glizzard's 'opes an' dreams. Just keep sitting there on the bed looking pretty an' combing yer 'air out all day, an' 'ope the dragon don't get yer.' She explained heavily: 'Yer don't fink Mr Glizzard wanted ter be the man 'e is, do yer?'

Gloria struggled to understand. 'Don't lock the door, that's all. Please.'

'Orders, luv. Nuffink personal. Listen,' Whitey confided, 'it's only until Willy comes ter 'is senses, I reckon.'

'Wot does that mean?'

'Until 'e gets fed up wiv yer,' Whitey said brutally.

Her footsteps plodded downstairs, the door closed, the key turned.

Gloria nibbled her supper, some sort of disgusting cutlet with a piece bitten out of it, but the vegetables in season were nice: it seemed that Reen, her employment subsidised out of Whitey's wage, was quite a good cook when she wanted to be. Gloria sat on the bed, listening as evening fell. Willy's place, quiet as a nunnery during the day, came to life at night, with doors slamming, feet tramping on the stairs, laughter, the occasional pop of a bottle. 'It's an 'igh class 'ouse,' he told her proudly when he came up in the early hours, hanging his suit neatly and taking off his shoes with a sigh, 'not like wot I started off wiv, I'll tell yer, a single room down Limehouse way an' two girls 'ot-bedding. Rough, that was. That's 'ow I teamed up wiv Strawberry, me mum knew 'is mum. Yer needed a bit of 'elp wot wiv them Chinese triads an' wotnot back then.'

He took off his breeches and woollen long-johns, and Gloria couldn't help giggling at the sight of him all naked and furry-looking.

'Wot's so blooming amusing?' he frowned.

She controlled herself. God forbid he should perceive what she was really thinking. 'Yer a funny bloke, Willy. I can't 'elp liking yer.'

'Don't be patronising, yer. Why shouldn't yer like me, it's only common sense. Got yer bread buttered an' a roof over yer 'ead.' He arranged two glasses on the dresser and shook the champagne to open it with a bang and a squirt of foam. 'I'd *love* anyone 'oo kept me in idle luxury all day an' bubbly all night,' he pointed out.

'Why d'yer tell Whitey ter lock the door?'

He laughed and kissed her mouth. 'Drink yer champers.' Afterwards he studied her over the rim. 'Yer the first girl I ever kissed on 'er lips. Not afeared of, like.'

He refilled her glass, his hands needing something to do while he spoke the difficult words. 'See, I love yer, Gloria, I fink. I've never bin in love but 'ere I am. I know men aren't supposed ter say it but I've always made me own way, an' that's wot I feel fer yer. I fink so. I never bin so 'appy in me 'ole life as these past few weeks.'

'Then why yer got ter lock the door?'

He poured her glass full to the brim.

'Because I'm afeared, Glo,' he answered her honestly. 'I'm afeared of losing yer ter another man. I'm afeared of meself.'

'Why?'

'The door's closed ter protect yer.'

'Wot, from the customers?'

'No. Don't let's be serious now, yer wasting the bubbly!' He grinned, eyeing her, and she could see exactly what was running through his mind. 'I got enough ter worry about at business all day. Well, I'm not working now. Let's 'ave fun!' He finished his glass and straddled her, guzzling her breasts with his mouth full of champagne while Gloria writhed and giggled. 'I love yer innocence,' he said sadly.

All afternoon Gloria sat alone staring from the window

at the drifting rain. Now that the harvest was in full swing, the streets were drained even of the people who usually filled all weathers with their cries: the match-seller gone from his corner into the invisible countryside to make money working in the fields; the knife-grinder and the pin-girl in her white bonnet gone too. According to a magazine brought up by Whitey, which had been left by a customer, the governing classes had retired to their country estates and the grouse moors for the Glorious Twelfth of August, and no one who was anyone was to be seen in the metropolis. The cabmen crawling Savile Row held up their whips hopefully for trade, but the middle classes had rushed on holiday to Railway hotels from Brighton to Bangor, Torquay to Scunthorpe and anywhere on a line in Scotland – until, at least, news spread of the epidemic in Glasgow. Gloria's hair had never been so finely combed, and she had never been so bored.

But there was Willy to think of.

More and more as the evenings drew in she looked forward to the time of night when he came upstairs, and she thought of him all day.

His feelings for her were obviously genuine and she was sure she had reformed him. He was the conqueror conquered, just a child really. She allowed him to lord it over her sometimes with his bragging and showing off, quietly getting her own way by making him pay court to her. The obvious pleasure he took in her company could not be false, nor could his thoughtfulness with a hundred small gifts, which she let him bring her from the fine shops of Regent Street and Old Bond Street. A dreadful scream echoed up from one of the alleyways below, reminding her of how lucky she was to have a roof over her head. Whitey's liking for her was obviously genuine, and she came up most afternoons, lolling back on Gloria's soft bed as though she, too, was loved. 'Willy's not a bad bloke. In another life I could see 'im doing somefink better'n running a knocking-shop, couldn't yer? Politics, maybe, 'e's got a great grasp of wot's wot, 'as Willy. Afore 'e lost 'is 'ead over yer 'e did, anyways. Why don't yer run away afore 'e comes ter 'imself an' don't protect yer no more?'

'Protect me from 'oo?' Gloria laughed, but with a stamp of her foot, not to be denied.

'From 'imself,' Whitey said. ''E's a rotten apple. 'E doesn't want ter be, but 'e is. Now yer know. But yer got too 'igh an opinion of yerself to listen.'

That night Willy made love to Gloria with intensity, hissing her name through his teeth, crying out openly at his climax as though she hurt him. He lay beside her, casually stroking her body that she had let him know so well.

'I love yer, but yer don't love me, do yer?' he said.

'I like yer. I do, I really do.'

'There's another man in yer 'eart, Gloria. The one yer love. There's no room fer me in there an' there never will be. I'm just a roof ter keep the rain off yer 'ead.'

'There's no one.'

'It's the one wot gave yer that coin wot's worth nuffink, ain't it? I saw the look flash in yer eyes when I took it.'

'No.'

'The truth, now.'

'Oh, I don't know,' she said impatiently, turning over.

'I do,' he murmured, taking his hands from her.

He slapped his forehead as she was on the point of going to sleep. 'Ah, bugger it, I'd forgot. Gloria!'

'Wot's up?' she muttered sleepily.

'Me uncle, Gilbert. 'E's coming down tomorrer an' I'd forgot, I'm out. Yer might make yerself look nice an' look after 'im, give 'im a few gills and a bottle of champers. Fond of oysters, are yer? First of the season.'

'Will 'e touch me?' Gloria asked, opening her eyes, staring at the dark.

'Special favour,' came Willy's voice behind her, but he didn't caress her.

'Just this once?'

'As God's my witness, I promise.'

'Yer don't 'ave ter go on about it, Willy.'

'That's me girl.' He slapped her rump comfortably, then turned himself the other way and went to sleep.

'It's not that I don't love yer, Glo,' Willy explained, putting her share on the dresser, 'but we couldn't 'ave kept it up between us at that 'eat ferever, now could we?'

'Couldn't we? I did everyfink yer wanted. Can't yer?'

'Whitey said the old boy didn't cut up rough or nuffink.'

'No, 'e was a game bloke, just as yer promised.' Gloria lay on the rumpled sheets with her eyes closed. ''E ate the Whitstable Natives, gobbling down oysters at two bob a dozen like they was two a penny, an' I downed a couple ter be polite, an' 'e drank the wine an' I 'ad a glass, then 'e walked around drinking 'is brandy an' taking 'is clothes off, 'is spats an' 'is cummerbund an' is white tie an' 'is God knows wot, then 'e did it ter me on this bed 'ere, where yer make love ter me.'

'No fuss then. Don't look at me like that, Gloria. Yer knew wot yer were getting into.'

'I trusted yer.'

'Anyone'd tell yer, I never bin able ter look at a girl yet wivout finking of customers. It's 'uman nature. It's nuffink ter do wiv us, Glo, it's business.'

He sat primly on the side of the bed.

'Sleep wiv me,' she said.

'Yer know better than that. Never give it away fer free,' he said.

'I even said no fer yer. I said stop, yer 'urting me, an' 'e looked so . . . *pleased*.'

'It's easier the second time. It's dead easy the third.'

'Did yer love me?'

'Yes, I do – not that it really matters ter yer,' Willy said with his strange honesty. 'I love yer just as much as yer love that bloke yer couldn't keep. An' I'll never forget the way yer was before I spoiled yer, just like the way yer'll never forget 'im. Idjit, yer is. It's yer fault, not mine.'

'Yer a bastard, Willy.'

'Yuss, but I'm a nice bastard. That reminds me, while I'm in a nice mood, I 'ad this done up fer yer.' He reached into his pocket and pulled out the coin in its claw, displayed it in his palm. The string had been replaced by a gold chain. 'It's pretty now.' He moved his hand so that the chain swung, flashing in the light from the candlesticks. 'I don't mean yer no 'arm, Gloria. I'd never 'urt yer, not if I could 'elp it.'

'I know.'

'Yer can keep me room fer a while.'

'While yer can still pass me off as Snow White, yer mean?' she said defiantly.

'I'll keep this then,' he grinned, pocketing it cheerfully, 'just as a safeguard.'

'Sin? There's no such thing as sin,' Whitey said, 'there's no such thing as come-uppance.'

'Isn't there?'

Gloria had come downstairs to Whitey's room, very different from her own, near the front door, where the draughts from the September gale were strong enough to set the single lantern swinging, as though they were in a ship. The floorspace was almost taken up by the double bed – Whitey took in a little extra trade on the side, and the sheets had not been changed, slick and greasy, still wet with wasted passion, dirty as skin – leaving hardly room for the broken deal dresser, or for Gloria, once she had opened the door. 'Close it, close it!' Whitey exclaimed, 'I'm freezing. Don't yer fink of a girl at all since yer got the run of the place?'

Her hair falling across her wide shoulders in stiff black curls, Whitey sat on a three-legged stool in a buxom black satin bodice, scarlet tassels dangling from the bosoms. Gloria watched her pucker her lips in the flyblown mirror, painting them with a waxy red substance to match the rouge on her cheeks, the way men liked it. Not that they appreciated poor Whitey's efforts probably; most of her trade was five-minute jobs of the poorest sort, but they were regulars, and she had her pride. She spent all her extra money on clothes. Gloria closed the door and edged around the bed.

'Wot's wiv the special togs?' Whitey asked the mirror, dabbing a red smear from her pancake-white face, then turned appreciatively. She reached up to stop the lantern swinging. Gloria wore a purple dress with black buttons and black braid lace, a broad purple hat topped with a fine fashionable curl of feathers. Despite the brim's shadow her blonde hair gave her face a glow, and her eyes looked very blue. 'Yer going out?'

'This is the only time of the day Strawberry sleeps.'

'I see.'

'Do yer?'

'Flattered by yer confidence, dear. I could blow the whistle on yer. It's me job.'

'Will yer?'

'Strawberry's snoring an' Willy's propping up the counter at the Burlington. I don't know nuffink.'

'Thanks, Whitey.'

'Coming back, are yer?'

Gloria shrugged. She carried a rolled umbrella, also purple, that Willy had bought to go with the rest of the outfit from Skinner's. It didn't quite match.

'Yer'll come back,' Whitey said, shrugging back her curls, black as boot-polish. 'Yer'll find yer will, Gloria. This is yer place now. Yer look really good.'

'I don't feel it.'

'Don't fret about feeling bad about yerself,' Whitey said. 'If yer don't get ter purgatory till yer dead, 'oo cares?' She took off her wig to reveal her bald, bloody skull pocked with sores. 'Nah, if yer gonner get punished, it's in this life. Yer look great.'

Gloria went outside and put up her umbrella, but the wind eddying along the alley was too strong, snatching and tugging. She furled it and walked through the girls who thronged the left side of Regent Street, and came to the underground station just opened at Oxford Circus. Going down, she paid her tuppence and waited for her train beneath an arch of antiseptic white tiles, quite impossible to keep clean in the days of steam trains underground; now the subterranean air smelt not of smoke but of electric sparks and hot copper windings. The Central tube, the first electric train she had ridden, arrived with a whine and a gust of wind, and she followed the girls like herself stepping aboard. They sat facing one another incuriously, swaying from side to side.

The line to Marylebone was not yet completed, so she got out at Marble Arch and took the General omnibus, travelling inside, for the slow clip-clop to the New Road and the turn right. Getting down by the Hôtel Great Central she walked up Great Central Street. The wind was racing the sunlight and shadow along Lisson Grove so hard that she had to hold on to her hat. The mansion blocks of Wharncliffe Gardens stood in front of her, huge, yellow, and invulnerable. She stopped in the shelter of the goods'-yard wall.

'Yer shouldn't 'ave come back,' she said to herself aloud.

Gloria felt herself. She was dressed in fine clothes, wore shoes of supple leather. Her hat alone had cost Willy seven pounds, as much as her father earned for his family in a couple of months, if what he said he was paid was true. In her purse lay fifteen or twenty pounds in sovereigns, perhaps more. She felt dreadful.

Gloria drew back into the shadow, watching and waiting as the sun swung down behind the buildings, hoping to see Mum come out on the balcony for the milkman, or Annie returning home from the Railway shop, or perhaps even the sight of little Jack's pale face pressed to the window; Wharncliffe Gardens children were not allowed to play outside during rough weather. The wind turned icy cold as darkness fell and the lights came on, but still Gloria watched. A silhouette drew the curtains across the lighted window-glass, Mum or Annie, so far away as to be unidentifiable. Bert Simmonds did not come home. He'd be working late, or more likely down at the pub with Ebenezer Mabb and the other men like himself.

Gloria slipped away, excluded from the homely company she had longed for. The wind blew hot and cold on her cheeks and she realised she was crying. What had she expected to find here, tea laid out and a merry welcome for the prodigal daughter? A girl tarted up like a posh lady with a feather in her hat and her purse heavy with sovereigns. She didn't want little Jack to see her. His child's eyes would have seen at once through these expensive clothes, and she couldn't bear him knowing what she had become. Gloria was a whore.

She stopped on the corner of the New Road and pulled

on her purple gloves, gave a sniff to clear her nose, then laid her umbrella on her shoulder like a rifle and headed for the bus stop. Doris Mabb came out of Great Central Street in front of her.

For a moment they stared at one another.

Doris stood with a confidence she had never displayed before, a woman, no longer a girl. She had grown up. Her clothes were old but neatly brushed, and her hat was plain but respectable. In the crook of her left arm she carried a shopping basket with a few purchases arranged in it wrapped in white paper: she had obviously been somewhere on an errand. But where was she going now, turning along the New Road when Wharncliffe Gardens was the other way?

Doris looked down her nose at Gloria. A couple of the girls round the side of the hotel pushed one another, and Doris looked at them, then back to Gloria. She looked Gloria up and down.

Doris held up her left hand. On the third finger, a wedding ring twinkled once, and she smiled. Then she turned and hurried away, and the crowd hid her.

'Yer getting up or wot?' a cad shouted, and Gloria realised the omnibus had pulled up beside her. She scrambled aboard, riding on top, but the horse-bus did not overtake Doris. Finally Gloria sat back and closed her eyes. Sam Hullabye's lodgings had been somewhere along the New Road. So it seemed likely that Doris had married Sam. Whatever, Doris had achieved a life as respectable as her parents' own. Everything Gloria would never have.

Behind her, coming down the steps outside the Great

Central Hotel, Willy Glizzard watched the horse-bus sway from sight, then popped a sweet in his mouth and whistled for a cab. He was back in Savile Row before her 'bus could have reached Oxford Circus. He waited in the coach yard, a shadow amongst the destitute bundles trying to get warm enough to sleep; but no one touched him. When he heard her tapping footsteps arrive he slipped after her, following her into the alley, then indoors, past Whitey's room with its floor shaking as she brought some customer to the point, then Janey's room, then the room Miz had got back now her baby was dead, Willy silently following Gloria's progress upstairs past Strawberry's lair, Strawberry's buckshot face peering out, then sliding back like an eel's into its hole as Willy held his finger to his lips, following Gloria's footsteps upstairs. The footsteps stopped and he heard her try the door.

He waited in the dark, listening to her shake the doorhandle.

'It's locked,' he called.

She came down into the candlelight. 'But yer can't lock me out,' she said.

'I can do wot I like. Yer tried to escape, even after I gave yer everythink, an' protected yer from everythink.' He treated her with contempt in his victory, having secretly followed her all day and watched her fail, knowing now that she was his possession and he could do what he liked with her, the girl he had once fallen for and made a fool of himself for. He really had loved her, for as long as such a thing could last.

'No one stays on top ferever, Glo. This is yer room now.'

He put out his arm, swinging open the door beside him with his fist, then followed her in. She looked at the rumpled bed, a cheap print of Giorgione's Venus on one grubby wall in a ghastly attempt at atmosphere, a tin tray to wash in afterwards. 'C'mere.' Willy clicked his fingers. 'This is the way fings are, right? Yer mine. Yer don't exist wivout me. Everyfink yer do an' say is mine. When I send yer out on the street, yer'll go. *Yes, Willy*. Say it.' He squeezed her loins through her dress. 'Say it.'

'I could kill yer,' she said, glaring straight into his eyes.

'Say it.'

She struggled. 'Yes, Willy.'

He let her go. 'I should get out of that dress, not quite such a nice class of customer down 'ere. Yer past yer best, I want production from yer. Don't worry, yer earning less, but yer'll still get yer cut. That's why people call me Mr Fifty Per Cent. 'Cause I'm generous.'

They were all the same – same trousers, same faces. She knew none of them. What they wanted was always the same. It all seemed unreal: the cheats, what they did to her, life itself. Gloria did not even form friendships with the other girls. Only Whitey stuck by her. Gloria lived to sleep, lying at the opposite end of the bed from the working end in an effort to separate her two existences. November hail beat down the window, sleet in December, falling three floors sheer to the slushy yard below. She lay looking at the glowing embers of the fire, forgetting in them who she was.

One evening she stuck her head into the corridor as Willy was going past. Strawberry eyed her.

'Fer God's sake, Willy,' she begged, laying her grubby hand on his Cording waterproof as though stopping a customer, 'let me out on the street sometimes.'

'Yer smell,' he said, pausing. 'Look at yer, when did yer last wash yer 'air? I 'ate it when yer girls let yerselves go. Get out of me sight.'

Whitey, bringing up supper on a plate, took Gloria's elbow and steered her past Strawberry to the safety of her room.

'Yer right ter be afraid,' Whitey said. She looked over her shoulder, put the plate down with a clatter, then closed Gloria's door behind her. She leaned back and crossed her plump white arms. 'There's nuffink worse than a man wot sees someone 'e loved turning into somefink ugly. She lets down the way 'e remembered 'er.'

Gloria ran her hands through her hair. 'But I'm not ugly.'

'Don't look in the mirror, then.' Whitey opened the wardrobe door, the big mirror screwed to its inside. 'Now or never,' she said. 'I'll get yer a toothbrush, some soap,' she offered. 'Scented, if yer want.'

'No,' Gloria said, 'I won't play Willy's game.'

'That's wot I meant,' Whitey said. 'Yer 'aven't got much time.'

Gloria hugged her so tight that the older woman grunted. 'Yer a wonder, Whitey.'

'Get off! Whatever yer do, yer got ter keep clear of Strawberry. Even Willy, because if 'e finds yer gone an' 'e's got 'is razor, yer can say goodbye ter yer face.'

''E'd never.' Gloria couldn't believe Willy would be capable of anything so terrible.

'It's survival. Trust 'im,' Whitey said, smearing her hands tiredly across her cheeks, 'or trust me. I'm not saying 'e'd want ter do it, but 'e'd 'ave ter, see, else 'e'd lose the respect of the other girls an' they'd all bolt wiv yer. Sorry, that's the way the system works.'

'I can't go anyway,' Gloria said.

'Oh, don't start that now!' Whitey raised her hand as if to strike a blow. 'I was so sure yer were gonner be the one of us that escaped. An' blacken Willy's eye too, maybe, the only girl 'e ever loved. Yer failed once. This is yer last chance, 'e won't give you another!'

Gloria shook her head. 'Yer know why,' she said.

A look of regret passed across Whitey's face. With a sigh she lifted her skirt and pulled a brass key from her garter. Gloria recognised the key to Willy's room. 'It's 'is spare, I knew where 'e 'id it,' Whitey said. 'I was 'oping ter keep it fer meself. Well, it's too late fer me. But it's not too late fer yer, Gloria, not yet. 'Urry, take it afore I changes me mind!' She clamped it in Gloria's hand and covered it with her own. 'I'm dying,' she said, not letting go. 'I'm dying, yer knows it. Don't ferget me.'

'Always.'

'I love yer, yer not soft!' Whitey chuckled, then opened the door and peered out. ''Ow long d'yer need?' she whispered.

'Give me 'alf an hour.'

'Reen'll 'elp, she's wiv yer too. An' the other girls. We're all in the same boat, Gloria. Mind the roofs; they're like ice wiv the frost. I remember one year a poor girl fell, that's all.'

'Thanks fer everyfink, Whitey.'

Whitey paused. 'Yer couldn't've done it wivout me,' she said, with a look of terrible shame.

Gloria hugged her, and this time Whitey didn't tell her to get off, the tears stood out naked in her eyes, trickling kohl-black lines down her cheeks, and her wig had gone crooked. 'God bless yer,' she mumbled, clutching Gloria again. 'Once I was just like yer.' Then she blew a kiss and clicked the door shut after her. Gloria heard her footsteps running downstairs.

Alone, Gloria drew a deep breath. She half closed her eyes for a moment of calm.

Behind her image in the wardrobe mirror, the purple dress hung tidily in its paper, the gloves neatly folded on the shelf, the hat in its own box above.

Moving quickly now, she knelt in front of the fire and stripped off her working clothes, pouring water from the pitcher into a bowl. With the point of the knife she speared a boiled potato from the plate Whitey had brought, chewing while she washed, determined to make herself clean. Her breath came fast as she doused freezing water over her hair, the strands leaking icy drops down her spine after she wrapped a towel round her head, unable to forgo her ritual even when there was no time. She flannelled her body and legs, dried them with her underclothes. Taking out the dress from the wardrobe, she removed the paper and slipped the garment over her head, unwrapping the wet towel, then running the heels of her hands down her waist and drawing a breath.

She looked at herself in the mirror. Already, even

without shoes or gloves or hat, she felt like a different woman, and her lips spread into a wide grin. She speared the last potato and shoved it in her mouth.

The door opened. Willy stood there.

'I couldn't let yer go,' he said, 'it's not love. It's sex. Everyfink's sex.'

The potato swelled in Gloria's throat as he approached. She tried to swallow but her mouth had gone dry. Willy took another step and she forced herself to swallow, but she couldn't help backing away. He was wearing that brilliant peacock-coloured waistcoat and there was the dangerous glint in his eye, as if he was on the street; but he was no taller than her, and here there was no Strawberry skulking behind his shoulder to reinforce his authority. She made herself watch his hands, and saw that he was bunching his fists. So he didn't have his razor on him. She bumped into the dresser behind her and could back away from him no further. Yet it was he who paused. She was absolutely terrified of him, but she had learned to fake pain or joy, to hide her real feelings deep inside her, and she had allowed no sign of what she felt to show on her face.

'Yer making a public fool of me,' Willy said.

She showed him the knife in her hand, holding it point-up, the way she'd seen it done. He laughed.

'I mean it,' she said.

He stared at her and she could see his anger evaporate. Her cheeks burned, her colour was very high, and she looked him right in the eye. In a moment, she knew, he'd grab her, so she got in first with a swing of the knife and he yelped, his waistcoat slashed, all but blooded. At once his demeanour changed utterly. He jumped back so smartly that he banged his shoulders on the edge of the door, then scuttled into the corridor.

'Next time we meet,' Willy Glizzard promised her, 'yer can ferget yer face.'

But he looked so spurned and inadequate, mean as a thwarted adolescent who had failed to get his way, that Gloria laughed.

She kicked the door shut with her bare foot and heard him go downstairs to get help. He was in no hurry; there was no other way out for her. Gloria threw the knife under the bed and flew for her shoes, jabbing them on to the wrong feet; but it didn't matter, the fine leather was so soft, and she plonked her hat on her head without looking in the mirror. He'd assume she'd lock herself in her room to keep him out for as long as possible, the way the girls always did in their terror. Gloria's last stand; Strawberry would take only thirty seconds, perhaps less, to come thumping upstairs with the set of skeleton keys, the way he always did when there was any trouble with a girl or a customer. It wouldn't cross their minds that she wasn't inside. At least, that was what she hoped, and she reckoned she knew the way their minds worked pretty well by now.

She twisted the handle silently, poked her head into the corridor. It was still empty, but she could hear Willy shouting downstairs. She remembered her handbag and ran back to the wardrobe for it, hanging it by its strap from her arm. Slipping into the corridor, she locked the door behind her then bent the key with all her strength, breaking it in the lock. Racing up to the next landing, she dropped the shaft cheerfully into the earth closet, and continued upstairs to the hardwood door.

The brass key slid easily into the Bramah mortice-lock, turning with those well-oiled clicks. She closed the door behind her and locked it, then added another half turn, cannily leaving the key in to jam the mechanism. She ran up the final set of stairs into Willy's room.

She stared at the bed and shivered. Nothing had changed, but now she knew for certain that there was no such thing as love.

From below came a terrifying splintering crash. Strawberry had used his shoulder on the thin door-panels of her room, found her gone. There was a moment of consternation, but Willy was bright, and he knew her: almost at once she heard his footsteps racing lightly upstairs, Strawberry thumping behind him.

She ignored the dresser, knowing that it contained only towels and dirty pictures, and crossed to the roll-top desk, though she knew it would be locked, it always was. She picked up the swivel chair and smashed it down on the roll-top.

'Gloria, yer'll pay!' came Willy's voice. He was beating his fists on the door below like a brave man, bellowing for help, as angry as a bull, as though Gloria had tricked *him*, deceived *him*. 'Get back in yer rooms, yer whores,' he was shouting now, 'she's cracked, she's gone crazy! She's got a knife. I'll look after yer!'

Gloria pulled away the broken slats and went through the drawers at the back of the desk. She found more money than she'd dreamed of – he'd been cheating on her all the time, and probably on the other poor girls for years. She felt a moment of guilt, it was their money too, but used her forearm to sweep as much as she could into her bag. There were rings too, gold, silver, she slipped what she could on her fingers. From the final drawer fell something heavier.

It was the talisman Jamie had given her, the old silver coin or whatever it was, on the false gold chain Willy had added. She held it for a moment. Yes, loss. Loss meant something to her. She ducked it over her head.

Heavy blows thudded into the door. Strawberry had brought up a sledgehammer.

Gloria went to the window whose view she had once known so well, then opened the window-catch.

It stuck fast, held by generations of matted, yellowed oil-paint.

Suddenly there came a babble of voices as though there was an enormous fight amongst the girls downstairs. Doors were being flung open. Strawberry shouted, but his yells were drowned by the rising tide of shrieks and catcalls from below. Gloria banged at the join in the window using all her strength and, with a crash, the whole frame broke, hanging wide. She knocked it out then hung her bag from her neck and scrambled over the sill, dropping down on to the steep roof; the toes of her shoes found no grip at all on the icy slope, her fingers gave way and she slid helplessly down the vee into the angle between the roofs.

She stood up. It was a fine, frosty, silent night with a lovely crescent moon sailing above the ragged rooftops. The crooked chimneys all around her were swirling cold blue smoke. She slithered amongst the icy rooflines, following the gutters, the narrow street swinging as far beneath her as a catacomb. A man was having his hair trimmed at a lighted attic window, and never sensed her figure slipping by less than a yard beyond his glass. Finally she felt an iron hand-rail and pulled herself on to a moonlit platform. Leaning over the edge, she saw a zigzag of iron ladders dropping below her.

She was at the back of an hotel, and clattered down the fire escape into an ostler's yard, the horses nodding peacefully over their stable doors. Gloria took the handbag from her neck and hung it from her arm, but she didn't stop running. She knew she had to get far away before dawn.

She followed the crescent moon. Regent Street was noisy but she didn't mind, and when she was accosted she gave back as good as she got, walking with a long swinging stride, afraid of no one now. Men were trailing out of the pubs, shrugging their coats around them, blowing on their hands made cold by beer and gin, feeling very full of themselves on a Saturday night, pockets jingling with hard-earned cash and the girls out to make a hard living. *How does a girl get on in the world? By selling herself, of course.* A man tugged at her sleeve and Gloria pulled herself away with ferocity, hating him. His mates laughed at his loss of face and he looked startled.

'Nah, she's cracked,' he told them.

'Yuss,' Gloria threw over her shoulder, 'but I'm cracked in the right place, chum!'

'Yer well out of it there,' one of the men comforted his friend, 'she'd 'ave eaten yer alive, that one.'

With her rapid strides Gloria followed the moon that was slowly falling among the rooftops. The river flickered into view down alleyways on her left, then a broad expanse of it twinkling with moonlight, cutting London in two. South of the river was the furthest place she could imagine to run away, and she recognised this for the Embankment along which she had followed Tib's ragged figure – it seemed like years ago, but less than six months had passed. Gloria did not feel like a different person; she felt exactly the same as that naïve girl who had run away from home, but people looked at her in a different way. The iron seats placed at intervals along the pavement sported ornamental iron arm-rests so that no down-and-outs could lie down to sleep, but she saw that each compartment was occupied by sitting, drooping figures crouched shoulder to shoulder. One man slept with white frost hanging from his nostrils. She knew these people now. Those still awake stared at her as she passed, as angry as she.

She hardly noticed Parliament.

Gloria gazed at the south bank of the river as she walked. It was a different world over there, a different London only connected to the north shore by most of these bridges within living memory; it was a place apart, and she had never met anyone who knew it. She remembered, growing tired now, Tib's voice saying sadly: *'There's millyuns an' millyuns of people in London, an' lots o' diff'rent Londons, as many as there are people. Most of us never see one another. Yer ever seen anyone twice in a different place? Not less'n yer wanted ter. An' I'll tell yer this, Gloria. Yer never see yerself, 'cept in every window.'*

Gloria came to a bridge, lights arching across to the other side. A motor omnibus drew up, rattling and clattering beside her on its iron wheels, pausing as if to nerve itself for the ascent to the apex, the driver sitting bolt-upright on the upper deck stirring the long gear-rod with his powerful wrists. Petrol exhaust-fumes poured over Gloria, a new smell and completely alien, catching her by surprise so that she held her breath. She saw that the inside of the converted horse-bus was lit by tiny bulbs, showing the passengers in yawning rows, bulky winter coats, a worried-looking older woman straightening the cap of a young boy travelling with her, a girl examining her nails, a man reading a newspaper. Gloria looked at the way his hands held the edges of the paper. With a crash of gears the motor-bus jerked forward.

'Jamie!' she called.

He could not hear her over the engine. Behind the glass his face was buried in the newspaper, absorbed in the reading of the tiny print; he flapped the paper irritably with the jerking of the vehicle, and she glimpsed his profile against the lights of Battersea. 'Jamie!' she shouted after him, 'Jamie Reilly!'

She clamped her hands to her breasts and ran, but the motor-bus ran faster than she, towing fumes behind it in a blue cloud into her mouth, and sparks, too, were jetting up from its exhaust as the driver changed gear. The cad standing on the steps at the back gazed at her, just another person running for the 'bus, then waved back as if to say there wasn't a stop for miles. The board above his head was neatly painted with destinations: Piccadilly, Strand,

Putney. The 'bus ran faster down the far slope, but so did Gloria, and when it slowed for the right turn off the bridge she jumped aboard.

Gasping like a boiler, she pulled herself forward between the seats. 'Hey!' she called, and he turned round.

This man was a stranger.

There was nothing of Jamie about him, and she did not know how she could have thought there was. In fact she did not know why she had run for this 'bus like a fool, because Jamie was far away and long in the past, and she felt nothing for him at all, nothing. 'Wot an idjit I am!' she muttered, putting her hands on her hips and collapsing into an empty seat. She leaned back panting through her open mouth, and a feather from her hat stuck to her lip. She spat it out and gradually her breathing returned to normal, but she knew Jamie would hardly have recognised her. She blinkered her cheeks with her hands so that they should not see her face if she cried.

'Here,' the man said, leaning across, 'you can borrow my handkerchief.'

'I know yer sort,' she snapped back.

The man looked unbelievably startled. He cleared his throat and the cad came forward. 'What sort of 'bus company are you running?' the man demanded furiously, puffing himself out. 'This woman is bothering me.'

'Leave off,' Gloria muttered. She opened her purse and held out a coin. ''Ere,' she told the hapless cad, 'I'll go as far as yer going.'

'That's a sovereign,' the cad said, finding his excuse. 'Yer fink I'm gonner change a blooming sov fer yer? Yer got

188

another fink coming.' He rang the bell twice. 'Off wiv yer. Right now.' The other passengers stared, rows of accusing eyes, and Gloria stared back. The girl with the nails looked down, frightened by her.

Gloria stepped off the rear platform with a flounce, then walked after the 'bus as it swayed out of sight. 'Yer all the same!' she blubbered, and now the tears really poured down her cheeks.

Dawn revealed countryside all around her, first the eastern sky showing a pale, smoking line of London, then white trees stark with frost growing out of the darkness over her like ghosts, and finally the outline of the strange wooden windmill by which she stood, its blades fixed motionless in the glowing air. Below her pale grass swept to an unfenced road lined with houses on the far side, good substantial dwellings dressed in red brick or cream stucco, but all with roofs made white by the frost. No lights were lit except in the servants' basements, and one house remained completely dark, but smoke rose from every other kitchen chimney as cooks began preparations for breakfasts. Gloria was starving. She watched a milkman plodding behind his dray, the horse stopping itself at each gate except one. A drink of milk would be nice, she thought.

She walked down and crossed the road towards the milkman, who blew white puffs of breath into his half-gloves, which were as black and stiff as pitch. 'Look out,' he called, then his eyes widened. 'Hey, miss—' Ridiculously, because he was well away from her, he ducked and clamped his arms over his head.

Gloria felt a numbing blow. Too late she heard the busy hoofbeats of a fine pair of horses, both of them going down around her on the ice with terrible screams, then the open carriage swung round behind them as though on a slingshot, the huge rear wheel spraying ice-chips from its iron rim as it struck her.

At first she thought she had escaped unhurt, but then she realised she was lying on the ground. She could not move her legs, and supposed she must have been struck with enormous force. A man's horrified face loomed over her.

The numbness spread through her and the screams died away. She was not sure if they were the horses' or her own.

That was her last thought.

PART III

His Father's Son

Chapter Eleven

Gloria's eyes flickered open on a high room. Above her a crystal chandelier hung from a brass chain set in a circle of alabaster roses, palest pink, very feminine. Looking up at them gave her pleasure.

Then she must have slept, because her eyes were opening again. The sunlight had moved from the chandelier and now painted a bright exclamation mark down the rose-covered paper of the wall opposite the window, which had its burgundy-coloured drapes pulled almost closed, revealing only a blinding stripe of the outside world. The light bothered Gloria and she muttered about it.

When she awoke again the drapes had been closed and the room was suffused with a lovely burgundy glow from the sunlight that had been excluded, apparently at her command. Where the ceiling met each corner, chubby plaster cupids frolicked with bare bottoms, bows and arrows and naughty smiles. Gloria's thoughts slowly drifted to her own situation. She was in a bed that felt as soft and wide as a cloud, her head reclining in soft down pillows. She was lying on her back, her arms crossed over the brightly coloured eiderdown covering her chest as though she was dead. The posture and its inference scared her and she tried to move her arms, but there was a stabbing pain in her chest and the memories came rushing back.

'Wot about the poor 'orses!' she cried suddenly.

A man's face appeared above her, no longer swaddled in a muffler and long-eared deerstalker cap; his expression of horror had been replaced by concern and guilt. He was about sixty, with white hair carefully trimmed but uncombed, a long, cleanshaven jaw, and mild blue eyes. He wore an oriental dressing-gown over a white cotton shirt with the collar unpopped, standing out in wings, and he had unknotted his necktie but not removed it.

'Are the 'orses chipper?' she asked.

His fine, mobile lips twitched with amusement, then he looked serious. 'Yes, they are indeed chipper. Pray do not distress yourself on their account.'

'Wot's wrong?' Gloria asked in a frightened, rising voice.

'If only you had escaped as entirely unhurt as they.'

'I'm not 'urt.' Gloria tried to move, then collapsed with a groan. Her body seemed unable to cooperate with her mind.

'I administered some opium for your pain.'

He leaned forward from the chair where he was sitting and took her hand gently in his long fingers. 'You are safe,' he said in a very kindly voice, as though speaking to a child. 'I pray you lie still, do not on any account distress yourself.' But he was a man, and Gloria wondered what he was up to, pretending to be so nice. She saw with contempt that his nails were beautifully manicured, they'd never known a day's work ... Then she noticed the forefinger of his left hand, marked with a shiny yellow callus such as hard-working clerks – she knew from the Railway offices – sport as badges of pride from their feathered quills; the edge of his palm was polished from its movement over paper. Gloria smiled. She already knew much more about him than he knew about her, she told herself, and that *did* make her feel safer.

'My dear young lady, you have taken the most frightful knock. Your left leg is broken.'

'Broken!' Gloria imagined how awful it looked, but could not lift the sheets to see – his hand firmly held her own.

'I can feel it now!' she complained. 'Oh. Ow!'

'I splinted it as best I could to get you upstairs.' He stroked her sweating forehead with an icy flannel. 'When he was a boy my son fell from his horse in the foothills half a day's ride from Simla, and I learned splinting on that occasion. Of course, he was tough.'

Gloria forced herself to lie quiet, glaring at him. 'I'm tough,' she said.

'You are a lady, Mrs—'

''Ow do yer know that?' she demanded suspiciously. 'We 'aven't bin properly interdooced. Yer 'aven't been through my fings, 'ave yer?' The opiate had loosened her tongue.

He chuckled, then put out his hand ironically: they shook hands like men and she realised her fingers were clustered with rings, at least half a dozen, and one of them was some poor girl's wedding ring. 'Arnold Handley, at your service.'

A proper gentleman and no mistake, but not stupid – those mild, shortsighted eyes hadn't moved from her own once, and he wasn't bothering to use the reading glasses which poked from his dressing-gown pocket. Gloria told him almost the truth.

'Mrs Gloria Paz.'

'I must inform your husband of your accident.'

'My 'usband's – gone!' Gloria stopped. The lie had come with astonishing ease, and she knew better than to over-egg the pudding. Arnold was looking down with genuine grief.

'My wife too is dead.'

She was touched, partly by her own guilt. 'I am sorry, Mr 'Andley.'

'The plans we had made. A whole lifetime of plans. *Dis aliter visum*, the gods thought otherwise. A long life alone, Mrs—'

'Gloria.'

'Gloria. Some of my friends I knew all my life, and never used their Christian names. You must call me Arnold.'

Gloria peeped beneath the sheets. Her bare left leg looked awful, swollen with bruises, strapped to a length of wooden rod, her shift rucked to the top of her thigh to accommodate it. 'Blimey, no wonder we're on first name terms. Looks like yer know me better than I know yer!'

'I would never – your modesty – propriety—' Arnold assured her, colouring. 'You screamed when you were picked up. I splinted your leg with a length of curtain-rail and carried you upstairs in my arms. I have called my doctor. I had by necessity to remove your lovely dress, it was torn and wet; you are a mass of bruises and I fear your

196

ribs are cracked. You were wearing so many layers of underclothes . . .'

'Wot ever would yer wife 'ave thought of yer?' Gloria said tactlessly, and he looked at her as though knifed.

'Emily has been dead these twenty-three years, and no other woman will ever live up to her memory in my mind. This is her room.'

'I'm sorry, Mr 'Andley . . . Arnold. Sometimes I just say wot I fink, it doesn't mean nuffink.'

'There's no such thing as nothing. This room has lain undisturbed, Gloria, until you. I would never defile it with any thought of desire for another woman.' He stared at her with his lips in a thin line.

'Well, that's a relief,' Gloria said.

For half a second she thought he would explode with years, perhaps decades of bottled anger, but then he burst out laughing. 'Well!' he exclaimed, 'what a homecoming this has turned out to be.' He held up his hand as a bell rang downstairs. 'That will be my old friend Doctor Lewis.' He went to the door, his slippers making no sound on the carpet. She caught a glimpse of a large carpeted landing, dark wallpapered walls crowded with pictures and photographs. He made no sound going down the stairs, presumably they were equally thickly carpeted. Gloria looked around her: Emily's room. It seemed a lot more cheerful in here than out there.

She spied her handbag on a chair just within reach, caught it with her fingertips and examined it eagerly: everything she had swept into it from Willy's roll-top desk was still there, a mess of pilfered coins and cheap jewellery:

Arnold could not know he had let a whore and a thief into his house. The talisman on its mock-gold chain lay undisturbed around her neck. She pushed her handbag back on to the chair as she heard voices ascending. 'Here she is, Lewis.' Arnold showed in the doctor, a bustling man in a Homburg and moustache, carrying a Gladstone bag. 'I'll wait outside.'

'Hallo! How are we?' The doctor took off his hat and examined her quickly. 'Cracked ribs, have to strap the little devils. Now for the leg. Oooo, a different kettle of fish, I think.'

''Strewth, I look like a sunrise,' Gloria moaned around the thermometer, and he grinned with his front teeth, testing the alignment of the bones. 'Yer won't 'ave to cut it off?' she asked in a little fluttery voice.

He laughed heartily. 'Like our friend Sarah Bernhardt, the actress? Gracious, no. Have to plaster it, but you shouldn't even be left with a limp. You couldn't have run into a better person than Handley.'

''E's a real gentleman, isn't 'e?' Gloria said quietly.

'Yes he is.'

The doctor shook the thermometer and replaced it in his bag, getting ready to leave without even taking off his overcoat. 'Bed rest. I'll come back later with a nurse and we'll sort out that leg. You're lucky, in fact.'

'Pull the other one.'

'Lucky to be alive. You have God to thank for that, you know. And Handley.' He picked up his Homburg and looked at her seriously. 'Yes, he is. He is indeed.' He tapped his hat-brim in salutation and promise of return,

198

then went out leaving the door ajar, and Gloria listened with her ears out on stalks. 'Well, my friend,' she heard the doctor saying jovially, 'you've found yourself an absolute treasure!' Their voices faded downstairs. 'Don't be so gloomy, man . . .'

In a few minutes Arnold returned. 'Feeling better now?' he asked, talking in a stilted way. 'Better to see the doctor, I always think.'

'I suppose so,' she said obediently.

'Lewis says you'll be stuck in bed for several weeks.'

'I see.' She didn't let him off the hook.

'This is terribly embarrassing for me. There must be someone who cares about you!' he burst out with genuine force.

'I don't have anyone, Arnold.'

'Everyone has someone.'

'Yer don't,' she pointed out.

'Oh, I have my son.' But he leaned his elbow on the marble mantelshelf, saying no more on that subject. 'To think that only six hours ago I was still aboard the P & O steamer in the Royal Albert Dock, making arrangements for the hire of the carriage from Gallions Hotel!'

'I bet yer don't remember when somefink unexpected last 'appened ter yer,' Gloria said. She laughed, then held her painful ribs. 'Yer phiz – the way yer looked at me out there! Yer was in more of a tizzy than I was.'

'Was I?' he said thoughtfully. 'You had plainly been distraught.' He held up her shoes, drying them in front of the fire. 'You were wearing them on the wrong feet!'

Gloria held her breath. 'Every girl has her mystery.'

'Yes. That's what I liked about Emily. I loved her but how deeply could I, a man, ever know her? Really know her. Yet she was my life.' He turned away suddenly. 'I'll let you sleep now.'

Gloria lay alone, giving a sigh of relief, looking around her at the feminine room left unchanged for so long. Her eyes began to close.

''Andley's 'Eaven,' she murmured, and slept peacefully.

And it was a sort of heaven. For the first time in her life Gloria had nothing to do. Arnold's house was a dream come true, lying in a soft bed all day in a nice room, a gentleman to dote on her, yet one old enough not to be any bother. She found she could just tell him to plump up the pillows a bit more, without risk of any hanky-panky; order a pot of Indian tea whenever she wanted it, stronger than the last time or weaker, according to her whim. It was sheer bliss.

At first she was on her best behaviour, but that lasted only a day or two after the nurse left, which was as soon as Gloria could reach the bathroom by herself. Her left leg itched unforgivingly beneath the plaster and she sat in there with the door locked and her leg stuck out in front of her, scratching her foot luxuriously with the handle of a feather duster.

But mostly she was bed-ridden, no rooms up here but bedrooms, the interesting downstairs of the house forbidden her by the long staircase and her plastered leg. When Arnold brought her *The Times* she asked for the *Daily Mail* just to see if he'd bring it. He did. Then she asked to see a woman's magazine, but when he had half a dozen delivered she couldn't be bothered with any of them. Her ears became attuned to the soft, muffled tread of Arnold's house-shoes approaching up the stairs, padding across the landing carpet, giving her time to prepare herself; and when he finally appeared, usually with his hands occupied by a tray or a pot of flowers that he thought she'd like, always knocking on the door with his elbow before letting it swing open, and always coming in with that smile spreading across his patrician features, she was ready to greet him with a frown. You got better service if you complained. It was a fact of life.

He had no butler or cook, having been abroad for nearly a year – including the months aboard ship – on his business trip to Bombay and Delhi and the various spice-havens of the East; all he did for her – and everything he did *was* for her – he did personally. Such an attitude from a man was so remarkable that she couldn't credit it at first, but gradually it dawned on her that, although Arnold never touched her, he liked her. He was no chinless wonder: he seemed to enjoy her company, and look forward to seeing her. Occasionally he visited his business somewhere in the City while she was taking her nap, but apparently his grown-up son dealt with all the day-to-day work and left him little to do. Sometimes Arnold looked a little sad after these visits. 'He can't help making me feel I'm in the way. Hugo has a fine business head on his shoulders.'

As always, Arnold wore his oriental dressing-gown to bring her morning tea. A knock with his elbow and in he came, a single beautiful bone-china cup and saucer balanced on a tray, various steaming silver pots, two biscuits slanted on a plate, and the *Daily Mail* neatly folded. There was no hint of any impropriety in what he was doing: he seemed to think of her as a companion, or perhaps the daughter who had never existed, since Emily had borne him only the single son before her death in India. Gloria had become his family, and because she realised his kindness was genuine she tried belatedly to respond to it despite his sex. He never let her down. Nevertheless, she found it hard living up to such a polite picture of a woman, and could never, she knew, step into the shoes of his dead wife. She tried to keep their relationship on a practical level. ''Oo does yer 'ousework fer yer, Arnold?'

''Ousework?'

'I won't be mocked by people like yer,' she warned, and he repented.

'Mrs – Gloria – I like you as yourself. Changing you is the last thing I want to do. I like you just as you are.'

'Why?'

'Because you are honest.'

'Do yer really fink so, Arnold?'

'It is a rare and wonderful quality. In answer to your question, I have the place commercially spring-cleaned once a year.' He glanced at the open books scattered on the eiderdown then sounded flattered. 'You really read them, don't you, those old things I brought you.'

'Yer can thank Miss Miller fer that, an' the Emmanuel Girls' School. Very proud of us, they was.'

'I'm sure.'

'An' I'll tell yer somefink else, I was 'Ead Girl. Yer fink

I'm stupid, an' I 'aven't got a brain in me 'ead 'cause I don't speak like yer?'

'No, Gloria,' he said, 'you certainly aren't stupid.'

But she had given herself away. Perhaps he wouldn't notice.

Later on each day, he wore a bottle-green velvet smoking-jacket to bring her breakfast, by which time Gloria had been awake for hours. She lifted the lid.

'It's proper kidgeree, not kedgeree,' he said. 'Not fish and egg with the rice like the British eat it. This is dhal lentils, cloves, cardamoms, cinnamon.'

'Curry powder!'

He shuddered. 'Exotic spices. Seeds, aromatics.'

'Imported by yer own company. Not bad.' She ate with increasing vigour. 'Yer'll make me fat,' she complimented him.

'I want to. Too fat to get out of bed,' he said, 'then I could keep you here for ever.'

'I like being 'ere. Wot else d'yer bring into the country?'

He shrugged; a gentleman didn't like to talk of trade. 'Essential oils – they turn up in all the things you never thought of, cooking, perfumes. And Hugo now imports dried 'erbs.'

'Airbs!' she laughed at his accent. 'Yer said airbs!'

'You're the second-best thing that ever happened to me, Gloria.' He looked away, afraid of showing emotion. 'I'm sorry. I didn't mean to patronise you, I meant it as a compliment.'

'I'll take it as one,' Gloria told him, 'but I'd better stay second-best, right?' He was so embarrassed that she took pity on him. 'Yer could always eat up 'ere wiv me, if yer lonely.'

That got him. He shook his head from the door. 'No. It wouldn't be right.'

All the clever things he knew, and he was shy! Gloria lay back with a sigh, alone, and scratched her foot with her other foot.

Christmas was almost upon them, but here in Athelstan House, the rain pelting down outside in utter silence beyond the thick walls, she sensed no sign of any forthcoming festivity. Arnold's son would not be visiting, there would be no turkey or gifts. 'Yer could 'ave a Christmas tree,' she chivvied him. 'Yer could put it in the 'all wiv candles on.'

'You wouldn't be able to see it.'

'I could if it was a tall enough one.'

'You see, Gloria, I don't celebrate Christmas.'

'Wot, not at all? Yer not a Scrooge, are yer?'

'No, in fact.'

'Yer poor old blighter! Not even 'cause I'm 'ere?'

He cleared his throat. 'Gloria, do you think I am ... old?'

'Yer don't say wot yer feel,' she said.

'In my day, people didn't, you see. My father was a very *severe* man, by today's standards.'

'I like yer just as yer are,' she said.

He broke into laughter. 'All right. A six-bob goose it is!'

'A twelve-bob goose, an' apple sauce.'

'Done!'

'An' I'll get meself down some'ow fer the scoff,'

promised Gloria, 'even if I 'ave ter slide downstairs on me bum. Oops, I mean me derrière.'

'Gloria, my dear.' He held her hands earnestly. 'If you yourself believe in Christmas, then surely you must believe that there is someone who cares about you?'

'No, Arnold,' she said, 'there's no one.'

He kept his word of course, and even more: the first thing she saw as she slid slowly downstairs into the hall on Christmas morning, step by step, her stiff leg bumping in front of her and Arnold fussing like a hen, was a fir-tree he'd cut down from the garden and put candles on. He had even thought to light them before helping her down.

Decked out in her purple dress and feeling like a real lady, Gloria looked around her, fascinated by this downstairs part of Arnold's house that she had wondered about so much. It was darker than she had imagined, tall rooms leading into one another, flock wallpaper and a dense underbrush of unused furniture smelling of dust. There was a family parlour and a parlour for best, even a small library stacked to the ceiling with books that had tiny gold titles. Each cold mantelshelf that she hobbled past – he had found her a cane – was covered with a yellowed lace lambrequin, and from the picture-rails hung watercolours of a hot, foreign land. For forty years Arnold had dabbled with a paint-brush – as an amateur, of course.

'There,' he said, watching her, his life revealed to her. 'Now you know everything about me.'

'Why no paintings of Emily?' she asked.

'Oh, I can't do faces.'

'Not even a photograph.'

He took her elbow and helped her down to the kitchen at the back, the best room in the house, warm to the point of hot, with a Russell gas range, and a worm's-eye view of the walled garden. Beyond the lawn and bare flower-beds Gloria saw a small summer-house, shut up, its pagoda roof gleaming with icy rain. Arnold handed her a glass of sherry but did not drink any himself. He put the vegetables into boiling water, adding soda to keep their colour.

'To me,' he said, 'she is still alive.'

He was as good as his word about the twelve-bob goose, too, but insisted on carrying it through to a dining-room, and they sat facing one another from upright chairs across a big mahogany table and the steaming wreck of the goose, the tall windows beside them showing the garden from a slightly different angle. Gloria could see a fishpond from here. Though Arnold had laid slices of meat politely on his plate, she noticed he ate only the vegetables.

'I don't know everything about yer,' she said.

'It's awfully boring. I spent much of my working life at the Colonial Office and on postings in India, where there is so much to admire, and so much to be done. For the first time in four or five thousand years the Indian sub-continent is united and at peace, and the administration of her government is uncorrupted. For me, that endeavour is past.'

'Yer sound like an old man when yer talk like that.'

'Perhaps I do. I am an old man.'

'Yer never are. Yer can't be a day more than fifty,' Gloria said with cunning.

'Sixty-four.'

'Never!'

He refused to look at her. 'The Hindu way of life is contentment. A Hindu is content with his lot in life and his class. Gloria, death exists only because without it we cannot be reborn.'

'Stone the crows, yer went native,' Gloria said.

'Only after Emily died. Life is evil, Gloria. I am tired of wandering. I believe in deliverance.'

'Yer mean, yer fink yer'll team up again wiv 'er when yer dead?'

'It is written in the *Bhagavad-Gita* that the wise in heart mourn not for those that live, nor those that die.'

'Yer do mourn her,' Gloria said. 'Why won't yer admit it fer the sake of the poor woman? Let 'er rest, Arnold.'

He looked her in the eye. 'You're very good for me, child. You have become so beautiful since you came here.'

'Don't come over all fatherly on me, Arnold.'

'You'll like my son, he's full of life too. His servanted childhood in India gave him a luscious irresponsibility, but business life has tamed him.' He waved his fork, lecturing her. 'You must have your own parents – someone, somewhere! I have been determined not to pry; your life is your own. Your poor husband plainly left you as a lady of some means, at least. But a family is the most precious thing in the world, Gloria. I mean to see you back with them. I want to help you.'

'Why are you doing this, Arnold?'

'Because I want you to be as happy as I am. At peace with yourself.'

She dropped her knife and fork and put her head in her

hands. 'Arnold, I don't deserve yer, I don't. I don't.'

He jumped up and ran to the window. 'Look!' he exclaimed. He turned to her grinning like a schoolboy. Beyond the glass, the rain was turning to fat, whirling flakes of snow, whiter than his hair.

Chapter Twelve

It was crystal clear to Gloria that, for all Arnold's kindness and intelligence, or because of them, he possessed no feminine insight whatsoever. He was incapable of feeling through Gloria's senses or seeing through her eyes: having classified her – *convalescent, daughter, housekeeper*, or whatever it was – he didn't bother to see her as she really was, living and changing and more of a woman every day. For all his clever ideas about religion and the world, he knew nothing about *her*; indeed as soon as he sensed something more to her, he seemed to shy away.

The January snows muffled the house, cutting them off even from milk and newspapers, and Gloria came to hate the boredom of her comfortable room and idyllic existence. Encased in its plaster prison, her whole leg itched mercilessly now. From her window she watched healthy laughing women – wearing 'short' sporting skirts and their hats tied down with heavy veils – ice-skating on the frozen gravel pit or skiing down the slopes of the hill-fort. Arnold brought her tea, but she wanted coffee. Next morning he brought her coffee, but when she saw the plate of eggs she said, 'Wot, no bacon?'

'I know that leg is hurting you,' he said mildly, holding out a small shaker-pot, 'I've brought some powder. I can't see myself it'll do any good, but if *you* believe it will, then it may.'

Instantly she forgave him everything. 'Fer a non-Christian,' she said, sprinkling her foot with a sigh of relief, then winkling as much as she could up the plaster with a knitting-needle, 'yer such a blooming Christian.'

'Lewis will have that cast removed,' Arnold laughed, 'when he gets through the weather!'

'Arnold, I love yer, yer a gent. Ooh, that's lovely. I love these eggs.'

His expression became serious. 'Just now you were angry with me about the bacon.'

'No I wasn't.'

'Gloria, yes, you were.'

'I didn't mean it, an' yer know I didn't,' she said airily.

'How could you say something you didn't mean?' He didn't want a real woman with faults and flaws, he wanted her as seamless and consistent as plaster, white all through, perfect.

'I'm sorry, Arnold, I won't do it again.'

Gloria sat at the window, her leg propped on a footstool, looking out at the snow on Wimbledon Common.

She wasn't sure if she could be, but perhaps she should be.

Early in February Dr Lewis's trap turned through the narrow gateway into the driveway below her window. He appeared upstairs as genial as ever and snipped at the plaster with a gigantic pair of clippers. The nurse removed his overcoat. 'Warm work,' he said.

'Yer watch yer don't clip me leg off by mistake,' Gloria said.

'There!' he exclaimed, satisfied. 'Now we'll have you dancing in no time, Mrs Paz.'

Gloria peered at her leg. It lay in the sheets like a piece of ham someone had left boiling too long, gone soft and wrinkly. 'Cheer up!' He patted her knee. 'You'll recognise it for your own in a day or two, and all this will just seem like a bad dream.'

'A wonderful dream,' Gloria said. 'I've been contented 'ere, more than I could ever 'ave imagined.'

'I hear you are to be Handley's housekeeper during your convalescence.'

So Arnold didn't want to let her go. 'First I've 'eard of it,' she said.

'He wouldn't want to ask you himself, of course.'

'So 'e got yer ter do 'is dirty work fer 'im?'

'Naturally!' Lewis chuckled, shrugging himself into his overcoat. 'Shall I just nod at him on my way out?'

'Tell him Gloria – tell him Mrs Paz sends 'er compliments, and is gratified to accept 'is offer, fer the duration.'

Lewis paused by the door. 'For all his advantages, Handley has led rather an unlucky life. Don't hurt him, will you?' He waved cheerily. 'Don't need to see me again. Bye!'

Arnold came in a little later, when Gloria was practising her walk in front of the window.

'So yer aren't going ter chuck me out,' she said.

'Thank you,' he said simply. 'Thank you for everything, Gloria.'

She set herself tasks to help her get better. The first was necessarily selfish: the utter joy of immersing herself completely beneath the bubbles of the huge white-enamelled bathtub, bobbing her head up into the steam to snatch a breath, then sliding back down with only her knees showing, her hair spreading around her like a golden fan. Later she soaped her left knee and calf-muscle with groans of contentment, then for hours sat in front of the bedroom mirror combing her hair with the lice-comb, until it hung as fine and gleaming as satin. The colour had returned in a flush to her high cheekbones, she saw, and her slanty eyes sent her bright glance straight back: she winked at herself, then flicked her nose in the mirror. 'That's yer lot,' she said.

The next day she turned to more practical matters. The first task was to get downstairs, the second to get back up. Within the week she could hardly believe the laborious effort of her first few journeys, she was running up the steps two at a time. 'Do you have to run everywhere?' Arnold complained tolerantly, flapping his newspaper. Each morning she brought his breakfast upstairs on the silver tray, leaving it outside his door, and collected it half an hour later while he was in the bath. She found the milkman had been cheating Arnold for years, and sorted that out. 'I'm not going ter take any lip from yer sort,' the man threatened, putting back his leather cap with his knuckles. 'Slap my wrist,' Gloria said. She held out her fist, then opened it. ''Ere yer are,' she said, 'sugar fer yer 'orse.'

The kitchen was a mess. Arnold had his one or two favourite small pots and pans, which were spotless, but the rest needed a good sanding. Except for the couple he had used regularly she found the cupboards were full of cobwebs. All the woodwork needed beeswaxing, the dining table came up a treat, and they ate in there so she could show it off. 'An' even if yer got ter be vegetarian, yer didn't 'ave ter boil yer veggies fer forty minutes,' she told him, 'yer brussels sprouts aren't supposed ter be so soft they slip through yer fork.' She had discovered Arnold's weakness for afters and brought in an enormous Delhi Pudding from the steamer.

'You're feeding me up,' he said afterwards, putting out his elbows to tackle the cheeseboard.

''Course I am. If yer take yer nap in the parlour remember not ter put yer feet on the seats.'

'But they're my seats.'

'But I 'ave ter clean them.'

'All right!' he grumbled good-naturedly, taking himself off with a last mouthful of Stilton.

The snow had melted and the Common was a pale waste of grass burnt by the cold, the trees like black lace. When Arnold complained she was feeding him too much, she cut down on his lunches, and he slipped off for his nap to find her waiting with his hat and coat. 'Wot yer need is exercise, an' it'll get yer out of the 'ouse fer a change. Yer 'ave a nice walk, an' when yer come back at four, I'll 'ave 'ot tea and toast ready fer yer.' She held out his stick.

He accepted with a good grace. 'You are very good to me, Gloria.'

213

'Quite,' she said, like a lady.

His walk became quite a routine with him, and got him out from under her feet, giving her an hour or two – he was so much a creature of habit – to finish up in the kitchen. On the sunniest days he insisted she accompany him on his walk across the Common, briskly along the path to the Windmill, him breathing deeply through his nose, then strolling past the old rifle ranges for the climb to Caesar's Camp, then briskly back again in time for tea. 'I wonder wot the neighbours fink,' she said as they returned one day: for the first time there was heat in the sun, and the bluebells made a haze.

'Think?' He was looking over his shoulder, seeming distracted. 'Why should they think anything?'

'Oh, yer know wot people are like.'

'No!'

'Well, wot they *fink* they see is more important than wot they *actually* see.'

That amused him, and he stopped looking behind them. 'You're starting to sound like me,' he said.

'Wot were yer looking at?' she asked, glancing back.

'Nothing.'

But a couple of days later he pointed from the parlour window, which held a view of the windy Common through the gateway.

'There – there, do you see it? The scarecrow. That's what I call him.'

Gloria pressed her nose to the glass, then wiped away the smear with her handkerchief, remembering Doris Mabb and the subject of nosy marks, and the Great Central

Railway clock inching its way towards eight o'clock. A shiver ran through her.

'Wot yer mean, a scarecrow? I don't see nuffink.'

'It's not there any more.'

'Yer saw it t'other day, didn't yer?'

'Several times. Once from an upstairs window. I went outside but he ran away . . . so many ragamuffins on market day.'

'Are yer sure it's a man?'

He hesitated. 'It's impossible to say.'

Gloria went round the room snatching the dirty antimacassars off the backs of the armchairs. 'Yer imagining it. No more cheese fer yer.' She eyed him furiously. 'I mean it, Arnold. *No – more – cheese.*'

He stared at her, amazed by her anger. 'For the first time,' he said yearningly, as if his words could reach out to her, 'I want to know *you*, and realise how little I can.'

'I've got ter wash these,' Gloria said.

There was a week of storms in a row, each one sweeping in from the Atlantic and pushing the one in front of it across the country, like mighty locomotives driving rain and wind before them. Today the air gusted with the promise of more to come; seagulls mewled for shelter above the Common, lifting like white crosses against the dark racing clouds. At first Gloria did not hear the knocking on the door, but Arnold had obviously cut short his afternoon walk, and no wonder. She hurried through to the hall, wiping her hands on a dishcloth. As soon as she touched the handle the door sprang open with the pressure of the wind. 'Quick, Arnold—' Gloria put her hand to her mouth. 'I'm sorry, sir,' she curtseyed, 'the master's not at 'ome.'

This man was as tall as she, wearing an Aquascutum cape that snapped and fluttered in the wind eddying about the porch. He held down his top hat with one leather-gloved hand, his elbow clamping a briefcase such as lawyers use to his side, while his other hand made a fist around the brass-topped cane with which he had been banging on the door. His eyes were Arnold's blue, but stared at her clearly and directly, and his black eyebrows were pulled into an irritable frown at her inefficiency. She reckoned he must be in his middle thirties, his dark moustache almost concealing thin, mobile lips whose impatience matched the irritation in his eyes. He was so angry, staring past her now, that it seemed he had hardly noticed her, except as an obstruction.

'Seen enough?' he shouted against the roar of the wind in the trees.

'I beg pardon, sir?'

'Trying to keep me standing out here all day, are you?' His lips tightened, if that were possible, and she realised she was blocking the doorway. She stepped aside and he pushed past her. 'Just shut it, that's all, I've had a hell of a ride, the horse-tram stops at Wandsworth, always impossible getting a growler south of the river.' He tossed his stick expertly into the stand together with Arnold's, his back to her, not bothering to turn round, unsnapping his Aquascutum and expecting her to be ready behind him to take it. 'I swear that Wimbledon is as far away from

216

civilisation as the South Pole, and the weather as hostile . . .' She caught the cape in her forearms and held it over the mat to save the parquet from drips. He took off his topper and dropped his gloves into it, then turned.

'Trust my father,' he whistled. 'Forgive me, my sweet, I did not see you properly before.' As if ignoring her had excused his arrogance! 'Never mind the parquet. He told me he had found himself a housekeeper to keep him in order – but not that she was a stunner. I clearly should not give you my hat!'

Gloria decided that she was too busy to pay him the attention he obviously wanted. 'I'm sure I don't know wot yer mean, sir,' she said, trying to get past.

'Oh, I'm sure you do,' he said genially, blocking her way to the kitchen corridor, giving her his hat to put on the hall table. 'However, since you're playing "housekeeper", you might nip the old Aquascutum off to dry and rustle up a pot of tea – two cups.'

'I don't expect Mr 'Andley back for an hour, sir.'

'Just do as you're told.'

'Yes, sir.'

'And don't keep calling me sir in that tone of voice, it's insolent.'

'Yes sir, sorry sir.'

His eyebrows drew together angrily, then he laughed. 'Off with you!' he chuckled, and she really thought he would try to pat her as she bustled past, so she circled this man of the world before going down the kitchen corridor with fast, loping strides. She knew exactly what his sort were like, and hung the cape over a chair in front of the

217

range, though not so close that the heat would crack the waterproofing, and busied herself with the kettle. He came in behind her, leaning across the kitchen doorway, one foot elegantly crossed over the other, his moustache almost in a smile as he watched her work.

'I'll bring it ter yer in the library, sir,' she said to get rid of him.

'Flying fingers.' He tapped his teeth with his thumbnail. 'I've got you now. Gloria, isn't it?'

'Mrs Paz, sir.'

'Hugo Handley.'

'I know 'oo yer are, sir.'

'My father must have talked of me?' He wanted that; to be the talk of the town. The self-centred vanity of an only child with everything he wanted dropped into his lap. Except, obviously, a mother.

'Talked of yer, sir?' she muttered, warming the pot, filling it, and placing it with its woollen caddy over it among the other tea things set ready on the tray. ''Ardly mentioned yer, sir.'

'A palpable hit,' he acknowledged, so vulnerably that she sent him a sharp glance. He let the moment drag out.

'And he has hardly talked of you, Gloria. Now I see why.'

'I'm sure *I* don't, sir.' She picked up the tray and waited, but Hugo did not move.

'Do you really know yourself so little?' he asked her. 'Do you not see how you affect people?'

'Excuse me, sir,' she said busily. He shifted and held out his hand: after you. She could feel his eyes following her.

'The library, remember,' he called, when she passed the library doorway. His eyes twinkled amusement now, looking at her directly as she laid out the cups and saucers between the books strewn on the table, staring at her wrists, her throat, her hair as she worked. She did not feel that he missed a single detail. She wished he would sit in one of the comfortable armchairs or on the sofa, where she could see the back of his head and not feel his eyes on her all the time. He made her very aware of herself.

'I see the fire is set: light it, would you?' he said. 'My father and I will be discussing business affairs for some hours.'

'Very good, sir.'

'He hates such matters, but they are necessary these days. Bring us a cold supper at six, a collation of meats, doesn't matter what.'

'Yes, sir.'

'I'm not like him, my sweet,' he said with a roguish glint. 'I eat anything that moves.'

'Will that be all, sir?'

'No. Pour two cups, drink one with me.' He leaned back against the broad table, his legs crossed. 'So, Gloria,' he remarked conversationally, taking his tea from her hand and blowing the steam, 'you are my father's little piece of stuff he's keeping on the side.'

'Yer lucky I gave yer that tea before yer said that, or I'd throw it straight over yer!'

He looked immensely pleased. 'I see that you know exactly what I mean. Girls like you always do, thank God.'

Gloria wasn't hurt for herself, but she was for Arnold.

219

'Never mind me, but if yer fink that about yer father, yer don't know 'im 'alf as well as yer fink yer do!'

'I do assure you—'

'Yer just a big-'eaded know-it-all, an' I don't care if yer tell 'im I said so!'

He held up his hands in self-defence against her tongue.

Gloria finished him off. 'An' that's all I've got ter say ter yer! I want ter get back ter me kitchen now, sir.'

'Wait! Please wait.'

She tapped her foot, impatient to be dismissed.

'May I tell you something, Gloria?'

'Yer do that, sir.'

'You see,' Hugo explained carefully, 'the male sexual urge dies completely at the age of thirty.' There was a silence. His mouth twitched. Gloria had to look down. The most awful urge to laugh was rising in her. She pressed her hand to her mouth.

'Stop it, I can't bear it,' Hugo said, 'you're making me giggle. I have an awful giggle, it's my worst feature. Don't. Oh, you've made me.' He pinched his nose until he had regained his composure, then unfolded a monogrammed HH handkerchief and wiped his eyes. Gloria stood by the fire with her forefinger curved over her lips, looking as serious as she could.

'I'm sure your relationship with my father is beyond reproach,' he apologised, 'but you are no more a housekeeper by nature than I am.'

'I've spent most of me life doing such tasks, sir.'

'Then you have been wasted. Don't call me sir any more.'

They both looked round as there came a whirr of the wind, then the sound of the front door slamming. Arnold's voice called, 'Gloria?'

'Go on then.' Hugo flicked the back of his hand. 'Run off and do what you obviously think you're best at, fawning over an old man.'

Before she could leave, Arnold came in, very windblown, unwrapping his scarf. 'Hugo, good to see you, my boy!' They shook hands. 'It's been too long. I was completely certain you were avoiding me. You've come alone?'

'South of the river and all that.'

'I've got awfully boring in my old age,' joked Arnold, but Hugo didn't laugh, and neither did Gloria. She took Arnold's coat and he rubbed his hands by the fire. 'Well, I trust you two found something to talk about?'

'You mean with your housekeeper?' Hugo turned his back on Gloria. 'This cup is dirty. Fetch us another, will you?' Without looking at her, he held out at arm's length the cup that she had put to her lips. He turned to his father, yawning. 'Yearly accounts again, Papa ... frightfully boring I know...'

When Gloria returned from the kitchen with a pot of tea freshly made and new cups and saucers, the two men had the briefcase open and their heads together over papers in front of the fire: one white-haired, one dark, Hugo doing almost all the talking. He ignored her. Arnold wore a pince-nez and was nodding. 'If you say so, my boy...' He looked up at Gloria with a relieved smile. 'Ah, thank you, my dear.'

'Don't forget,' Hugo gave her instructions without

taking his eyes from a column of accounts, 'supper at six.'

'Gloria usually joins me . . .'

'Actually it's a working supper,' Hugo said. 'Annual General Meeting.'

Gloria, put in her place, busied her hands in the kitchen, but her mind was busy with Hugo Handley. What an ego, turn your lights off and there was Hugo still glowing by the light of his own self-satisfaction. She could not recall when the sight of knife-edged creases in a pair of trousers had annoyed her more. She took some cold roast pork and a chicken from the marble slab in the meat-safe, and jointed the chicken imagining it was Hugo. By the time she carved the pork she was beginning to wonder whether he preferred thick cuts or thin, lean or fatty; she decided to give him thick and fatty, not to her taste at all, and not, she suspected, to his, just to teach him a lesson. Then she relented and added a few lean slices. By this time she was sorry she'd been so rough with the chicken and arranged it more artistically on the salver, then added a nut salad so that the collation would appeal to both men. As an afterthought for Arnold, not thinking of Hugo at all, she added the Stilton that Arnold loved even though it gave him bad dreams, and the roundel of Koboko that had been hanging about in case Hugo liked it, and took the collation to the library. Hugo spoiled her entrance immediately.

'Where's the salt and pepper?'

It was the one thing she had forgotten, and he cast her an amused glance to catch her out so completely when she thought she had prepared everything with such house-keeperly perfection. She fetched the salt-dish and pepper grinder with a red face, knowing he wouldn't let her off the hook, and he didn't. 'Don't forget the pickle,' he ordered, not even looking up from the folder he was consulting. She plodded back for pickle and fetched the mustard pot too, giving him no excuse to put her down again.

'Ah, Colman's,' he said with a wonderful smile, satisfied with her at last, taking the mustard-spoon from her hand and applying a generous dollop. 'Mr Colman made his fortune from what people leave on the side of their plate – just like us.' She gave him a look, saying with her eyes, *I'm not stupid, yer know*. 'Off you go!' he chuckled.

She waited in the kitchen for an hour, then collected the leftovers and helped herself. By the time she finished the washing-up, complete dark had fallen over the garden and the invisible storm rattled the glass, beating around the house. The gas flue made a whistling sound in the strongest gusts, and she sat listening to it, waiting for the next to arrive.

The bell-register tinkled and flagged red for the library. She put on her shoes and found them sitting back in the armchairs, their work obviously finished. 'Brandy,' Hugo ordered, 'Napoleon VSOP. A whisky for you, Papa, like you always used to drink?'

'No.' Arnold looked sleepily at Gloria. 'It's such a filthy night,' he yawned, 'I've insisted Hugo stay.'

'No, really, Papa,' Hugo disclaimed, and Gloria stared at him suspiciously. Modesty wasn't his style.

'My boy, I absolutely insist. She'll make up a bed for you.'

'Then how could I refuse?'

'My head is spinning.' Arnold stood tiredly. 'The room at the back of the house, would you, my dear?'

'Of course.' First things first: she brought the cut-glass brandy decanter and snifter on a silver tray, knowing Hugo would not be satisfied with a plain glass. The spare-room took rather longer to make ready than she had thought; instead of dreaming with her elbows on the kitchen table and just listening to the angry weather, she should have anticipated that Hugo would stay over. As she hurried downstairs Arnold was coming up. He wished her goodnight.

She knocked on the library door and told Hugo his room was ready.

'Stop it,' he said, the flames flickering on one side of his face.

'I beg pardon, sir?'

He was standing very close to the door, not letting her in. Gloria was afraid their voices would carry upstairs. '*I beg pardon, sir,*' he mimicked her, even the curtsey. 'And don't say, *I dunno wot yer mean, sir.* Not again, Gloria. Stop it.'

She leaned forward into the doorway. 'Wot else am I supposed ter say?' she hissed.

'Stop lying to me, that's all.'

She swallowed.

'You knew this would happen,' Hugo said reluctantly. He held the brandy glass in one hand. With his other hand he touched her wrist, then took her fingers in his own. Almost he was pushing her away, and again Gloria looked towards the stairs. 'You know that you are the most beautiful girl I have ever seen,' he murmured. 'You know what you have been doing to me all evening. Don't lie to me, Gloria, don't pretend. Let me just kiss your hand, like this.' But he didn't kiss her hand. He put his lips to the tips of her fingers and kissed them one by one, and not once did he take his eyes from her own, staring into her. 'I see you deeply, Gloria. You're so full of life, and so sad.' She tried to say something but he put her hand to her mouth. 'Whatever you are going to say to me, Gloria, don't lie to me.'

'I won't lie.'

'There's never been another you.'

'I shouldn't be 'ere.'

'Will you stand out there in the corridor all night?'

She shook her head, he tugged her gently, and she slipped through the doorway into the firelight.

'Yer were awful ter me earlier,' she snuffled, her head down, fiddling with a button on his shirt so that he could not kiss her mouth. 'Yer said terrible fings. I'm not like that.'

'I know.' He put his arm around her, holding the stem of the glass between two fingers, offering the fragrant bowl caressingly to her lips. She looked up and he kissed her.

'That's what you've been waiting for all evening, isn't it, Gloria?'

'Just put yer arms around me.'

'Don't lie to me, Gloria, you know that isn't enough. I felt the truth in your mouth. Don't let me down. You know I'm not the same, don't you? Oh, Gloria!'

She looked at him wonderingly. 'It's really important to yer, isn't it? Yer really do mean it.'

He kissed her hair, her eyes.

'Prize yourself as highly as I prize you, Gloria,' he said. 'Can you?'

She lay on the rug with her head on one side, looking at the fire. The flames were dying down and Hugo ceased the urgency of his passion. She clasped him instinctively and he stretched out beside her, exhausted, then pulled her face on to his chest, her mouth against his tiny nipple. 'You've wasted me,' he congratulated himself.

'Don't be like this afterwards. 'Old me. Look into the fire with me.'

'I'd much rather look at you,' he said, as his passion returned.

He sat up, his unbuttoned shirt hanging from his shoulders, his feet still in the thick woollen socks held up by elasticated straps just below his knees. He ran the palm of his hand over her body from her thighs to her throat. 'Now I know everything about you,' he whispered.

'Do yer?'

'I believe some women can experience a similar ... symptom,' he said. 'Moment of passion.'

'Wot woman would want ter be as selfish as a man, Hugo?'

'I know that love is more important to you,' he said sincerely.

'Do yer love me now?'

'As a man loves a woman, you lucky thing.'

'I'm in love,' Gloria said.

He stopped doing up his shirt buttons. 'With me?'

'Yer the only bloke 'ere, aren't yer?'

'Don't let it mean too much to you, Gloria. There is a gulf between us. A social gulf.'

She sat up and put her elbows on her knees. 'Wot does that matter?'

'I am a gentleman, and you . . .'

'I'm not a blooming gentleman, that's fer sure!'

'You are plainly not a lady.' He crawled to her and kissed her mouth. 'And I love you for it. Look at you, you're seducing me again.'

''Ow? I'm just sitting 'ere. I wish men were as nice as the things they say, but it's all a bluff wiv yer, ain't it? Yer don't see us the way we are. Yer don't really care.'

'Believe me.' He sat in front of her and slipped his knees beneath her own, then put his arms around her and clasped her tight. 'Believe me. I love you.'

'Would yer love me if I was ugly?'

'Yes.'

'Will yer love me when I'm old?'

'Yes.'

'Liar!' she said affectionately, lying back and letting him come into her, giving herself with all her strength: because in her excitement, while the moment lasted, she believed he spoke the truth. And that was worth it.

Chapter Thirteen

In Hugo Handley, Gloria told herself, her dreams had come true, and she was sure that her gifts of the night before would make him fall in love with her. His concentration in her had been total: she would never forget that furious, yearning look in his eyes. She was in love! She had him to herself to cuddle for half an hour afterwards, then he had to go upstairs to get his sleep alone in case they were found out. *She* couldn't sleep, and imagined him tossing and turning as uncomfortably without her as she did without him in her own room. He was up bright and early and let her button his collar in the kitchen. She kicked his feet under the breakfast table, accidentally brushed her warm hip against him when she put his dish of scrambled eggs in front of him. Her dress swished on the parquet as she put everything on the table within his reach. She felt enormous pleasure in watching him eat so hungrily, because she knew that desire – love – for her was the root of his hunger. But he was going to leave at any moment.

With a smile she wiped a smear of toast and marmalade from his chin, so that he knew she was thinking about him, that she was caring about him; showing her feelings in any way she could think of to cement him to her. Finally she came to a decision and sat on the chair close beside him. Last night he had said, *Don't lie to me*. That meant most to him.

'Listen, I want ter tell yer the truth.'

He looked surprised. 'What truth?'

'All about me. See, I don't want there ter be anyfink about me yer don't know.'

'I must dash,' Hugo said, finishing his coffee.

She wanted to ask him if she would see him again this evening, but instead she heard herself saying: 'I am not a widow.'

He looked serious. 'I see.'

'I never 'ave been married.' She wriggled the ring on her finger. 'It's a lie,' she said earnestly, but he didn't put his arms around her.

'Why are you telling me this, Gloria?'

'Because I don't want any lies between us.'

'There aren't.'

'So yer do love me, even if yer afraid ter admit it.'

He laughed and kissed her without restraint, which was what she liked about him: he got what he wanted, even her. 'Of course I do!'

She brushed his jacket and brought him his dried and aired Aquascutum, imagining the *if only* so vividly that she was sure he must feel it too. If only she was doing this for him every morning, seeing him off to the City, shrugging him into his jacket and fetching him his hat and cane – not like a housekeeper, not like a lover: seeing him off with his clothes neat and no marmalade on his chin, as prosaically and habitually as a wife.

'I won't wake my father just to tell him goodbye,' Hugo decided, saying none of the things that needed to be said, that Gloria sensed filling the air between them, but that he seemed able to ignore.

When she opened the front door she couldn't bear the silence any longer. She followed his broad back on to the porch.

''Ow soon will I see yer again?'

He turned, chuckling. 'Do you remember what you forced me to say last night?'

'Yer loved me for not being a lady, that's all I remember. At first yer wanted ter talk about 'ow far apart we were, but we aren't.' She tugged his lapel. 'Not now we aren't.'

He spoke in a kindly undertone. 'Gloria, not even you can change this world of ours.'

'Would yer love me if I was ugly?' She looked into his eyes. 'So yer do remember?'

'Yes.'

'Would yer love me when I'm old?'

'Passionately. But you'll never grow old. You'll always be as you were last night.'

'Is that enough for yer?'

For a moment he closed his eyes. 'If only there was more,' he said with genuine longing.

He touched the knob of his stick to his hat-brim in salutation of her, then went quickly down the steps and turned out of the driveway before she could run after him.

'There is more,' Gloria said, but she was speaking to herself. She found herself staring at the necklace clamped in her hand, the coin in its claw, the silver flashes clashing with Willy Glizzard's fake gold chain, and felt a momentary hatred for it – hating herself for keeping the thing, for letting it mean anything to her, hating its worthlessness. Last night, she told herself as she went back into Arnold's house, she had glimpsed something of infinite value: love. Hugo would be back, because he had glimpsed it too. She put the back of her hand to her cheek and ran down to the kitchen to fetch Arnold's breakfast.

The elder man must have sensed a change in her mood, but put it down to the wrong cause. 'Your convalescence is complete by any measure, yet you are plainly unhappy,' he told her as they took their afternoon walk on the Common.

'I'm 'appy!' Gloria tried to distract him by pointing at children playing, but contrarily the sight of them reminded her of home and all she had left behind her. There was no word for it, only feeling the emotion bobbing like a ball in her throat: home and childhood; all that had to be left behind and could not be brought back.

'You move like a person in pain, and I see it in your eyes,' Arnold said gently. 'You know, you cannot continue for ever in your duties as my housekeeper.'

'Why not?'

'Because, as Hugo mentioned to me, and he always sees such things more clearly than I, you are plainly *not* a housekeeper. He was worried about your good name – and mine. You know what people are like. Hugo's right. You really must consider your future.'

'Yer mean yer want ter get rid of me?'

'I mean I wish to see you reconciled with your parents, whom you never talk about.'

'Yer never talk about 'Ugo.'

But Arnold was not to be distracted. 'It is the one great, good thing I can do for you.'

Gloria watched her feet walking. 'Yer don't understand,' she said.

'I won't take no for an answer,' Arnold insisted. He stopped, making her face him. 'I owe it to you. You see, there is only one Emmanuel Girls' School in London with a Miss Miller as Headmistress. I checked in the reference library. The address is in North Street, NW8. Were I to write to her—'

'Yer don't need ter do that.'

'I thought tea,' Arnold said, 'in the garden. I like you very, very much, Gloria, but I cannot be your father.'

It was a gorgeous Sunday afternoon, spring mellowing into summer, and Gloria waited for her parents to arrive. She watched in agony from her bedroom window, which was open to let in the distant chime of church bells and the sound of dogs yapping on the greensward of Wimbledon Common, laughing children in spotless smocks and bows throwing sticks and coloured balls. The elegance and domesticity of the scene passing across her sparkling sash-window, spring-cleaned and freshly repainted, had become almost unendurable to Gloria: smart horses stamping, some decked out with patriotic plumes, open carriages rattling to and fro with white dust trailing from the tall, thin wheels. With better news arriving from the war in South Africa, the policy of concentration camps obviously a success, and the period of mourning in black for the death of Queen Victoria finally over, the ladies' fashion colour of the moment had brightened to a very fetching pale brown with matching gloves and veils, and spectacular feathery picture hats.

Now that the time had come, Gloria was consumed by nervousness, and when her father's green Great Central Railway dray appeared plodding bluntly through the elegant display of money and class, billycock hat clamped on his head, whip flicking in his hand and scowl on his face, she almost died from embarrassment. Dad was going to go on about Sunday drivers not knowing one end of a horse from another, he was going to stand with his hands in his pockets clenched like fists, and that challenging glint would be in his eye. Albert and young Bill would hang about behind him, not saying a word. And Mum would cry. Even now, Gloria wasn't sure that she could resist her mother's angry tears, her tearful clasping and, finally, her remorseless Christian reconciliation. Gloria didn't want to be forgiven; she could not admit she'd done anything wrong.

She'd laid out the tea things in a huge wicker garden-tray on the kitchen table ready to take out to the summerhouse, with the milk-jug that she must remember to take out of its cool hiding-place in the larder, and the kettle left simmering on the side of the range so that bringing it back to the boil wouldn't take a trice . . . and yet now they were almost here she couldn't bring herself to go down. She combed her hair then patted her cheeks to sting some colour into them; she looked as pale as a ghost. Peeping from the window again, part of her hoped the dray would drive straight past. Mum was holding a piece of pale blue paper in front of her face, Arnold's letter, reading the address, and young Bill was counting off the house numbers – his voice sounded much deeper, it had broken. Albert, wearing a suit and his hair parted in the middle, pointed at the path to the Windmill and they all looked round, obviously knowing they were close. Gloria saw no sign of little Jack with them, and her heart sank. Her frail smallest brother, who had witnessed her departure and probably alone understood it, had been the one she had most wanted to see. If he was ill she wondered what she could give Mum to take back as a present for him.

The meeting, she knew, was bound to be supremely awkward for everyone. Only Arnold didn't feel it, yet she was enduring this for him – and to prolong her stay until Hugo came back, she admitted. Arnold didn't attend church, wearing his lavender-blue velvet smoking-jacket and his usual calm, slightly remote smile as though Sunday was any other day, and this a visit by any ordinary guests. Gloria drew back from the window as Albert pointed at the house, and Mum put down the letter – she was wearing glasses! Perched on her beaky nose, the wire frames flickered as she looked up at the house, but her expression changed neither for better nor worse. Gloria watched her fold the letter and put it in her bag, then fold her glasses after it. Mum was wearing her favourite bottle-green dress with the leather hem to keep the dust off, and despite her fringed parasol must have been sweltering in the heat, but she allowed no sign of it. Gloria peeped from the shadows of the room above them: Dad dropping the whip in its holder and tying on the brake; then, with the economical, almost unconscious movements of long practice, not even looking at what he was doing, slipping the nosebags on the horses and standing the bucket of water between them. He handed Mum down without looking at her either, then the boys jumped down leaving Annie to fend for herself. She was wearing Gloria's green Great Central Railway dress, taken up. 'Boys!' Mum said, and they ran back to her as though she had jerked them on wires. ''Elp yer sister down.'

'Do as yer mum says,' Dad ordered.

The group disappeared from Gloria's sight beneath the window-sill and, too late, she heard the sound of the front door opening. She ran down belatedly, but Arnold was already welcoming them inside. Mum snapped her parasol shut, which must only just have fitted through the doorway. 'Thank you fer looking after 'er,' Mum said with domestic determination, keeping up her front with a stranger, 'yer know wot they're like nowadays, the young, don't know where she gets it from. She ran away from 'ome, Gawd knows why, we couldn't do enough fer 'er. Yer didn't 'ave ter go ter all that trouble, Mr 'Andley, I'm embarrassed.' They all stared at Gloria on the stairs.

''Allo, Mum,' she said. 'Dad.'

'There she is,' said Mum. There was an awkward silence, the family standing around Mum like statues. Arnold closed the door.

'Perhaps you'd like to take tea in the garden?' he murmured. 'Then I'll make myself scarce. You must have so much to talk about.'

''Ammersmith Broadway's a nightmare any day of the week,' Dad informed him without budging, bracing his hands in his pockets. He stood too close to Arnold in that way he did, balancing himself up on his toes. 'I cut through Sands End, back-doubled behind Peterborough House, didn't stop once, slipped slick as a goose across Fulham Bridge.'

'You must mean Putney Bridge. I see you're a north London man.'

'I see exactly wot yer are,' Dad nodded, tipping the wink, talking man to man as if he was outside the pub with one of his mates. 'Not that I'm saying anyfink against yer, mind.' That meant he was. He turned to Gloria for the first time. 'Got it pretty cushy 'ere, girl.'

'I never thought yer'd come,' Gloria said.

'Nah, come on downstairs ter us if yer like, don't stand there above us like a bleeding lady.' He grinned. 'Wrong again, am I? I s'ppose that's just wot yer are, now. A fine lady ter this fine gentleman. No offence,' he assured Arnold. 'We're plain working folk, honest in our way.'

'I'm sure. Gloria has made an excellent housekeeper.'

''Ousekeeper my arse.'

'Dad, don't,' Gloria said.

'Dad don't,' said Dad, turning on his heels with the smile that meant real trouble, bunching his fists so that his knuckles showed bumps through his pockets. ''Asn't she done well? I never believed it of yer, Gloria!' She had never seen him so angry, his voice was shaking. 'I never listened ter wot they said, all them wagging tongues: Gloria coming back from the Irish wiv 'er tits 'anging out, Gloria leading the kids a merry dance across the goods' yard an' some of them youngsters crossing the rails 'ardly old enough ter walk, God's mercy no one was 'urt or killed, an' I said, that wasn't my Gloria. I stuck up fer yer.'

'I never done nuffink wrong, Dad.'

'Oh no, it was us wot was wrong, was it? Lay it all at our door. An' where did I go wrong wiv yer, I wonder? Wot did I do wrong? I'll tell yer. I didn't do nuffink wrong. It was yer. A bad apple spoils the barrel.'

'Dad—'

'I'll tell yer wot's wrong. Yer let me down, that's wot's wrong. Yer can't deny wot 'appened, yer was seen! But still I wouldn't believe it, that's wot's worst. I wouldn't listen ter wot they said in the pub or at work or wot the kids shouted in the street. I said I know my Gloria, an' I stuck ter it. I know my girl.'

Gloria held out her hands. She came down step by step.

But Bert Simmonds just stood looking around him. 'Now this,' he smiled. Gloria realised he wasn't really listening to her, any more than he was really looking at her. 'Mum was right about yer.' He chewed those words as though they choked him to spit out.

'I always told yer I was right,' Mum said, drawing herself up.

'Don't start on it in public,' begged young Bill with something close to terror.

238

'See, Mum's taken out the copyright on it since yer left, Glo,' Dad said bitterly, with a big, broad smile. 'Always right, she is, these days.'

'It's not *my* side of the family, Bert,' Mum said, putting her arms around young Bill and Annie who were closest, 'it's that grandfather of yers, that Simeon wot got transported ter Australia an' came back wiv a criminal 'clination. An' yer father, Arthur, wasn't a saint by all accounts, shingle-splitting out of London one step ahead of the constabulary. If only I'd known when I married yer wot I know now.'

'Yuss, go on about it,' Dad said, turning to look at the spray of flowers that Gloria had set in front of the mirror.

'Perhaps we could conduct a calmer and more useful discussion in the garden,' Arnold suggested, gripping Mum's elbow firmly. He guided her out. 'Your daughter has green fingers, did you know? Whatever Gloria touches, grows . . . I must show you the roses she . . .' His charming, irrelevant conversation, that wouldn't fool Mum for a minute, faded towards the rosebeds, and Annie trailed after them with a pale look, the hem of her dress dragging on the floor.

Gloria crossed the parquet to her brothers, keeping her end up. ''Lo, Albert. Young Bill. Nice of yer ter come.'

'Ooo, *nice*,' young Bill mimicked her, with a glance at his dad, safe to take sides now they were alone.

'We're very impressed, Glo,' Albert said, growing up into a steady young man, though his face was still shiny from some serious shaving. 'Rich, too.'

''Andley's a very kind bloke,' said Gloria, but found

herself thinking of Hugo, 'and that's all there is ter be said.'

'Yer go on out back, boys.' Dad nodded them away. 'Just the two of us, Glo.' Alone, he held up his hand when she tried to speak first. 'Wot made yer do it, Gloria?' he said in his low, smiling voice.

'Do wot, Dad?'

'That don't matter, wot. I did everyfink fer yer, I gave yer everyfink.'

'Everyfink except proper love,' said Gloria.

He ignored her; he'd already decided he wouldn't believe a word she said, he wasn't listening to her, only to his own bitterness. 'All the plans I 'ad fer yer, it was all fer yer. Yer was the apple of me eye. Yer was me pride, Gloria.'

'Yer so sure I'm living in sin wiv 'im, aren't yer?' Then the worst possible thing happened to Gloria: she blushed, remembering Hugo saying to her, *don't lie to me, don't pretend*, and him kissing her mouth, and everything that followed. She could still feel his fingers, the unutterable relief of knowing someone loved her, that she was worth something.

'Yer face tells the truth, Gloria.' Dad lifted her hand: the wedding ring on her finger. 'Stolen? Yuss, I bet, not that I blame yer. It's an 'ard world an' yer me clever girl, I'd've done the same in yer place.' He dropped her hand as though he never wanted to touch her again, and stepped past her.

Gloria flung after him: 'Then yer worse than wot I am.'

He came back and struck her casually across the face. 'That won't leave a mark,' he said, very calm, and she knew he was screaming inside. 'Go and throw yerself in the river, that's all yer good fer.' His lips pulled back from his teeth. '*Yer let me down,*' he said, enraged. '*Look at yer! I just wanted yer ter know, yer let me down!*'

He fell a step back from her, and she stared in the mirror. The hallway smelt very strongly of flowers. 'Yer wrong,' she murmured, touching her swollen lip. 'Yer 'ave left a mark.' He shrugged. They'd just think she'd been crying.

'Yer made my life like an 'ell wivout yer,' Bert said, taking off his billycock hat at last, turning it over and over in his hands as though it had been lost and he had found it. 'I want yer ter know that, in case it's any satisfaction ter yer. It's not an 'ome, wot we got. Mum's got uppity an' full of 'erself, it's not the family sticking together. Even if yer was born innocent, yer ain't now, yer can't grow up wivout growing guilty. An' that's got ter be hid, Gloria. I'm sorry.'

'Yer never knew me,' Gloria said.

'All I know is,' Dad said, 'I never deserved yer.' He was gone before she could reach out: the moment of truth had passed, and left her feeling as though her father had died and she had found no time to tell him something.

What did she really feel? She wasn't even staying here for Arnold now. It was all for Hugo. *Prize yourself as highly as I prize you, Gloria – can you?*

'Yes,' Gloria said to herself, 'I can.'

She went down to the kitchen, fetched the cucumber sandwiches and chocolate cake she had prepared earlier, and carried the teatray into the sunshine, crossing between the rosebeds to the summerhouse. She set it down on the white wrought-iron table, trying to conceal every emotion she felt beneath the layer of domesticity she knew Mum expected of her, but inside she felt like the most wicked person in the world.

'Why's little Jack not 'ere?' she asked, putting a brave face on it, pouring the milk with a hand that she prayed would not tremble, but it did.

'I'll take my tea in the house,' Arnold said. Dad had joined his sons kneeling on the paving around the fishpond, pointing out the golden orfe, carp, shebunkins. Only Mum and Annie sat at the table, Annie with her head bowed, looking at her hands in her lap, that awful dress, and Mum's face shadowed by her parasol she was holding up. Mum's gleaming eyes watched Arnold going away between the shrubs.

'Dirty old man,' Mum said, 'the gall of 'im, getting me 'ere ter rub me face in it. That's the upper classes fer yer. Look wot example the Prince of Wales set, our present King, God bless 'im. One law fer the rich an' another fer the rest of us. I could spit.'

Gloria kept silent, busy cutting the cake. She knew Mum on principle wouldn't respond to any direct question that she was asked.

'Jack's no better,' Annie murmured. 'I said, Jack's no better, Gloria.'

''E's just the same,' Mum told Annie. 'Wipe yer nose.'

'Sometimes I fink 'e's worse,' Annie said with a sniff, 'I really do.'

'Left 'im wiv a pillow fer 'is 'ead, an' one fer 'is feet,' Mum chided her, 'an' Mrs Mabb lookin' in too.'

'I ought've stayed,' Annie said unhappily.

Mum frowned, wanting to preserve family unity in front of Gloria. Annie's face was scrubbed spotless. Mum stirred sugar in her tea holding the silver spoon between finger and thumb. 'See, fings 'ave worked out pretty well fer us wivout yer,' she told Gloria.

'What a terrible thing ter say, Mother.'

'Don't yer mock-lady *mother* me, girl. We're a family now, Albert an' Bill stick tight, an' Annie's not left 'ome.'

'I work in the Railway shop now,' Annie explained, sipping delicately at her tea, but her eyes were a living reproof.

'In my place,' Gloria said.

'Albert or Bill walk yer 'ome, don't they, love?' Mum said. She pushed her hand on her knee and got up, took Dad his tea.

'She's like this all the time.' Annie bent forward, whispering. ''Ow could yer do it, Gloria? I'd run away like yer did, but I 'aven't got the guts. An' I never will.'

Gloria passed the plate of cucumber sandwiches. ''Ere, take 'alf a dozen, slip some in yer bag fer later.'

'I couldn't,' Annie giggled.

'I s'ppose yer the queen of Charlie Brewer's marriage list now.'

'I'll choose my own man!' Annie said.

'Good fer yer, show a bit of spirit.'

Annie spoiled it. ''Sides, Sally Kean already got 'im ter the altar.' She burst out, 'Little Jack does miss yer, Glo, don't let 'er tell yer otherwise.' She jerked her head at Mum, her boys gathered around her now telling *her* about the golden orfe, and it was Dad's turn on the outside. 'See,

243

it's a sort of competition between Mum an' Dad. There's no love between them personal, like. It's all fer us kids. It's a sort of battle.'

'Wot will yer do?'

Annie shook her head.

Gloria sighed. 'So nuffink's changed at Wharncliffe Gardens, an' never will.'

'Doris Mabb moved out when she married Sam 'Ullabye. She 'ardly comes in ter the shop, big wiv child. Any day now.'

'Lucky Doris.' Gloria remembered Doris, no longer a girl, standing with the confidence of a married woman on the corner of Great Central Street, the wedding ring twinkling on her finger, the grin of vindication on her face. Her victory over Gloria. 'I feel so sorry fer 'er, ter be honest.'

Annie looked down. 'Didn't she know about Sam?'

'We both knew.'

'Sam's an 'orror,' Annie murmured, and her cheek reddened.

'I 'ad thought, if she could make 'im 'appy, maybe 'e'd settle.'

'No one could make 'im 'appy, 'cept yer, Gloria, an' 'e was frightened out of 'is wits of yer. It was Doris wot betrayed yer, wasn't it? She made a rod ter beat 'er own back wiv. 'Er own punishment.'

'I 'ope not. I'm sure she'll 'ave a beautiful baby.'

'That's wot I mean,' muttered Annie. 'It's the kids I feel sorry fer.'

Gloria helped herself to a second wedge of sticky

chocolate cake; she had hardly realised she was eating. Annie looked at her with admiration. 'I wish I was yer,' she said.

'Wot, a fake ring on yer finger, an' everyone finks yer living in sin wiv the old bloke 'cos of 'is nice 'ouse, posh walled garden wiv fishponds an' wotnot, an' 'is son is the most 'andsome man yer ever met, and yer want 'im wiv a passion?'

Annie grinned. 'Yuss, an' all the chocolate cake I could eat. Yer got yer little piece of 'eaven 'ere, Gloria.'

'No such fing on this earth, Annie.'

Annie helped herself daringly to the biggest slice of cake, pushing the crumbs into her mouth with her gloved fingers. 'Well,' she said daintily, 'maybe it's just yer wouldn't recognise it if yer saw it, Glo. Maybe if it was biting yer on the nose yer still wouldn't see it.' She gave a ladylike burp, then turned her sad young face to the sun. 'Only 'uman nature, that's wot. Never satisfied.'

'I'm never going back,' Gloria said. 'They can't 'urt me now.'

'Yer proved yer can manage wivout them,' Annie told her, 'they'll never forgive yer fer rejecting *them*. Wot did yer expect, 'ugs an' kisses?'

The tea was cold, and the boys brought back the milk-skinned cups and saucers awkwardly to the table. They stood looking over their shoulders. 'If only they'd brought Jack—' Albert said.

'Maybe it would've bin different,' young Bill said.

Everyone went back to the house. Gloria picked a spray of red roses, wrapped the stems in paper, and asked Annie to give them to Jack as a present from her. 'I'll put them in a vase by 'is bedside,' Annie said. ''E'll love looking at them an' thinking about yer.'

No one else said anything, Mum getting into the cart without a word. The family had done its duty. There would be no reconciliation, not even a word of kindness for Gloria. Her parents simply could not see themselves. Dad took the nosebags off the nags and hitched the empty water-bucket to its hook, then came forward, wiping his hands on his jacket, pausing between Gloria and the dray.

'Comfortable as a worm in a nut, eh, luv?' he murmured with a conspiratorial wink, swinging himself up on to the hard bench-seat where he passed his life. 'Watch out fer that chocolate cake,' he called down, leaning across Annie and contentedly plucking the head from a rose to adorn his lapel, 'or yer'll end up fat as a pig.'

He cracked the whip and Gloria watched the dray shrink into the distance until it was gone from sight, lost in the press of traffic. People returning from a day in the country, white road-dust drifting slowly across the Common, greying now and becoming indistinct in the fading light, and cold creeping into the air.

'You're shaking all over,' came Arnold's voice.

'I didn't know yer was there.'

'For you I'm always here.' He hesitated, then put his arm around her shoulder. 'Gloria, I'm so sorry, I didn't mean to put you through that.'

'Mum's going ter cry all the way 'ome,' Gloria said. 'Yer know, that's wot really 'urts.'

* * *

246

Next day she got up early as usual and, before going to the bathroom, went downstairs to put on the kettle to take up Arnold's early morning tea. The weather had turned sour with a vengeance, real Monday-morning mist clinging to the trees, rain trickling down the glass. A businesslike double knock sounded on the front door and she went through.

'Who is it?'

'Telegram fer yer!'

She opened the door and the local GPO boy gave her a cheeky grin. He held out the folded piece of paper in his hairless hand, running on the spot to show how busy he was. She gave him a penny and stood alone, looking at the rain-spotted outside of the message, then remembered to close the door with her foot. The office of origination was filled out as Marylebone Station, and Gloria remembered the booth a couple of arches along from the Railway shop, run by a man in shirtsleeves and green visor who never seemed to sleep. She couldn't remember his name. She knew she didn't want to read this message.

She opened it enough to peep at the end of the last line, but she was already sure who had thought to send it.

STOP ANNIE

The Wimbledon Hill post office clerk's capitals in indelible pencil were neat, yet at first Annie's words struck Gloria completely without sense.

JACK DIED LAST NIGHT WITHOUT PAIN STOP
LAST WORDS OF YOU STOP

THANK ROSES STOP NOT SAME WITHOUT
YOU GLORIA STOP LOVE YOU
STOP ANNIE

Their youngest brother, the mistake. Gloria read and re-read the message. Something in her died. This time more than a black mourning dress was required. Jack was dead, the only one who knew the truth. *It wouldn't be the same wivout yer, Glo. But nuffink would change, yer know. Not Mum or Dad or anyfink. I dreamed yer went.* The only one who understood about Jamie Reilly. *Yer got a little devil in yer somewhere, 'aven't yer, Gloria?*

'Yes,' Gloria said aloud. 'A little devil called love.'

Love. She told herself she was thinking about Hugo. But she burst into tears.

Chapter Fourteen

'*The wise in heart mourn not for those that live, nor those that die.*' Arnold's fatalism, his blind acceptance of whatever life threw at him, was a strange comfort to Gloria because it ran so against her own instincts. There was nothing, he said, that she could do now her little brother was gone – she could not bring him back – so nothing was what he urged her to do. No displays of grief – 'What good can that do, wearing mourning for the dead?' No weepy attendance, even from the back of the crowd, at the funeral in the ostentatious black dress, black veil, black gloves, black mourning handkerchief specially made for weeping. Arnold did not even believe in heaven, only that Jack would be reborn. So Gloria stayed at home, though at the last moment she weakened and sent some flowers. Living up to Arnold was the hardest thing she had ever done.

'Not 'aving gone – it'll finish me wiv them, Arnold. They'll fink I'm cruel an' totally beyond redemption an' all that – an' they'll be right, this time.'

'Let them rest,' he said, ending their discussion. 'You can't go back. The past cannot be brought back to life or lived another way, Gloria. I realise that now, and you must face it. Only his body is gone, and your life goes on.'

'I don't 'alf feel guilty about it, though.'

'It has been almost twenty-four years since Emily passed on. I do understand, Gloria. When I married her she was hardly older than you. I felt the same age that I do now . . . I came back to England to marry her, you know.'

'Yer didn't meet 'er outside the East India United Service Club, did yer?'

'I beg your pardon?'

'Nuffink.' She looked at him, marvelling. 'Yer really don't want me ter leave yer now, do yer, Arnold? Not even fer a few hours, in case yer lose me.'

'I have had too little, and lost too much. I want you to stay,' he said, 'with all my heart. Will you?'

'I will,' she said.

She kept herself busy with a hundred household tasks to make herself useful to Arnold, so that he smiled whenever she came into the room, believing it was for him.

Partly she thought of Hugo because she could not bear the thought of little Jack lying dead beneath the ground.

Gloria had held nothing of herself back from Hugo Handley. Giving her body had been easy for her, she knew all too well what men wanted. Hugo was exciting, a man of the world, and though she was sure he was capable of cruelty, she had felt safe with him. And he was fun, with those bright, brittle eyes and his soft mouth, his sometimes hard words contrasting with the vulnerable Hugo she sensed beneath his skin – the man she had touched, from whom she had hidden nothing of herself. Sharing herself with him felt like a kind of immortality, and she had sworn always to tell him the truth.

Yet she realised how little she knew about him – not exactly where his office was, not even where he lived, except that it must be north of the river, and she imagined a set of bachelor chambers like the Albany, somewhere he couldn't invite a woman. She wanted to know everything about him, but it was difficult to fish for information from Arnold, because she was sure her voice would give away her eagerness. It was difficult to imagine two men more different than Arnold and his son, and if it weren't for the business, she thought, they would have had no common interest to bond them: only Gloria, she told herself, saw them both.

Every weekday she walked to the shops. Arnold kept his account with the small emporium in the High Street, and they had delivered to him for years, but she preferred to look out for season's bargains from the street-stalls or the little fancy-goods shop run by two maiden ladies, who in their treasure-trove of tiny drawers behind the counter stocked everything imaginable for the housewife: threads, bodkins, hooks and eyes, bolts of Madapollam cotton cloth from India. Gloria was returning from the greengrocer's stand with her daily basket of perishable shopping over her arm – mostly vegetables, beetroots for the pressure cooker that would retain their sweetness, some green peas and mint, and a few stalks of rhubarb, the last she would find this year, for marmalade. She'd forgotten she would need ginger for that and had to go back for it. Tired now with the heat, rather than follow the dusty pavement with the squeaking, rumbling cartwheels passing her too close for comfort, she chose the grassy track just within the Common boundary. She had her eye on a bench beneath a shady tree when suddenly some boys went running by her, their hoops and skimmers forgotten, even a girl or two caught up in the excitement. There was a terrific bang like a gunshot. A horse reared, older ladies put their hands over their ears, and nannies quickly rocked their prams before looking round accusingly. A red light flickered between the treetrunks, warning of the approach of a motor car.

Gloria followed the tall vehicle, moving silently now on its air-filled tyres, the engine properly regulated to a soft chugging noise after the startling backfire as it turned into the driveway of Arnold's house. Two children jumped down from their place beside the chauffeur, relegated to the rumble-seat on the back, and stared at Gloria. The young chauffeur, wearing a flat hat, scrambled over the rear mudguard with some difficulty and helped down the woman riding beside the driver. She was short and quite plump, with a pert parroty nose and damson cheeks, her hat tied down with a long piece of crêpe-de-chine against the slipstream of the York Phaeton. Her automobilist's ulster hung almost to the ground, so that only the toes of her boots, in a stocky shade of brown that did not match the cream serge, showed on the gravel. She held a bundle wrapped in a cloak that it took Gloria a moment to realise was a baby.

'Hallo,' the woman greeted her, giving a very pleasant, unaffected smile. 'You must be Gloria.'

Gloria looked at her blankly.

The newcomer held out her hand. 'I'm Kittie.' She laughed, all bobbing cheeks and a row of tiny yellow teeth, at Gloria's baffled expression. 'Mrs Hugo Handley.' She looked concerned. 'Is something wrong? Do you feel all right, Gloria?'

Gloria swayed. Her legs felt as though they were sinking into the gravel. She put down her shopping, almost dropped it.

'Don't be familiar with the servants, Kittie,' grunted Hugo up on the car, sitting as high as their heads. 'She's a housekeeper, don't address her as if she was a parlour-maid.' He wrestled with a lever on the steering-wheel, his face smudged with oil and exhaust-smuts, then grimaced a triumphant smile as the engine finally stuttered to a halt.

'Hugo's contrivance,' sighed Kittie indulgently, bobbing the baby now, because the little fellow had obviously decided on milk, turning to the warmth of the invisible breast. 'I don't think men ever grow up, do you? They're always little boys at heart.'

'I told you we should have had a wet-nurse,' Hugo grunted, 'it would stop him bothering you. Go inside, for God's sake, it's indecent.'

'Hugo's told me all about you,' chattered Kittie to Gloria. 'We're so grateful for what you've done for Arnold . . .'

Gloria looked up at Hugo. He had goggles on and she could not see his eyes. 'You've dropped your shopping,' he said.

He jumped down, grabbing Kittie's elbow and steering

her towards the house. Arnold came down the steps and Gloria heard him saying excitedly, 'What a wonderful surprise to see you!'

'Trying out the motor-car,' Hugo said. 'What do you think of her?'

'So this is my new grandson.' Arnold parted the swaddling with his fingertips, gazing into the baby's face with a rapt look, and Gloria couldn't bear to watch. She dropped to her knees and pushed the scattered pea-pods and rhubarb stalks into the basket anyhow; the beetroots had rolled like balls, some of them under the vehicle, and she smudged her hair with sticky motor-grease getting them.

'Oh no,' she said, 'oh *no*.'

She walked slowly into the kitchen and put her basket down carefully on the table. What a fool she had been. She made the tea, but that routine task did not comfort her now. She did not know which she hated more: Hugo for fooling her or herself for wanting to be fooled. She made a jug of lemonade for his children, who were playing pirates with sticks in the summerhouse, then took the tea into the best parlour, set it down between the two men, and took herself off without a word. The thought of tea made her feel sick. Kittie was upstairs feeding the baby and Gloria calmly went up with a teacup, two lumps of sugar in the saucer, and knocked on the door.

'I thought yer might like a cup of tea, ma'am.'

'That's very kind of you.' Kittie said. She was sitting on the bed, her son clamped to her breast, guzzling at her with hungry sucks. Her sad expression brightened at once, and

Gloria sensed the woman was eager for company. Kittie patted the bed with her free hand: sit here beside me. 'Have my other two killed themselves yet?'

'They're repelling boarders in the garden, ma'am.'

'Do sit! Don't be stiff. What's the matter? Do you always sit with your arms folded like that, like a wooden indian? We're going to be such friends.' The baby turned his head from Kittie's nipple. 'Here, do you want to hold him?'

Gloria held Kittie's baby. Automatically she put him on her shoulder and burped him, just as she had Jack. Some things you learned and never forgot.

'Oh, I see you're an expert!'

'No, ma'am.'

'You're not at all as I imagined,' Kittie said perkily, buttoning her dress with quick, practised fingers. 'Of course, the age gap between you and Arnold is considerable, but—'

'Is *that* what yer think? That I've set my cap at Arnold?'

'Isn't it obvious what he feels? You'll be one of the family,' Kittie said contentedly.

'I shouldn't think yer 'usband finks much of that!' Gloria burst out.

'Of his father remarrying after all these years? Oh, I know boys can be funny about that sort of thing, and Hugo has many faults, but jealousy is not one of them. On the contrary, he says it may bring him closer to his father.'

Gloria closed her eyes. Hugo had it all worked out. He could see her anytime.

'Yer make me feel so bad,' she whispered, 'so ... *wanting*.'

The chauffeur knocked on the door. 'I'll put the suitcases in 'ere, ma'am, will that do it? Then Mr 'Ugo said ter find a chemist fer some petrol fer the run down ter 'Ampshire tomorrer.'

'We're staying overnight,' Kittie explained to Gloria. 'My mother lives in Hampshire, on the old farm. I'm just a country girl. When I first met Hugo,' she said fondly, 'he swept me off my feet. I'd never met anybody who mattered before, and I thought he was a god. I still do.'

After supper the house fell quiet. Kittie had almost fallen asleep at the table, worn out by the baby's demands, then excused herself and took him upstairs to give him his last feed and get herself ready for bed. Hugo didn't lift a finger, watching Gloria. He sat with a cigar clamped between his white teeth, his thumbs pressed in his waistcoat and his chair leaning back on two legs, and she knew exactly what he was thinking. Gloria cleared away the plates. The older boys came to say goodnight and Hugo nodded them to bed without taking his eyes off her. Arnold mumbled conversation, sounding very old, unaware of everything going on around him. Gloria put soda in the sink and did the washing-up with red hands and red eyes. By the time the plates were clean she could not even remember what they had eaten. The stalks of rhubarb were still on the draining-board; she'd planned to have them simmered, sieved, and ready for cooking by now, but there was only enough for Arnold and her, and anyway she'd forgotten to make the pastry.

She heard footsteps behind her.

'He's gone to bed,' Hugo said, so close that she could feel his warm breath on the muscle of her neck. 'You can get off your high horse. Just you and me.'

'Yer bastard, yer never told me yer was spliced!' She turned fiercely.

'Would it have made any difference?'

'Yer know it would.'

'I know you, Gloria.'

'No, yer don't,' she said, 'not in the way that matters!'

He held out his hands for her to come into, but she backed against the sink. 'Gloria, you've seen what Kittie's like. How could I love a dowdy creature like that?'

'Yer married her, she's yours, she seems lovely ter me. I won't be wot yer want ter make me.'

'I know what you are,' Hugo snarled petulantly, childishly.

'I never wanted ter 'urt anybody,' Gloria said.

'Kittie is sweet, but she's not a patch on you. She doesn't know anything about men.'

'Yer were romping wiv me when she was 'aving 'er baby, weren't yer, yer bloody swine!'

'Never mind her; she understands.'

'I bet she does not, Hugo.'

'I'm rather afraid I've fallen in love with you.'

Words failed her. Quickly he followed up his advantage. 'You can't resist a rogue, Gloria. Neither can I.' He took a step away from her with his hands reached out, but she stayed where she was, not following him into his trap this time. 'She just bears my children, that's all,' he said. 'That's what a wife's for, she doesn't mean anything more to me

257

than one of her brood cows, she bores me to death and her breath smells of apples. But you. You'll never have children or a family, Gloria. You're just like me. You're my match.' He dropped his hands to his sides, his eyes furious and yearning, wonderfully handsome and thickheaded, totally unaware of the pain his arrogant prophecy caused her. *You'll never have children or a family.* Her lover could look her in the eye and say something so dreadful. 'You see, I know you'll never love me,' he murmured. 'I know there is someone else.'

'An' I know wot yer want,' she said contemptuously, going round the table to pass him, into the corridor.

'So there is someone. I've always sensed it. That's what makes you so hard,' he called, then followed her as faithfully as a lapdog. 'Gloria. Stop.'

'I don't need yer,' she said, and slammed the door between them.

There were various dresses hanging in her wardrobe, half a dozen by now – the mourning black bombazine for Queen Victoria, not Jack; a pale brown one with lovely chocolate-brown trimmings, a couple of others with fashionable stripes, the come-hither purple dress that she had arrived in, and a hardwearing tweed with a businesslike jacket, all smelling of camphor against the moth. By the morning sun streaming through the window she chose the tweed, removed the dress-weights and aired it, brushed it to get rid of the mothball smell. Going to the bathroom she cleaned her teeth, then brought back both toothbrush and toothpowder.

258

Now she took off her nightdress and folded it, squeezed it into the little carrying-bag. She drew on the gorgeously soft but practical Milanese silk drawers Willy Glizzard had given her; she had not worn them since she had arrived here. From the drawer she selected a pair of black cotton stockings with white feet – some black dyes stained hot feet, and she didn't know how far she must go. Plain white petticoat, cambric chemise, white blouse. She stepped into the dress and combed her hair.

There came a low knock on the door. Arnold was standing there.

'Don't go,' he said, bowing his white head.

She went across. He wouldn't come in. They spoke through the doorway.

'I'm sorry, Arnold. Yer bin so wonderful ter me an' all I done is 'urt yer.'

'You haven't hurt me. Or if you have, I wouldn't have it any other way.'

'Yer knew I lied ter yer,' she whispered. 'Right from the start yer did. Yer knew I never was married.'

'Mourning the living,' he shrugged. 'Age has its advantages. One of them is wisdom. I'll do anything you ask, Gloria.'

'I can't ask anything more of yer,' she said gently.

'You see, I am addicted to you. All the littlest things. The way you put up your arms to comb your hair, the way you turn your fingers, the way the light catches your eyes. I glimpse you in so many different ways, to me so magical and inaccessible. I don't want you as my housekeeper . . .'

'Yer know why I've got to go.'

259

'It's not Hugo's fault, it's mine. For never remarrying. His mother—'

'It *is* his fault, Arnold. I don't want ter be ashamed of meself fer letting yer down in yer own 'ouse,' Gloria said decidedly.

'Is there nothing I can say that will persuade you to stay?'

'I've made up me mind.'

'Gloria,' Arnold said. 'Marry me. Be my wife.'

She held him tenderly, but he flinched at the heat of her physical touch here in his first wife's bedroom.

'It wouldn't work,' she explained. 'I won't be second best. There's got ter be more.'

'I can give you everything you want. A marriage in name only. Separate bedrooms, no . . . nonsense. To be near you is enough.' He stepped back. 'I know you'll turn me down. I won't push myself. But I wanted you to know. You'll always have a home here, Gloria, however far your life takes you.'

But Gloria told herself that what was past was past.

'Thank yer,' she whispered, leaving her – Emily's – cheerful room for the last time.

She hurried into the sunlight, her bag swinging from her hand, slipping past the York Phaeton parked in the drive. The chauffeur lounging against the wheel watched her with a bored expression. She turned quickly to the right along Parkside Road; Hugo's departure for Hampshire should take him in the opposite direction.

Instead, the motor-car appeared in the distance behind her. It came towards her, almost obscured by the busy traffic, then dodged into sight again, horn parping, heedless of the rearing horses. She stopped, head down; but Hugo in his cream serge driving-coat drove by with hardly a glance. The vehicle barely slowed its furious velocity as it took the first turn left ahead of her, on to the Portsmouth road.

So Gloria went right, her footsteps taking her past genteel villas set in rhododendron parklands bordered by monkey-tail trees, but still she could not shake off a feeling that she was watched.

As she came to the Trinity Church she stopped, then turned suddenly.

There was no one. The pavements were empty. The hospital was silent.

She was alone: as alone as she wanted to be.

Then she saw the lone figure standing maybe half a mile back, on the green swell of Putney Heath. Dressed in black, it was too far away for Gloria to see if it even had a face. She was sure it was the scarecrow Arnold had sensed dogging him on his afternoon walks.

Just as it had then, a shiver ran through her. It was not interested in him, but in *her*.

Why? she wondered.

Perhaps it was Willy Glizzard.

Yet she did not feel threatened as she walked on, and the next time she slowed her footsteps and looked back, the figure was gone. The heath was hidden by the maze of new sidestreets thrown up on the far side of the Railway line.

'*Why?*' she whispered, looking back from every road junction. '*Why?* 'Oo cares about me?'

Chapter Fifteen

A girl's got ter get on in the world, thought Gloria as she walked, *even if the world don't like it!*

Those words were such a mockery, because it was a man's world, and they made the rules. The river on her left shimmered and stank like a sewer under the August heat-haze, a slimy grey-green ribbon sucking at the mudbanks between the bridges as the tide fell. A man could always turn up a job somehow, but for a girl the world was harder than men could imagine. Across the river she saw the sooty Houses of Parliament, where a girl could neither vote nor be elected. Ahead of her rose the jostling cranes and warehouses of Lambeth and Southwark, jobs for a hundred-thousand working men. They didn't earn much – that was the privilege of the men like Hugo who worked in the fine offices of the City, beyond the black dome of St Paul's, commuting back and forth to detached residences in the suburbs – but they had pride in themselves. A builder's yard and ramshackle outbuildings were propped hard against the wall of Lambeth Palace, every butcher's shop had its sleeping dog, and so many people were swarming around her that they seemed to float in the heat. Here everyone obviously knew everyone else, and Gloria's mood brightened like the sun. Their cheerful shouted greetings and the casual grumbling that immediately followed was a different world, she realised, as far as another planet from those grand, dull façades only a few yards away, curving into the distance along the north shore of the Thames: the government buildings, then New Scotland Yard for the police and the Temple for the Law, and beyond it the banks that financed them.

Here, south of the river, was the hard work that paid for all.

No one was still, everyone running, or hefting bales with their muscles, cursing and shouting. Everything was dirty, alleyways like black caves. Above the narrow, teeming turnings and smoking chimney-pots a train roared slowly overhead from Charing Cross, and no one looked up – here were houses, whole streets beneath the railway arches. Gloria walked among working men stumbling under the loads on their heads, steam-cranes shrilled, suddenly the buzz and screech of a sawmill filled the air, then slowly its sound fell behind her as she walked. Heat and an acrid smell billowed from a limekiln, the shovellers popping their lunches into niches in the stone-work to keep piping hot, and smoke of vivid filthy colours plumed from tall industrial chimneys into the haze over Bedlam.

She saw no parks, no squares, only railway lines looping above the houses and the huge main roads, locked solid with traffic, that divided the district. Yet between these boundaries, she discovered, lay hidden communities that seemed to hark back to an earlier age, of quiet little streets and yards like sheltered oases amidst the turmoil around and above. Suddenly she found herself returned to the river, with a wonderful close view across to St Paul's Cathedral on its hill, standing in its reflection in the muddy water.

The excited screams of children attracted her. She followed their cries to a strip of green grass at the water's edge, almost overhung with warehouses, where a troupe of players clowned *Macbeth* on stilts. The beards of the grandly-named 'Great Pike Gardens Open-Air Theatrical Company' were held on by sticking-plaster, and they waved broomsticks for swords. 'Wot's this about?' Gloria asked the woman beside her in the crowd, who wore a loud blue and yellow coat impeccably brushed, and was rewarded with an expression of freezing contempt from a powerful, wrinkled face and piercing eyes.

'Shakespeare, of course, young lady. Don't the young know *anything* nowadays?'

'Be like that,' sniffed Gloria, 'sorry I asked. Southwark, is this? Never seen so many pubs.'

'Be quiet now.' The ragged acrobats hobbled and swayed on their cheap wooden stilts with amazing skill, and on cue the ghost swung past on a long frayed rope hung from a tree, sometimes deliberately swinging back to cause chaos, which the crowd loved. Gloria howled with laughter and surprise when the rope broke and dropped the ghost in the mud. The old lady, as straight-backed as though she carried books on her head, glanced at her and thawed a little to see

Gloria's enjoyment. 'That's an old, old trick. This is Shakespeare's home ground. Rose Alley here is where the Rose Theatre once stood; once this area was all theatres. Bear gardens and theatres – the Hope built there – and houses of ill-repute, and inns. Over there–' she gestured with a flourish – 'stood the Globe, where the Bard acted in his own plays. *Macbeth* was performed there, open to the sky. That, you understand, is the limit of my interest in this nonsense.'

'Not enjoying it at all,' Gloria said innocently.

The older woman gave Gloria a sharp look, and when the actors came round with begging hats she moved away smoothly. Gloria got the picture. She opened her purse and took out a sovereign, dropped it with a clang into the hat, and joined the woman in the bright coat at Punch's penny theatre stall, where she was standing like a statue among laughing children who had eyes only for the show.

Gloria watched her out of the corner of her eye. Mr Punch had got a string of plump sausages for his supper and asked the children to make sure Toby the Dog didn't steal them. 'Behind you!' shrieked the children as the dog's nose appeared, then his open mouth. But Gloria watched the woman. Those pinched, joyless lips had slipped for a moment into a smile, which immediately withered when she saw Gloria's amusement.

'Miss Gloria Simmonds,' Gloria said.

'You give away your money too easily. You'll find it doesn't do to flash that much around here.' To get away from Gloria's grin she moved to the pitch by the railings occupied by Sallementro the snake-swallower, who wiped the scales of the reptile he held with a clean white cloth. She watched with an expression of absolute disgust as he rubbed the snake with sweet oil from a bottle and held it up by the tail, about to commence the most revolting part of his act, the bit the children liked most, but she found herself hemmed in between the railings and Gloria and could no longer escape.

'The snake likes it,' Gloria assured her, 'it's warm down there.'

'I have never liked them,' said the lady, in a tone which made it unclear whether she referred to snakes or children.

'It's all right so long as the bloke don't cough, I reckon.'

'Miss Lily Alhambra, since you insist.'

'Wot a lovely name.'

'You've heard of me?' The lined face was transformed into a kind of pathetic hope at odds with her eyes, hard as shells. 'Desdemona at the Princess's in Oxford Street? No, you're not old enough to remember. In Oscar Wilde's *A Woman of No Importance* perhaps?'

Gloria was embarrassed at her lack of knowledge, because at heart the old dear seemed an all-right sort of stick. 'Nah, sorry, we only ever went as far as the Edgware Road, ter the Met.'

'But I know that slaney well! I had face-entry there for many years, since I played the girl in Zola's *Drink*, a very coally rôle, but that would be . . .' she turned away suddenly, clamping her mouth shut as though she had already said too much. 'That would be before you were even born, my dear.'

'Coally?'

'Strong, worthwhile. Plenty of heat to it.'

'I'm looking fer a rooms ter stay. Yer wouldn't've heard of anywhere going round 'ere?'

'Certainly not.'

'Yer don't like me, do yer?' Gloria said cheerfully, with the devil in her.

The hard eyes looked directly into Gloria's own. 'Thirty, forty years ago, God help me, you remind me of myself,' said Lily Alhambra. 'Young and not needing to lie.' She turned with a shudder from the Sallementro's act. 'There. You have won. I could not bear it after all.'

'Let's sit down beneath that willow fer a minute.' Gloria waved a couple of children away from the bench by the water's edge. 'Clear off. Yer sit down 'ere beside me, Miss Alhambra.'

'You really are quite bossy!'

'That makes two of us. Alhambra's yer stage name, ain't it? And yer was a dancer, I bet, 'cos yer still move like a dancer.'

'You have a streak of wickedness in you. You watch people so closely. It's intrusive.'

'I think Lily's yer real name, though,' Gloria went on. 'Yer don't mind if I call yer Lily, do yer?'

'Why do you keep looking behind you?'

'I didn't know I did,' Gloria lied, and Lily looked at her sharply and with real interest.

'Yes, my dear, I was a dancer, and I started my career at the Alhambra Palace, as it was in those days. You know what I mean by dancer. One was not allowed to raise one's foot higher than one's head, which of course was what the crowd came to see. Every last one of us is a hypocrite, Gloria – may I call you Gloria?'

'Fill yer boots.' Gloria turned her face to the smooth caress of the sun, half dreaming, letting Lily's words wash over her. The willow waved its fronds beguilingly over their heads, sending shadows rippling and jerking down Lily's harsh features, her nose hooked by age, the folds of her dry skin. But Lily spoke of events of thirty years ago and her eyes gleamed grey-green, ageless, remembering.

'Someone denied they enjoyed the show and reported us to the Lord Chamberlain. Mr Strange's licence for music and dancing was revoked. I even got parts in opera, but prima donnas talk about themselves all the time, even in their sleep, to the detriment of their vocal chords. In the end Mr Strange was allowed to put on stage plays. However, my name stuck.' She opened her handbag and unwrapped some sandwiches in greaseproof paper, offered one without a change in expression. 'Cheese. Don't pretend you're not hungry.' She watched Gloria eat. 'You have a tiny hard line on each side of your mouth that I think is new. There's a hardness in your eyes, yet it makes you attractive. I usually sum people up in two seconds, Gloria. But you defy me. Are you on the run?'

'From the law? No.'

'A man, then.'

In her mind's eye Gloria saw the sun's blaze fade to a single candle in a darkened room, and she remembered Willy Glizzard tugging at his belt, hearing his voice grunting self-righteously, *Don't look at me like that, Gloria, I never bin able ter look at a girl yet wivout finking of customers.* She heard Hugo demanding, *Stop lying to me, that's all. Prize yourself as highly as I prize you.* The bloody liars, they hadn't cared for her at all; she was only a trophy under their belts.

'No one's going ter turn up,' Gloria said. 'No men. None of those bloody liars. Don't worry.'

'Good!' Lily said.

Gloria clasped the chain around her neck, feeling the weight of the coin hot and heavy between her breasts. 'I can't even remember 'is name,' she claimed.

'Can't you?'

They sat in the sun, the old woman and the young, while the falling sun swung the shadows of the willow-tree around them, and the tide covered the mud.

'Often we don't know why we do what we do.' Lily stood up, then held out her hand. 'I'll break my own first rule of the house.'

'Wot's that?'

'No female lodgers.'

Gloria followed the blue and yellow coat through the choking aroma of bad eggs blowing from the gasworks across the nearby houses, into alleyways threading between a confusion of sawmills and glassworks, then ran to catch up.

'No women at all?'

'Men are less trouble, my dear, and being more used to discipline are more easily disciplined. I take no nonsense,' Lily snorted. 'I know what I look like now. On my retirement from the boards while my small capital sum was still intact, I swore to myself that I would put up with no more of the hysterics and fainting and spitefulness which accompany the hothouse condition of actresses' lodgings.'

'Yer mean yer don't like women?'

'I mean I run a tight ship.'

'Crystal clear,' Gloria said.

'I've made an exception in your case.'

'Why?'

Lily halted between a brewery and noisy boilerworks, trying to stare Gloria down with that intimidating coldness, then her expression softened into almost a girlish grin. 'I told you,' she shouted above the racket of hammers and rivet-guns. 'Old times' sake!' The tea-up bell went, and in the abrupt silence she stiffened her face into its previous sternness, as though ashamed of providing a loud glimpse of her true feelings – as if that gosh-bright coat and eyewatering hat weren't a loud enough statement. Lily Alhambra couldn't lie her way out of a paper bag to Gloria, but she had her pride.

She turned right by the lead-and-colour works, past a very fine pub on the corner, down Wagstaff Alley into one of those sudden, surprising streets of paving-stones sloping to a trickling gully along the centre and standpipes at intervals, a Southwark oasis.

'This is Zoar Street,' Lily said. 'It is an ancient word, meaning refuge. A Baptist sanctuary used to stand here. Welcome.'

Chapter Sixteen

A guinea a week, four weeks in advance, was to be left discreetly on the mantelshelf – Lily Alhambra did not like to be seen to stoop so low as actually to touch rent-money. Gloria thought this was a decidedly steep sum for a lodgings in Southwark, but on the other hand she enjoyed spending that bastard Glizzard's stolen money. She was shucking off the past like a second skin, she told herself, emerging new and gleaming, her own woman: new clothes, new shoes, an irresistible passion for hats. Each time she opened her purse in a glossy Newington Causeway millinery she felt an emotion of sweet revenge against types like Willy Glizzard and Hugo Handley, all men, in fact. In Arnold's house she had made better her broken leg and cracked ribs; here in Zoar Street, she told herself, she would recover from her disillusionment. The more she spent, the better she felt, and the more herself. And the better she felt in herself, the sweeter her revenge. Each time she touched the gold, she mentally kissed her fingertips.

Lily Alhambra, with her iron countenance and secret smile for Gloria, instinctively shared the unspoken secret.

The two women, though separated by a gulf of years, had a good understanding of one another. Lily opened the door and stepped back, watching Gloria. *It's very sad*, her eyes said.

Gloria, too excited to notice the older woman's expression, stood in the centre of her room. She held out her arms and twirled. It wasn't much compared to Emily's room in Wimbledon, perhaps, but it was her own, paid for by herself – a year ago her situation would have seemed like a dream come true. Her very own room with a russia mat at the foot of a sturdy iron bedstead, a hard mattress and bolsters like rocks; it was clear which sex Miss Alhambra expected her lodgers to be. She was allowed as much cold water from the standpipe in the street as she could carry, and a pitcher of hot water once every two days, to be collected from Jenny in the scullery. Gloria slipped to the window, loving every moment of it, and grinned across the rooftops to the hop warehouses of Southwark Street, the railways looping above them in every direction, the South-Eastern driving eastward from Waterloo Junction Station, the London Chatham & Dover striding on its journey south; at night the train windows seemed to fly clattering across the sky. Yet, though almost surrounded by the railways, Zoar Street remained a safe refuge.

'Yer done well,' Gloria murmured to herself, 'yer done very well.'

She doubted the other lodgers held Miss Alhambra in the same affection that she did. On Gloria's first night those nervous gentlemen had stood waiting quietly in the lace-and-overstuffing parlour, amidst dark brown walls and the smell of cabbage, a copy of *The Times* on the table, none of them under fifty-five or with much hope left in their lives. At seven p.m. the parlour clock gonged and a ripple started as Miss Alhambra, her wrinkled neck clotted with what appeared to be real jewellery, though it was awfully sparkly, descended from her quarters to supper. Captain Villers had manners and usually escorted her from the foot of the stairs, but he was a soapy old devil behind his military demeanour, fooling Miss Alhambra no more than Gloria: they exchanged glances about him. Mr Poulton was a clerk at Morgan's chocolate factory in Tooley Street, and always rubbed his knife and fork with his napkin however spotless they were, his napkin squeaking the only sound at the table. Mr Rutt, with a shiny bald head and nervous mannerisms, was a manager at the lead works; he called the captain, whom he hated, 'Half-Pay'. Miss Alhambra cleared her throat and the squeaking napkin stopped. She said grace and sat; they all sat. Jenny, pasty-faced and frantic, rushed in the wooden nugget of roast beef, and Miss Alhambra turned to Captain Villers and inquired, as though for the first time, whether he would be so kind as to carve the joint. 'My pleasure, ma'am.' As always, Villers stood and sharpened the carving knife as seriously as he would a sword, his chest puffed out, representing his tiny, impotent army around the table. 'Get on wiv it,' hissed Mr Rutt through his teeth, but the captain would not give up his pathetic privilege.

'Mr Rutt is our local historian,' Miss Alhambra said, and everyone sat up.

'Southwark? Really?' drawled Captain Villers, directing his conversation as always to Miss Alhambra. 'Goodness gracious, who'd've thought it? Fine beef, ma'am; not showy, but well up to standard.'

'Not 'istorian, I'd put it more like hamateur hantiquarian,' insisted Mr Rutt, trying to sound like a gentleman, lording it over Gloria. He ran his heavy hand through his short grey hair. 'An hamateur hint'rest. I'd be tickled ter show yer some corners of our historic an' dignified diocese, Miss?' he grinned, wiping his palm on his lapel.

'I'll find things out fer meself,' Gloria said, and he stared at her, chilled.

'I say, steady as she goes,' said Captain Villers, turning to Miss Alhambra, 'I said, steady on, what?' He passed her the salt, filled her glass with water.

Lily Alhambra couldn't see what was as plain as the nose on her face: Captain Villers was in love with her.

The days were long and Gloria increasingly stayed out, buying herself a Waterfall umbrella for rainy weather; soon she became a familiar figure striding purposefully past the women doing their washing outside, their voices carrying like birdsong over the roar of the washboards along the street, their reddened arms pumping into the suds that filled the broken-hooped, cut-down tubs left for dead by the Great Guildford Street cooperage. These indomitable women weren't stuck-up, they dressed anyhow, third-hand, clothing their children from the rag-man, yelling gorblimey this and gorblimey that, sweeping back the sweaty tresses from their foreheads with hands like boiled hams. It was a kindly, dirty area and going downhill – Lily's doorstep was the only one dubbined, Jenny the tearful maid scrubbing on her knees with the brush with her eyes closed as if she was asleep while she wept, and the concrete surround of Lily's door and windows the only ones in the street licked with fresh cream paint. Mostly everyone eked out the housekeeping by taking in washing, cursing a southerly wind that blew smuts from the iron foundry chimneys and covered the morning's clean wash that had been hung out, so that the work must be done again in the afternoon. Gathered around the standpipes, they nodded cheerfully to Gloria and passed the time of day. 'Wot's that pong?' yelled Gloria, and they yelled back, 'Wot pong's that?' then broke up in laughter, pretending not to notice the stink they lived with, the oilcake factory hidden behind the houses. The braver urchins old enough to walk followed Gloria as far as Southwark Street before she turned them back.

Gloria's smile faded. She walked alone. Tired now of the shop windows of the Causeway, she began exploring as far south as the Blind Asylum, then on Saturdays she roamed as far west as the Cut, lined to bursting with cheap stalls, where poor people with Saturday's cash burning a hole in their pockets came to buy their Sunday lunch and anything else between a penny and a bob, from a pig's trotter to a woman's body. 'Wot's the matter wiv yer, luv?' called someone when she could not bear to look. It was the dull acceptance on the women's faces that was so awful, neither pleasure nor pain, filling her with dread, and she began to avoid these busy, ghastly places.

From Zoar Street it was only a short stroll through the Liberty of the Clink to Southwark Church, its quiet enclave dwarfed by the soaring arches of London Bridge. Builders were adding bits on to the original building to make it the size of a cathedral. She wandered inside during the peace and quiet of the lunch-break, finding at first everything to be dust and shadows; gradually the gloom cleared as her eyes adjusted.

'There has been a church standing here at St Mary Ouverie for over a thousand years, perhaps much longer,' the verger whispered. 'Observe how finely carved the stone altar-screen is – the gift of Richard Fox, Bishop of Winchester, nearly four hundred years ago...' Gloria stared up at the statues, row after row of them, at their stony faces, which seemed so human. The verger followed her, white stone-dust coating his hat and shoulders, his soft words firing her interest in the things of the past hidden to her before. From two centuries earlier, she came across an effigy of a sleeping man, as bright as though he were still alive, of a poet called Gower.

'Never 'eard of that one.'

'A friend of Chaucer,' murmured the verger, and the familiar name gave Gloria a sudden pleasure, a sense of connection. 'The *Canterbury Tales*? Perhaps at school.'

For a moment, there in the dusty gloom inside St

Saviour's, everything looming at her half seen, half sensed, Gloria felt as though life was an invisible web in which everything touched everything else.

'More than five hundred years ago Chaucer and his pilgrims departed for Canterbury, just over the road there,' the verger pointed through the doorway, 'from the Tabard Inn.'

Gloria went out into the glaring sunlight and he followed her, shading his eyes.

'Is something the matter? Does the name of the Tabard mean anything to you?'

'No. Why should it?'

He shrugged. 'No reason.' The builders were wiping their hands on their trousers and yawning, starting their racket of hammers and chains again. 'Perhaps Madam forgets her Chaucer?' Out here in the light the verger's glance took Gloria in with contempt, undeceived by her hat, seeing she was not educated. ' "All that is given, take with cheerfulness. To wrestle in this world is to ask a fall. Here is no home; here is but a wilderness." ' He held out his hand for sixpence.

Gloria gave him a penny.

She climbed the steps to London Bridge, looking for her way, crossing the road and exploring down the Borough High Street, peeping through the covered arch-ways leading to the decrepit stagecoach-yards of Long Southwark: the King's Head, the White Hart, the George – complete with St George on horseback, killing a rather small, petulant-looking dragon. Then she came to the sign of the Tabard.

Obviously this was an ancient coaching inn, and the place seemed to be waiting for a return to those days, as though it had forgotten the present. Through the archway Gloria spied crooked galleries lining a long, cobbled courtyard, and a mess of straw blowing everywhere which a miserable boy was sweeping. The place looked very dilapidated, with tiles slipping from the stable roof and grass growing through an old cartwheel leant against the wall. The boy started his task again, defeated by the wind. A huge fat man, his beer belly overhanging his greasy white apron worn like a loincloth, his lower lip swinging pendulously above his chin, waddled from the tap-room doorway and slapped the boy to make him work harder. Someone called from a window, 'Mr Wittle, trouble in the bar!' Mr Wittle hitched up his belly with the palms of his hands and waddled back into the shadows.

The boy swept frantically.

Gloria looked up at a sign swinging over her head, meant to attract customers, and a sudden frightening sense of the strangeness of the place almost overwhelmed her, for all its apparent ordinariness, looking at first glance much like any of the other shabby inns lining this road: they had all seen better days. The Tabard's peeling sign-board depicted the white shirt or smock, now a sort of sun-faded dirty cream colour, presumably once called a tabard. Instead of medieval heraldry and coats of arms, all the usual stuff, the flaking paint seemed to show a dog's head, a pile of silver money, other things she could not make out.

Gloria's lips moved, as though she heard a voice with an Irish swing in it.

'Twas a lodging-room in London, Southwark I believe, she were a barmaid at the Tabard Inn, a poor place where they were in love.

'Oh my Gawd,' Gloria whispered, 'it's the place.'

The child of the woman he loved was born there: poor Tilly O'Neill's baby. Jamie Reilly.

The wind gusted, blowing the smell of the Bermondsey tanneries around her, and the sign flashed the sun behind it as it swung. She gave a shout as someone bumped into her, giving her shins a terrific bang.

'Why don't yer watch where yer going!' she shrieked, rubbing her leg. Her eyes watered, and she looked up through tears, though they were as much of shock as of pain.

The young man who stared down at her, whose cared-for but slightly threadbare black jacket could not conceal the gauntness of his tall frame, had large eyes which held her with a steady, serious gaze. His mouth was small, his complexion pale – made paler by gingery hair and eyebrows. With his shy, deep brown eyes this man looked more used to reading books than knocking over women in the street. Neither was that a mouth made for smiling, and she wondered if he hid bad teeth behind his tight lips. The tip of his tongue separated them uncertainly, but still she could not see.

'I'm terribly sorry,' he murmured. 'Can – can I help you at all, ma'am?'

Gloria, standing straight again, almost laughed; he was

as deferential as if he hoped she would order half a pound of peppermints or an item of hosiery. She winced so as not to let him off the hook too easily, but his mouth twitched in response to her, seeing through her, yet not quite sure what he had said that was so amusing. Still, he did seem genuinely worried about her. She scented the piece of pungent licorice he was sucking, which explained why he kept his lips shut.

'Nah, I'm walking wounded,' she reassured him.

'You're sure there's nothing I can do?' he inquired, still staring at her. 'I don't know what came over me – I must have been thinking.'

'Forget it, chum,' she said, and in farewell he politely lifted his bowler hat, which seemed one size too small for his head, looking so lonely that Gloria was sorry for him.

'Daniel Fox, at your service,' he said. She glimpsed his fine white teeth.

He put his hat back on, turned, and walked off the kerb. With his steady tread away from her, Gloria glimpsed that the soles of his shoes were worn to holes. He crossed the road and went into a chemist's corner-shop. Gloria put her hands on her hips and shook her head.

She turned back towards the Zoar and Lily Alhambra's house.

Coming back to Zoar Street, Gloria ducked beneath the rows of washing that crisscrossed the narrow haven from side to side like white flags. The street was filling with shadow as the sun dropped behind the factory roofs; for most people it was a short respite before getting the washing in and putting the supper on. A boy with his cloth cap half over his face had fallen asleep on the still-warm paving; the other children were seeing how close they could jump over him without kicking him awake. The women sat out on their doorsteps, elbows on their knees, a few of them smoking, and several had got together in a group to run the lice out of their skirt-seams using the corner of a hot brick, which they shared. 'Where yer bin an' gone this time, Gloria?'

'Ah, it's no good,' Gloria said. 'Money's running out.'

''Ave ter take in washing, won't yer! Like us, yer lucky sod.'

'Stash it, wouldn't mind if I did.'

'Go on, wouldn't yer!' They roared with laughter, and Gloria ducked forward beneath the washing wearing a cheerfulness on her face that she did not feel. Other girls who hadn't finished up so early, who had rushed to finish hanging out while there was still some sun, were coming back and with strong kicks of their feet pushing over half-barrels of cold, filthy suds into the central gutter. They sat on their doorsteps, slathering their arms to the elbows with quantities of the thick white grease that was supposed to do good, waterproofing their skin for tomorrow's repetition of today's work. Yawning with youthful, lined faces ingrained with dirt, their open mouths showing terrible teeth from the jam sandwiches and sweet tea that they lived on, these young girls hardly noticed Gloria in the slackness of their exhaustion. Many of them were unmarried, not from choice, but because there were so few men around. The work was cruelly hard and for most of them, Gloria knew, there would be no end to it.

Gloria stopped in the doorway of Lily Alhambra's house, looking back. The grease was of the cheapest grade and there was a slight but distinct odour of fish.

After supper Gloria, carrying dirty plates on a tray, followed Jenny to the scullery. It was an awkward little room at the back of the house, the doors and windows in the wrong places, dirt and washing and washing-up everywhere. 'I'll give yer a 'and, I never could sit still,' Gloria offered, pushing up her sleeves, but Jenny turned with an expression of fierce resentment.

'Yer get back up front, I'll look after it down 'ere. This is my 'ole an' I like it, an' it might not be much compared ter the likes of some, but I know where everyfink goes, an' I don't appreciate no interference!'

'I want ter 'elp,' Gloria said.

'Please,' Jenny begged, 'please don't. 'Elp yerself if yer want ter 'elp someone, get back where yer belong, miss, I don't want nuffink changed round. I got work ter do, an' I got ter get meself going all alone while it's still dark tomorrer morning, while yer all snoring yer 'eads off.'

'Where d'yer sleep?'

'Down 'ere. The nights is getting parky an' it's warm by the stove.'

'I'll wash the plates up, an' yer can put them away where yer know where they go, if it means so much ter yer.'

''Course it does!'

'Listen, girl,' Gloria demanded, 'yer fink I never got me 'ands wet before or somefink?'

'I don't know nuffink. If I was yer, *I* wouldn't.' Jenny wiped her nose on the side of her hand then put back her greasy black hair. 'Yer talk like us an' yer pretend yer like us, but yer diff'rent from us.'

'That's a 'urtful fing ter say, Jenny. Everyone's diff'rent.'

'Everyone's the same!' Jenny said, coming out of herself. 'Less'n they got money or class, that is. We're all the same. We was talkin' about yer, us in the street.' She looked at Gloria with liquid, envious eyes. 'I dunno 'ow yer done it but yer are diff'rent.'

'Come on,' said Gloria busily, 'let's be friends, why not?'

Jenny pulled up the sleeve of her dress just as Gloria had, putting her forearm beside Gloria's, matching their hands. 'See wot I mean, Gloria? Yer white.'

'Wot yer trying ter do, make me feel guilty?' Gloria remembered her sister Annie's work-reddened hands. Jenny's were even worse because she had scratched the irritated skin, and her nails were bitten back – except her thumbnails, always easiest and most useful to preserve, which she had left almost religiously long for the ecstasy of scratching.

'I got me 'ands in 'ot water four hours a day,' Jenny said proudly. 'It's longer fer them other women wiv children, or wot got ter take in work. I'm gonner be 'appy when I die, 'cos then I'm not going ter char no more, an' yer know wot? There's no chapped 'ands in 'eaven. Yer missed a smear there,' she pointed, returning the offending plate.

'Why d'yer work 'ere, Jenny?'

'Lucky ter get it,' Jenny said quickly. She took back the cleaned plate, examined it, approved it, then added, 'Wot choice do yer fink I got, anyways?'

'Yer 'aven't got no family?'

'I wasn't *that* lucky, Miss Simmonds.'

'Yer can keep calling me Gloria, if yer like.'

Jenny sighed. 'See, I never knew me ma.'

'Yuss,' Gloria sighed, 'I s'pose I wasn't that lucky neither.'

'Wot yer never 'ad yer don't miss,' Jenny said fiercely.

'Well, I do miss 'er.' Gloria pulled the plug and patted her hands dry on Jenny's towel. 'Me mum gave me a tip, I know it sounds funny. If yer can't afford rosewater, rub a bit of carrot on yer 'ands an' see if it'll stop that trouble yer got.'

'I ain't got no trouble,' Jenny said defensively. ''Sides, all our carrots is sprouty. I don't like the sound of it, that's the truth. Why'd yer 'ave ter come down 'ere an' spoil fings?' Her lower lip trembled. 'I'm just a maid, I don't want ter pong like a blooming carrot.' She looked so frightened of what Gloria might do that Gloria burst out laughing. Jenny put away the plates in a huff. 'There's nuffink wrong wiv me 'ands,' she said.

Gloria found a carrot from the old sack by the potatoes

and rubbed it over her own hands with every appearance of enjoyment. 'It even pongs quite nice.'

'It looks silly,' Jenny resisted her, 'an' I don't care fer the look of it, an' I'm not going ter do it, an' yer can't make me, an' that's that.'

That night Gloria lay awake watching the train lights flash across the ceiling of her room, her hands behind her head. Of course she had rinsed them as soon as they dried, oddly coloured and sticky as sugar from the vegetable. But she was sure it had done good, or at least no harm. Yet Jenny had preferred to suffer her chapped hands as they were: probably they had been like that for years, and her discomfort was part of her by now. Besides, she had a low opinion of herself – *just a maid*, as though that was all there was to her. Gloria pulled the pillow against her cheek, irritated.

This afternoon she had seen them use whalegrease on their arms, cheap and effective no doubt, but smelly and ugly too. Who wanted to look ugly? Only people who didn't care about themselves, people who had an ugly picture of themselves, like pretty little Jenny, frightened of trying to improve herself. Frightened even of dreaming, so downtrodden were they by their remorseless toil, so accepting of their servitude. That must suit the ruling classes across the river very well.

Gloria thought dreamily, *carrot juice would work better*. Root vegetables lasted longer than any other, she knew, the stuff would keep at least a month in cool weather, she could make up a batch ... and by selling it she would be helping people as well as making her money last a little longer. Carrot juice! – no, she could just see them laughing their heads off on the doorsteps, she would have to present it attractively so that people would *want* to be interested by it, look at it, touch it, feel it. She'd have to make it into something just a little bit intriguing. Something just a little bit different so that people thought they needed to buy what she was selling because ... because there was nothing else quite like it.

The fascination factor, she thought dreamily.

Gloria sat up in bed, realising she had almost been asleep. She didn't sleep again. She could hardly wait for morning.

By daylight, hurrying to the Borough fruit and vegetable market by St Saviour's, hard in the shadows of London Bridge, she soon realised that her task was more formidable than it had seemed in her night thoughts. Buying a pound of fresh carrots was easy – though in her enthusiasm she changed her mind about how much she needed, first from a pound to a couple of pounds, ending up buying a stone because then they were half the price per pound: starting off as she meant to go on. But fourteen pounds felt like a ton to carry, so she got the smallholder's boy to deliver them to Zoar Street for a penny, while from the oilman she purchased a gallon tub of grease and tottered home with it clasped in her arms. Jenny was busy with the housework upstairs so Gloria busied herself at once in the kitchen, grating a pound of carrot into the grease. She surveyed the results excitedly.

'It looks revolting,' Lily Alhambra commented that

afternoon. 'What are we meant to do, put it on our skin or eat it?'

'At least the carrot takes off the fishy smell.'

'I can see you know nothing about greasepaint, my dear. It never sinks into the skin, you know. You need something much finer.'

'I know what I need,' Gloria said with determination. 'I need something that looks better.'

'You, my dear,' said Lily, 'need something that works.'

After supper Gloria chivvied Jenny into smearing it over her hands. 'It's lumpy,' Jenny said tearfully, bobbing to Lily whom Gloria had brought in on her side, 'an' it looks odd, an' it feels funny, an' I don't like it very much, if it please yer, ma'am.'

'Stop that silly whining,' snorted Miss Alhambra, who wouldn't touch the stuff. 'Really, Jenny, I've just about had it up to here with you, you miserikins.'

'Try it every night fer the next week,' Gloria suggested to the sobbing girl in her friendliest voice, 'an' if it 'asn't done wonders ter yer at the end of it, yer can 'ave yer money back.'

'But I 'aven't given yer no money,' Jenny snivelled. 'Oh! I see! Yer mean it's a present.' She brightened visibly. 'That's lovely! No one never gave me a present afore.' She surveyed her hands with pleasure.

'That girl's got no more brains than a guinea-pig,' confided Miss Alhambra, irritably returning to the front parlour.

'I'm trying it out on meself too,' Gloria said.

But in a week, Jenny's hands were smoother, even Mr

Poulton agreed. Jenny admitted that the irritation had eased, and because she was now more aware of her hands she took better care of them. 'There,' Gloria said, 'now no one would ever know yer was a skivvy.'

But the men resisted the excitement which could now be felt running through some rooms in the lodging.

'You females and your vile potions,' said Captain Villers, flourishing his Kitchener moustache.

'Wot about you men wiv yer shaving-soap an' yer moustache-wax an' sticky macassar hair-oil?' demanded Gloria.

'I certainly do not wax my moustache, only Frenchmen do that.'

'Poulton uses heau-de-cologne,' Mr Rutt accused slyly.

'I never do!' claimed Mr Poulton hotly.

Gloria left them to it. 'We know it works,' she told Lily with satisfaction after supper, 'and if this stuff does the job, believe me, anything will.' She had already experimented with the mixture: having thrown away loads at first, she'd learned to make up only very small quantities. She now pounded the carrot with pestle and mortar, mixing it like a roux, and she'd tried substituting the grease with unsalted butter, but it turned rancid in half a day. 'Now I've just got to have something that *feels* that it works.' She snapped her fingers. 'A touch of magic.'

'If only yer didn't 'ave ter take it off,' Jenny said, 'it's a real bind when yer sleepy, an' it's 'orrid sticky goo.'

'There's something called lanolin that sinks into the skin,' suggested Lily. 'Lanolin wasn't available when I started my career, but later I knew some actresses who swore by it. Comes from sheep's wool, I believe.'

'Where would I buy it?' asked Gloria, but the others shrugged.

'Hany chemist's shop would 'ave it,' said Mr Rutt, who knew about such things. 'A pharmacist's hundoubtedly would. There's one hin the Borough 'Igh Street, slap hin the middle of the road where St Margaret's Church was.'

Gloria remembered the shop, and in the morning she put up her umbrella and walked through the pelting rain to London Bridge. Opposite the tumbledown Tabard Inn, where Southwark Street ran at an angle into the Borough and the road was at its broadest, a huddle of buildings half-way across the cobbled expanse made a sort of traffic island. Now carts and drays were stalled on every side of it, a wagon had broken its swivel-post attempting a U-turn in the worst possible place, in front of the bank at the north end. A policeman arrived and held up his arm, then waved Gloria across for something to do. Cobbles, tarpaulins and the drivers' hard hats gleamed waxily under the rain, and the starry shoplights glowed yellow as dandelions. Past a tiny confectioner's and an empty Eel Pie shop, Gloria found the wedge-shaped pharmacy on the southern extremity, its entrance no wider than the door.

A bell above the door *tinged* softly as she went in. The shop was surprisingly deep, and the angry shouts of the drivers were shut out by the click of the latch. She shook her umbrella over the mat, then placed it loosely in the rack, and the boards creaked as she walked between the dark counters. Colza-oil lamps gave a cosy glow. Glad to be out of the rain, she looked around her carefully. What a place!

It was all counters and shelves – shelves were crammed along all three walls, stacked to the ceiling with bottles and glass jars and tubs of every shape and size, with a ladder on wheels for the assistant to attempt the upper layers. Along the broad back wall the coloured bottles carried mysterious alchemical labels to make their contents deliberately obscure, it seemed to her, and the pharmacist seem very clever: HYDROX, PERM.POT, HYD.SULPH, H_2CO_3 – Gloria reckoned that *experts only* was what they were really saying. The counters prevented customers from touching what they wished to buy; they had to know what they wanted, or be able to identify it from a distance. The assistant would know best.

All Gloria could see of him was the top of his gingery head, bent over a ledger placed on the longest, innermost counter. Such was his concentration on the figures and the scratching of his pen that he had not heard her approach, yet Gloria could not imagine, sniffing the dusty odour of the place, that the bell rang very often. There was a raised pulpit with a cash-till and seat, but though dusty Lamson overhead railways ran to it for the payment of bills and the return of change, it too was unoccupied and dull.

She cleared her throat. Still no reaction.

'A pound of gobstoppers, please,' Gloria said.

He looked up with a start. 'It's you,' he said.

'Oh!' She clicked her fingers. 'Mr Daniel Fox.' He stared at her and she felt sorry for him because he looked like he needed a square meal. ''Ow are yer terday?'

'How are you? I was just thinking about you.' He glared at her legs, then remembered to cap his pen. 'I see you have remembered me too.' He smiled shyly with his small mouth. She waited without expression. 'Oh, gobstoppers?' he said at last, pulling his jacket straight. 'Gobstoppers! You have to go next door for sweets.'

'Only joking,' she sighed.

'I see,' he said seriously. 'As you see, the place is not very busy at the moment, but one still has to keep abreast of affairs.' He patted the ledger, nodded at the enormous leather-bound pharmacopoia on a bookstand.

''Ave I got yer full attention now, Mr Daniel Fox, or do I 'ave ter call the manager?'

'I am the manager,' he said as though it was obvious. 'The sign is above the door, "Martin Fox (1871) & Son, Pharmacists." But it *is* rather faded, even though the "& Son" was added later,' he continued apologetically, as if not to give offence. 'I am the addition.'

'Yer sound an educated bloke, but I'll speak ter the organ-grinder, if yer don't mind, not 'is monkey.'

'My father died in March last year.'

'I'm sorry. I didn't mean ter be rude.'

'But it doesn't seem to bother you,' he said quickly, flickering his smile. 'Let's start again. I'm twenty-eight years old, and fully qualified, I assure you. How may I help you?'

'I want lanolin.' Gloria was determined not to do things by halves. 'Lots of lanolin.'

'There's not much demand for it round here. In the West End ... but here people like to see stuff working.

And it is comparatively expensive.' He took down a pretty pot with gold chasing. 'Four ounces of Lady Olivia's Beauty Cream, as supplied to gentlefolk of town and country, etcetera. Lanolin. Nothing but lanolin. Yours for a shilling and sixpence.'

'One and six! There's only an 'andful!'

'But a very gorgeous pot, don't you think?'

''Ow much is it wivout the pot?'

'I can sell you a ten-pound tin of commercial cholesterin-fatty matter for only a guinea.'

'Chol . . . wot's that when it's at 'ome?'

He laughed. 'Lanolin!'

Gloria hefted the pot thoughtfully. 'That's quite a wheeze, ain't it? Money fer jam.'

He refused to be drawn. 'May I ask for what you require two years' supply of lanolin?'

Gloria turned away. 'Yer father was a dreamer, wasn't 'e,' she said, looking around her: the overhead railway that could not ever have been justified by the turnover of a shop this size, the bulky typewriter that sat unused on the desk in the back office. 'But yer not, though.' Daniel followed her eyes.

'My father, Martin, was the oldest of six brothers,' he admitted. 'All of them were brought up as gentlemen. There was a sister too, Jemima. When my grandfather died – this was before I was born – they found that their inheritance . . . there was no inheritance. The family scattered.' He tightened his lips as though there was more to be told, then shrugged. She wouldn't understand. 'My father ended up here. He was brilliant at everything except figures. Thus he never earned money, and the little he did earn, he could not keep.'

Gloria wandered around the shop. She checked her purse furtively. She did have a guinea, but it was next week's rent.

'Now I know everyfink about yer,' she said over her shoulder.

'And I don't even know your name.'

'See, Daniel, I've been finking about the people nobody never finks of,' she said, turning towards him decisively. 'The people round 'ere wot everyone takes fer granted, not worth anyfink 'cause they can't pay. People like yer and me.'

'My books balance,' he said precisely.

'I bet they do, yer that sort of bloke. But only because yer don't spend no money on suits and shoes, nuffink on yerself. I bet yer socks are darned 'alf ter death, an' yer do 'em yerself. Look at all this stock yer carrying, though.'

'Necessary for the business. But I do not have expensive tastes, it's true, and I live over the shop for nothing.'

'No wife, no children? Yer look like yer could do wiv a good square meal, Daniel Fox.'

He fiddled with his pen. 'What's your point?'

'I've got a secret ingredient.'

He stopped. 'What is it?'

She leaned her elbows on the counter. 'That's why it's a secret,' she taunted him with a smile.

Still she couldn't get him out of himself. 'I see,' he repeated patiently. 'Like your name which you won't tell me.'

'Gloria. Yer can 'ave that one fer free.'

'But not your secret ingredient.'

'The fascination factor.' She snapped her fingers. 'Pure magic.'

'Witchcraft. Eye of newt, toe of frog. The same old story.'

'Yer right,' she said slowly, 'yer right, it's a long tradition, Daniel, yer put yer finger on it. People will believe,' she said urgently, 'because they want to believe. They're desperate, only they don't know it yet. If yer believe in somefink 'ard enough it comes true, did yer know that?'

'I hardly think that proposition would stand up to scientific examination. Something either works or it doesn't, it can be analysed and tested, any doctor will tell you—'

'I'm not going ter talk ter yer any more if yer won't believe. Go on, get me yer tin of fatty cholesterin, 'ere's yer guinea.'

He rolled the ladder across and ascended it slowly, fetched a large tin on the top shelf. He tucked it under his arm, then laid it carefully on the counter beside her guinea.

'No charge,' he said.

He looked so thin and sad that she felt guilty. 'Come on, yer sure yer can afford it?'

Daniel amazed her. He laughed.

'I'm much poorer than you are,' he said, and Gloria knew she held him in the cup of her hand.

'Yer'll see,' she promised him earnestly, 'it works.'

'It had better,' he said, fetching her umbrella and holding open the door, fastidiously polite, grimacing at the rain. 'When you've made up a batch, you might bring some in to me. I might even sell some.'

'My very first customer!' she laughed.

He watched her figure bobbing across the road, her feet kicking her dress, drops of shining water scattering from her umbrella in the coming sun. The tin gleamed in the jaunty curve of her arm.

'If you want to know what I really think,' he said to himself without rancour, 'I think you've made a fool of me. I didn't even ask for your address.' He closed the shop door and leaned back against it. 'And I don't think I'll ever see you again, Gloria,' he murmured.

Chapter Seventeen

Though he was relieved and surprised to see Gloria return a week later, he allowed no sign of these feelings to show on his inscrutable face – he thought he never did let anyone get an advantage over him. Nevertheless, Daniel had a feeling, which he hated, that she knew exactly what he was thinking, that he had no secrets from her. She was a hot potato and he wasn't quite sure how to handle her.

'Oh, it's you,' he said with politeness, trying to show no sign of pleasure. It was a windy day outside, September gales rattling the door and scattering newspapers along the street, blowing umbrellas inside-out, and Gloria's laughing face looked buffed and rosy-cheeked as the wind banged the door open and seemed almost to blow her into the shop. Such was her vivacity that he frowned to counteract it, and fiddled some packets of soap straight.

'Surprise surprise,' she called. 'Don't pretend yer not surprised ter see me!'

'I knew you'd come,' he said, alarmed now by the wind rushing around the shop, sending papers flying. He struggled the door closed behind her. It was suddenly quiet.

'Why?' she asked. 'Why should I come back?'

He looked startled, then tried not to. Even her grin was provocative. 'I trusted you,' he explained.

She laughed with a harshness that surprised him, the hardness seemed so at odds with the rest of her. 'Trust always works, does it?' She gave him a wise look, that blue gaze of hers catching him right in the eye so that he couldn't help responding to her. He felt himself redden to the tips of his ears under the spotlight of her attention and hastened past her, but she was way ahead of him again, tossing him her umbrella so that he had to catch it and put it in the rack for her, then meekly follow her striding figure up his own shop. He walked slowly, adjusting a couple of items of stock that the wind had dislodged on the way, to show that he wasn't impressed by her exuberance, he wasn't going to let her push him around, making her wait for him.

But instead, without even noticing he was not there, she was rummaging in the huge sewing-bag she was carrying, setting out a row of tiny frosted-glass pots along the counter. 'I got a job lot of these off a barrow in the Cut,' she said busily.

'You don't know where they've come from,' he said, alarmed. 'They might be stolen, or—'

'A thousand fer 'alf a crown, but some were broken, the packing-case 'ad fallen off a cart I reckon. I got a coster ter push 'em back ter Zoar Street on 'is barrow fer tuppence.' She winked. 'Did I let that slip out? Now yer know where I live as well as me name.'

'I don't think you let much slip out by accident, miss.'

'Don't pretend ter be stand-offish.'

'I'm not pretending,' he said, annoyed, and even more annoyed when she laughed as though he had said something funny.

'Gloria,' she said. 'Come on, move yer lips, take the medicine, it won't 'urt.'

'Gloria,' he said through his tight little mouth.

She shook her head and flicked a piece of lint off his shoulder. 'Yer a funny one,' she said, but turned back to the bottles before he could respond. ''Ere yer are, an' it works. Lanolin an' the secret Gloria-ingredient. Go on, don't 'old back, dip yer fingers an' 'ave a go. Yer know yer dyin' ter.' She twisted the top off one of the little pots and held it under his nose.

'You could sell coals to Newcastle,' he said grudgingly, trying another tack with her. Carefully he took the open pot between two fingers and examined it his way, whatever she said, taking nothing for granted. He sniffed cautiously, then touched his fingertip lightly to the surface of the cream. He grunted and took it to the window. Gloria followed him anxiously.

'Wot's the matter wiv it?'

'Discolouration of the surface layer.'

'They all do that.'

He glanced at her then went to the back of the shop, took a dropper and allowed a couple of drips of liquid to fall on to the lanolin.

'Your secret ingredient,' he informed her, 'is vegetable matter.'

'Wild 'orses wouldn't drag the recipe out of me,' she

recited her spiel gaily, she must be selling the stuff already, 'it's a secret passed down the family for generations, mother ter daughter, jealously guarded.'

'Yes, most people would wish that was so.'

'That's why I tell 'em.'

He put a tiny dab to his tongue. 'Carrot juice?'

Her face fell. 'Well, it works.'

'You are trying to pull the wool over my eyes and the eyes of the populace of the Borough with *carrot juice?*'

'An' of Bankside, an' a shop along the Newington Causeway wot said they might take some.' She tightened her mouth, riled by his nit-picking scepticism, his refusal to see the obvious. 'There's a bit of cucumber in it too. Miss Alhambra said actresses swore by it.'

'What you make up for in enthusiasm you certainly lack in professionalism.'

'Daniel, I wish yer'd just talk to me properly, in English, an' look at me. I'm not saying I'm perfect, but I wish yer'd 'ave some vision. Wot am I doing wrong?'

He stopped his examination of the silly pot of cream, and looked her in the eyes. 'To me you can do no wrong,' he murmured.

His awkwardness and unhappiness were so funny and lovely that this time she didn't knock his words back at him like lightning, as she usually did, her feelings flying straight out of her mouth: she thought about what she wanted to say before trying to put it into words.

'If that's so, maybe that's because yer don't know me,

Daniel. I don't fink yer've known many girls, 'ave yer? Not even one maybe. Now yer going ter tell me yer were close ter yer mother.'

They both turned their full attention to the pot.

'I can help you,' he offered, 'if you want me to.'

'Yer'll put some pots out on yer counter fer me?' she said eagerly. 'I got two different sizes, I thought the bigger's good fer a bob, yer get a heck of a lot—'

'The average income around here is less than eighteen bob a week.'

'Fer those 'oo can't afford the Bob Pot—'

'Nearly everyone.'

'There's this one. The Penny Pot. That's enough fer people ter try out, sort of a sample, like, and it lasts a week if yer don't go wild.'

'It wouldn't keep more than a week anyway.'

'Yer right,' she said thoughtfully, 'maybe small is better.'

'I could stabilise the vegetable matter to make it last a little longer—'

'No Daniel, it wants ter be fresh, we don't want people taking it fer granted, got ter keep 'em finking it's special. Always buying a new one – diff'rent colours an' smells ter make a change, cucumber maybe. But wot about that nasty colour it goes on top?'

'That's just oxidation, Gloria. I can easily do something about that for you. But a penny is an awfully tight price. That means you have to sell it to the shopkeeper for a halfpenny or less.'

'The pots cost almost nothing, a French firm stamps 'em out by the million, an' Jenny fills 'em from a barrel.'

'You're going much too far, much too fast,' Daniel warned her.

'But that's the only way to go!' Gloria tried to make him understand. 'Everyone in the street wants some. Jenny's pals came knocking round the door on Saturday afternoon when they got paid.' He looked at her blankly. 'Ladies is supposed ter 'ave soft 'ands,' she explained.

'Are they?'

'Soft an' ladylike, that's wot I told the girls. Why? 'Cause that's wot they wanted to 'ear. 'Oo do yer fink wants to put a scaly paw in the 'and of the boy they're walking out wiv ter the Surrey Theatre or the Palace on Saturday night? Yer don't care the first thing about us, do yer? Men are supposed ter 'ave work-callused 'ands, yuss, but we're supposed ter be . . . yer know. A bit more int'resting.' She had a strong feeling that he didn't know.

'Sugar and spice and all things nice.'

'See?' she said cheerfully, 'yer a brain-thinker.'

'I won't buy this batch,' he said, 'it's got to be better than this is.'

She got round this setback cunningly. 'Yer the only one 'oo can 'elp me,' she complimented him.

'Oh, the chemistry side of it is easy. But if your commercial strategy is to sell your product for a door-to-door price of a penny – half that to a shop . . . well, you have to use ingredients that cost almost nothing. It's simple economics.'

'Wot yer saying is there's no point in selling fer a penny if it costs a penny ha'penny ter make.'

'Especially if you were buying by the ton and selling by

the million,' he said sadly. 'It's an easy trap to fall into, I suppose. I'm sorry, Gloria. I wanted to help.'

He looked at her silently.

'Right,' she said angrily, the hot colour rising in her cheeks. 'We need ter find something cheaper than lanolin, that's all!'

'I don't know of anything,' he said gently. 'Not that's been scientifically proven.'

'Yer do yer job,' Gloria said with determination, pushing the dropper into his hands, 'an' I'll do mine.'

It wasn't that easy. Gloria leaned glumly against the scullery door, watching Jenny Rouse wash the lettuce for the evening meal in dilute permanganate of potash, the lurid purple drops standing out on the girl's hands and wrists. 'See, lanolin goes into yer skin,' Gloria sighed, 'it keeps on protecting it, that's the fing.'

'Liza got a rash,' Jenny said suddenly. 'I was afraid ter tell yer.'

'Oh Gawd. From the lanolin? Daniel never warned me about that.'

'Nah, don't worry about 'er, Glo, that Liza Chase comes over in bumps at the drop of an 'at, an' 'er mum was delicate too.' Jenny rinsed the savoy cabbage, grunting at the weight of the water-pitcher. 'Ever so posh in 'er ways, Grandma Chase was, by all accounts. In 'er old age she wore a tea-cosy on 'er 'ead. She swore by cocoa butter, when she could get it. Very exotic-like, but she were a peculiar old bird, everyone remembered 'er. That was thirty years ago, 'course.'

'Yuss, but we tried butter an' it don't keep.' Gloria busied herself helping out, adding tarragon vinegar to the salad-oil.

Jenny put the lettuce in the colander and swung it briskly from the doorway, spraying the yard. 'Maybe cocoa butter's diff'rent. Keep yer beady on the eggs while I fetch more water, would yer?'

At the far end of the supper table, the men sat almost in silence picking at their lettuce and hard-boiled eggs. The women sat in a group at their own end now that Jenny was allowed to join them at table, talking amongst themselves. 'Foreign,' muttered Captain Villers loudly enough for them to hear. 'I said, *foreign*, is this?' He was glowering at the greenstuff on his fork. 'Really, Miss Alhambra,' he appealed to the bejewelled matriarch at the head of the table, 'I can't imagine what's got into you recently.' He cast his eye accusingly at Gloria, knowing perfectly well.

'I'm quite sure you buckled down to worse on the north-west frontier or wherever it was,' hissed Mr Poulton tartly.

'Rabbit-food,' murmured Mr Rutt, and everyone knew that first thing after supper he'd be off to the George for a fat mutton cutlet at Mrs Murray's table. 'Hafter an 'ard day's work, yer can't hexpect a man ter live on rabbit-food.'

'You're such stick-in-the-muds!' remarked Lily Alhambra, 'you men never want to try anything different, anything new. Well, this is *my* house, and things have changed. If you don't like it, then you know what you can do.'

'*I* like it,' said Mr Poulton, chewing with satisfaction, and his companions threw him hot looks.

'Miss Alhambra – Lily – be reasonable,' pleaded Captain

Villers, but the women were talking among themselves, and ignored him.

'Maybe we could add cocoa ter butter, see wot 'appens,' Gloria said.

'I'm hoff!' exploded Mr Rutt, throwing down his napkin. 'Hexcuse me, ladies.' He pushed past them and the front door slammed.

'Now look what you've done,' said Captain Villers reproachfully, but Lily ignored him.

'Maybe the cocoa stops the stuff going off so fast,' Gloria said.

'I couldn't help overhearing,' Mr Poulton offered when the meal was over, moving his chair beside Gloria's with a small bow. 'You were talking of cocoa butter?'

'Yer 'eard us.'

'Well, as you know, I am employed by Morgan's chocolate factory.'

Gloria looked at him blankly.

'I'm sure I could obtain a quantity of cocoa butter for you, if you so wished.'

Gloria's spirits leapt. 'Yer mean a chocolate factory uses cocoa butter?'

'Yes, in huge quantities, and I'm sure Mr Morgan would quote you a most competitive price – in the number one building alone, I daresay ten tons is blended at Morgan's every day. Would a fifty-gallon barrel be enough to get you going?'

'I suppose so.' Gloria hid her elation. 'If the sample works, that is.'

'It worked fer Mrs Chase,' Jenny whispered, 'an' she 'ad

delicate skin. If'n it works on that Liza, it'll do the job fer anyone.'

'And I'd need it fully delivered,' Gloria said, 'sixty-day account, naturally.'

'But only our best customers get sixty days.'

Gloria smiled at him, using her most feminine smile, all but fluttering her eyelashes. 'Well, I'll see what I can do—' Mr Poulton visibly melted, like a bar of chocolate on a hot day.

'Thank yer very much, Mr Poulton,' said Gloria, as firmly as a dismissal.

'That's right, my dear,' Lily Alhambra said when they were alone, laying her hand on Gloria's wrist. 'You've got the hang of it, I see.'

'Wot's that, Miss Alhambra?'

'Making use of them.'

'It's pretty good stuff,' Gloria said, hoisting herself on to the counter with a sigh of relief, taking the long day's weight off her aching feet. 'That was the first key to selling it. And the price is right, that was the second key. And people wanted it, they just didn't *know* they wanted it. That was the third key.' She yawned. 'It wasn't one thing, it was lots of things. The right place at the right time.'

'It smells odd . . .' Daniel Fox demurred, sniffing the dab of cocoa butter on his finger, 'very odd.'

'Well, yer odd too, but that's not necessarily saying anyfink against yer. *It* costs 'ardly nuffink.'

'I was surprised to sell any of your silly pots at all,' he confessed, 'especially as you insisted they be flaunted on the counter like that. I thought people would never waste a penny on them.' The shop had closed for the evening, the door a black rectangle holding their reflections, and he had gone so far as to take off his jacket. His grey flannel trousers had a shiny bottom, she now saw, as well as shiny knees. They were held up by perfectly horrid dark red braces. He was so clever in some ways but he couldn't see himself as she did. 'But it's certainly a distinctive scent,' he said, getting her attention, 'and not unattractive.'

'Distinctive.' Gloria seized on the word. 'That's just what we want. It's got ter pong right, it's all part of wot makes yer feel it's doing yer good.' She snapped her fingers. 'The fourth key.'

He looked round, frowning. 'What's all this about keys, Gloria? You're always flying away ahead of me. And of yourself, too, I think,' he added. 'You're a brilliant saleswoman, and you have a silver tongue, but all you are selling is dreams.'

'Wot's wrong wiv that?' she said blankly. 'Don't yer dream, Daniel?' He shrugged. 'Daniel, I've bin looking an' learning, I've bin in more chemists' shops than I've bin inter in me life,' she said – forgetting for a moment that he was a disciple and trying to convert him; she couldn't stop working – 'an' listen, this week I wouldn't sell ter anyone 'oo wouldn't put the stuff out on the counter. *On the counter*,' she emphasised. 'That was the most important thing. I wouldn't let 'em 'ave it unless. An' ter make sure they did I even gave 'em me little Gloria stand fer free, though they cost me a bob.'

She was sitting beside the cheap'n'cheerful Penny Pots

she had insisted he display here, swinging her legs, not realising, no doubt, that she was showing her ankles. Daniel tried to ignore her lack of gravity. He hated her counter display too, the little brightly-painted stand spoiled the clean line and serious demeanour of the shop's counters, which she called dull. Worse, customers tended to collect around the stand, drawn to it, making him come over. But what he really hated was that the price was marked in large black letters, bold as a Wanted poster: ONE PENNY. It was the only marked price in the shop and it lowered the professional tone of the place. On the quiet he'd tried to detach the board from the stand, but instead of screws it had been cunningly tenon-and-morticed in place by the cabinet-maker she employed in the Newington Causeway railway arches. From the amused glance she'd thrown Daniel when she returned this afternoon he suspected she knew exactly what he'd been up to. There were no flies on Gloria, but she had no financial sense.

'You've spent all your money, haven't you?' he reproved her.

'Every penny,' she said cheerfully.

'You didn't need to risk everything. You should have started slowly and built up within your means.'

'Yer dad didn't, did 'e? 'E 'ad style.'

'He had been brought up to do whatever he wanted. The Fox family have always had a streak of arrogance.'

'But yer can't build up a business within yer means, it's impossible. Yer can't get the cash back fast enough. Without that sixty-day settlement of account Poulton slipped through I'd've been sunk afore now. Mr Morgan's financing my business, though 'e doesn't know it.'

'Business, now, is it,' he mocked her. 'Proper accounts and business theories and everything.'

'Yer jealous because I'm making money, even if I do 'ave ter spend it faster'n it comes in, but that's ter grow. We do 'ave businesses, 'aven't yer cottoned on? 'Alf the milliners' an' dressmakers' shops along the Newington Causeway are run by women, an' the dining rooms. Amelia Murray rules the George.'

'But the bank wouldn't lend you any money.'

'He was a frump! He wouldn't lend money to anything wearing a skirt if she was the Queen of England.'

'Neither would the London & Manchester when you asked, or—'

'Bankers are like generals, they're always fighting the last war.' Impatiently Gloria kicked off her shoes and waved her hands over her feet. 'I was doing door-ter-door this morning, all them tiny streets from St Saviour's Union Workhouse ter the prison, they're only much good on a Saturday. I 'ate those tenement blocks, nuffink but up an' down stairs, an' the kids pee off the balconies at yer when their mums aren't looking. This afternoon I walked ter the South London Chronicle office ter put advertisements in fer Monday, some people will 'ave a bit sneaked by, see, an' the old man will be out. Then I was off ter the Railway advertising offices, the South-Eastern as well as the London Dover and Chatham. An' even in the middle of next week it'll be worth burning shoe-leather in the three rich squares – Nelson Square, Trinity and West. Then it all starts again.'

'You're exhausted,' he said from the door, looking through her reflection.

'No I'm not, I'm too excited ter get tired, I just pass out.' Gloria yawned. 'Jenny fell asleep over the barrel last night, even Miss Alhambra does 'er bit, she broke a nail, an' she says I'm going ter 'ave ter buy 'er a new maid. I wish we *would* get a new maid, she could 'elp wiv the filling.' She rested her arm over the stand, dropped her head on her shoulder for a moment. 'It *is* a success . . . it's a success, Daniel . . .'

He looked round, hearing only the hard wintry sound of the rain falling outside. She was asleep. 'Yes,' he murmured, 'but I wonder if the possibility that you might fail has even entered that pretty little head of yours.'

Daniel Fox approached Gloria silently and stood looking at her, the counter putting her almost on his own level: he could have touched her nose with his own, she had lovely smooth eyelids with long curved eyelashes, very black, her slanty eyebrows losing themselves in the brassy cascade of her hair now slipping forward; he tried to hold it back from her face but it flowed down over his hands, warm and scented. She murmured in her sleep. He withdrew his hands and looked at the ledger. She had no idea of double-entry bookkeeping – everything about her was so full of life and yet flawed – but he could do her accounts for her, he had only to look at a column of figures to add it up . . . it would be a small weight off her mind, surely. He peered into her face behind its veil of curls. Her mouth had slipped into a contented smile, and he wondered what she was dreaming.

She could not possibly remain asleep on his counter!

He pulled down the blind over the door, then put his arm around her shoulders and grunted as she rolled into him, her forehead hot against his neck. He made sure her skirt was demure, then lifted her legs and took her weight, all soft curves moving against him, and tottered upstairs with her a step at a time, all he could manage. He stood trembling in the tiny first-floor parlour, not sure he had the strength to put her down, then managed to get the bedroom door open with his shoulder, and laid her on the bed feeling his back would break.

He stood looking down at her. The pub gaslights threw their familiar pattern over the ceiling; this had been his room since he was a boy. She rolled over in her sleep and pushed her face into the crook of her elbow, making her mouth look silly.

He draped the coverlet over her, then watched her sleeping with a mixture of emotions chasing through his mind.

'Yes,' he murmured, 'but I wonder if you can afford to be a success.' He did not dare say her name in case it woke her, but lingered in the doorway, fascinated by her even asleep: she was such a strange, instinctive, provocative creature.

He went out and closed the door softly behind him, then made up the parlour couch for his own bed, to come back to. He needed little sleep and rarely felt tired. Scratching his head, he went downstairs to try and work out the complete mess she had made of her accounts.

Chapter Eighteen

The mums were jostling for position in the pecking order around the water standpipe near the bend in Waterloo Street, a narrow turning sandwiched between the Phoenix Gas Works and the steaming smokestacks of the distillery. They were rubbing their elbows from the cold of the winter's morning, frost sticking to their slippers, the sun not yet peeping above the huge rusty gasometers that towered over the rooftops, pregnant with a summer's worth of coal-gas for the coming winter. The ladies farted and yawned, excuse-me, while they waited for the pots to fill. All were short, and all had discoloured, decaying teeth, except the oldest, who (like the youngest) had no teeth at all. Lifting their feet to rub their bunions on the backs of their legs, they stood one-legged like shaggy African birds, not realising how strange they looked. They knew each other so well, having all lived in this street all their lives, that they thought they had nothing left to pretend about. They complained about everything under the sun; their husbands, their children, other people's children, and – with a disapproving jerk of the thumb, and a shake of the head for what things were coming to – the young girls at

317

the next standpipe. The older women, clucking their disapproval, had forgotten that these willowy, vulnerable girls were themselves, separated only by twenty-five years of time.

The youngsters, still second-class citizens of the age to be sent out while their mums stayed in their nice warm kitchens – which was the point of having children, so that they could help out – had been relegated to the spigot further down the dead leg where the pressure had dropped. 'Bloody fing's 'alf froze,' Gail swore, but not in so loud a voice that the group of oldsters heard. She gave the thing a kick, and it stuttered and spat air.

'Me mum won't 'alf give me one if she finds out about last night,' Mary repeated, obsessed. She glanced fearfully at the women by the other tap: you never knew who might have seen you, and tongues were made for wagging.

'She'll give yer a kick like that, Miss Mary Cox,' Gail goaded her, giving the spigot another whack, 'I shouldn't wonder if she wouldn't, an' chuck yer out quick-sharp – kissing Teddy Farebrother!'

'I never ever did. Well, 'ardly.'

'We 'eard the suck from 'ere,' Emma joined in, seeing the way the wind was blowing against Mary.

'Yer all know me better'n that,' Mary said miserably.

'Yuss,' Gail said vindictively, 'we know yer *much* better'n that.' She'd got her hooks into Mary and now she kicked the spigot again, with a laugh. 'Just like *that*, she will.'

Mary quivered. 'I just wanted 'im ter treat me wiv respect.'

'Emma! Stop yer jawing an' get on wiv it,' roared Mrs Wardle from the upstairs window. 'Slack as a length of string, yer are. I can't put 'is,' she jerked her head back significantly, ''is kettle on til yer pull yerself tergether.' Dad was back from the sea, and there were certain things he expected on his return.

'It's the bloomin' tap!' Emma shrieked despairingly, and Gail gave it a couple of obliging kicks to demonstrate. Miss Ingledew came outside, looking very neat in her housecoat, put down a coconut mat to kneel on, and started scrubbing her doorstep with a piece of hearthstone.

'All I 'ave ter say is,' she threw over her shoulder, 'in my day girls wasn't quite so noisy in a nice quiet street.'

'Don't ferget the Brasso fer yer doorhandle too,' whispered Gail in a voice that could not be heard. Miss Ingledew would put a word in your dad's ear if you were rude.

'I'd bought a packet of five "My Darlings" ter smoke when we went out,' Mary confessed.

''E's never even noticed yer was alive,' Gail snorted, ''e don't care.'

'I bet 'e took yer ever so serious-like, Mary,' Sarah said shyly, only fifteen. She carried a pail in one hand and the other held her little sister, just toddling, who in turn held a rag doll with a mop of ginger hair exactly like her own.

''E was impressed,' Mary said, 'but I 'ad ter sneak some of me Mum's cuttlefish powder ter get the stains off me teeth afterwards.'

'She'll kill yer if she finds out!' Gail said. They quietened as Mrs Nutting sailed up, pushed into the head of the queue, filled her kettle and sailed back again with a slam of her door. Tom Smeed was at it again, repairing some old cart tilted over on wooden blocks, one wheel off; the older women waiting around their tap frowned at his mess mucking up their street.

Albert Bushell came out on to his mum's doorstep, home on leave from the Army, stretched his back and stuck a fag to his lower lip. He strode past the group of girls, but held them in the corner of his eye. 'Morning, me young ladies. Mary. Emma.'

'Morning, Corporal Bushell,' they murmured.

He paused, eyeing them. 'Keepin' busy, are yer?'

'Out of trouble,' Gail said, pushing herself forward. He winked at no one in particular, but Gail giggled when he'd gone round the corner. 'Did yer see 'im pretend not ter look?'

'Talk of looking,' Emma said, pointing, 'look at *her*.'

Gloria summed up the street in a moment: young ones first. She was getting very expert about manipulating people.

Yesterday she had covered the Peabody Buildings, up and down the big tenement blocks across the Blackfriars Road until her feet felt as though they were being squeezed in a vice, and today she had set herself the task of working these terraced estates between the highway and the Railway arches.

'Bloody freezing, innit,' she said, knowing she looked smart, in control, and not at all cold. Three up to her, yet the way she spoke made her one of them.

'Fingers falling off,' confessed the girl with stained teeth.

'Wot yer got in yer bag?' demanded Gail, the one who'd shown a bit of leg. 'Yer don't look like yer need ter sell fings.'

'Me? I'm not selling. Yer couldn't afford wot I got in 'ere,' Gloria said combatively, but let the bag be pulled open before slapping their hands. 'Tell yer somefink, turn that tap off a minute, let the pressure build up an' blow the ice out. In 'ere? Beauty creams, that's all, yer wouldn't be int'rested. Yer too young ter look int'resting. All right, yer can turn the tap on now.'

'Wot yer mean, I can't afford it!' Gail exploded.

'Only a penny each, but it must sound like a lot ter yer,' said Gloria, following the eyes of the two quiet girls who also fancied the bloke with the military walk. 'Change yer lives, though. Boys like ter walk out wiv girls 'oo know 'ow ter make themselves look right, they take it as a compliment. If yer don't take the trouble ter care about yerself, no one else will, that's only common sense. 'Oo's that woman kneeling?' she pointed.

'That's Miss Ingledew,' Emma said. 'Yer won't get nuffink out of that sour old snit. Look, really makes a difference, this stuff, does it?'

'Gives yer that certain fascination, but more'n that, it's good fer yer. I'll come back next week an' if yer not blooming fer some more I'll eat me words.' Gloria knew when to stop – she knew she'd got them. Emma reached into her pocket, hesitating, but by then Gail had taken the plunge and they both held out their pennies together.

'It's only a penny,' Gail said nervously, 'but don't let me mum see.'

321

Gloria smiled, hiding her tiredness.

Last night her eyes had been red and inflamed with exhaustion, and she had bathed them with the solution of boracic that Daniel had insisted she take back to Zoar Street to try – she had never slept at the pharmacy after that one night. Nevertheless, she was beginning to find Daniel indispensable, his enthusiasm now matching her own. He never showed any sign of interest in her for herself, or even awareness of her sex, which was a blessed relief because they had no time for anything but work, and having to tell him no would have been very sad – and he looked so sad anyway! Besides, he was ten years older than her. *All you are selling is dreams*, he'd told her once, and she never forgot it, but for herself she now had no time to dream. She'd been at work in the scullery filling pots last night when these girls were starting their beauty sleep, and this morning she had been up since five, long before it was light or they were awake, to catch the cleaning women returning home across London Bridge, and then the factory girls leaving home for the early shift. Business had been poor, of course, but so near the end of the account month, with a sheaf of bills fluttering on her dresser to be paid, every little helped – and the seeds had been sown, she told herself, to be reaped next month. Already by seven-thirty she had been on her way back to Zoar Street for a bite of breakfast, washing her face in cold water to tighten her skin, taking out the tired lines beneath her eyes with white wax, then changing into smart clothes and the elegant hat – which would have made her a laughing-stock with the already weary early crowd in their overalls – but impressed people so much in the sunlight, on their own doorstep. When she was asked in, *she* was never invited into the back parlour, but always to the front, kept Sunday best, and perhaps even offered a cup of tea. Many housewives felt awful, after all that, if they didn't order more than they really wanted from the woman who had become a friend in their own home.

Gloria had seen at once that the daintily housecoated Miss Ingledew finishing off her doorstep would ask her into the front parlour, if properly handled, and the invitation would be noted at the senior standpipe by the blunt ladies in print dresses and slippers. Slippers was a good sign, meaning they had at least two pairs of footwear, and they probably sold to the ragman rather than the other way around, and had a few pence left over after the house-keeping and the funeral club. They'd need a different approach to catch their interest; but whatever Miss Ingledew bought, they would – eventually.

'Miss Ingledew?' Gloria introduced herself politely but firmly. 'My name is Miss Simmonds, and I have been given your name as the person I should speak to in this street.'

Miss Ingledew glanced at the housewives, relishing their attention. She put her fingers to her cheek and smiled.

'Of course,' she said, drawing Gloria into her spotless hallway. 'Come on in, do. I do apologise, the place is such a mess. Perhaps we should go into the front parlour?'

Even on Saturday nights, Gloria found she could not relax, because she'd got to the point of exhaustion where she felt guilty even about sitting down for a minute, but Daniel insisted. 'I bin experimenting wiv new ways of selling ter see wot works best,' she told him, putting her feet up on the furniture in his little wedge-shaped room and closing her eyes, leaning back in his armchair. He drew the curtains, shutting out the February night, the rooflines of the Borough ragged with blue snow under the moon.

'Just sit still for a minute,' he told her.

'Aye-aye, cap'n.' She knew him well enough to kick off her shoes, then she let her hands dangle almost to the bare boards to show him how tired she was; but he'd gone to the sideboard and his back was to her. 'I wish yer'd get some carpet in 'ere!' she complained, picking a splinter out of her heel.

'Can't afford it,' came his voice.

'I'll make it a present. An' a quid's worth of coal,' she shivered, 'yer must 'ave ice fer blood.'

'I don't want your money, Gloria. You haven't got any, anyway,' he added, and she gave an exhausted smile. How right he was.

'I've been experimenting too,' he said, clinking a glass rod in a pharmaceutical beaker, then poured the mixture into two glasses. 'This is just a start, it's a tonic to buck you up. Fox's Patent Cocktail.' He turned. 'I don't know how you can keep smiling. You look awful, Gloria,' he chided her.

'Only yer could say that, Daniel, an' mean it.'

He glanced at her blankly, then put the glass into her hand. 'You're a fool to yourself.'

'I don't 'ide it from yer.' She squinted at him through the liquid. 'Is this good fer me?'

'Tonic syrup and neat surgical alcohol.'

She tossed it down. 'Yer right,' she gasped, 'it is.' She held out her glass at arm's length, and he refilled it reluctantly.

'I was going to make the toast "to us",' he said without looking at her.

'I don't know about that, Daniel.'

'I meant as a team. We make a good team, Gloria.'

'To us.'

'I'm good at what I do, too,' he said.

'Yer worked out my account books fine. Yer got a business brain.' Gloria saluted him with her glass, then brandished it between her fingertips, and Daniel emptied the last of the beaker into it, obediently. 'Yer never thought of the cocoa butter, though,' she said. For a moment her exhaustion filled her, overwhelming her, so intense that her limbs felt as though they were made of lead. Only her tongue moved, and her ceaseless, sleepless mind – she couldn't stop herself. 'Yer never tramp the streets from dawn ter dusk an' yer fingers an' toes getting so cold yer could cry. No one ever turns *you* down, Daniel. No one ever ignores yer. Yer never go out an' 'ave ter cold sell. Yer just stick in 'ere in yer little shop wiv yer books an' bottles, an' wait fer 'em ter come in yer door.'

'You've done an amazing job. Shush now. Relax.'

'Don't patronise me!'

'I shouldn't have let you have that third glass,' he said.

She grinned at him, daring him to take it back, then polished it off before he could.

'I know what you're doing, deliberately needling me,'

Daniel told her mildly. 'It's your wicked streak talking and I'm not going to respond to it.'

'Don't yer ever get miffed about anyfink, Daniel? Are yer always cold an' calm?'

But he refused to stand up to her in the way she demanded. 'You're tired,' he said. He put down his unfinished glass on the sideboard. It was time for her to go. 'I'll show you in the morning.'

'Show me wot? Yer not going ter ask me wot *I've* bin doing, are yer! No, yer bloody aren't!'

'I know what you've been doing. You've been selling those Penny Pots, as always,' he said calmly.

'Yer so blooming perfect. Go on, then, show me! Never mind *me*.'

'Back in a minute.' He disappeared downstairs to the shop, and she slipped over to the sideboard and finished off his glass. Like the cat that got the bird, she was sitting back as though she had never moved by the time he returned. He showed her some white goo in a beaker. 'You see, I've been working too,' he said enthusiastically, 'it took me all day to get right.' She realised she'd struck home with her remark about him sitting around the shop all day, which she had never meant seriously. She had only been trying to strike a spark from him, to get a bit of verve into him and make him react. Instead poor, serious Daniel took it as a challenge to his masculine pride, taking everything at face value. Not for the first time, she wondered what he would be like angry, what he would be like red-faced and shouting and really screaming, furious and caring about something. Passionate.

'In yer quiet way,' she said, 'yer a fanatic, too.'

'I tried thirty-two other formulae before settling on this one.'

She rubbed the cream between her fingertips. It felt lovely, and the scent was creamy and lingering. 'Yer and yer 'undreds of bottles, yer really enjoy mixing an' trying fings out, don't yer? Wot've yer magicked inter it?'

'It was simple in the end,' he said proudly. 'Eight parts finest spermaceti oil, eight parts white wax, then *thirty parts* of sweet almond oil.'

'An' lemon?'

'Lemon oil.'

'Somefink else?' she sniffed.

'Aloe vera. The merest pinch.'

'It niffs pretty pricey. I don't want nuffink too fancy.'

'But it's good.'

'But I couldn't sell it.'.

'You'll have to expand your range,' he said.

'Don't tell me wot I got ter do,' she said. 'I know wot I do best, and yer do wot yer do best.'

There was a silence. 'What have you been up to today all by yourself, then, Gloria?'

What a strange man he was, she thought – he almost sounded jealous, except she couldn't imagine anything he had to be jealous about. 'Thought you'd never ask,' she said. 'See, I can't do everything myself—'

'Victory.' He toasted her again, then saw his glass was empty. He sat against the arm of the other chair, examining his knees. 'At last you've realised you need someone.'

'So I've been appointing agents.'

'What! You're paying wages, not only committing yourself but others to the success of your venture – suppose you fail?'

There was nothing she could say. Gloria had never even thought of failing.

'I thought you just wanted to help people,' he said calmly, 'that's how you started, wasn't it?'

'Yer know that, Daniel.'

'What are you up to? You're just running to waste, like a tap that's been left on, because you don't know what else to do, you've no business experience. Letting it get out of control, Gloria. It's taking you over.'

'Oh, Daniel, of course it's not!'

'When did you last have a day off? When did you last have even a Sunday morning off to go to church?'

'I dunno wot's the matter wiv yer,' she said. It was the first inkling she'd had that he was religious and offended by her absence; he kept himself so tucked into himself. 'Anyway, they're on commission, not wages.'

'Commission.' He wore his penny-pinching look. 'Commission of how much?'

'Well, I thought twenty-five per cent of retail price was right,' she told him, but his mouth turned down as though she'd done wrong, and Gloria wondered if she ought to have squeezed the girls harder.

'They'll take advantage of you!' he said.

'Twenty-five was 'alf-way between doing it meself an' getting a shop ter do it, an' I thought it was fair,' she justified herself, but he didn't look satisfied. Because she wanted his approval she added, 'But they have ter buy their own paper bags, of course, an' samples, even pay fer their order book.' His expression didn't change. 'Each girl's given her own street ter see right,' Gloria explained, 'then a few more in their area – four or five 'undred 'ouses. The best are Peg Loman, she's smartly turned out an' works the district from St George's Circus ter the Cut, an' Miss Ingledew 'oo covers east of Blackfriars Road ter the Railway. Me girls soon get ter know wot people are int'rested an' ter go back ter; some even get upset if they're forgot.' Her smile twitched, but he didn't respond. 'I call 'em the Gloria girls,' she bragged.

'I see you've got it all worked out.'

'It worked itself out, Daniel. It was the right fing ter do, that's all.'

'You just blow with the wind and swim with the tide,' he said. 'What drives you? Where are you going?'

'Who cares? I *enjoy* selling, Daniel. It's fun. It's exciting. I know my customers, and if I like somefink, probably lots will.'

'Stop,' he said. 'Just stop a minute, will you, Gloria?' He leaned forward and touched her hands. 'You need me. We mustn't hurt one another any more.'

She didn't understand. 'Yer 'aven't 'urt me, Daniel.'

'But you have hurt me. You do, Gloria. I hardly see you.'

'That won't do yer no 'arm!' She laughed at him for being so serious, but he just looked at her straight in the eyes, holding her hands, until she stopped still.

'You see,' he said with terrible awkwardness, 'I've fallen in love with you.'

'I know, Daniel.'

'From the first moment I saw you, Gloria, outside the Tabard. I don't mean love at first sight, necessarily,' he had to add precisely, being Daniel Fox, so that she had to struggle to contain her amusement, 'but I couldn't forget you. Even when you're unkind to me I still don't want you to go. Sometimes when you're unkindest I want you most. That's all I have to say.'

'Are yer asking me ter walk out wiv yer? I'm flattered, Daniel, but—'

'I'm asking you to take me seriously,' he interrupted. 'As seriously as I take you.'

She gripped his hands tight. She didn't want to say *I love you*, because she didn't love him; yet she did want to be honest, because he was honest. And she wanted to be sincere, because he was being sincere with her.

' "To us",' she repeated, and he smiled openly, showing his teeth, thinking he understood her.

Crouching, he kissed her hand shyly, and she did not have the heart to snatch it away.

Chapter Nineteen

Jenny walked with stars in her eyes. Freed at last of domestic service, she was wearing a smart ladylike dress – green with a dark green stripe, secondhand and strictly speaking last summer's fashion, but you'd never know to look at it, obviously hardly been worn – that made her aware of her body with every step she took. She hung her umbrella properly from her wrist like you were supposed to. Blokes said good afternoon to her now, knocking their caps politely with their forefingers, and the ladies of Paragon Crescent and Newington Causeway no longer looked down their noses at her. Jenny liked that because she knew they were responding to what they saw – no longer Jenny the maid, Jenny Wot's-this-mess, Jenny Clearitup, do this, do that. Her hands were smooth and her eyes were clear, and she radiated confidence.

She looked behind her, thinking she heard footsteps, but there was no one there, only an old bent-over tramp in a tattered straw hat, filching something from the slime in the gutter; it had been a wet summer.

'C'mon fer Gawd's sake, Jenny, stop yer woolgathering,' Gloria called, setting off in a new direction across the High

Street, tossing a penny to the crossing-sweeper to keep their skirts clean of the mounds of muck, and Jenny had to hurry after her. Gloria walked like the wind, St George the Martyr was striking four, there was never enough time – Gloria walked as though time was no longer manufactured. Jenny hated being made to run to catch up. She ran.

'We've done enough fer today, miss, 'aven't we?' she puffed. 'I mean, I 'aven't 'ad a moment's sit-down.' She'd discovered that Gloria even ate lunch standing up, a sort of meal-in-one from a working-man's stall in the Cut, meat in one end of the pasty and marmalade in the other, brushing away the flakes of pastry – with a little brush she carried, everything planned! – and all the while that Jenny's jaws struggled with the lumps of indigestible gristle, Gloria's bright blue gaze was searching the faces around them as if for customers, potential saleswomen, already plotting the next item on the itinerary; then she was off with Jenny running after her again. 'This is the only way ter learn the ropes,' Gloria said, twisting her way along the turnings that shimmered featurelessly in the heat, talking to everyone she saw as if she knew them. 'Follow me round, see 'ow I does it. 'Allo, Sophia, luv, remember me ter yer mum. Listen, Jenny, it took me long enough ter develop a style, Gawd knows, but it'll be easier fer yer. Second time round the 'ard work's bin done fer yer.' Jenny helped to deliver a district order by hand to Peggy Loman, now living in Kennington since her husband got a room over his work: so Kennington had been added to Gloria's map on her bedroom wall, Mrs Loman's red District Representative pin in a gathering circle of smaller green pins, the Area

Representatives as she appointed them, a task Gloria had been forced to delegate, though she had written down a long list of rules. Gloria Girls were always smartly dressed. They never trod dirt into a house. They must be friendly but never fawning, sociable but not demanding. The list was long, and getting longer.

'No time fer sitting down when there's work ter do,' Gloria said.

'Yer could afford a drayman an' cart, surely, miss.' But Gloria didn't answer, and Jenny followed her thoughtfully. For nearly a year at the Zoar she – *they* – had helped Gloria, who had landed amongst them like a glowing meteorite, it seemed, from nowhere, turning everything they knew topsy-turvy to make this extraordinary and growing success. A girl who never talked of her past, but with those hard, hurt eyes. By sheer force of will Gloria had made her dream come true, but it was changing their lives. Mr Rutt had handed in his month's notice and left, but the rest of them had become as enthusiastic as she about her enterprise, taking over his vacated room as a storeroom, and they felt themselves to be contributors to her achievement – even Mr Poulton had decided that Mr Morgan was no longer a god. Chivvied and bullied by Gloria's exuberance, they had willingly clung to her coat-tails, Jenny filling pots in every moment of her spare time and happy to do it, even Miss Alhambra rallying round to stick on labels, as swept along by the excitement of expanding the business as Gloria herself was. It was their achievement too.

But Gloria lived to work, she had no time for anything else. These days her smile was only for customers. Jenny had worked hard for almost no money in the early days, Gloria owed her; but even so when Gloria agreed to put Jenny in as the salaried District Representative for the streets of Bermondsey, where Jenny had been brought up by the Chase family and still had her friends, Jenny had thought she saw not so much friendship as cool calculation in Gloria's eye. Local people liked to work for and buy from local people, and Gloria had decided Jenny's face fitted, that was all.

And now, running after that determined figure striding along the Borough High Street, Jenny wondered what drove Gloria. Was it really just a wish to help people? Did she *really* believe in the product she was selling? Jenny began to wonder if Gloria was interested in money at all. Gloria, she decided, was after something else.

'Miss Simmonds?' Jenny called.

Gloria turned impatiently, and Jenny saw that cold businesslike gleam set in her eye.

'I wondered—'

'Yuss, Jenny? Yer can talk ter me.'

'Nuffink,' Jenny said, intimidated. She decided it was more rewarding to think of herself in her smart green dress instead, and the people looking at her. Gloria was walking out with Mr Fox who had his own shop, perhaps she would even marry him and settle down. If so, that would give Gloria everything a girl could desire: a husband, status, a family. As they passed the Tabard he came out of the pharmacy in his shirtsleeves. Jenny giggled as he sent them a friendly wave across the street, the sun glinting on his plated Spandex armbands and the buckles of his braces, somewhat stylish presents from Gloria; she had prevailed on him to get a new pair of trousers from Read's too. Everyone said Daniel was a bit of a cold fish, but Gloria had warmed him up. He still looked a little uneasy in them, Jenny thought; as though the gifts wore the man, not the other way round.

Gloria's footsteps tapped along the arcade leading into London Bridge Station, and Jenny hurried to keep up. 'Let's see 'ow we do 'ere,' Gloria said, stopping at the chemist's. ''Ang back an' pretend yer a customer just looking: most shopkeepers point-blank won't talk ter two representatives, let alone' – she used the sneering phrase they heard so often – 'two bits of crumb.'

'If yer don't think yer'll make the sale, why bother trying?'

'Because if I don't make the sale today, yer'll come back next week an' try again. An' then keep trying 'til they give in an' we make 'em some money. Then they'll believe in yer when we bring in a new line, 'cause it showed we bits of crumb was right.' She sighed, looking sadly at Jenny's soft skin, her large, untried, uncertain eyes – yet Jenny thought she looked so confident. 'Listen, Jen,' Gloria said gently, 'yer got a lot ter learn. Selling ain't easy, especially not fer a girl, 'cause women are admired more than men, and yet despised more too. A woman's never taken at face value, she's always a woman. Sometimes people are terribly rude. So use yer femininity to yer own advantage. Water off a duck's back. Yer can't never let them get ter yer, that's all. Never let 'em make yer cry.'

'I admire yer,' Jenny said. 'I do.'

'Yer a sweet.'

'Nuffink ever gets yer down, does it, Gloria? Nuffink's got yer down in the whole of today.'

'Selling cold cream's never going ter be an 'uge industry,' Gloria shrugged, ''cause women 'aven't got enough money ter spend on themselves. If there's anyfink left over they're always finking about another pair of shoes fer their kids or getting the old man a bit extra fer 'is tea. It's just an 'obby fer me, Jen.'

But the business was her life. Jenny said nothing. It was the first time she had caught Gloria out in a lie.

'Let's go in.' The chemist's shop was much less stuffy than Daniel's pharmacy, and obviously designed for passing Railway trade. 'It'll open up a wider market fer us,' Gloria whispered, 'commuters coming an' going from the new towns like Orpington and Bexley wot we don't cover yet, women up from the country shopping, holiday specials.' She went and chatted to the lad behind the counter, making a friend of him, then took out her card, fancily and expensively printed by Troughton's on Bristol-board, and asked if it was convenient to see the manager. The man who ducked out from the back office had rough sallow skin and short grey hair, and his polite manner evaporated when he realised Gloria was not buying but selling. He looked her up and down with a kind of rage when she told him how successful the Penny Pots were. 'Yer display 'em on the counter,' she told him, 'we even give yer a stand, yer'll find they sell 'emselves.'

'Cosmetics, is this?' he demanded, then would not let her answer. 'Like tarts put on?'

336

Gloria's mouth tightened. 'We call these women's toiletries.'

'Put that stuff on my counter, out in the open? Where male customers can see 'em? And just what d'you think they'd think of me? I'll tell you. You've got a nerve, miss,' he said, taking Gloria by the elbow. 'I'll show yer where I sell that sort of thing.'

He led her round the back where a woman was scraping some pots, opened a door, and showed Gloria the toilet.

'I see,' Gloria said.

'I should make you clean it, you bint.' He called over his shoulder, 'Aren't I right, wife?'

The woman, scrubbing harder, didn't hear.

Gloria asked the sallow-faced man politely, 'Wot's yer name?'

'I'm Mr Dagworth, I am.'

'Thank yer, Mr Dagworth,' Gloria said, and when he stood aside, walked past him.

''E's always like that before the evening rush,' whispered the lad, letting them out of the shop. 'Try 'im after 'is elevenses.'

'I'm not going back in there,' said Jenny in a trembling voice.

'That's the sort of manager we're up against,' Gloria told her with a smile, hiding her bitterness as they walked between the tanneries into Bermondsey, and Jenny, in her smart green dress on tick, and carrying her pawnshop umbrella, began to wonder if by coming out from under Miss Alhambra's wing she had exchanged one kind of servitude for another, with Gloria Simmonds as an even more ruthless employer: those looks that saw right through you, and that utterly determined smile. 'They've done things the same way all their lives, Jenny,' Gloria said suddenly, as in the cool fragrant shadow of the leather market they came to the old stable Jenny would use as a storehouse. 'They 'ate change. Well, I'm going ter enjoy changing that one. I'll tell yer wot we'll do.'

Gloria was back at Zoar Street early in the evening, for her – she was in time for supper, and Claire Michaud, the new maid, fetched Gloria's plate which by habit she had already learned to leave to keep warm in the oven. She was a French girl from Bethnal Green, small, pretty and pert, with a turned-up nose and a very pale complexion that made her eyes seem unreadably dark. Her mother was a singing teacher who had fallen for a pupil with a beautiful voice. 'Baritone,' Claire jerked her shoulders indifferently, while her fingers remained busy with the cutlery; her body moved in French but her voice was Cockney. ''E got 'er so she din't know wot way was up, an' I said so, an' she said, Girl, yer got yer father's terrible 'abit wot 'e 'ad of speaking 'is mind. So fer me it was move aht or get thrown aht—'

'An' yer jumped before yer was pushed,' Gloria said, eating hungrily.

Claire cast her a grateful glance. She was another misfit who had wandered the streets of London before ending up, like a fragment of tattered driftwood, at the Zoar, and of course Lily Alhambra had taken her in. No more questions had been asked, and Claire had turned out an efficient little thing, no tears, yet that pale, hiding sort of face, if you knew how to look – and Gloria looked at her thoughtfully.

'It is my hope, Gloria,' Lily said, putting her elbows on the table and flashing the paste jewellery that coated her wrists, 'that you will not appropriate *this* maid.'

'Cross me 'eart!' Gloria laughed. 'Yer know me better'n that.'

'That's what I mean,' Lily said suspiciously, then remembered her table manners and put her elbows to her side.

'What's this foreign matter in my cabbage?' demanded Captain Villers, picking at the crunchy boiled vegetables on his plate. 'Black bits. And it's undercooked.'

'It's cooked proper,' Claire assured him briskly, jabbing some with his fork and eating it herself, 'an' caraway seed's lovely in it.'

'I don't think I can stand much more of this,' Villers said quietly. 'I've had enough of this, Lily.' They knew he was really serious this time, because he had used her Christian name.

'Now, don't be like that, Captain,' fussed Lily, 'you've been here longer than anyone.'

'Lily, I think you should bear that in mind.' He got up with dignity and went into the front room, putting himself not in his favourite armchair but on the hard upright one by the reading-table, and they heard him flap open his newspaper.

'He's quite right of course,' Lily murmured worriedly. 'We have been treating him rather badly.'

''E'll come round,' Gloria said. 'I wonder if there's somefink yer could do fer me.'

'I suppose so, but—'

'Yer know Dagworth's, near the station? Go in tomorrow an' ask fer a Penny Pot, an' look disapproving when 'e
can't sell yer one. Don't overdo it, yer know wot I mean,
but yer such a beautiful actress.'

'I'll see what I can do,' Lily preened, always incapable of
saying no to a compliment.

'Jenny's going, an' I'll get Miss Ingledew on it, an' she'll
get 'er girls going. The more the merrier. Claire, yer might
pop in sometime, too.'

'Don't mind 'tall, Miss Simmonds.'

'I think we should consider Captain Villers's feelings in
all this,' Lily sighed. 'He is right you know, Gloria, you
have turned my house virtually into an industrial premises.
You have become very unfeeling of his point of view.'

Gloria shrugged her hands obligingly. 'All right, if 'e
means that much ter yer.'

'Claire, you are a domestic servant and you are not to let
her bamboozle you into filling any more pots.'

'But I don't mind 'tall, Miss Alhambra – it's a nice bit of
extra.'

'Oh, get on with you, girl, and see to those dishes,' Lily
Alhambra said crossly. She put her hand on Gloria's arm.
'My dear, I really need that room you've been using for
stock – I heard of a poor girl today—'

'It's a bit of a blow.' Gloria thought of the store she was
now renting in Bermondsey, then hugged the older woman
impulsively. 'I bin taking yer fer granted, 'aven't I?'

'You can't help it,' Lily Alhambra grumbled fondly.
'That's how you were born.'

Gloria wondered how much longer she could stay at the Zoar.

Though beset by all these problems and demands on her attention, she left Dagworth to stew for a couple of weeks, all the while making sure that each day he received a visit, or two, or three, from different girls innocently asking for a Penny Pot, until Claire returned to Gloria, chuckling, with the news that he now ducked into the back room as soon as the request was made, leaving it to the lad to make his excuses – the sort that shopkeepers always make. Sorry, ma'am, never heard of it. No call for that sort of thing, ma'am. Not very much demand for it round here. Been unable to obtain supplies. Sorry ma'am, we just sold out.

Gloria walked into Bermondsey. 'Wash yer 'ands. Time we paid our friend a visit,' she told Jenny, who was stacking boxes of stock ready to be sent out at the end of the week's sales campaign. 'I'll stay outside fer starters. We don't want ter 'umiliate 'im all at once, do we?' she added grimly.

Jenny had gained real confidence by now. 'I could sell twice as much as I am,' she chattered as they walked. 'More, if yer made the pots brighter, an' we 'ad nice colours. Yer know, cool green fer cucumber, warm yellow fer almond, all that sort of thing. People like a change, it gives 'em a different feeling.'

Jenny had started thinking for herself, Gloria realised with pleasure. *I'll get Daniel on that idea*, she thought.

'It's an overnight success, Miss Simmonds,' Jenny chattered.

How young and naïve she sounded in her easy faith that everything was now marvellous, that life would keep on getting better and better! Yet hearing Jenny talk like this, so bright and full of hope in her certainty that all was for the best, was for Gloria like listening to her younger self, of only a year ago perhaps . . . but already it felt to Gloria, though the year had passed in a flash, as if a much, much longer time had passed. She tried to remember what she was really like then, but it was gone; the memory of her days had merged into a featureless blur, and only the nostalgia for her youth when everything was possible and she had achieved nothing remained.

'Overnight success?' Gloria shook her head. 'It only seems that way, 'cause yer growing up so quick now, Jenny. An' I'll tell yer somefink worse. Time passes quicker as yer get older, did yer know that?'

But Jenny was too excited to believe her.

'Yer not much older than me,' she said shyly, as they crossed Weston Street. 'I love yer, an' I'm going ter make meself just like yer.'

They came to the station where Claire was waiting with a counter-stand, the photographer, and a mean-looking little man with a ratty mouth, who wore an overcoat despite the glaring sun: it was a few minutes before eleven o'clock. Gloria turned to Jenny. 'Good luck, girl, see yer in a minute or two. 'Old up yer thumb ter tip us the wink.'

Jenny went into the shop and the door closed. Gloria crossed her arms, irritated by the photographer who was picking his teeth. While they waited she watched the jumble of traffic in the Railway approach, growlers and hansoms jockeying for position, commuters weaving impatiently between them, urchins shining shoes in rows along the kerbstones, old men jealously guarding their pitches, shouting, 'Piper! Speshul! Four-turty, latest wire!' To Gloria's itching eyes, made tired by smoke and traffic-dust, they seemed to wave their racing extras like white fans amongst the black top hats, the vivid sea of brilliantly coloured hoardings above their bobbing heads advertising Bovril and half a dozen different makes of cocoa, Nestlé's milk and Quaker Oats... In the shadows beneath the hoardings she discerned bundles of rags huddled against the bricks, each bundle holding out a grimy hand, or with a battered hat between its feet. One of the bundles moved and through the white hair a face turned up at Gloria.

Jenny came out the shop and held up her thumb in victory.

A young policeman, his belt-buckle shining, strode towards the beggars. As one they scrambled to their feet, clothes flapping, scrabbling up their spilt coins, and evaporated in the crowd.

'Wot's the matter wiv yer?' Jenny said.

'She's 'ooked the fish, Miss Simmonds,' said Claire, then suddenly, 'Are yer all right? Yer awful pale!' She slipped her arm around Gloria's waist, realising how thin she was – much thinner than she looked, wearing those nice clothes. Why, there was hardly nothing to her! Claire could have counted her hard ribs.

'I'm all right. Leave me alone,' Gloria said, and Claire watched her pull herself together, hands over her face for a moment, then standing straight. 'Thank yer, Claire, I dunno wot came over me. Come on!' she called to the photographer, and Claire ran after her with the gaily-coloured counter-stand. The ratty-mouthed stringer for the *South London Chronicle* opened the door for her and Gloria swept into the shop just as Dagworth, in his waistcoat, came out of the back room wiping biscuit crumbs from his lips. He goggled at the crowd invading his shop, seeming defensive without his jacket to bolster him. Gloria took his hand in hers and shook it, holding the counter-stand in front of them with her other hand.

'What's going on?' Dagworth stuttered as she pulled him in front of the camera.

'Free advertising,' Gloria told him, then squeezed his hand tight. 'Smile!'

There was a flash of photographic powder and everyone coughed, then broke up in laughter at themselves. But Jenny was watching Gloria's face: Gloria's smile showing all her teeth, Gloria's cheeks stark white and her eyes far away and dulled, as though something terrible had happened and she was looking backwards into herself.

Jenny shivered. It was a haunted face.

Chapter Twenty

In the Borough, every November was the same: as the weather turned bitter, the smoke pouring from the forest of factory chimneys lost its velocity, congealing into an overhanging mass of filth above the rooftops. Midday barely glowed through the lid of industrial fumes – the tall chimneys standing into it as though they were legs built to hold it up – then night fell in the cold mid-afternoon as the smoke came sliding down the chimneys, thick as treacle, first making them shorter, then blanketing everything entirely. Fog had come to London. Fog catching at eyes and throats, fog filling lungs and streets. Fog seeping like an exhaled breath through drains and manhole-covers from the marshes below the warren of houses, and the smoke from their chimney-pots flowed downwards into the narrow turnings instead of rising upwards. The gigantic fog-flares and braziers mounted on London Bridge and at traffic-junctions seemed only to add to the confusion. Sight receded and deceived, and the Borough began to dissolve into strange shapes, becoming almost an alien location, its streets unfamiliar even to those who thought they knew London best.

The church bells that came clanking and tolling into Gloria's sleep, calling people to worship, seemed to echo from every direction, even from the river.

It was Sunday! Gloria woke with a jerk – Daniel, as always on a Sunday morning, would accompany her to church, the only time off they had together, and in her opinion he did it as much for the excuse of walking with her, slipping her arm through his, as for prayer. But he was nothing if not punctual, and she realised how late she was by the clatter of breakfast dishes and cutlery being rushed back to the scullery by Carys, the breathless Welsh girl who had quit her black industrial valleys for the streets of London paved with gold. There were no golden streets in London, but there were some golden hearts to be found, a few, and one was Lily Alhambra's. Lily had taken Carys in as a new maid when Claire moved out – she now lodged, for the moment at least, with Jenny above the stables in Bermondsey.

'I suppose, Gloria,' had been Lily's comment, 'that it is only a matter of time before you appropriate poor little Carys too.'

'Would I do such a fing!'

'These days I'm not so much your landlady as your employment agent, for girls with broken hearts and bruised hopes.'

'They work best,' Gloria had told her sadly. 'Shadows lie around every corner, an' those girls know it. When they knock on a door they'll understand the 'opes an' desires they find in the front parlour. There's more ter being a

346

Gloria Girl than selling cucumber-scented face cream, Lily.'

'That's why I let you stay, even though you could afford better now. So that I can keep an eye on you,' Lily Alhambra had confessed affectionately. 'I do wish you'd look after yourself better, Gloria.'

Now Gloria slipped her Sunday best dress over her head, a respectable dark indigo from the Newington Causeway, and pinned on a hat in matching velvet. Draping a black woollen cape around her to keep out the fog, she went downstairs. 'Your young man's just coming down the street,' Captain Villers called to her from the window, ready in his military overcoat and muffler to take Miss Alhambra to St Saviour's. ''E's not *my* young man,' Gloria said testily, but skipped to the front door and opened it just as Daniel raised his hand to knock. 'Surprised yer!' she said, 'I'm ready.'

But Daniel, a figure standing fog-wrapped on the doorstep, a slightly too-small bowler perched on top of his head, was never surprised by anything Gloria said or did. He looked rather lost in the beautiful Burberry she had insisted on buying him as a present. He had complained about the cost (typical Daniel!), but she had never paid him for all the work he did for her in the pharmacy, or for keeping her accounts in order, and being Daniel he never asked. In this he was just like his father, she guessed, no businessman; or maybe he had another plan. Gloria struggled not to laugh. He raised his hat politely, which she knew was a genuine indication of his pleasure in

347

seeing her, though he was much too self-controlled to say so. He looked glumly over his shoulder, as though apologising for the fog that filled the street like grey jelly.

'We'd better not go too far,' he said as they pushed into the stinking murk. 'I thought St George's?' That was in the next parish, but Daniel sometimes walked miles for a different face giving the sermon, and once as far as the Southwark Park Road, then across to listen at the bandstand in the park afterwards, sitting beside Gloria on the abysmally uncomfortable folding chairs. She had stood up with relief, but he looked disappointed. She'd hardly noticed he had been holding her hand.

He put her arm into the crook of his elbow, guiding her through the fog, warning her when a kerbstone approached as though she didn't have eyes of her own, until her laugh burst out of her. 'You're a funny one,' he said arrogantly. 'I don't think there's anyone else like you.'

'That's 'cause yer 'aven't looked at any other women.'

'I hate the way everything looks different in fog,' he said. He had developed a cough and she pulled his lapels up under his chin to keep him warm.

Along the Borough High Street no traffic moved. Gradually they became aware of figures trudging alongside them towards the church, overcoats smelling of mothballs or the ragman's cart, puffing their white breath through moisture-beaded mufflers or clenched hands held over their mouths, stumbling their way through fog thick enough to touch. The gaslit church clock appeared like a glowing face above them. Coughing and complaining, they all went up the steps between the pillars. Inside, the church stank of fog and old, cold wood, the pews creaking as people shuffled for a place. Someone sneezed and a voice demanded, 'Have you got a cold?' Gloria looked through the hymn book, bored, then up at the painted ceiling. 'The Glory of God breaking through the clouds,' Daniel whispered. 'That's not clouds, that's fog,' she told him, and the large woman in the pew in front looked round. She was wearing a brown coat and green hat. Ahead of her a figure sat slumped as if she had been there for hours, weary beyond endurance, black clothes and battered straw hat streaked down one side with stone-dust as if she had slept on the vestry floor, as very poor people sometimes did. 'What are you looking at?' demanded the lady in the brown coat, then tutted at such rudeness and turned her broad back. Gloria peered around her.

'What's the matter with you?' hissed Daniel. The organ got down to business and everyone started singing. Daniel pressed the hymn-book into her hand. The man beside her sang too loudly, showing off, holding his personal hymn-book at arm's length. Gloria mouthed the words standing on tiptoe, trying to see over the awful green hat. The figure in the front pew was standing, peering into the hymn-book, flicking the pages with grimy fingers sticking like claws out of the half-gloves. Daniel budged Gloria's elbow and frowned at her. She was pushing against the singing man in her efforts to see.

Sensing that someone was watching, the figure in the front pew turned round, and her eyes met Gloria's.

It was the same face, the same exhausted eyes, but all the hardship and misery Gloria saw in them, the beggar's stock-in-trade, had become real in the years that had passed – her face was even older than Gloria remembered, only one savage tooth remaining now, a yellowed splinter hanging from the old woman's upper jaw.

'Gawd, save us,' Gloria whispered. 'Tib. It's Tib.' The figure that she had denied to Jenny that she had seen at London Bridge Station and a dozen times before; had denied even to herself.

Neither of them moved, and Gloria stared, dazed.

She remembered Tragedy Tib's voice cackling cheerfully: '*Everyfink's worth somefink!*'

Gloria tried to get past the person next to her, but he was singing more pretentiously than ever, moving his lips as extravagantly as a man trying to dislodge a sweet stuck to the back of his tongue.

Tib threw down her hymn-book, snatched up her rotten bag and did a bunk, hobbling, along the aisle: for a moment she was close enough for Gloria to think she smelt her. The man in a hymn-induced trance eyed Gloria but could not stop singing. She gave him a shove, the seat caught him behind the knees and he sat down with a bang. Everyone looked round. Gloria struggled along the row, knocking against everyone, and somebody said, 'Wot's got inter 'er?' The woman at the end of the row wisely sat down before Gloria reached her, casting up a polite, terrified smile as Gloria pushed past her.

Behind her everyone was struggling up, embarrassed about sitting while the singing was going on, casting apologetic glances at the vicar. The organist stopped and now everyone turned as Tib's boots, no longer muffled by the matting on the aisle, rattled on the flagstones and she tugged at the main doors. Gloria had half fallen from the pew; some upright burgher was actually trying to hold her back, and she would have hurt her hands but for the matting. She heard Daniel saying something angrily, the church was silent now, then there was the sound of a push and another bang from the seat. 'She's sick,' Daniel said, clever Daniel. Gloria ran to the open doors. Fog poured in.

Daniel skidded behind her.

'Thanks, Daniel,' she said, trying to see into the fog.

'I'm not going back in there,' he told her, looking alarmed. 'What on earth's got into—'

'Shush.' Nothing moved, but she heard footsteps fading between the walls on their right, up the Borough High Street. Gloria lifted her dress and ran. The inn taprooms looming out of the mist were still shut up and dark, it being church hours; her own footsteps drowned any other sound. Gloria ran alone in her circle of fog. She must be getting along much faster than an old woman with a dicky knee, surely? She stopped, panting. When Daniel ran up she held out her arm to stop him. No sound, and nothing moved.

'I know yer there, Tib,' Gloria yelled angrily.

A shape moved from behind the latrines in the middle of the road, slipped into the shadows beneath the Railway arches, and Gloria ran after her. Tib was gone. A train rumbling overhead towards Waterloo Station, gaining speed, sent down a flashing illumination from the carriage windows, making the fog seem more opaque than ever. Gloria ran beneath the spokes of light.

Dark again. London Bridge rose up ahead of her, a great arch of fog-flares. For a moment on the slope Tib was silhouetted, close, running to the left, and Gloria dashed after her almost close enough to touch. She glimpsed the four pinnacles of St Saviour's church growing out of the fog ahead of her, on her own level. She reached out to grab Tib's shoulder but was left holding the hat.

There was a cry and Tib plunged from sight as though the earth had opened.

Gloria screamed. There was a terrible, almost musical sound, like someone making an iron railing ring as they fell. Then silence.

'Don't!' Daniel said.

Gloria stopped. She was holding her own straw hat, the one that Tib had stolen from her long ago in St James's churchyard.

'Why did she run?' Gloria whispered.

'Don't look,' Daniel said. He coughed, going down carefully, but Gloria pushed past him, taking the steps two at a time – they were very steep, of stone, turning sharply half-way down to the church precinct below.

Tib lay with her head between two steps, quite motionless, not shivering. Her eyes followed Gloria, but she showed no reaction when Gloria picked up her hand. She was very far gone.

'All this time,' Gloria said. 'It was yer, not Glizzard, following me! Yer bin watching over me. Why?'

Tib's lips moved. Gloria held her breath, leaning close.

'Guilt,' Tib exhaled.

'Guilt?'

'Ninepence,' breathed Tib.

'That doesn't matter now.'

'It does, see,' whispered the voice. 'An' yer 'at, too, I stole. An' almost the most valuable thing of all ter yer. I even tried ter take that from yer.'

Gloria stared at her blankly.

Tib's fingers trembled and rose, touched the chain at Gloria's neck.

Gloria shook her head, surprised. 'I even forget I'm wearing it. I don't remember ter take it off, that's all.'

'I knows the truth,' Tib said.

Daniel held Tib's wrist between his thumb and forefinger like a doctor taking her pulse. He looked Gloria in the eye.

'I came back,' Tib groaned, 'I would've made it up ter yer. I'd bin like yer once, Gloria. But I never wanted ter make yer like wot I became. The Club doorman said 'e'd seen yer, but yer was gone, an' I knew yer'd gone down, yer was lost, an' it was my fault.'

'Nobody's fault. Just the way things are.'

'I couldn't find yer, though God knows I put the word out. I paid, but I didn't find out about yer an' Willy Glizzard 'til it was too late – 'e's a respectable gent now, got married an' runs a fine classy pub across the river, the Londoners' Arms.'

'Sssh, don't talk now,' Gloria whispered.

'Then one day I was talking ter Larry, yer wouldn't remember 'im, wot'd bin a milkman, though never a kind word fer 'is 'orse. An' when I described wot yer was like 'e knew yer at once. Yuss, 'e did! An' so I came ter Wimbledon fearing the worst. But yer'd set yerself up real fine, a gentleman's 'ouse, a real lady. Wot did I feel? Guilt, an' envy too. I'd made yer: it ate me up. I imagined I was yer, I looked like yer, I lived through *you*. Then yer threw it all away again, fer no more than 'cause of yer pride, yer damned pride. I 'eard 'ow it was wiv 'Andley's son, an' it was plain enough ter see. Yer could 'ave 'ad everyfink everyone dreams of, except a 'usband.'

''Ave yer called a doctor?' Gloria called to Daniel frantically, but he shook his head.

Tib gripped Gloria's hand with the last of her strength. 'Now yer done it fer yerself, all by yerself. Yer can 'ave it all, Gloria, an' I 'ope it makes yer 'appy.' Her touch was light as a feather, but insistent, and Gloria could not have pulled away. 'Remember the young lady wot rode the tiger.'

Gloria looked at Daniel.

'The tiger ate her,' Daniel said.

Tib's voice faded. 'I'm not worth much, but everyone's worth somefink, an' I can make yer ninepence up ter yer a little. I wanted ter 'elp.'

Gloria entwined the filthy fingers in her own, as though she could drag Tib back to life.

'I'm only sleeping,' Tib said. She stared at Gloria. The fog swirled around them. Her fingers fell from Gloria's grip.

'She's dead,' Daniel said. He started unbuttoning his overcoat to cover the body. 'Who was she?'

'I don't really know.' Gloria stood up and stopped him. Unclasping her cape, she laid it over Tragedy Tib, hiding the staring face.

'I wonder what she meant?' Suddenly Daniel Fox held Gloria against him, very tight, feeling her body shuddering against him. 'Are you afraid?' He pressed his face against her own, not trying to kiss her, just holding her so close that their eyelashes fluttered against each other's flesh. 'I knew there was more to you than you showed me,' he said.

Chapter Twenty-one

There had been no question of a pauper's grave for Tib, though Daniel raised his eyebrows at the money Gloria splashed out instinctively and so without thought, as it seemed to him.

'Didn't you consider your expenditure at all?' he lectured her a few weeks later – she was sitting on the shop counter, swinging her legs: she had dark brown shoes and slim white ankles. He tried to take his eyes off them. 'Four black horses with black plumes, a mahogany coffin with brass handles, a silly amount of flowers and all that public show – for a worthless old woman?'

'She wasn't. Not to me.'

'You can't possibly put all that down as business expenses,' he said.

'I'll pay the undertaker's bills out of me own money then, but stop nagging at me, Daniel!'

'And the church's fees, and the monumental mason, *and* every Tom, Dick and Harry you let latch on to you. And you do realise you are now liable for income tax, Gloria? Don't you think things out for a single moment before you rush into them?'

Gloria looked at him rebelliously. 'Yer right, Daniel,' she said heavily, 'I didn't consider it properly.'

'You don't seem to realise that your financial position—'

'I don't care, just see it's paid, will yer?' Gloria snapped.

She dropped by the shop for the early-bird coffee that Daniel now always kept ready and steaming for her, 'should you just happen to be passing', knowing her habits: they had discovered a shared distaste for tea, and to please her he had unearthed an enormous siphonic machine invented by his father, that bubbled boiling water through glass tubes and filters and made delicious coffee. Usually the ceremony relaxed her, but today was very early on a frosty, misty morning shortly before Christmas, her busiest time of the year, and Gloria knew she had an enormous day stretching ahead of her, and already they were on the verge of having a row. Rows with Daniel were always serious.

'Just pay it,' he said, mimicking her explosive gesture, 'all right, I'll do whatever you say – I always do!' He held up his hands as though she had drawn a gun on him – though he did not realise how funny he looked, because he was as angry as he ever got. 'Do you realise how badly you treat me, like you're just giving me orders?'

She shrugged and blew the steam off her coffee.

He sat on the stool and rested his arms on the counter.

'What *do* you care about?' he murmured, looking up at her. 'Nothing. You never speak of your family. Of where you have come from, of your childhood. What do you really care about, Gloria? Just yourself? Looking good. You do, you know, you always look perfect. You're a perfect self-centred woman, you think only of yourself.'

'Wot do yer care about? Yer coffee machine . . .'

'You.'

'An' yer shop . . .'

'You.'

She stopped swinging her legs. 'An' mixing up yer potions.'

'Don't cut me off,' he said. 'I'd do anything for you.' Daniel always spoke this seriously, and he always meant every word he said. He was probably incapable of a lie, and that was what Gloria liked most about him – because with Daniel, what you saw was what you got.

'Yer a wonderful friend,' she said.

He wasn't having that. 'You know what I really feel for you. Tib said she envied you because you'd made a success of your life – all by yourself, she said. But you're not doing it all by yourself, Gloria, you're doing it with Jenny and Claire, Lily Alhambra . . . and me. Admit it, Gloria. You need me.'

He was right, of course, Daniel was always right. She knew Tib's death had changed a lot between them. Gloria fascinated him, the look of her, the idea of her, a woman. He couldn't let her go, went over and over her in his mind – she could sense it. It was a rather nice feeling, but a responsibility. It wasn't Daniel's way to fantasise, but she was sure he invented a picture of her in his mind, a Gloria of his very own. He'd never known another girl, and she could tell that the poor boy – ten years older than she! – was still a virgin, because of the way life flushed into his face when she entered the shop. And there was his curiosity. *I knew there was more to you than you showed:* he desperately wanted to believe in Tib's dying words. Why? Was this how all men felt about women, or was it special to Daniel? – because *he* never spoke about *his* family, either, or *his* childhood. Daniel felt closer to her, now: he behaved as though he had seen beneath her skin that day by the bridge. Perhaps he had. He wanted to; to make sense of her. Perhaps, Gloria thought mildly, it was this easy. He talked in a way that tried to show her there was more to him, too. He wanted her to fall in love with him.

'I've been going over your figures,' he said unromantically, and she howled with laughter. He frowned. 'It's no laughing matter, actually.'

'No, I'm sure it isn't, Daniel, I'm sorry. I thought yer were going ter talk about somefink else – that's all!'

'You spilt your coffee.' He wiped it from the counter with a cloth, touching her hip by mistake before lecturing her. 'There was no obligation on you to believe that Mr Morgan sacked Poulton simply because of you when the affair of the unauthorised sixty-day account came to light, yet I see you are now employing Poulton as if you felt some guilt over the matter.'

'Well, I do.'

'You feel guilty about everything!'

'It was my fault. I needed that credit extension so bad I never thought about Poulton's neck being on the block. Making up 'is job was the least I could do fer 'im. An' the old boy's turned up trumps, 'e knows all the sweetshops and newsagents—'

'You are selling our cosmetics in common *sweetshops* and—'

''Cause there are *thousands* of them, Daniel. It was only an idea at first, but Poulton's done wonders. 'E talks ter 'em man-ter-man, gruff 'n' sensible, it'd make yer laugh.'

'I'm not laughing, Gloria, because I see here that we now have to pay Morgan cash on delivery. We've lost two months' worth of money, and now we're running an overdraft at the bank.'

'It isn't 'alf depressing, listening ter the way yer go on.' Gloria sipped her coffee but still burnt her lips. 'Anyway it isn't us, it's me. Anyone'd fink I was making a blooming failure of it.'

'Yes,' he said. 'You are.'

'I'm shifting the stuff by the cartload – yer may not believe in this sort of fing, Daniel, but there's lots of us do. A bit of brightening in our lives. It doesn't do no 'arm – it's not against the law, yer know, fer a woman ter care 'ow she looks.'

'I hate it when you sound so worldly-wise, when you can't even settle down to a consistent selling strategy. You seem to take pleasure in not making up your mind – in deliberately chopping and changing! I'd like you to be—'

'Are yer talking about me or the business?'

'Simply Gloria.'

'Come off it, Daniel. Sounds like a perfume.'

'What I see in your eyes.'

'Depends wot yer seeing.'

'Innocence,' he said. 'Mystery.'

'Blimey, is that the time? I must rush – I'm presenting Beatrice Ingledew with the gold-'eaded pin. Campaigner of the month.' She made to slide down from the counter.

Daniel put his hand lightly on her wrist, an assertion so unusual for him that he forced her to stop. 'Look at me, Gloria. Just calm down for a minute. Let's get down to business, if that's all that means anything to you. Exactly what have you been doing all this year?'

'Me? Rushing about like a blue-arsed fly!' she laughed, but he shook his head.

'Think about what I'm saying. What's the point of all this activity of yours?'

'Selling fings. Giving people what they want. Building up the business.'

'Isn't the point of it to make money?'

'Yuss, 'course it is, 'cause wivout the spondulicks nuffink else 'appens.'

'Look at this.' He brought out some sheets of paper, costings, it must have taken him weeks to be so thorough – since the day of Tib's death, perhaps. Gloria put down her coffee and riffled through the sheaf to show willing. 'They're called cost breakdowns. I know you aren't interested in the ghastly details so I'll spare you. The upshot is, Gloria, you're selling too cheap. Here, the bottom line. There's hardly any profit.'

She turned to him immediately. 'Wot can I do?'

'Double your price. That's what you need to do and I've always said so.'

'But if we doubled the price,' Gloria argued back, horrified, 'we couldn't call it the Penny Pot. We'd never sell it across the doorsteps.'

'You could halve the size of the pot.'

'Oh, I wouldn't want ter take advantage of people.'

'The thing is, Gloria, at the moment they're taking advantage of *you*. Your customers are buying at barely more than cost, no wonder they're lapping it up.' Again he touched her wrist. 'What I'm saying, Gloria, is that – forgive me – your amateurish, intuitive operation has to be put on a businesslike footing if it is to survive.'

Gloria had forgotten her coffee. 'Wot's a proper businesslike footing?'

'A proper company—' Daniel looked round in irritation as the door rattled. 'Closed!' he shouted.

The top-hatted man outside had flattened his belly against the glass, peering into the shop with his hand over his eyes like a sailor surveying the horizon. Spying Daniel and Gloria inside, he took off his spectacles and rapped on the glass with the wire frames, then peered again with mole eyes. His loose overcoat, with a spotted handkerchief dangling out of the pocket, revealed a baggy, dusty suit beneath, and beneath *that* a waistcoat streaked with egg. God knew what his shirt was like, Gloria thought, it had probably never been changed.

'Open at nine,' Daniel called through the glass. He took out his fob-watch and pointed at the hands. 'Nine!'

The man outside beamed broadly, shaking his head. Daniel unlocked the door.

'My pleasure, sir, and madam,' the man greeted them as he came in, but with his watery eyes fixed on Gloria, crinkling himself around the weighty curve of his belly with the best bow he could manage. 'Miss Simmonds, of course. Charmed,' he said, sweeping off his hat with a flourish. 'My name is Thomas Snapper, of Snapper and Wells. Solicitors, ma'am, notary publics, commissioners for oaths.' Patting his white hair, he looked for somewhere to place his hat, but a large stand of Penny Pots obscured the counter. He rested his briefcase awkwardly against his knee. 'I pass through London Bridge Station, you see, on my way to my chambers, and fancied I'd save myself a journey back later in the day by going straight to Zoar Street.'

'Why Zoar Street?'

'Obviously, that is the address I have for you. But Miss – ah – Alhambra, the landlady, informed me that I would most likely find you taking coffee here at this hour.' He peered at the coffee machine and licked his lips, squeezing the brim of his topper with inky fingers. Gloria ignored the hint.

'Why yer gone ter all this trouble to find me, Mr Snapper?'

'I am executor of the estate of Miss Elizabeth Snapper.'

'Never 'eard of 'er. She sounds more a relative of yers than of mine.'

'She is – was – my sister. Twelve years younger than I.' He sighed. 'Tib, Miss Simmonds. It was her vanity to disguise herself with that name, it is a low form of Elizabeth. She would take nothing from us, not even her name. We did our best for her, but she rejected us all. I believe you knew her.'

'She scavenged the streets of London, sir,' Daniel said with contempt, 'I have to tell you that she was a tramp.' Tramps sleeping in the doorways were a perennial problem for ratepayers like him despite all the police could do – they were always trying it on in the street, too lazy to work but scheming to keep themselves out of the Workhouse. They seemed unable to see that crime was illegal. They stole things out of boredom, feelings of alienation, frustration or bravado – but, as always, it was the honest citizen who paid.

'It wasn't our fault,' Snapper assured Daniel, who nodded. 'You are right, sir, but some people just won't be helped.'

Gloria slid down from the counter. She took Thomas Snapper's hat and put it up where she had been sitting. 'No, Tom, I didn't know Tragedy very well, but she knew me.' She poured a cup of coffee and held it out. 'That's the way it was.'

'Thank you so much!' Snapper sniffed the aroma with enjoyment. 'Brothers and sisters are the most different people in the world, you know,' he chuckled self-indulgently. Gloria leaned back on her elbows, watching him. 'Elizabeth – Tib – my dear departed sister – was a most difficult woman. A disappointed woman. Our father had died when we were very young. She grew up too wild and wilful for us to help her – deprived of love perhaps, with no one close to her own age – and after an unhappy affair she lived the life she did from choice. Some people do, you know. A few.'

'What has this to do with us?' Daniel said.

The solicitor bowed again to Gloria. 'Tragedy left her fortune to you, Miss Simmonds.'

He sipped noisily, beaming.

Gloria laughed out loud. 'But Tib didn't 'ave no fortune! She was as skint as a rock. I should know.'

'How much, Mr Snapper, if I may ask?' Daniel said.

Both men looked at Gloria.

'Mr Fox 'andles all me financial side,' Gloria said offhandedly.

'Very well then. I'm afraid that death duties were recently raised considerably, Miss Simmonds. The sum in question has regrettably come down to about twelve hundred and fifty pounds.'

''Strewth!' Gloria exclaimed, 'yer aren't telling me she kept that much up 'er skirts?'

'In care of Prideau's Bank, actually. It was part of a legacy in South American mining shares which was originally much, much larger, but she refused to sell at a loss. I have now realised this amount in cash.'

'Twelve hundred and fifty pounds,' Daniel told Gloria, as though it was supposed to mean something to her.

'I can't take it all in,' she murmured, thinking of how the bells sounding everywhere through the fog around them had been calling the worshippers to the invisible churches, and of Tib's dying face.

'After my handling commission and legal fees,' Snapper gave a small cough, 'the sum comes down to a little under a thousand.'

'You have deducted two hundred and fifty pounds of your own sister's money for signing a few papers?' Daniel said sharply.

'Ah,' said Snapper with a cunning light in his eye, 'it is the legal matter of knowing what papers to sign, sir, is it not?'

'Why me?' Gloria demanded.

'You realise the difference this makes,' Daniel said urgently, coming back to Gloria after shutting the door behind the solicitor, locking it. He followed her between the counters. 'You do realise it, Gloria.'

'I keep thinking of 'er, that's all.'

'Gloria, I don't think you understand—'

She turned on him fiercely. 'I do understand. I've got capital. Capital!'

He followed her again.

'It's time to put everything on a proper footing,' Daniel said calmly over her shoulder. 'A proper company. You can do it now.'

'Wot d'yer call a proper company?'

'A limited-liability enterprise, so that you aren't at all personally liable, if everything should go wrong one day.'

'My own company?'

'Your very own.'

Gloria leaned on the counter, her imagination caught. 'Wot, wiv a proper name an' everyfink?'

He took her hands. 'Especially a proper name.'

Gloria said, 'We'll call it Gloria Simmonds!'

'No,' Daniel told her across the counter, 'we'll call it Gloria Fox.'

They stared at one another, breathing heavily, and suddenly she realised that he had proposed to her.

Chapter Twenty-two

For a single moment, before she said yes, Gloria had wondered if she was making the worst mistake of her life. But Daniel was right. She did need him. He was interested in the things that bored her, those bloody accounts that would have driven her crazy in an hour, and he actually enjoyed the dry meetings with accountants and solicitors to settle on accounting practices for this and legal conventions for that, the wording of the Articles of Association, all the bits and pieces Gloria could never have been bothered to give a second thought to, but without which the business – a *proper* business – could not function. Daniel knew he was important. He often came to supper at Lily Alhambra's now, arriving as late as Gloria, as tired as she, but permitted to kiss her on the cheek – which made Lily simper, it being her conceit that she had arranged it all – now that they were officially engaged, although no date had been set. Sometimes they were so late back that everyone had gone up to bed, but Carys, who was by far the best cook Lily had ever had, left a cold collation on the table. Often Daniel fell quietly asleep with his face on his arm on the tablecloth, unused to the pace at which Gloria lived, and she sat twining her fingers sleepily in his hair waiting for the mantelpiece clock to wake him, chiming eleven or midnight or whatever it was, to pack him off home to the shop.

Four days of the week, Daniel employed an old boy in a stiff white apron – Mr Cory, who had kept a chemist's for years on the Newington Causeway – to dogsbody for him in the shop, leaving him free for what he did best, organising Gloria. Almost at once Daniel made her realise how haphazard her organisation had previously been, and within a few months he had the operation ticking like a watch. Orders were properly sent out in writing by a part-time clerk in the back office of the shop, and bills were paid on time. Gloria had not realised how heavy her burden had become until Daniel helped her take the load. 'We're more than a team,' she told him, meeting him by chance at the Railway arches by London Bridge when he was coming back from a meeting, 'we're a partnership.'

'Not legally.'

'Yes, just when *are* we going to name the day at St George's?'

'I meant the company is all yours, Gloria. Technically I'm just your employee.'

'Yer honest ter a fault ter yerself, Daniel,' she said as they walked. 'I thought we was going ter be equal about everyfink, no secrets, equal shares.'

'I know how much what you have achieved must mean to you,' he said shyly. 'It's your dream. I understand how I would feel in your situation, and I won't come between you and your company.'

'Yer called it mine. It's *ours*.'

'All I want is you.'

'Daniel, I don't deserve yer,' she said, and gave him a kiss on the lips.

He stopped her at the end of the island of shops. 'I thought I'd better get this. It's secondhand, but the shop will take it back if you don't like it.' It was an engagement ring, dark gold. 'It's probably the wrong size,' he said.

'Yer awfully kind,' she said, making him slide it on her finger himself. The sound of hammers came banging around the corner. 'Somewhat premature, perhaps,' he said, leading her round by her hand with the ring on it, 'but I went ahead anyway.'

Workmen were nailing up a new signboard over the doorway. Gloria stood beneath it looking up. In elegant italic letters she read:

The Gloria Fox Pharmaceutical Co., Ltd.

'Well, yer done it now,' she said. 'We'll 'ave ter get spliced pretty quick an' make it come true.'

'Half your name,' he said, adding with satisfaction, 'and half mine.'

But somehow they never seemed to have the time. They could afford not to be quite so close now. They set the great day first for July, Daniel insisting on a proper honeymoon, but then they remembered how much the heat of that month shortened the stock's shelf-life, making it difficult to handle and needing extra staff; then in October there was a fire in the number one building at Morgan's, the cocoa-butter burning like explosive, and though no one was hurt the building was gutted, so another source of supply had to be found – not so close, unfortunately, and Gloria now employed a drayman, his nag and dray full-time. Not until afterwards, walking back to the Zoar, did she remember that had been her own father's job. She was employing a man who could have been her father, one more little nail that made her realise how far she had now come. And she had beaten down his price fearlessly, too.

Christmas was their busiest season, and then in the New Year there was the campaign to extend their franchise as far west as Battersea, and to Greenwich in the east, now covering a hundred thousand doorsteps – all of them in rows of houses much the same, under smoking chimneys much the same – and all of them south of the river.

'This is ridiculous,' Gloria told Daniel, 'yer worse than I am, we've got ter let it go fer a week. We'll just make a time an' stick ter it.'

The wedding was set for St George's at the end of May – 'Come wot may!' Gloria said, but Daniel carried on with what he was doing, he hadn't got the joke. She gave him a hug because he was so funny. 'Tell me,' she said, tickling him, making him splash the mixing beaker.

Daniel tried to get away from her, shielding the fragile glass dropper but losing his dignity – he was terribly ticklish. 'I surrender! Tell you what?' he gasped.

'Where we're going fer our 'oneymoon, 'course.' She looked disappointed that he didn't want to be tickled any more.

'That's my surprise,' he said. 'It's all arranged. You've made me spoil this mixture,' he told her.

'Then wot dresses should I take, fer warm or cold?'

He hadn't thought of that. 'Oh, hot, definitely,' he said. 'Though I suppose it's bound to rain. And the evenings will be cool. Now, *will* you let me get on with this?' He was working on what they called the jewellery – making cheap basic ingredients look or smell slightly different, so that they became special while costing virtually no more to manufacture.

'Walking shoes or opera glasses?'

'Oh, Gloria, please!'

'Yer a great 'elp. Yer don't understand 'ow important it is.' She sniffed the mixture. 'This is somefink completely new, isn't it?'

'Ginseng,' he sighed, slopping it down the sink. 'It has – or had – rather remarkable properties.' He hated showing her anything before it was ready.

'I like getting yer going,' she told him, but he didn't rise to the bait, though she was sure he wanted to. His reserve, his coolness, enticed her. When he broke it would be like a dam going, irresistible. 'I wish I 'ad that brain of yers,' she said.

He looked startled. 'But you have talent,' he said. 'You have a talent for selling. I wish I could just go up to people and—' he clicked his fingers. 'Sell yourself. I love to watch you, Gloria.'

'Blimey,' she said, pulling on her coat to get back to Zoar Street, 'that was almost as good as a kiss.'

But in truth she was glad there was not such a physical side to their relationship, because it made what she felt for him all the more real and true. Round here, Gloria was sure, many of the women she sold creams and powders to were common-law wives, with little more than sex, cooking and habit to keep their man coming back to their arms, but Daniel – although he had no more money than they – was educated, and men of his class did not sleep with the girl they would marry. Besides, Miss Alhambra would never have stood for it.

In March Mr Poulton was in an accident with a motor-car, though the driver claimed he was doing no more than twelve miles per hour, and Daniel had to waste time taking over the sweetshop sales until Poulton recovered. 'It seems everyfink's against us getting married!' Gloria exclaimed. To cap it all, at the end of April, Jenny Rouse abruptly quit, to set up a competing business on her own, a betrayal which she must have been planning for months; she was even using the same cocoa-butter supplier as Gloria. 'That bitch!' Gloria stormed, 'I taught her everyfink she knows, she's taken advantage of me – and ter fink I sent 'er a wedding invitation.'

'We're going to stick to the date come hell or high water,' Daniel soothed her. But he looked at his future wife with interest. He had never seen Gloria angry, really angry before, with her cheeks on fire and her eyes flashing, kicking at the tassels on the rug as she stormed up and down. 'Remind me not to get you annoyed,' he said. 'Are you always like this?'

'Oh, shut it,' she said.

'Only if you don't get your way,' Daniel noted. 'She'll come back to you, don't worry.'

More dressmakers specialised in funeral dress than

374

bridal clothes, but when Gloria was walking to place her monthly order at the wholesale perfumer in Blackfriars Road, then went on to the nearby herbalist by the corner of Great Charlotte Street, she found herself stopped in her tracks by a very elegant shop window: Wedding Trousseaux a Speciality. As soon as she opened the door Gloria was lost in an avalanche of white tulle and flounces, gloriously embroidered skirts and all the things she could hardly know the names of – soft lace berthes and fichus, veils with chenille spots, picture hats and princess bonnets. This wonderful chaos was in the care of the sisters Jane and Liza Shellshear, equally thin and elegant, and impoverished. No trouble was too much. Prices were not marked, which meant they could be beaten down. All Gloria's bad spending habits, suppressed since soon after her arrival at the Zoar, came over her like a hunger. Gloria indulged herself shamelessly, and the sisters could not have been more helpful. 'Convent made,' they trilled past the pins in their lips, holding the dress against her, moving around her with their measuring tapes as swiftly as dancers. Three evening chemises, two boudoir caps, a feather-light Japanese silk dressing gown – two pounds, nine and sixpence, that, but beaten down to a little over two pounds – drawers trimmed with lace and ribbon. 'We call them knickers now,' twittered the sisters, 'it's so much more fashionable, don't we think?' Lace evening nightdresses for a guinea, and fifteen-bob nainsook ones for the morning after. 'Ladies consider six of each the utter minimum.'

'They don't last long, do they?' Gloria said.

The sisters glanced at one another. 'Garters, black, with

clusters of fruit,' they said, and would not take no for an answer, throwing them in for free to be delivered as part of the deal. Gloria left the shop poorer by sixty pounds but happier than she could remember, and the sisters turned to one another and shook hands.

The wedding day at St George's didn't turn out rainy after all, but continued the heatwave with peerless sunshine and not a single cloud. Even inside the church was hot, the warm shadows smelling of flowers and beeswax. Gloria's parents, though they had been sent an invitation, had not even given her the courtesy of a reply. Yet she nursed a hope that they would turn up at the last moment, her father at least, to give her away. But, as the open phaeton drew her slowly along the Borough High Street, Gloria saw no sign of Bert Simmonds – it was a Saturday, and he was working. He would say she should have been married on a Sunday to get him. Gloria closed her eyes.

It was stiflingly hot behind her veil.

Last week, with still no reply and time almost run out, she'd taken a hansom from the cab-stand by the Hop and Malt Exchange in Southwark Street for what felt like an endless journey across London to Lisson Grove: Wharncliffe Gardens looking so smart and modern and invulnerably smug with its shining glass windows and rows of glossy balcony-railings. The littl'uns had all been at school, the mums forty-winking no doubt because of the heat; no one was to be seen. Gloria had asked the hansom to wait and slowly climbed the concrete stairs and landings – it seemed so strange that they still felt as familiar, gritty under her shoes, the iron railing running smooth beneath her hand, as though she'd left here yesterday. She could hardly remember exactly what she had been doing last week, but everything felt from her childhood seemed to last a lifetime, as bright and vivid and alive as when it happened all those years ago – as much a part of her as though it was still happening inside her. But when Gloria had raised her hand to the Simmonds' door and knocked, there was no reply.

The cabbie had still been waiting for his money, his weary horse munching a dream of oats, yawning like a human when the cabbie cracked his whip. 'Marylebone Station,' Gloria had told him, but he wouldn't wait there without being paid off. Then she'd gone in and stood for a moment sniffing the pungent odour of smoke and iron; even the shadows on the concourse had been hot, and the potted plants were wilting. When the train lumbered out, silence had fallen, and she'd even heard the birds singing in the roof.

As she came into the Railway shop – which seemed much smaller – Gloria had seen her sister Annie working alone with her back turned, restocking the jars of boiled sweets that travellers, even if they didn't have sweet tooths usually, always wanted to suck as soon as they got in a Railway carriage. The shop was stocking flowers now, too. Annie looked taller and she'd grown her hair, the pale brown curly mass of it pinned up tightly. She was wearing the green Great Central Railway dress.

''Allo, Annie!'

Annie turned with a shout.

'Gotcha,' Gloria said.

'Can I 'elp—' Annie, her hand still clutching her chest, peered. 'Gloria?'

'Wot, 'ave I changed or somefink? Give us an 'ug!'

'Yer different.' Annie's face wrapped itself in a grin and they hugged, then held each other at arm's length. 'Ooh, yer do look smart,' Annie said.

'An' yer've grown up, Annie.'

It was true. Annie was nineteen, an adult now, and her spots were gone. She wasn't beautiful, but she was pretty and she walked prettily, and she looked kind. She was going to make someone a lovely wife one day. Gloria hugged her again, enviously.

'I love yer clothes,' Annie said, inhaling the expensive smell of them.

Gloria shrugged. She had learned how to wear a dress. 'There's a little place, a couple of old dears wot does me all right. They just run 'em up an' I wear 'em.' Her underclothes were from Lucile in Hanover Square, as delicate as cobwebs and beautifully tinted as flowers, and nowadays she never spent less than five pounds on a dress, she didn't have time. 'Dad all right?'

'What wiv the Waterloo rebuilding being finished, 'e got the push an' 'e works fer Leibig's Emporium now, that big place in Old Bond Street. 'Is cousin 'Awk 'Awkins got 'im in.'

'Yer still working 'ere, then.'

'I'm acting manageress now,' Annie said. She still hadn't congratulated Gloria on the forthcoming wedding.

'Congratulations,' Gloria said, but Annie didn't respond.

'I won't keep it long. 'Ullabye got the push fer drinkin',

an' they'll find a man ter put in 'is shoes soon enough.'

'Wot's 'e doing?'

'It was a relief ter 'im, see, 'e doesn't 'ave ter 'ide it now. Doris still lives wiv 'im, but she's twenty years older in the face, an' she's got the two young 'uns. She feeds 'em by charing-work, takes 'em wiv 'er so 'e don't get at 'em. 'E might kill 'em after a few. It's not 'is fault, 'e's not responsible when 'e's drunk.'

'I'm sorry fer 'er,' Gloria said.

'I'm not,' grunted Annie. 'She got wot she asked fer, an' that's more'n wot most people get.'

'Are yer walkin' out?'

'There's a nice boy works at the library. Nothing special, but 'e's got a way about 'im.' She said nothing more.

'Don't yer know?' exclaimed Gloria, 'yer mean Mum an' Dad 'aven't even told yer? I'm getting married!'

Annie clapped her hands to her cheeks. 'Glo, I'm so pleased! 'Oo is 'e? Is 'e rich?'

'Nah, that's all past, 'e's the one 'oo's marrying *me* fer me money!' A customer came in and Annie dealt with her, then dragged Gloria into the back room. Gloria told her about Daniel Fox.

''E sounds all right,' Annie said, with a kiss. 'I approve.'

'But Dad won't come, yer fink?'

'Yer know Mum. She won't let 'im, I'm sure.'

'She don't rule the roost, do she?'

'If yer fink that yer don't know nuffink.'

'But why didn't they even let yer in on it?'

'Yer know wot fings are like,' Annie shrugged. 'They got ter finish wot they started.'

'They can't admit they were wrong!'

'Albert's left 'ome, so they don't 'alf keep tabs on young Bill, fer all 'e's old enough ter shave now. Where yer going? When yer coming back? Yer know Mum, an' she gets Dad ter put 'is foot down.'

'So there's no chance of them turning up on Saturday afternoon?'

'I'll come, but why should they, when yer all that's 'olding 'em together as fings is? Don't imagine they've forgot yer, Gloria. Never, never. Mum'll be sitting on the sofa lookin' at yer invitation in 'er 'and, come Saturday afternoon, while Dad's at the cricket.'

'I wonder if I should invite poor Doris, if she's so un'appy, just ter show there's no 'ard feelings.'

'Yuss,' Annie said agreeably, 'that'd be cruel.'

'Then I won't. Promise me yer'll be wiv me, though, Annie.'

'Wild 'orses couldn't stop me!'

'No, I want yer ter do more'n come along an' 'ang about. Annie, I want yer ter give me away.'

'Oh, I dunno,' Annie had said doubtfully, with a lingering touch of Gloria's beautifully coutured sleeve, each stitch by hand and each of them as equal as if by machine. 'I'd be out of my depth, wouldn't I? Lot of toffs lookin' down their noses at me.'

'Oh, they're not posh!' Gloria had assured her. 'Promise me. Promise me . . .'

Sitting together holding hands, the phaeton drew Gloria and Annie along the Borough High Street. Daniel's best man, his cousin Peter, pulled down the step. Annie fussed nervously around Gloria's dress, then slowly they walked up the aisle. Gloria struggled to hold back her tears: although she had deliberately not asked Arnold Handley, because he was part of her past and would have remembered her as she had been, she found that her side of the church was almost empty, as though she had no friends at all – except for the brave peacock figure of Lily Alhambra in her brightest blue and gold, absolutely drenched in jewellery, Captain Villers standing ramrod-straight beside her in full military dress, and behind them, with a pew all to herself, little smudge-eyed Carys in her black maid's uniform, without the frilly white apron.

But the guests crowded into the pews on the other side were an amazement, seeming to fill the place with their murmuring. Each wore the lapel nosegay of malmaison carnations made popular by the King, for which she'd placed an open order at the florist's, and there seemed to be a whole hothouse of them here: the Fox family was enormous, hundreds of them, covering every age of life from a bawling baby to an uncle with an ear-trumpet. All their faces turned to look at Gloria as she passed, acknowledging her, and she wondered if she hadn't been wrong about Daniel's extended family not being posh. There seemed to be every sort of expression here – a woman with piercing brown eyes – and a fortune in hats, Australians and a loud Canadian voice that was trying to sell the others life insurance, but some of those noses had definitely been made for looking down. She squeezed Annie's hand reassuringly and lifted her veil the moment they reached the minister, feeling half boiled.

'Why are you crying?' whispered Daniel.

'There seem to be rather more of you than there is of me.'

'You're allowed to cry on your wedding day,' he said. 'And then no more.' She shot him a grateful look, envying his control over his emotions. Whatever he felt in front of all these people, Daniel was able to hide it inside himself. Gloria tightened her lips, unconsciously imitating him. She answered the questions in a clear, high voice, but Daniel's replies were croaky, because he was really nervous, and he cleared his throat with a grin, then kissed her before she had realised it was over.

'I'm allowed to now,' he said, 'any time I like, Gloria Fox.'

The signing in the vestry, which had been swept but still smelt of poor people, took only a moment. They returned to the body of the church, deserted on one side, full to bursting on the other. Her new relations smiled and nodded to Gloria as she passed, Daniel with his arm through hers, patting her hand.

Then they came out into the sunshine and Gloria stopped with a gasp. The Borough High Street was full of faces – the Gloria Girls – all looking at her, women's clothes of every colour, parasols, dresses, prams, barking dogs. She recognised Peggy Loman with her smart daughters, Maria with her long red hair curled in a trubichon over her shoulder, Miss Ingledew primped to the eyebrows as ever, Claire laughing and carefree, for once, with her arms held out to catch the bouquet. A cheer went up. Confetti streamed down and lay like snow on the hot stones.

'It's all for you,' Daniel said. 'Every one of the Gloria Girls is here. They couldn't *all* get in the church, so none would. Chin up, Gloria. Didn't you know how much they love you?'

Even Jenny was there.

At last Gloria held up her arms for quiet. 'Thank yer fer being 'ere! Seein' yer took me breath away. That's the first time in me life I bin lost fer words.' She threw the bouquet and Jenny, the traitor, caught it. She stood holding the flowers with the tears streaming down her cheeks.

'Come on,' Gloria yelled, setting off towards the Tabard Inn, 'come one, come all, yer all coming ter the breakfast!'

The Tabard was one of the great coaching inns of England, all crooked walls and cranked roofs, a warren of rooms, landings, nooks and crannies, panelling and secret places impossible to fill, or even to find, for people who had not been here before and who had not time to be familiar with its ways. Mr Wittle laughed deep in his belly, mine host of good cheer with his carmine, bristling features contorted into an expression of crafty bonhomie. 'Well met,' he cried, leaning his shoulder around the ash staff which held up his great weight, 'hail an' well met, sirs an' ladies, an' welcome!' The crowd bustling into the tap-rooms over-flowed into the private parlours, except that nothing was private today – the ancient wooden stairs thumped and creaked with footsteps, guests in their best clothes led by scampering, shoeless urchins in threadbare breeches, the adults swarming after them along the open galleries overhanging three sides of the courtyard below, then up more stairs, following the children's excited cries, to the upper storeys of galleries, laden like the others with food and drink.

But still, around and below the chattering voices, the place was ancient, and kept its mysteries to itself.

As the party settled, old folks sat calmly, husband and wife together, the wife with alert social eyes. Men in their prime leaned their elbows on the wooden railings, smoking, surveying the scene below. The courtyard was full, but people ran under the arch to the inner court, where more tables were set out among a hastily cleared mess of hay and pitchforks and a broken wagon. Horses looked out curiously over the half-doors, snuffling the sweet scent of beer. The children in suits asked their mamas if they might feed the horses sandwiches, and the ostler's brats watched from the attic windows thrown open high above, their chins in their hands. Their mother had locked them in, but they would be allowed down to clean up later, and there would be sandwiches and pies, roast meats and wedges of cheese left over, if Mr Wittle did not get to them first. Their mouths watered and they looked at one another, making plans.

Daniel was fetching Gloria a glass of port, so she found herself with a few seconds of peace. She looked around her, ducking beneath the low ceilings, room after room leading away from her with oak-beams warped and split by age, blackened and made grimy by hundreds of winters of fires, tobacco-smoke and moist beer-breath, so that the windows thrown open today hardly seemed to dispel the fug. The babble of talking died away behind her and she stopped with a sudden chill, imagining she heard old Seamus Reilly's Irish voice, gruff and weatherworn: *There's such a thing as love, I know. Love can exist, like a flower, for a day or a month, before it dies. An' the more beautiful it is the more its dying hurts*.

She wondered which was the room where Tilly O'Neill died, the baby dragged from her loins by Seamus's strong, loving hands. The baby had lived, and she imagined she heard its cry. Gloria covered her ears with her hands.

'*I love her*,' she heard Jamie say.

'Stop it,' Gloria whispered to herself. 'Wot yer doin', girl, finking this?' There was no reply from the peeling walls of the room in which she found herself, that was for sure. Gloria turned to go back to the party – *her* party.

A woman of about fifty years old was standing in the doorway, watching her. 'The Pilgrim's Room,' the woman read in a sonorous voice from the wooden plaque hung splitting above the fireplace. 'In Southwark at the Tabard as I lay, ready to wend on my pilgrimage to Canterbury, at night was come to that hostelry nine and twenty in a company, sundry folk, by chance fallen on fellowship, and pilgrims all . . .' She turned with a smile.

Gloria remembered those piercing brown eyes from the church, and they burned in a face accustomed to getting its way. Her clothes were not very expensive, but in solid good taste, and she wore a lovely silver brooch in her lapel, not the nosegay. A woman who decided her own mind.

'Yer must be one of the Foxes,' Gloria said.

'Originally.' The woman's voice was cool, sharp, elegant, with no trace of upper-class drawl. 'I was to have been

Arthur Fox's seventh son, you see, but – here I am.' She
held out a fresh drink. 'Jemima Summers, and have been
for the last thirty years. But I was born a Fox indeed. My
eldest brother was Martin, Daniel's father.'

Gloria took the drink gratefully and finished it in a gulp.
'Yer a woman after me own 'eart.'

'Am I?' Jemima said. 'Let's sit down, my feet are killing
me.' There were a couple of musty chairs by the cold ashes
and both women took off their shoes, wriggling their toes.
'My dear, when I came in . . .'

'Yes, Mrs Summers?'

'Jemima.'

'Gloria.'

'May I be frank? You looked distrait.'

'Did I?'

'And now you are hiding it.'

'Oh, it must be one of those days.'

Jemima's smile twitched. 'Yes, Gloria, every woman is
entitled to be a little distraited on her wedding day. I'm
sorry if we seem intimidating. Our name *does* have rather a
lot of relations. Not all of them are called Fox; in fact, by
now, few of them are, what with the girls marrying. Our
family goes back for hundreds of years, all at Holywell. But
we have become rather widely spread out, in the nature of
things. Holywell is long past. We do enjoy a good get-
together occasionally.'

'Just because yer fink I'm working-class doesn't mean yer
'ave ter justify yerself.'

Jemima laughed aloud. 'I like you after all! Let's not play
high horses with one another. We both have sharp tongues

and we must make an agreement not to cut one another. Pax?'

'That's fine by me,' Gloria said.

'Thirty-four years ago,' Jemima said calmly, 'my brother Reuben, who was youngest and closest to me, had his throat cut a few yards from here.'

'Gawd, Jemima! I'm sorry, Daniel never mentioned it.'

'I doubt he even knows. It was in his father's time. So much is forgotten, and so quickly, is it not? And yet,' Jemima murmured, 'so much is remembered.'

'Yuss, it is,' Gloria said quietly.

'I never thought I should come back here.'

Daniel stuck his head round the door. 'I've been looking for you everywhere!' he told Gloria with relief.

'We were just talking,' Gloria said.

'The carriage is outside to take us to the station – the train won't wait, you know!' he chivvied her.

Jemima slipped the shoes on Gloria's feet. 'I expect we'll have another chance,' she said. 'My husband Henry is a gynaecologist. Our house is in St John's Wood. Perhaps one day, in the course of nature . . .' She pressed her cheek to Gloria's. 'Good luck. I hope you can make Daniel happy. He was such a miserable little tyke as a child,' she said with cool fondness. 'He could do with some fun.' Her own grown-up sons, Alex and Gerald, arrived: Alex stern and Gerald tipsy.

'I'll try, Jemima,' Gloria said.

'Bye-bye, Auntie Jemima,' Daniel said, then opened another door and hurried Gloria through a roomful of people, who parted for them with a genially tipsy air, then they came through into the archway by the road. The crowd gathered to wish them goodbye, but first Lily Alhambra, hard-eyed but trembling and sentimental, leaned over the side of the carriage and gripped Gloria's arms, staring up into her face.

'Goodbye, my dear,' Lily said hoarsely, 'God speed and look after you!'

'An' yer, Lily.'

Lily dropped back, waving. 'You don't need us any more, but there'll always be a welcome for you back in Zoar Street. Always.' Her voice faded in the distance. 'Farewell, Gloria! Farewell!'

PART V

Holywell

Chapter Twenty-three

'Brighton!' Gloria gasped, embracing Daniel with a hug that made him grunt, ''ow did yer know?'

'Know what?'

'We used ter come down 'ere when I was a sprat! 'Appiest time of me life!'

'How could I know?' he said, following her. Gloria insisted on taking the tram down to the sea – a cab would deliver her trousseau to the hotel – and much later that was how Daniel always remembered her, Gloria running away after the London Road tram in her excitement, laughing as she held down her hat-brim that the sea breeze lifted and flapped, her ribbons fluttering behind her, one hand clawed to catch the rail. So he ran after her, and a dog raced after them both, snapping at his heels. Daniel really thought she would fall flat on her face, but then Gloria swung aboard, reaching back to him past her flying hair, and he couldn't give up. Red-faced and puffing, he jumped aboard with his trousers torn, leaving the mongrel killing a fine piece of tweed in the roadway behind them.

'Bloody idjits,' the conductor snorted as she ran on to the

upper deck, and flakes of confetti spilled from Daniel's hand as he held out the fare-money. His face went bright red and he threw the man a furious look. 'Oh, bloody 'oneymooners, that explains it,' the old sailor said tolerantly, winding out the ticket. 'Go on, chum, get swarming after 'er.'

Gloria was standing at the front of the top deck, gripping the curved railing above the searchlight of the rocking, swaying vehicle. She held out her hand to Daniel, pointing with both their hands. 'We'd stayed over there in Kemp Town – I remember we could see 'cross the rooftops down ter the sea. Oh, Daniel, this is the perfect place!' She gave him a splonking kiss. A boy trotting beside a goat-cart looked up at them and whistled. 'It's a piece of 'eaven, Daniel, I was young 'ere. They'd started building Marylebone Station, but Dad'd got moved down from up north before, wot wiv all the work fer drivers.'

Daniel looked uncomprehending. 'I know nothing of you – I mean of your childhood.'

'Nuffink special, us. Then we didn't come 'ere fer years, only Dad an' the boys, but Annie an' I always remembered wot it'd bin like.'

'Is that why you offered your sister that job?'

'Getting the Gloria Girls started in Marylebone? First time north of the river. Why not?'

'I thought you felt no loyalty to your family, yet you indulge in childish sentiment rather than make a proper business decision.'

'Annie'll cope. She 'eld down the job of acting manageress at the Railway shop 'til they could get a man in, she's got a 'ead on 'er shoulders an' she'll do a great job.' Gloria pointed. 'There's the Chain Pier! We used to beg a penny from Dad fer the Italian ice-cream man what lived in one of the towers . . .' her voice faltered. She was pointing at the Palace Pier; the Chain Pier was gone, demolished.

They swung down from the tram by the Aquarium. Magnus Volks's Railway was still running, squeaking and sparking as Gloria remembered, but the Daddy Long-Legs railway in the sea was also gone, and she couldn't hide her disappointment. A nanny pushed a baby in a six-wheeled wicker-basket pram, an old lady drifted silently past them in a dog-cart, her huge black umbrella raised against the low sun glaring from the sea – the wind blew, catching the umbrella like a sail, and the dog began to run lest he be overtaken by his burden, the barefoot boy scampering alongside him. One of the fishermen, the Spaniards whose boats were drawn up along the beach of Madeira Walk, knowing Brighton much better than she, told Gloria the Chain Pier had been blown down in a storm. They walked along the promenade; King's Road as always dug up for repairs, a tangle of carts, queues and piles of crushed stone ready to make mayhem of the height of the summer season. Below the raised esplanade thousands of luggers, drying their brown, salt-streaked sails like leathery wings, were beached by the rope-huts, and glowering fishermen hawked their smelly wares near the bathing machines. Nets were tangled everywhere across the pebbles, even hanging in pongy drapes along the promenade railings, and Daniel, somewhat repulsed, looked into Gloria's face.

'It means a lot to you, doesn't it?' he marvelled as they strolled. 'Coming back here.'

'Wot of it?'

'So it means a lot to me.'

Outside the Hôtel Metropole, all the working mess was left behind them. The elegant Brighton Sailing Club was set in ivy-clad arches, the club flag bannered from the mast, and the day-sailing boats were pulled up in apple-pie order. This was the view from their room, a corner suite filled with the setting sun.

Gloria tipped the bellboy. In bed, Daniel overcame his nervousness, pretending he knew everything about everything, and she submitted to him demurely. She had meant to be clumsy but it was difficult, and she could not bring herself to cry. She knew that there was so much she couldn't tell Daniel about herself, he'd only misunderstand. There was only one awful moment: when she tugged at his jacket in the passion of his kiss, a pile of wedding confetti fluttered on to the bed from beneath his lapel, and she laughed.

Daniel was so full of himself and the marvel of his possession of her that he could not lie still in bed. She struggled not to laugh at him again; as enthusiastic as a little boy, he'd forgotten all about supper now being served in the dining-room, for which they had paid in advance, and he was usually scrupulous about making use of anything he'd paid for whether he wanted it or not.

'I'm so aware of you,' he murmured. 'Thank you for sharing your memories with me this afternoon: it makes me love you even more.' He was trying to shed his stiff upper lip – the only time he had screwed himself up to the point of actually saying *I love you* was just now, when he had been lying on top of her, and her still in most of her clothes too. What with the sheets that covered them, and the drapes drawn almost closed, she still couldn't see anything of him below his pale freckled chest.

'Daniel, I'm starving!'

'I couldn't go down to supper now,' he said, ashamed. 'Everyone would know what we've been doing.'

'But I'm so 'ungry me stomach finks me throat's been cut.'

'Gloria, may I say something?'

'Fill yer boots.'

'It's all very amusing talking like that between the two of us, but I wish you wouldn't in front of other people. It's embarrassing.'

She ordered a seafood supper from room service and Daniel dressed ready for the arrival of the waiter. Gloria went into the bathroom and put on the evening nightdress that she had definitely *not* bought from the Shellshear sisters: she had gone especially to Hanover Square, to Lucile's, and purchased an almost transparent confection of a nightdress, the sort that Victorian husbands put their foot down about and made their wives return to the shop. It lifted in the lightest breath, flowing around her like mist, so romantic that its touch made her skin as hot as a caress. She remembered also to pull on the garter with the cluster of embroidered fruit – grapes and cherries mostly. Going back into the room, she tried to show him that she was determined they should not be contracted together just as husband and wife, but as real lovers.

Supper had been laid out on the table and she sat. Daniel turned from the window and sat down with a scrape of his chair, concentrating on his cockles and mussels, local winkles, shrimps in their shells, anything but her breasts. He had not grown fully used, despite his crack about her accent, to the fact that she was now his property. But when she poured him a third glass of Chablis, his tongue loosened.

'What are you wearing?' he said.

'Yer allowed ter look at me now, Daniel. D'yer like it?' she preened her nightdress provocatively, 'went specially ter Maison Lucile, ever so classy.'

He pointed in her cleavage with his knife. 'No, that.'

He meant the coin hanging on its fake gold chain between her breasts. She lifted it out and laid it in his palm, still warm, as if to make her closer to him.

He shrugged. 'What is it?'

She changed her mind. 'It doesn't mean anyfink,' she told him into his eyes, 'it's just an old silver guinea or somefink.'

He simply didn't understand. 'Well, you should have it valued, then you could borrow against it as security.'

She took it back. 'No, I wouldn't want ter do that, Daniel.'

'You look very fetching in it,' he said, putting down his fork. She supposed his mind had moved on to her nightdress. 'It's almost indecent.'

'That's wot I 'oped yer'd fink,' Gloria said, and they left

their supper half-finished. This time he held the edge of the coin between his lips while they made love, not understanding why she gently took it from him, or why her eyes gleamed in the dark as she turned her head away.

When she woke he was standing by the drapes. Through their half-opened curve she saw his body silhouetted against the moonlight on the sea, the black pagoda roofs of the West Pier's toll-houses. A cross-Channel packet was getting up steam from the landing-stage at the end, shooting sparks from the funnel. Daniel didn't seem to see it. He was talking to himself as though, in his despair, he was talking to her. 'There's so much I haven't been able to tell you, Gloria.'

'Yer aren't the only one,' she said, surprising him. '*Us* is all that matters now.'

'But there's so little between us.'

'Isn't that the way yer wanted it?'

'No, no, I know how wonderful you are, in your way. And yet ... but for an accident of fortune, I might have married a duchess by now.'

She laughed quietly, but of course, he wasn't joking.

'My father was a failure.' He lifted his leg and scratched it, a peculiarly human gesture at this moment when he was estranging her, and she wished he would come back to her and whisper these nothings in her ear in bed, not across half the room. 'You've married a failure, Gloria. What Jemima said is true, our family goes back further than we can find—'

'Everyone's does,' she said, sitting up, 'that's common sense.'

'And it's true that for generations they lived in the same house. Hundreds of years, perhaps.'

So he really had been listening behind the door while his Aunt Jemima talked. Gloria held out her arms, but the sheets fell off and he wouldn't return to her, and she remembered she was naked, except for the garter.

He was silent for a while.

'I know why you married me,' he said at last. 'Because you can control me.'

Gloria went to Daniel at once, padding across the thick carpet to him. She put her arms around him, her head on his shoulder, her hair falling down his chest, and the coin pressed hard between them.

'I know the name of the place yer talking about,' she said. 'Holywell.'

He sighed. 'Holywell Manor was our family's home. It was the place where we all came home, sooner or later. All the Fox family. I cannot remember it directly, it was sold in 1870 before I was born, but I remember my father, Martin, remembering: when he was drunk he talked . . . Is it possible to live through the memories and stories of one's father's childhood, so vividly that in a sense they become one's own, more real and true than one's own childhood memories?'

She kissed his collar-bone. 'Yer little piece of 'eaven,' she said quietly. A boat's sail crossed the moon.

'I've never been back there,' he said, 'but I imagine it.' He was the only son of the eldest brother; the house would have been his by now. 'The Hundred of Blackheath, the green valley of the Vaudey cleft running down from the high moor north almost to the Thames, near where the county of Kent crosses the water to the other side. There were oak trees, and a fountain, a huge view over London . . . God, Gloria, they threw that glorious inheritance away! It's probably all covered with housing estates and train stations nowadays. When the six brothers and Jemima had to sell, who knows what they were letting go?'

'Now yer got ter put up wiv someone like me, is that wot yer saying?' she whispered, hurt.

'Oh, Gloria, I didn't mean it that way. What a fool my father was. He was the one and it was all his. He should have hung on somehow. It was his birthright. It was *mine*, and my own children's.'

'Don't take it all so seriously, Daniel.' But she knew he had meant what he said, and she covered how much he had hurt her by kissing the hard bones of his shoulder. Perhaps as Daniel Fox, squire of Holywell, he really would have married a duchess's daughter by now. What he'd actually ended up with, due to his impoverished circumstances, was only a London girl with a winning way and a common voice, standing as tall as him but with not a stitch on her, a piece of fake jewellery around her neck and a silly fruit garter on her leg.

'Instead, my father divided the portions equally between his siblings – even Jemima had her share – and they scattered to the winds.' Daniel stood up tall. 'My father threw away his little share purchasing a chemist's corner-shop in slummy old Southwark!'

'There's nothing yer can do about that,' Gloria said. 'Now we're together, we got ter stick together tight.'

'Yes,' he said calmly and coolly, the Daniel she knew. He stared into the moonlight in her eyes. 'The past is past. It can't hurt us or change us.' He went back to the bed and lay down, leaving her at the window.

Then held out his hand and she went over and lay beside him, trying to love him.

They both tried hard to make their honeymoon a success, to make it something to look back to. Next morning Gloria winkled Mr Seaman the photographer out of his premises, him half falling over his camera tripod and shroud, to take their picture on the Esplanade: Gloria with her tongue around an ice-cream and Daniel smiling at her; Gloria with a pointing finger, laughing her head off at Daniel who'd spilt his ice down his suit. Another year it was Gloria with her parasol tugging in the wind, blurred, the stormy sunlight making a slant down her face. She looked happy. They had decided to come back to Brighton every year to celebrate their anniversary – it had been Gloria's idea, that very first morning, nudging him over breakfast in the Metropole's dining-room – 'an' yer can be like yer were last night, every year.' She smeared her butter-knife over the back of his hand because he wasn't paying attention to her. 'Passion britches,' she'd leered. Daniel had looked horrified; there were people eating toast at tables all around them. 'Wot do they matter?' Gloria had whispered. 'They don't understand us anyway. I love it when yer go red ter the tips of yer ears.'

She got her way, of course. Every year they came back, even if only for a night or two, to the same room. Daniel loved seafood, and once she had caviare served to him in a silver bowl, with champagne, but he said it was too rich for his stomach. The memories of their times together here in Brighton became so intense for her, remembering when she was a young girl on holiday here with her brothers and sister, and later how on her honeymoon night, grown-up, she had felt so alone here and decided to be loyal to her husband, and do her best for him. But Daniel seemed unaware of these feelings she hid inside her, which were so strong. He thought everything was as easy for Gloria as it was for him.

But at first everything was wonderful. Their business life and home life took off in tandem, she and Daniel working together to promote their hopes and dreams, and every little step seemed to lead them gently upward on a spiral of commercial and domestic success. Daniel was right. They were a good team, their personalities perfectly matched: Gloria did the selling and generated the ideas, Daniel had the technical knowledge to make them happen. And he had the financial discipline, which Gloria could never learn. Their business success made their marriage also a success.

Each year Gloria dragged Mr Seaman out of his shop – and, later on, his sons who had taken over the business – so these photographs could be taken on the Esplanade. Gloria had them framed and hung them up on the stairs of the pharmacy, where they lived at first, like a stop-motion of their married life. She paused, remembering this one: sheeting with rain, them sitting in the shelter next to the old dears with their little dogs, and Gloria had borrowed one and held it on her lap like an old woman – Daniel hated dogs and the camera caught his expression perfectly, half curiosity, half disgust, afraid the pug-nosed peke would somehow wet his coat. And the mischievous light was caught in Gloria's eyes.

The trouble was, Daniel worked all the time.

Another creaking step, and here was another May, sea-misty, the sun gleaming around their figures in the more flowing clothes that were now becoming fashionable, Gloria holding out her arms to dance, Daniel with his face averted.

Another year Gloria and Daniel were standing hand-in-hand, with hundreds of day-trippers crowded along the pebble beach behind them, the mums sitting on blankets in long dresses and hats, children wearing smocks and straw hats, adolescent girls turning their faces to the sun: a fresh, toned complexion was the coming thing, and a pastry-white face that never saw the sun – once delicately promoted by Gloria's brochures as 'creamy' – was no longer the badge of rank of a lady. Perhaps in any case the young cared a little less nowadays what ladies looked like. They began to dress up their faces. Pale-faced girls flocking to Brighton from the sunless factories believed a sunny complexion was the mark of a leisured life. Looking at those poor burnt cheeks and blistered arms on the beach gave Gloria a wonderful idea. She rushed Daniel home to start packaging a moisturiser with an ingredient to filter harsh rays from the sun – bergamot oil, which smelt nice, had been known to do this for years – and lest they missed the summer they rushed into production with a huge order. The weather broke; the last week of July and the whole of August teemed with rain.

It was the Gloria Fox Company's first really big marketing disaster and she had to rent a warehouse in Bermondsey to store all the merchandise returned by retailers. Daniel swore the stuff would keep until next year, but it went off and had to be destroyed.

He worked out to the penny how much they had lost. 'I don't want ter know,' Gloria said, slumped in the armchair with her eyes closed.

'All right,' Daniel said. He dealt with all that side of the business, a thankless task for which she was never grateful. He closed the door behind him.

She wished he would understand how shattered she felt – the exhaustion of this first defeat was quite different from the overworked, frantic success they had known before, where tiredness was banished by excitement. But now Gloria couldn't sleep. Finally she wrapped her dressing-gown around her and went and spoke to him in bed. 'It's thousands of pounds, ain't it. Are we going ter go under?'

He looked surprised, putting down the papers and glancing at her over his reading glasses. 'No, of course not.'

'Yer mean we can afford it?'

'Oh yes, easily. You're quite well off, in fact. If you sold the business today you would be talking tens of thousands of pounds.'

'All from a farthing profit on a penny pot,' she said wonderingly, then shivered. He always kept his bedroom so cold.

'I'm married to a wealthy woman,' he said in a neutral tone, picking up his papers, and she returned to her bed. Perhaps Daniel was right to be like this, she thought

403

fretfully. Only the laboratory that had taken over the pharmacy premises was his personal property, passed down to him from his father. Everything else was hers. Mr Snapper, her solicitor, had proved intensely loyal to Gloria's interests and even more, she saw now, to her growing fortune. If the lawyer felt any sentimental connection between her and his dead sister Tib, his loyalty may have been reflecting that fact, though his charges were swingeing. Perhaps he thought Daniel would not have been so generous – and he would have been right. Daniel cared about money.

'Daniel,' she demanded over breakfast, 'Listen, if we're—'

'Oh-oh,' he said, folding his newspaper, 'you've been thinking.'

'All last night. I couldn't sleep.'

'You didn't stay with me.'

'Oh, Daniel, don't make me feel guilty, I thought I was tired.'

'I wanted you to stay,' he said quietly.

'Yer see, listen. If we're so stinkin' rich, right, then wot we doing living in this crummy 'ole?'

'I thought you liked it.' The rooms above the pharmacy had proved surprisingly spacious once they opened up the attic, where Gloria had her bedroom, and they lived comfortably. The back room downstairs, which Daniel had had panelled like a real boardroom in miniature, was where they held their meetings. Claire Michaud, still unmarried and totally dedicated, her brown hair combed straight and a cigarette smeared with lipstick constantly in her mouth, was now a director. Jenny Rouse's business had failed in the recession of a couple of years ago and she had returned to the fold. She'd sworn she was sorry and she'd do anything for Gloria, but Gloria had looked at her with a scaly eye. In the end Daniel had won her over. 'Come on, Gloria, she's learned her lesson,' but Gloria was once bitten twice shy, and Jenny would never be allowed to sit in a director's chair. Annie might; Gloria's sister was transformed since she had left the Railway shop and married Bob Devine, her gangling young man from the library, and they'd moved into a top flat in St John's Wood Court, newly built. Dad came over sometimes, Annie said, flattered at first, then she had realised it was not really to see her: the flats had been built between Wharncliffe Gardens and Lord's cricket ground, blocking his prized view, and he brought his telescope with him to spy on the matches. Annie said that of all the children Mum had started with, she had only young Bill left at home now, and he wasn't as young as he was – Dad had got him in with him as an assistant delivery driver at Leibig's, and they left for work together. That was all Annie knew: Dad obviously didn't let on any more to his second-best daughter now than when she was a child, 'too young to understand.' But Annie had taken to the task Gloria had set her like a duck to water, and now the network of Gloria Girls north of the river was seeping into the well-off suburbs – every middle-class home contained at least one little maid in service, young, lonely and impressionable.

Gloria dropped her elbows on the breakfast table, her hair in her hands. Sometimes it seemed so difficult to separate her work from her life at home. She even ran Daniel like a business. They worked at their relationship instead of feeling it. She had always hated the size of this tiny kitchen, and now she felt the walls closing in around her. One of the drawers hung open like a tongue.

'I want a nice 'ouse,' she wailed, 'I'm fed up wiv doing everyfink meself, an' I'm not going ter!'

'Is this one of your moods?' Daniel suspected she used her moods deliberately, a woman's privilege. 'You're tired, that's all.'

'I'm not going ter be put off,' she said, 'I've decided.'

That look came over Daniel's face, a smooth shell with a sort of petulant resignation behind it. He hated the way she rushed into decisions, because he thought she only let him in on what was going on when it suited her, but in fact her ideas just boiled up on the spur of the moment and rushed her along.

'Darling, I just wish you wouldn't be so calculating about getting your way,' he said.

'But I'm not. I want a proper 'ouse, an' children.'

Here she goes again, his face said. 'We've had this discussion before. We've been perfectly content here.'

'I don't want ter be *content*, I want ter be 'appy,' she said impulsively. Daniel stood there like a piece of wood; doing nothing was the best way of ensuring nothing happened.

'Where's my boiled egg?' he said suddenly. 'Why can't you even do my egg at the proper time?'

She supposed she could run back to the Zoar, but Captain Villers had at last popped the question to Lily and been graciously accepted. Whatever Lily told Gloria for friendship's sake, she had come too far to go back – even Carys the maid now trod the yellow-brick terraces of Stoke Newington wearing a gold Gloria Girl pin in her lapel.

'Listen, Daniel, we'll keep the pharmacy on as a laboratory,' she offered, filling the saucepan then sitting again, 'yer can still 'ubble and bubble ter yer 'eart's content.'

'As it is I only have time for that in the evenings and at weekends. And don't forget there are the new season's colours to be worked on now.'

'Yer got 'alf a dozen blokes wot can 'andle that as well as yer.'

But Daniel looked unhappy. He liked to be busy with his hands. 'Why do you always have to belittle me?' he said out of the blue.

She was aghast. 'But I don't!'

He shrugged.

'I don't mean ter,' she said.

He shrugged again. 'It's always my fault that we don't have children.'

'I've never said that, I've never even thought it!'

'It's not *my* fault!' he said. '*You* don't really want them. How would you ever have the time for them?'

They sat with a silence between them.

'Oh Gawd,' she exclaimed, ''ow long's that water bin boiling?'

'Don't goad me, Gloria!' he shouted. 'You always goad me, *and you always go too far!*'

Gloria turned off the gas, then reached across. 'Let's kiss an' make up,' she said.

'Don't change the subject. Perhaps it's *your* fault we don't. Your fault. That beautiful body of yours is no good inside. Have you thought of that?'

'Give us a kiss. We're both so tired.'

'Maybe you should have yourself checked up, Gloria. My Aunt Jemima's husband, Henry Summers, is one of the finest men on women's matters in the country. He advises childless women from the very best classes. But you aren't from those, are you?' It burst out of him. 'What did you do, Gloria, before I met you?'

'Don't, Daniel, fer God's sake.'

'Don't you start that crying act. I knew on our wedding night that I wasn't the first man you'd had. I'm not a fool, you know, though you treated me like one.'

'Yer behaving like one.'

'My own wife dressed for our marriage bed like a woman of the night.'

'But yer liked it, back then. Yer came ter me. I wanted ter please yer! Wot did yer expect?'

'Not that, of my own wife. In a whore perhaps! You felt no pain, Gloria.'

'Should I 'ave lied ter yer? I showed wot I felt.'

'Since when is holy matrimony about pleasure? That's all today's women seem to believe in, not the time-honoured things: duty, or responsibility, or behaving properly.'

'I did it fer *you*. I did behave proper. Yer didn't grumble.'

'I know why your parents threw you out, Gloria. I learned that the day we were married, at the Tabard. While you were prattling with Jemima in the Pilgrims' Room I cornered your sister Annie, and she let it slip. She took your side, of course, but I read between the lines. You were guilty as sin.'

'Nuffink ever 'appened.'

'And what about that ghastly woman, Tib? How did you fall in with her? And what happened then?'

'Once yer wanted there ter be more ter me,' Gloria said miserably.

'But now you are my wife.'

''Ow did we get ter be so far apart?'

'That was always our strength,' he said. 'Look how successful we were.'

She stopped him getting up. 'Where are yer going, Daniel?'

'I don't know,' he confessed. 'Nowhere, without you.'

'Stay wiv me. Wot do yer want?'

'You finally got your wish,' he said dully. 'You finally made me angry. Well, here I am.' He threw his arms around himself. 'You're good in bed and no good out of it. What is there, really, between us? I don't know what to do.'

She stood matter-of-factly. 'Do yer still want 'Enry Summers ter test me fer a venereal disease?'

'So I was right,' he said sadly. 'You *are* a woman with a past.'

''Ave yer never done nuffink wrong, Daniel?'

'No, nothing wrong. Things I've regretted, I suppose. No, for God's sake, not Henry, he's one of the family.'

'Yer won't get dirty touching me, Daniel. Promise.'

'Don't hurt me any more. I've never regretted marrying you.' He hugged her fiercely, making up. 'We need each other, even when we fight. It's just you instinctively seem to know how to say the wrong thing.'

Gloria stared over his shoulder through the rain-specked window, the dull traffic crawling along St Margaret's Hill, motor-cars with steaming radiators splashing through the puddles, horses standing patiently in their own reflections.

'I want people around me,' she said. 'It's not enough ter work: we got ter work at us too, Daniel. I'm sorry fings came ter this pass between us. We mustn't fail at anyfink again. I bin selfish, I should've seen that 'is wife owning everyfink would get ter be a burr under a man's saddle. I'll 'ave 'alf the shares in me company made over ter yer name.'

'But Gloria – you don't even know what they're worth!'

'Don't argue,' she told him. 'I want a proper 'ouse, an' children. An' I need a marriage wot works.'

Chapter Twenty-four

But still, there were no children.

'Come on!' Gloria had chivvied him, trying to warm Daniel up as the motor-car crunched over the slush of Newington Causeway, 'we were bound to make mistakes from time ter time! We'll get up again. Don't be sad, just because yer showed me wot yer felt. Everyfink'll be the same again between us.'

But it wouldn't, and she knew that would be more her fault than his. She would never forget those dreadful things Daniel had said to her with fury in his tongue, driven too far, becoming almost a different man in his rage, the man she had made him; not because they were dreadful lies but because everything he had shouted at her was true. She did have a past, and when he accused her she had not been able to deny it. Perhaps it was even true she was rotten inside, because beauty was only ever skin deep. Because they had no children.

It was true he'd married beneath him, and that mattered, but she had been so full of herself in those days that she had simply not seen it, though it must have been obvious to everyone else but her. Gloria had gone over and over this in her mind like a nightmare, every detail of her wedding day too perfectly preserved in her memory, not now to be unremembered. The Fox family, who claimed they could trace their ancestors back to William the Conqueror, must have been watching her gauche mannerisms and listening to her brassy laugh and thinking of little else, and the friendliness she had sensed in Jemima had been mere self-deception – Jemima had all the social graces, and simply been kind in talking to her. Henry Summers had been knighted for his medical services in the New Year, and Gloria wished she could be a woman like Lady Summers, who was never frightened and never laughed too loud or got caught with the wrong knife and fork, who could quote Chaucer from memory while her eyes searched Gloria's face.

'Fings'll be the way they were again between us, Daniel,' Gloria lied.

'That good,' he said, putting her down, and she felt more guilty than ever. He showed no sign of being aware of her real thoughts.

'Yer my 'usband,' she said cheerfully, papering over the cracks, 'so yer must mean somefink ter me.'

To cheer herself up she'd gone out and bought herself the motor-car that they were sitting in, a maroon Lanchester, and she'd insisted to the dealer that it come with a properly certificated Lanchester chauffeur too. Splashing out the money had been a real tonic, but the expense had horrified Daniel. 'If you want to go somewhere why not just hire a cab?'

'Because a cab 'as no style, an' these days 'alf of 'em are motors. When did yer last catch an 'ansom? Anyway, I forgot,' she said, ''alf the money I spend is *yours* now.'

'Give it a rest, Gloria,' he said shakily.

'Go left 'ere,' she instructed the chauffeur through the speaking-tube, then re-plugged it. 'We got ter keep fighting. Fighting ter keep together, Daniel. Yer got ter 'elp me, we got ter work at it.'

'I suppose so.'

'I know so,' Gloria said, squeezing his hands as the car turned into the square. 'Look!'

The fine rows of cream-painted houses enclosing Trinity Church Square were old and beautiful, with the spacious rooms and high ceilings of houses from a golden age of, she supposed, candles and periwigs, built almost before coal-gas or electricity were thought of, and certainly long before motor-cars. Gloria, visualising how they would live, decided at once that her Lanchester would have to be garaged in the mews stables, whatever the old horses thought of it. Being on the south-east side of the square, the ample back garden was well supplied with trees, which she imagined waving their shadows over the rear of the house on sunny summer days. Daniel, with typical thoroughness, pointed out that the pickle factory on the other side of the garden wall would send a cooky aroma floating through the rooms on an easterly breeze, but he ascertained from the Admiralty that such a wind could be expected to blow up the Thames only once every ten days. By the time that reply reached Daniel, Gloria had long ago bought the place, of course.

She bought it, in fact, within four minutes of walking in through the front door: the downstairs rooms were obviously perfect for entertaining, and the beautiful carpets that came with the place gave it the muffled, classy air of Arnold's house. Best of all, the leasehold was running low, so she beat three hundred pounds off the asking price. The bedrooms needed a lick of paint, and that was worth another twenty-five. The agent escaped gratefully, and Gloria jumped the last three steps off the posh stairs, just as every day she had from the concrete steps at Wharncliffe Gardens when she was a schoolgirl. She twirled in the hallway with her arms flying, her eyes closed, now that they were alone.

'We don't need Victorian herds of servants,' she called, 'we'll knock together a couple of the attic bedrooms ter make a nursery.'

'You don't realise how you frighten people when you look at them that way,' came Daniel's voice from one of the front rooms. 'You're no longer a young girl, you know, you're a mature, forceful woman. You don't realise the effect you have.'

She went through and hugged him with one arm. 'Yer embarrassed 'cause I 'aggled 'im down, aren't yer?'

'I should have handled the negotiations.'

She realised he'd been making a list. 'Yuss,' she said, 'but yer'd 'ave taken six months beating the bush wiv 'im, an' meanwhile someone else'd 'ave got the place, but this way it's ours.'

'For what it's worth.' He tapped the boards with his stick – this was the only room without a carpet, and his voice echoed after her as she went up the stairs. 'Whatever do you want something this big for? There's only two of us. It's a shell,' he said, 'not a home.'

She leaned over the top banister. She could see just how the decorations would be: striped wallpaper for his bedroom and something flowery for hers. 'We're goin' ter 'ave parties 'ere.'

'I don't think we're well off enough for the plans you're making, or that we have the time, do you?'

'Dinners and dances. Masques, everyone in disguise! An orchestra serenading. I'm goin' ter fill it up wiv people. An' children playing. Noisy, naughty children 'oo don't want ter go ter bed.'

Daniel called up: 'I've already put him down for Eton.'

'Yer counting yer chickens before they're 'atched, aren't yer?' But she leaned back against the wall upstairs where he could not see her, delighted that they were still dreaming the same dream, still a team. Still together.

'It's only a matter of organisation,' came his voice grumbling up the stairwell. 'The school expects it. Everyone does it, except you, and you know no better.'

'We got ter keep close,' she whispered, shutting her eyes tight. 'I got ter keep 'im close.'

But still, there were no children.

By the time the bedrooms were papered and they had moved in to Trinity Church Square, making it the headquarters of the business, the end of May had come, and they cleared their diaries for the annual pilgrimage to Brighton. On the Esplanade young Mr Seaman proudly displayed a strange machine called a cinématograph, wound at a steady rate by a large handle and a skilled hand, sometimes assisted by a ticking metronome, that took photographs which, although flickery, actually appeared to move. This time the Brighton Road Board, busy as usual during the tourist season, was having King's Road laid to tarmac, and the stink of boiling pitch and crushed stone overhung the promenade. With the lantern clattering in the darkened room at Trinity Church Square they saw workmen toiling grainily in the background, then Gloria's figure walking jerkily towards the audience in her mink coat – which the weather had made far too hot to wear, but it was a gift from Daniel. She stopped, looking at someone off the screen, and her face went out of focus then returned. She waved, then blew a kiss, showing off.

That coat makes me look fat, Gloria decided, sitting in the dark, and returned the chocolate she had been about to eat to its tray.

The guests applauded and Daniel, smoking a cigar, clicked his fingers for the lanternist to rewind and run it again. Plump Gloria walking. Stopping. Waving. Blowing a kiss. Showing off. Letting herself down, in Daniel's opinion, in front of people they knew. He cared about her enough to be a little cruel to her, at least.

I hate that coat, Gloria thought. *It makes me look nouveau-riche*.

She skimped her meals to fit the coat, and next summer made Mr Seaman use his glass-plate still camera, and insisted Daniel be beside her against a stormy sky, hand-in-hand. Husband and wife, come what may. Gloria's determination to keep him was visible in her face, in the lines beside her mouth. Not to be defeated. It was not in her nature for one moment to acknowledge failure, accepting his small humiliations and inflicting them, knowing she needed Daniel personally as well as in business. After all, she had married him of her own free will, and she told herself that he was her anchor. Her husband was her life.

More and more she concentrated her energies on these Trinity Church Square parties, a classy address to entertain at, taking pleasure in the arrangements even though they were more than they could really afford. But she never could resist temptation, they were such terrific fun, and she wanted people to think well of her and have as much fun as she did. It was an excuse to dress up and meet old friends, Captain Villers arriving with his wife Lily – Gloria's tongue slipped and she called her Miss Alhambra instead. Lily leaned on a stick nowadays, and the two women, the old and the young, competed in bright, inexpensive jewellery, as gaudy as birds on the arms of their husbands, who were exchanging the stilted grunts men used by way of conversation.

The border between home and business life became almost indistinguishable when new seasons' product lines were shown to the gold-pin Gloria Girls at the morale-boosting bashes here at Trinity Church Square. The girls came from as far away as Bradford and Exeter now, even Lewis's Bon Marché of Liverpool. The breakthrough into the department stores had come when Gloria simply walked into Selfridge's of Oxford Street, newest and most innovative of the great retailers. Cosmetics were, of course, sold under the counter. She persuaded Gordon Selfridge to display them in the open near the doors, and in return paid for the stand and the shopgirl's wages. It was a flop, the department turned over only five hundred pounds in its first year, but Gloria never gave up on anything now. She worked the stand herself and soon found out what was wrong: respectable ladies disliked being seen purchasing toiletries, it was 'low', or 'not done', but they snapped up lily-of-the-valley scent – made respectable for years by Yardley in Old Bond Street – by the middle-class gallon. Running a lily-of-the-valley promotion to draw them in, Gloria renamed a whole eye-catching range of creams Lily's Valley, with a full colour picture painted by a Royal Academy artist of a shepherdess glowing with health, and next year turnover doubled. 'Not classy,' Gloria told Annie with a satisfied sniff, 'but it sells.'

Annie's second baby arrived, christened Lily 'in honour of the new range', but thanks to a bigger house in St John's Wood and a nanny, Gloria's faithful lieutenant didn't stop working. Like most people who became successful, Annie went to an elocutionist and had learned to speak properly, and soon she looked down on people who spoke as she once had. 'One does it for one's children,' Annie said, aware that she had risen a class. 'You are what you speak, and they deserve every chance in life.'

'That rules me out then,' Gloria said, pretending cheerfulness. ''Aving no kids, I mean.'

'That doesn't mean you won't,' Annie said, and Gloria had to acknowledge to herself that Daniel was regular in bed. Sex was habitual for him, a physical need rather than an emotional one. They never made love on the window-seat where she could lie seeing down into the garden, blossom on the apple tree, and he never took her by surprise, covering her with kisses like in the best novels. The opera at Covent Garden was the closest they came to passion. He bought her chocolates and she simply had to eat them. When they dressed up for Shaw's play *Pygmalion* at His Majesty's, about a plain-speaking flower girl who was passed off as a Cinderella by Professor Higgins, and taught correct speaking, Gloria felt Daniel's eyes on her. He was saying, *Don't let me down*. She disregarded his message, applauding Mrs Patrick Campbell's performance as though a play had nothing to do with their real lives. Did Daniel really believe himself superior to her? Of course he did: he was a man for a start, never mind his lost inheritance. He passed her a second box of chocolates in the interval and was watching her eat as the lights went down. He was making Gloria what he didn't want her to be. In truth he wanted her suddenly to collapse into his arms and confess, 'Yes, Daniel! I'll be the woman you wanted me to be! I'll go to a speech school and slim down and look twenty-one years old and learn how to be the wife you should have married!' She didn't, of course, and when the lights came up, she'd eaten all the chocolates.

That night he came to her bed, of course. It was Friday.

When the Gloria Fox Pharmaceutical Company's per-fumery wholesaler in Blackfriars Road raised his prices for the second time, and then the herbalist climbed on the bandwagon, Gloria decided she was being taken for a ride.

The Penny Pots and Beauty Bottles sold because they were cheap to people who simply could not afford to pay more. They would not buy if her prices went up, so her profit margin was always on a razor-edge. She invited bids from other suppliers, but their prices were no lower, so she decided to economise by cutting out the middle-man and buying direct. A few minutes poring over the Post Office Directory was sufficient to send her walking across Tower Bridge armed with half a dozen addresses. She enjoyed a brisk spring day with the wind whipping green waves along the river, and as always on a Saturday the steamship *Royal Scot* lay at the Hermitage Wharf, foam beneath her stern, seagulls already whirling there, about to depart on her regular run to Edinburgh. Tapping the steps with her fashionably long-handled parasol, her Fragonard-blue chinstrap hat cocked over one eye, she walked down to St Katherine's Way and turned left past the dock into Burr Street. The sign for HH Aromatics was a few yards along, pointing towards King Henry's Yard. Skirting the puddles in the courtyard, she looked around the brick warehouses with their identical shabby arches, but there was no one to ask the way, it being after midday. Bits of paper blew around her, then she saw a notice for the office pointing up rickety wooden stairs on the outside of a building. She climbed carefully, not wanting to dirty her gloved hand on the filthy railing.

Inside she found a front office with a deal desk and scattered papers, a corridor leading away. 'Hallo?' she called.

'Closed!' echoed a voice from the back.

She went down the corridor and opened a door on a comfortable room with red overstuffed chairs, no curtains on the window, and a fine antique desk. For a moment she stared at the man sitting behind it, her business card hanging from her hand, hardly recognising him. She was only sure it was really Hugo Handley when he stood up and said, 'Gloria! You haven't aged a day.'

Had so long passed? This man, who had been her lover, must be about fifty years old, but he looked older – his spanking black Kitchener moustache had gone grey and his eyes and nose were veined with drink. His belly had filled and tightened, pulling down his belt: he must have put on fifty pounds, and he had been so trim. That was how she had always thought of him: trim and fierce and sweeping her off her feet, so very long ago.

'Yer bastard,' she said. He was still damned handsome, though in a ruined sort of way. Without that moustache his bare lip would look weak. There was nothing wrong with his hair – except that he had slicked it to conceal its thinness.

'The sort of man you fancy, as I remember,' he said, trying to make his eyes twinkle.

'Yer past it, 'Ugo,' Gloria said, but her angry stare bounced off him. She turned to the door. He was still pretending he was the bee's knees and the cat's whiskers all rolled into one, but she no longer believed him.

'Wait,' Hugo said without pride. 'You always did rush off like there was no tomorrow.' He held up a glass. 'Just one.' A desperate stare instead of the old roguish glint. 'For old time's sake.'

'Not that one,' she said, and he frowned, realising the glass was dirty. She wiped the chair and sat, her hands clasped over the handle of her parasol while he went through the drawers in his desk. 'Don't bother,' she said.

He helped himself. 'I wish you wouldn't sit like that.'

'Do yer?'

'It's so businesslike. I prefer to remember you the way you were.'

'I'm not that young girl any more.'

'Yes, I suppose you're all hard edges and sharp corners now,' he said hurtfully. 'Cheers. Up the suffragettes.' He toasted her. 'I'll wager you haven't changed underneath. You feel exactly the same, don't you?'

'Yer lied ter me, 'Ugo. Yuss, I feel exactly the same about that. Kittie, isn't it, yer wife's name?'

'You must be the wrong side of thirty, but you're as beautiful as ever, you could pass for ten years younger,' he said casually. 'Except for those edges and corners I see in your eyes.' He raised his eyebrows, then finished his glass in one. 'What happened to you, Gloria?'

'Oh, I learned 'ow ter survive.'

'It's a rotten world, isn't it?' he said genially, putting his hand on her knee. 'Come on, don't pretend,' he grinned.

'Take yer 'and off me, this instant.'

'Ah, I see the female sexual urge also dies completely at the age of thirty!' But his joke didn't work twice, and she stared him down. Hugo looked around him nervously, then began to giggle. He knew he was making a fool of himself and went back to the drinks cabinet.

'Yer 'urt me once,' Gloria said. 'Yer can't 'urt me again.'

'You expected too much.'

'Yuss I bloody well do!' Gloria shouted.

'I promised I'd love you if you were ugly, I promised I'd love you when you were old,' he said quietly. 'But I cannot love you when you are ... unflinching like this. Hard.'

'Spare me the tears, 'Ugo. Yer never loved me, yer just came ter believe yer own seduction routine.'

'It's different for a man. You wouldn't understand.'

He sounded so weak and pathetic that she wanted to kick him. 'Special, are yer? An' I suppose yer still love yer poor wife wot turns a blind eye ter wot yer get up ter? Kittie even wanted ter be friends wiv me, she was so desperate not ter believe it, as though by being nice enough she could make a nasty bastard like yer all right.'

'Kittie?' he said, surprised. 'Don't you know? It seemed everyone must know what had happened,' he said sadly. 'I thought she was rational. Sane. Charming. Sufficient. Oh, she was a strange creature, Gloria, I misjudged her. I'm afraid she turned! I was indiscreet and I was, as they say, caught *in flagrante delicto*. Trousers down. It wasn't funny, Gloria.'

''Oo was she?'

'A nobody. But Kittie went perfectly crazy, you have no idea. A madwoman – as though she hadn't always known the way it was with me!' he chuckled indulgently, trying to make his wife a willing, conniving accessory to his years of infidelity. Hugo probably didn't even feel guilty; he would have imagined all the blame into being Kittie's now, for making a fuss. 'It got frightfully messy. Ghastly. The idiotic woman sued me for divorce even though she knew that would lose her everything – name, respectability, children. A *divorcee*. Still, she went through with it, dragged me through the courts. The legal fees alone . . . she certainly hit me where it hurts. She had to marry a foreigner in the end, lives in the south of France I believe. The children are with me, I'm blooding 'em in the business.'

''Ow did Arnold take it?'

'I'm afraid that until the day he died he believed everything I had done was his fault.'

They both looked up as a siren whistled on the river.

'The *Royal Scot*,' they both said together.

Hugo sat behind his desk, propped his hands over her card on his blotter. 'What really brings you here? I see you are *that* Gloria Fox. You must have married a very clever man to have got on so well. Perhaps you and he could throw some business my way.'

'That depends on your prices.'

'For you they will be lower than for anyone else.' She stared at him until he coughed. 'Times have been a little tricky lately. I can supply direct and the Gloria Fox Company has the potential to be my biggest customer.' It was the closest he had come to admitting he was broke.

'I wouldn't have it any other way,' purred Gloria. 'Now listen—'

'Are you sure you wouldn't rather your husband carried out the negotiations with me?'

'No, because I know 'ow ter deal wiv yer,' Gloria said.

'I'm afraid I don't terribly much like your tone.'

'Yes yer do,' Gloria said, 'that's exactly wot yer like. Yer stay afraid, chum. Yer can take it or leave it as far as I'm concerned.' She stood up.

He looked alarmed, fluttering his hands for her to sit down.

'Listen ter me,' Gloria said. 'I sell in volume. I don't drip titchy quantities of cream or flower perfume into beautifully crafted cut-glass bottles for a classy clientèle. I shift the stuff across doorsteps, I'm wot a girl buys instead of 'alf a pound of sweets. I sell good stuff an' it works. I get through beeswax, glycerine, lanolin an' cocoa butter by the ton, carotene, rose oil and almond oil by the barrel—'

'In stock in my warehouses.' Hugo gestured through the window at the courtyard.

'All those basic products sell big, an' that sells the Gloria Fox name. By now yer workin' 'ousewife knows she can trust Gloria, she can trust the product 'cause it's got Gloria on it. But it's not enough. The Gloria Fox Company can't move upmarket, that's closed off 'cause we're too basic an' popular, so I got ter broaden me mass-market ranges sideways. Tryin' out new stuff all the time. Win some, lose some, keep movin', strike lucky. See, a girl don't buy cosmetics only ter do 'erself good or look good.'

'Oh, I assure you I am an expert on female vanity.'

'Yer a real bore, 'Ugo.'

He laughed, startled.

'It's for 'er ter *feel* good,' Gloria said. 'It's partly in the mind, see, but it's real – not only ter look but ter *be*. So we're launching a new range called BE. That's our slogan too. Don't *look*, BE.'

'I can imagine how it will be plastered all over your sort of shop,' he said sourly.

'We'll need more different ingredients to keep changing,' Gloria said, not hiding her enthusiasm now. 'I got ter keep ahead of the game. All the stuff yer 'ave, ylang-ylang, zdravets, coriander and sandalwood oils—'

'I assure you, we import the widest range, peach-kernel oil, cardamom—'

'An' botanicals too, witchhazel an' cinchona, quince seeds, black hellebore root fer freckle lotion—'

'Only the finest hellebore, from a single valley in Devon.'

'Then yer better get ter work,' she said.

Hugo looked up at her as she stood to go. 'I am your slave,' he said.

Chapter Twenty-five

Before that summer had ended, war was declared.

'It won't make any difference to us,' Daniel reassured the girls at the boardroom table – actually the dining-room table at Trinity Church Square, but with the lace table-cloth replaced by severe green baize, and place-mats giving way to blotting-pads and sheaves of paper: the effect was suitably businesslike. 'I mean,' Daniel corrected himself, 'it won't make any difference to the company.'

'Are the doors closed?' Gloria asked. This was always how she opened meetings, step by step. She took her place at the head of the table. Daniel pushed her chair in, then went back to his place at the other end. 'Are we all here?' she asked.

There was no doubt about who was in charge. There was a flower arrangement in the centre of the table, a gift sent by one of their suppliers. Annie had been talking with Claire about whether they were really orchids. Maria Loman, the striking ginger-haired girl who had taken over retail sales when Poulton retired, sat on Gloria's left. None of these fashionable girls' dresses reached the floor, coming only halfway down the sweep of their calves, revealing silk hose. Daniel, as financial secretary, had once very late on a Friday night confided to Gloria, after several glasses of wine, that these meetings made him feel like the only cock among the hens. 'Why?' Gloria had frowned, not understanding his titillation. 'Because I am the only man,' he pointed out gently. 'Oh!' Gloria had laughed, 'I'd never noticed!' She'd left him feeling subtly cut off at the knees, something she seemed unable to avoid doing these days. You couldn't change Gloria, Daniel thought shaking his head ruefully, she was what she was. Only a woman would allow these flowers at a business meeting, sent by the jovial Mr Hugo Handley of HH Aromatics. Personally Daniel distrusted him as a bit of a wide boy, despite the man's gentlemanly but rather overbearing air. Daniel suspected that Mr Handley did not respect him as he should, but there was nothing he could do, the fellow carried Gloria's stamp, she had vouched for him. The Gloria Fox Company, she had explained, was by far Handley's largest customer, and the service was invariably as keenly-priced and attentive as such a position enabled them to demand. And Gloria always demanded the best. Daniel couldn't argue with her logic, but still he didn't like the man.

He flicked his pen along a row of figures, lost in thought, but Gloria was looking into their faces around the table one by one. Jenny Rouse, who had never found the right man, sat on Gloria's right with gaunt cheeks, forgiven or partly forgiven at last for her ancient treachery of setting up her own short-lived company, and brought into Gloria's inner circle – Gloria's inner *business* circle, Jenny corrected herself. Gloria would never fully extend her friendship again. Jenny's knowledge of the trade and sheer hard work had allowed her to climb back so far, but sometimes she felt as if she was only hanging on by her fingernails.

Claire had developed, or was affecting, a white streak in her hair. She felt Gloria's eyes on her and stubbed out her cigarette.

'Hm-mmm.' Gloria opened the meeting by tapping a tiny silver wand against a glass bell, a gift from her sister Annie. Annie had recovered her figure fully from Lily's birth and she looked slimmer than Gloria now, flawlessly smart and efficient but lacking her sister's fire.

Gloria asked for the minutes of the last meeting to be read, then they covered today's agenda item by item. She watched the top of Daniel's head, his flicking pen. 'Any other business?'

Annie jerked as though her mind, like Daniel's, had been elsewhere. 'This dreadful war.' Bob, her husband, had volunteered at once and was marching with the drum somewhere in France. She was worried about him because he knew nothing at all about fighting except what he had read in books; he would never hurt a fly. She had wept bitterly waving goodbye at Charing Cross Station. Most of her friends were proud to see their husbands go, and started scrapbooks to paste in the war news and their letters home, but when Bob was gone she wondered if he'd left because her work was more important than his at the library – she, after all, was the breadwinner. None of the men had been home by Christmas as promised, and Annie felt that she had failed him.

'It's business as usual,' Daniel said. 'I told you, it won't make any difference to us.'

Gloria held up a piece of paper, and everyone looked at her. 'This is a cutting from this morning's *Daily Mail*.'

'What of it?' Daniel said.

'It says more than a million men are under arms.'

'Gloria, I fail to see—'

'They've left their jobs behind them. These jobs are being filled by women from the Register for War Service. Women driving carts, delivering milk and coal, even driving cabs and buses maybe. Look at this photograph of munitions workers filling shells.' She held it up. 'A hundred girls at least. Only one man, the foreman.'

'I still don't see what difference this makes,' Daniel sighed. 'These women are always drunk, according to the Government.'

'The war is costing two million pounds a day, Lloyd George says so 'ere. It occurs to me that a soldier receives one shilling in the same period of time. So where is the rest going?'

'Last night I heard the guns firing in France,' Claire said.

'Munitions,' said Gloria, tapping the photograph. 'These girls won't work 'cause they're sober, they'll work 'cause they're paid. I went down to the Woolwich Arsenal yesterday, waited about beneath that 'uge lamp on the arch, an' I 'eard the girls complaining comin' out 'cause they were paid *only* two pounds a week, goin' up. Now, if these poor sods, their faces canary-yellow with lyddite an' chemicals, can't spend their cash on drink 'cause the Government shuts the pubs early . . .'

'Pianos,' Daniel said. 'Apparently every munitions girl's dream is a piano in the front room.'

'I have one, actually,' Annie said.

'Yuss, yer gone up in the world, but they never 'ad the lolly before,' Gloria said. 'They was stuck at 'ome like our mum, an' if they got work at all they was paid a pittance. Now fer the first time in their lives they got their own money ter spend – an' they're not going ter be backward about coming forward ter spend it. That's a big diff'rence, Daniel, a big change. An' change is an opportunity ter be grasped.' She closed her hand tight. She wasn't one for letting an opportunity slip past.

'You mean we'll be competing with pianos for their money?' Daniel actually laughed. He couldn't see it.

'A battle we will win,' Gloria said. 'For the first time, Daniel, they *got* money. Whatever their accent or their table manners, they're earning money now. There's real money out there among our people.'

'Our customers, you mean,' Daniel corrected her.

Claire scribbled busily. 'Advertising? Free samples? Competitions? Prizes?'

'Glamour,' Gloria said. 'I saw a girl at work yesterday wot was wearin' enough eye make-up ter be Mary Pickford. Did yer see our Mary in *The Violin Maker of Cremona*? Millions did, an' we fell in love wiv 'er, the World's Sweetheart. Whatever Mary wears, they'll wear in Woolwich. A ciné camera needs plenty of make-up to pick up eyes an' lips, else yer look like a faceful of milk. So it's eyes an' lips, Daniel.'

'I'll look into it.'

'No, get yer kettles an' pots steamin' at ninety miles an hour. Crack the whip over the boys. I want samples on me desk first fing Monday morning, strong an' feminine. No wishy-washy stuff. Umber pigments, red an' yellow oxides. Mascara wiv Carnauba wax, strong colours fer the lipsticks. Plenty of top notes in the fragrances.'

'All this is going pretty far, pretty fast,' Daniel warned her.

'Always 'ave done,' Gloria said, ignoring him the way she always did when he tried to slow her down. 'We'll call it the World's Sweetheart range.'

'Maybe we could ask Mary Pickford to endorse the product,' Maria said.

'She took 'ome a million dollars last year,' Gloria said, 'we couldn't afford 'er. Charlie Chaplin earned ten times that, an' I remember when 'e played Billy the page-boy at the Met fer a few bob a week an' 'is supper. It's not the play now, it's the player.' She shook her head, closing the meeting.

When they were alone she went down the table and put her hand over Daniel's. 'See wot I mean? Everyfink's changed.'

'You would see it that way,' he said. 'You like those flowers, don't you?'

Gloria looked at them. 'I suppose so. Wot's yer point?'

'Nothing,' he said, gathering up his papers. 'I'll get down to the lab for you and crack the whip.'

Daniel hated Gloria's parties. He hated them invading his

home, and he hated the guests she invited: glossy, shallow people as bright and hard as buttons, with glassy laughter and malicious tongues. He stood against the wall swirling his punch in its glass. The women pushing past him smelt of crushed flowers, and the men in their white ties and tails looked hungry and hatchet-faced, like German spies. Real men were in short supply, Daniel told himself, having his glass recharged at the silver bowl, smiling politely, nodding and bowing, sweet as a tooth to people he did not know and did not wish to know. There was an enormous Christmas cake on the table beneath the chandelier, tiers of white icing and a base large enough to hold a person. Gloria was having it sent to the boys at the Front for a moment of Christmas cheer and memories of home – God knows what they'd do with the great gauche thing. 'Some officer's mess'll nick it, wot else?' Gloria had said, but first cameras would click and correspondents would be given a paragraph of good cheer to write up. The gesture must have cost her a hundred pounds. Daniel spilt his drink as someone pushed past and Daniel apologised. There was something rough and nasty just beneath the grinning veneer of the fashion world.

Gloria no longer needed to worry about money – not that she ever had worried, he told himself bitterly, helping himself to a slice of kidney toast, it had been he who spent the sleepless nights fretting over their finances – but now that she was rich these lounge-lizard types were attracted to her like flies, and she appeared to revel in them when there was no need. The way Gloria behaved by instinct appalled him, flirting shamelessly; she had also taken to smoking a cigarette in a long jade holder. As always, of course, he had to admit that she was right. These parties were important, now that so many newspapers had stopped their women's pages, or replaced them with heroic articles about a lady porter at Marylebone Station doing the work of two men, or women dentists, or women county councillors standing for election – women were taking over the country while the men were gone fighting. Gloria's parties had taken advantage of this beautifully, he couldn't deny, but the thunder of gossip and nudges-and-winks in this closed, perfumed, influential world still irked him. Last year, Daniel remembered, he had brought Gloria official figures showing over a million more women than men in the country, and in many southern counties – their main commercial market – one woman in five would never find a husband. Now the war was subtracting its further ghastly toll from the male population. She had frowned over his figures; the way he presented them, they simply meant nothing to her, and he had not been able to explain their significance in words she could understand.

But Gloria had sensed what was happening to the market by sheer feminine intuition, seen her opportunity and seized it. The World's Sweetheart range had been an enormous hit, and yet the almost random way she had arrived at her inspiration appalled him. To Gloria business decisions weren't an intellectual process, she picked up any old snippets from the *Mail*, or women's pages, trade papers or God-knows-where, they went into her subconscious and she ended up just following her feelings. He glimpsed her on the far side of the room, laughter trilling, smile working,

434

always selling. She poured the love she didn't feel for him, Daniel thought self-pityingly, into her business and her success.

'Cheer up,' Annie said, 'it won't look so bad tomorrow.'

'Was I looking glum? I'm sorry.'

'This lot's enough to give anyone the glums,' Annie commented cheerfully. 'Still, that's the way it works, isn't it?' She was wearing a smart, simple dress and glanced round as Gloria's laugh echoed above the crowd of heads. 'You've got to admire the way she pulls them in.'

'Yes, I just was,' Daniel lied straight-faced. He had seen Hugo Handley arriving, taller than the others but stooping to kiss Gloria's hand. He was wearing a crimson cummerbund around his waist, his chest bulging above it, his belly below. Daniel stared coldly, wishing Gloria wouldn't play Handley along; the man was besotted with her and voracious. He saw Daniel watching and raised his glass in salute, so Daniel turned back to Annie. He made conversation. 'I heard your husband Bob is up for a gong?'

'Military Cross.' Annie showed her pride. 'Something frightfully brave to do with a machine-gun post. I'm trying to come to terms with a husband who started the war as a librarian, returning home on leave as a hero!'

'Leave?'

'Dover packet, home in the early hours. That's why I'm going to dash off any minute. Bea, the nanny, saw that the children were given extra-long naps this afternoon so that they may be woken, they're so excited.'

'You're excited too, aren't you?'

'Yes, I am.' Annie's face lost its freshness. 'I just hope he isn't changed. They are, you know, some of them. You can see it in their eyes. They come home to their wives changed and they don't talk about what they have been through. I don't think I could bear it if Bob wouldn't tell me everything.' She pointed, smiling again. 'Look, there's Gloria's old lady from the Zoar. Thank goodness for someone real.' Her eyes shifted again to the ormolu clock.

Lily saw them and waved. She hobbled over on her sticks, then lowered herself with a sigh on to one of the fake Louis XIV chairs set along the wall. 'Having as much fun as I am? I can't party like I used to. What a wonderful circus Gloria puts on.'

'Indeed,' Daniel said.

'She even lets me hold court, when I can get a word in edgeways.' Lily tugged his sleeve for him to sit beside her. 'That's better. You give me a crick in my neck, Daniel.'

'I have that effect on people,' he said without a smile. 'How are you?'

'Better than one fears at my age.'

'I have a horror of growing old,' Daniel said insensitively.

Annie went away to fetch a glass of punch. Lily surveyed the swarm with hard eyes. 'You hate this, don't you?'

'The circus?' Some girl gave a squeal of laughter and staggered tipsily. You never saw that sort of behaviour in the old days. Gloria had even invited his aunt, Jemima Summers: incredible as it seemed there was some sort of affinity between those two. Jemima's upper-class, old-money frown spoke reams to Daniel. 'Yes, I do hate it,' he told Lily. 'But my wife is so very good at what she does. Bound up in it, you see.'

'That answers my question. Do you worry about Gloria?'

'No, Lily, why should I? She's old enough to look after herself.'

Lily grunted. 'She's a child inside, Daniel. That is her strength, never to grow up.'

'She is powerful and she can be cruel.'

'Because she knows what has to be done.' Lily shook her head. 'She is making her way in a man's world. But you are her strength too, Daniel.' She patted his knee, such a Gloria gesture that for a moment he felt disorientated.

'Am I her strength? I wish I could believe that.' He looked jealously at Hugo Handley.

'Gloria loves her marriage,' Lily said simply. She lifted her stick in welcome as Gloria came over. 'I was just bending your husband's ear.'

Grinning, Gloria wiped her forehead with the heel of her palm. 'Whew, I'm boiled. Did yer know the salmon never turned up?' A woman dressed like a man in collar and tie, wearing rough tweeds with poacher pockets, sauntered up. Gloria kissed her, introduced her as someone terribly influential; nobody caught her name. Gloria pushed her in the direction of someone else and returned trailing Hugo. Daniel was still sitting beside Lily looking glum, and there was no response from him. Hugo tried to look rakish and commanding.

'Come on, Daniel,' Gloria said, kicking his foot and trying to cheer him up, 'everyone's come 'ere ter see yer.'

'They've come to see the great Gloria Fox,' Daniel said. Hugo was openly diplomatic. 'I'll buzz off and see if I can't rustle up that salmon for you, Gloria.'

'I can't stand that man,' Daniel said, watching the hall door close behind Hugo.

'Neither can I!' Gloria tucked a canapé into her mouth.

'You make it so obvious.'

'Yer, my love,' Gloria said, patting his head, 'are not a woman. An' if yer fink I find that fat bloater dishy, yer got another fink coming.'

'Excuse me,' Lily said, struggling to rise, 'I know you two enjoy arguing in public—'

'Sit down, Lily,' Daniel said, 'we're sorry.' Annie forced her way through the crush with Lily's glass of punch.

'Sorry,' she said, 'I spilt it.' Gloria saw Hugo beckon from the door and went over.

'The telephone,' Hugo said, with a jerk of his head. He had found the salmon and had two waiters in tow.

'I'll deal with it.' Gloria went to the booth in the hall. ''Oo's that?'

A girl's sobbing voice said, 'It's me, ma'am, Beatrice.'

It was on the tip of Gloria's tongue to say she didn't know any Beatrice, then she remembered plump Bea, Annie's Norland nanny. 'Bea, wot's up wiv yer? Yer sound awful.' A cold hand closed on Gloria's heart. 'It's not the kids, is it?'

'It's their father, ma'am.'

'Bob? Bob's not 'urt, is 'e?'

'He is dead, ma'am.'

Annie's husband Bob had fallen under a late motor-bus outside London Bridge Station, half an hour from home. Gloria put down the earpiece. Her hand couldn't make it hang up properly so she just left it swinging there.

Gloria opened the door. She didn't mean to go in, but at once Annie's eyes met her own across the crowded room.

Gloria didn't breathe. She ran all the way to Annie and held her as tight as she could. Annie trembled: she knew.

'How shall I tell the children where their father is?' Annie said in a lost voice.

Six months later that feeling of loss, though it was her sister's not her own, had not left Gloria. Annie had recovered quickly, the funeral was quick and businesslike – a carriage with glass sides but not too much show – even then the war had been changing the way all of them felt about death, and these days it had become a very quiet industry. No tears or wailing mourners, the great displays of the early days were gone and people felt they should hide their grief inside themselves. Even mourning black was going out of fashion.

Annie, with a simple black armband, her young children beside her with uncomprehending faces, had shed a tear at the graveside. The minister had hurried off, he had a dozen other funerals; the mourners, a few soldiers on leave, glanced at their wristwatches, accustomed to death; Bob's friends from the library had to hurry back to work. The sun flickered through the bare trees. Bob's mother had arrived, a kind-looking woman Gloria had never met, her own family insulating her.

On the Simmonds side, Mum and Dad were supporting Annie – Bert in Leibig's purple and gilt, with cropped silver hair now and an assertive pot-belly, standing first on one

439

leg then the other to favour his veins. Young Bill had volunteered before he was conscripted and was now a driver-mechanic somewhere in France, and Albert apparently drove a locomotive for the Great Western Railway, had got married and lost touch. Mrs Simmonds, underdressed to the point of ostentation – for Gloria's benefit, Gloria was sure – glanced at her eldest daughter across the grave as if she was looking at something the cat had brought in. Then Mum, towing Dad, gave an ostentatious, tearful kiss and a sobbing hug to Annie, but cast not even a nod of acknowledgement in Gloria's direction. Even Gloria's success, no doubt, was held against her by those two, and they probably distrusted Annie for having joined the enemy's camp. Everything that had ever gone wrong in their little world they probably blamed on Gloria. Perhaps they believed that, but for Gloria, they would have spent the last day of little Jack's life with him, and maybe he wouldn't have died. Gloria had done so well – but there was more to life than money, said Mum's speaking glance, with a sniff for Gloria's clothes and arty manners, and especially her big red Lanchester behind her. Big cars and chauffeurs were unpatriotic, the National Organising Committee for War Savings had said so, and to set an example to his staff Mr Leibig, Dad's guv'nor, had had his Rolls-Royce garaged on blocks and the wheels removed. Mum thrust her arm through Dad's, towing him away.

'Yer can 'ave as much time off work as yer want,' Gloria told Annie, 'yer know that.'

'I want to come back at once,' Annie said fiercely. She tousled the hair of Edward, her eldest, nearly six and already taller than her waist. 'Bea is so fond of them. I want to bury myself in my work.' She looked up appealingly. 'You do understand, don't you?'

'Yes,' Gloria said, 'I understand.'

That was the trouble, she understood all too well. She thought Annie was making the wrong decision, throwing herself into her work instead of her children. Yet Gloria told herself she would have done the same thing ... she *would* have done, but perhaps would not do so now. Her business life was sufficiently successful that every day was not a battle for survival, and Daniel dealt with all the daily worries of supply, production and financial control: he was a superb manager. And Daniel was right, Gloria had decided, in his distaste for her splashy parties – as right as Mum's disapproval of her gleaming Lanchester. On impulse she had it mothballed by the local garage and let her chauffeur go to the war. Her parties would no longer be purely for business, now they would carry the veneer of some fundraising effort or other: raising money for warm flying clothes for the poorer pilots of the Royal Flying Corps, sending out free cosmetics for nurses and the Women's Legion in France.

It was a strange situation: she had worked so hard for what she had achieved, could buy anything she desired; but now that she had everything Gloria was left with a feeling not of gain but of loss. Annie was missing her children growing up because she was working for Gloria. Her parents were passing into old age alone. Gloria looked around her, trying to see with fresh eyes what was really happening to them all. Incredibly, without her noticing, even Daniel had changed. In his forty-fourth year his hair was losing its gingerness, softening into grey, and his forehead was higher than she recognised in the Esplanade photographs – now old photographs, she realised with a jolt, of a much younger man. She touched her own face, but that was the same – even though it was no longer quite the face she saw when she looked at herself first thing in the morning. She told herself that she still looked ten years younger than her true age. She smiled at herself in the mirror, "the smile that smiles", then dabbed at the lines.

It was a Monday morning and Gloria had a week of work in front of her. The birds had been singing outside her bedroom window since first light, at a little after four-thirty now because of Daylight Saving Time. When she went down the early post was already lying on her desk. Her appointment book was full. The phone was ringing.

She ignored it and on the spur of the moment walked outside without her coat.

And suddenly the birdsong was bright and loud. She took a deep breath. She was wearing a loose green summer dress that flowed as she walked, its hem stroking the backs of her legs soothingly. The morning was brilliantly sunny and already warm across the rooftops, the air tangy with smoke and breakfasts. She didn't know what she was doing or where she was walking, had not the faintest idea. She couldn't imagine Daniel doing this – running across the Newington Causeway even though no traffic was coming. She passed the shop windows with pleasure but no inclination to buy, then cut through the backstreets that she knew so well from those wonderful early days when she had

442

set the business up, when it had seemed that everything was possible. The housewives were kneeling in rows washing their steps, their daughters setting off for the factories. There was no sign of their brothers, who were at the war. The fathers and grandfathers had stern, withdrawn faces: the telegraph boy brought no good news these days. Gloria found herself in Zoar Street.

It had grown dirty, some of the houses boarded, the windowsills covered with bird-droppings. When Gloria knocked on the door it was answered by a maid she didn't recognise. The silly girl got flustered and finally Gloria went upstairs ahead of her. The bedroom door was open.

'Surprise,' Gloria said.

Lily looked terribly thin. She was propped up against the plumped pillows, wearing a lurid green and gold bedgown, playing solitaire instead of eating her breakfast. 'It's all right, my dear,' she beckoned, 'I've got my teeth in.' Gloria kissed her and sat on the side of the bed.

''Ow yer gettin' on? Still not eating?'

'My hips have given up,' Lily grumbled. 'They are very irritating things, my dear, hips. Don't talk to me about doctors.' Her face was immaculate, her eyes bright with the hardness Gloria liked about her. 'I suppose you've come to pinch my maid.'

Gloria chuckled and helped herself to Lily's fried bread. 'The good old days.'

'They don't come back.' Lily shifted, and her face contorted for a moment into a mask of the pain she concealed. 'You're welcome to that girl, totally useless!'

Captain Villers came from the bathroom in his trousers

and shirt with one brace dangling, shaving-soap clinging to the lobes of his ears. 'Eat your brekkers, Lily,' he grunted dotingly.

'He's more senile than I am,' Lily said happily, waving him away. 'Go and get dressed, you old fool.'

'She's a good cook though,' Gloria munched, 'crispy bacon.'

'Don't eat it all,' Lily said, alarmed.

'I'll have some of that egg, though.'

Lily dropped her cards and grabbed for the knife and fork. Gloria hung on then let go gently. 'Well?' Lily said.

'Well wot?'

'You come here just to eat my breakfast?' Lily asked around her mouthful of egg, eating obediently.

'I've taken the day off.'

Lily swallowed. 'What's wrong, then?'

'Maybe it's that time of life.' Gloria picked up a rasher of bacon and ate half of it without thinking. 'Sometimes I wonder if it's worth it.'

'What?'

'Everyfink.'

'That's my last rasher,' Lily said hungrily. Her lips trembled. 'Oh God, Gloria, you fool. He's an *old* fool—' she gestured at Villers's door with her fork – 'now you're a young fool. Everyone's a fool but me. Of course it's worth it!'

'I don't feel so young any more.'

'You're a spring chicken from where I'm sitting. I wish *I* was your age again, I can tell you!' Lily snatched at the bacon but Gloria twirled it out of sight behind her fingers.

'Yer can 'ave it only if yer eat every last mouthful,' she said.

'I'm *starving*,' bleated Lily. 'All right, promise. You're the cunningest woman I've ever met, Gloria Fox. You always get what you set your sights on.'

'Your maids.'

'Wealthy women all, now,' Lily said. 'Jenny and Claire wouldn't be on a thousand a year if they'd stayed here with me.'

'They might have been 'appier. I don't know they're 'appy. But Carys is, yer remember 'er? She done well, was goin' up, then fell in love wiv a Welsh lad, married, opted out. Followed 'im back ter the Rhondda, now they're living 'appy as sandflies in a two-up, two-downer wiv I don't know 'ow many kids running all over the place.'

Lily swallowed. 'Are you really so very sad, Gloria?'

'Do I look sad?'

'You look exactly how one expects a woman in your position to look. Healthy. Beautiful. In control of yourself.'

'That's Gloria fer yer – done everyfink right, got everyfink everyone wants, ain't I?'

'Have you, Gloria?'

'Thanks fer the eats,' Gloria said. She slapped her knees and got up, then bent down and kissed Lily's cheek.

'Have you, Gloria?' Lily murmured.

Gloria walked to the river. The sun was very hot now. Across the oily water the outlines of the government buildings were softened, swathed in steel nets like spiders' webs against the threat of bombing from Zeppelin airships.

She could see volunteers clustered high on the platform of the Monument, their telescopes turned to the east even though the day was so lovely; an east wind like this was a Zeppelin wind, blowing them over from Germany, and then the usual westerly would reassert itself to blow them home. Motor-omnibuses rattled here, there and everywhere, you never saw horse-drawn 'buses these days, Gloria realised, they were part of history already. So were many of her memories – it seemed the world was driven onward pell-mell, changing too quickly, there was already so much she didn't recognise. She walked past St Saviour's, now a cathedral, and up the steps beyond. Pausing on the stone landing where Tib had died, she continued upwards to London Bridge. The prostitutes, many of them foreign refugees, had gathered around the entrance to London Bridge Station to pounce on a returning trainload of servicemen.

A man walking down the pavement from the bridge threw her an amused glance. She stared after him. She felt the blood rush through her.

She had seen Jamie Reilly.

Chapter Twenty-six

It couldn't be him. There were millions of people in London; you never saw anyone unless you were looking for him.

Yet he was Jamie Reilly to the life.

He must have changed more than this – that dark hair, straight and unfashionably long, almost to his shoulders, was just as she remembered. But she hadn't thought of him for years – had she? Gloria stared after his tall, broad-shouldered figure ambling, *loping* into the crowd, which seemed to separate in front of him. A way of walking, of affecting people, of *being*, couldn't lie. That glance in his eyes hadn't lied, any more than her own could. He had known her for who she was. His lips had moved, saying her name. Gloria.

Gloria thought desperately of how much time had passed. Sixteen years ago they had been children – different people, surely. Now they were grown up to be adults, with long lives and different experiences behind them, and they and everything had changed.

Except that everything about Jamie was the same. He'd lost the threadbare donkey-jacket, frayed trousers and cracked fourth-hand boots with clay on them – she remembered him in her mind's eye as clearly as she was looking at him now: but now he was wearing a tweed shooting-jacket with big useful pockets – who wore a shooting-jacket in the centre of London, for God's sake? Long leather boots almost to the knee, highly polished but strongly made, as though for a farmyard rather than the metalled streets of the City.

The crowd closed behind him and Gloria had lost her opportunity.

She knew what she must do.

She must turn her back on him, run back down the steps off the bridge, forget she had seen him. Walk around for a while to get a grip on her feelings, then go home to the office. She could still do a full afternoon's work. She and Daniel had their routine.

If she followed Jamie anything might happen.

Gloria ran after him through the crowd, pushing aside their dull faces, running down Long Southwark. The Tabard Inn was under a mess of scaffolding for repairs, but she glimpsed Jamie turning under the archway. By the time she reached it he was gone. Gloria stopped, appalled. The galleried court was a builder's yard, baulks of timber everywhere, some of the balcony support-beams being cut away by chippies with saws and chisels and replaced. Tilers were at work amidst the ancient cranky rooflines, stripping off rotten pantiles and dropping them into the yard with cries of 'Below!' where they exploded like bombs; Gloria's shoes crunched across the fragments as she made her way to the inn's entrance. It being the lunchtime drinking period, the usual women were waiting around the door, in the shade of the gallery, for their men to come out. They thought Gloria was coming to join them, then stared at her when she went in alone.

The windows were as small as Gloria remembered, with warped panes, and the scaffolding platforms outside cut out even more of the light. The first door led to stairs rising into gloom, a hallway that twisted and turned out of sight. She went back and tried again, this time finding herself among tables and chairs with not a straight edge among them, under crooked adze-hewn beams. The room smelt of dust and old dark wood that had never known beeswax polish. There was a barmaid showing more breast than face, her lips a provocative crimson slash. It never ceased to amaze Gloria what men found attractive. The barmaid eyed Gloria up and down.

''Ooever yer lookin' fer, ducky, yer won't find 'im 'ere.'

Gloria ducked into the next room, and there he was.

Jamie Reilly was leaning against the bar with one foot on the worn brass rail, his elbows on the counter. From the way he was standing she could see the taut line of his thighs in his breeches, and the vent in the shooting jacket revealed the curve of his bottom into his slim waist. He was joking with Mr Wittle, the landlord, whose overhanging face seemed made of rusty red iron. A blotched white towel thrown over his shoulder, Wittle was still rumbling with amusement at something Jamie had said, but the watchful look in his eyes changed not at all. Women, except for the busty barmaid, did not come into his inn alone, and never,

ever, women without coats, like Gloria. Jamie didn't look round, but his laughter abruptly stopped as he sensed her.

'I knew ye'd find me one day at last, Gloria,' he said, his back still to her, and she realised he was looking at her in the mirror behind the rows of bottles.

'It's really yer?' She tried not to sound foolish and lost as he turned slowly towards her. 'Do yer remember me?'

'Every night of me life, Gloria, for ye stole me heart when we were children.'

'We can't start talking like this at our age,' she said.

He held out his hands, hot and hard from the sun. But he only took her gently and guided her to a bar stool. She had dropped her handbag. He picked it up and put it in her lap. She couldn't take her eyes away from him.

''Tis an offence under the Defence of the Realm Act,' he murmured, 'for me to buy ye a drink.'

'If she's not wiv yer, she's out on 'er arse,' Wittle rumbled, 'or it's the lounge fer yer, me luv.'

'Port,' Gloria said.

'I'll vouch for her.' Jamie spoke without looking at Wittle, only at Gloria. 'Vintage Dow's. Two glasses.' They sat watching each other. Wittle heaved up a trapdoor and went thumping down into the cellar, leaving them alone. Tiles crashed distantly in the courtyard.

'Vouch fer *me*,' Gloria said. 'Where did a bloke like yer learn about Dow's?'

'Ye've still not quite lost yer snobbery against me, it seems, Gloria. 'Twas part of the pleasure for ye, wasn't it? Defiance. Ye just didn't want to do what ye were told.'

She needed to talk of real things. 'I lost everyfink fer yer.'

'I came back an' ye were gone.'

She said suddenly: 'I'm still in love wiv yer, Jamie.'

He said nothing as footsteps sounded from below. Wittle came up, grunting, wiping his face on the towel, then slammed the lid. He held out a bottle white with cobwebs for Jamie's approval. Jamie paid with a pound note and took the uncorked bottle and glasses to a table by the window. He gestured her amiably into the bench seat opposite his, only the narrow table between them. Holding the bottle by the neck with proper manners to fill her glass, he looked at her with that amused glance. 'Good health to ye. Live dangerously.' He sipped, then unbuttoned his jacket because they were sitting in the sun.

She was having a drink together with Jamie Reilly. Gloria could hardly believe it. She wanted to hold his hands and squeeze everything out of him, all he'd been doing. 'Wot yer bin up ter all this time? Wot 'appened ter yer? Yer look so well an' so ... *cared* fer.' Her heart thumped. 'Did yer marry someone else?'

'Have ye still got it?'

She reached inside her dress and pulled out the coin he had given her so long ago. It rotated slowly on its chain in the sunlight, sending silver flashes into her eyes.

'So much happens,' he said, putting down his glass. 'Our lives are so short. I'm never sorry I gave it ye, Gloria. 'Tis thy own for ever.'

'An' still yers.'

These words were awful, intoxicating. They were talking like lovers. She hoped it wasn't just the port, she never wanted it to stop: this moment by the window with the frames casting sun and shadows down their faces and over the rough wood between them, and the talisman of his feelings for her flashing like a beacon. Suddenly he laughed with her.

'Aye, ye're the same starry-eyed Gloria Simmonds ye always were.'

'Gloria Fox.'

'Aye, I know that.'

'No, yer don't know anyfink about me now.' She stopped because she sounded so odd saying that; so obviously telling a lie. She told him anxiously, 'I ran after yer, that day.'

'I know,' he said. 'I knew ye would.'

'But yer knew I'd turn back.'

'Ye're a girl of spirit, yet of common sense too.'

'But I nearly didn't.' She raised her eyebrows. 'I very nearly didn't.'

'Now ye do frighten me,' he said.

She rubbed his tweed cuff between her fingertips. 'Yer did well wivout me, up north. I'm pleased.'

'Aye, money makes me respectable even in the English community these days.' With his little finger he pointed at the builder's sign outside the window: S. Reilly & Sons, Building Factors. ''Tis a piece of nostalgia now. Seamus, me father, died soon after we started.'

'I'm sorry. I liked 'im.'

''Twas his great heart. I an' me fine brothers, Fergus an' Declan, built up the business with sheer muscle. The dear fellows had not a brain between them, 'twas all for the contest of it with them, they had their fun. I bought the lads out years ago when I moved the business back to London. There's always work here. But they set up happily again on their own, and there they still are, digging up the streets of Hull for gas-pipes when they get the work, repairing driveways when they don't, drinking in the pub in the evenings, then home to their mother.'

'She's still alive?'

'They never die, do they?'

'An' the first girl yer fell in love wiv? Wot about 'er?'

He refilled her glass.

'I married a kind and gentle lass whom I would not hurt for the world, Gloria, an' she is the mother of my children.'

Gloria swallowed loudly. 'I see.' She wanted to ask politely how many and whether they were boys or girls, but she wouldn't trust her voice.

'I married her because in the dark her flesh is ye.'

'Jamie, we're both married. We can't talk.'

'When I touched her, I touched ye. When I loved her, I loved ye. She was hurt by a fall a couple of years after we were wed . . .'

'Don't make me feel like this.'

'My love for ye is greater than thine for me, Gloria. Why do ye lie to thyself?'

'I don't. I know wot I feel. I do love yer, I always 'ave.'

'Ye never see me, Gloria.'

She stared at him. 'Wot yer talkin' about?'

Jamie pressed his hand over her own on the silver talisman, hiding it beneath them. 'Ye mean ye really don't know? A dozen times ye've walked almost into me, ye were close enough to touch. I was the man buying something in a chemist's shop, ye brushed past an' I breathed ye, I felt the warmth of ye. But ye ignored me an' so I let ye go by. Once I was looking at ye plainly out of a cab window, but ye wouldn't see me. I came out of a dining-room pulling on me coat an' ye literally walked around me – ye hands full of bags an' samples an' I don't know what else, ye mind was a million miles away. At a Rotary dinner I heard someone call to ye across a room – Gloria is not such a very common name,' he said mildly. 'Not every girl is named Gloria, now, is she?'

'Yer making me feel terrible.'

'Good,' he said, 'Gloria Fox.'

'I bin married fer twelve years.'

'An' I for eleven.'

'Oh Gawd, Jamie.'

'I saw thy face in the newspaper photographs. Ye are older, Gloria, but the same.' He didn't mention how much plumper she was – maybe, she wondered, she wasn't, except in her own mind. 'There's no need for that stuff on thy face, ye have nothing to hide from me. Ye are still beautiful. Still hot.'

'It's all right fer a man. Yer 'aven't changed at all, Jamie.'

'I haven't changed because thy feelings about me haven't changed.'

Suddenly she tried to pull her hand away. 'We can't go on like this, we're not still children.'

He let her go. She glared at him, rubbing her hand. There came a sound from outside of sliding rooftiles crashing in the yard. Another emergency, she saw. Someone coming running for Jamie.

'Only one thing lasts for ever,' he said, without even a glance at the window. 'What I am feeling now.'

She ducked her head through the chain.

'Love,' he said. 'I am in love with ye always.' He put his finger to the spinning coin, setting it to rest. He did not even touch her. 'Ye are still mine.'

She denied it.

Gloria was afraid to go back to her house in Trinity Church Square. She couldn't behave normally, Daniel would know everything. The phone would ring in her office; it might be Jamie. She kept looking behind her as she walked down the High Street, as though part of her was sure she would see Jamie coming after her, but of course she did not. She stopped and turned. The pavement was empty but for the vacant faces of shoppers, cursing men unloading casks from a brewer's dray, the echoing shrieks of a costerwoman selling tomatoes. Gloria would not let herself look back again, made herself walk along the shop windows of Newington Causeway as though nothing had happened. She went into Dunn's the tailors and bought the first thing that came to hand, a shooting stick.

'Present fer yer,' she told Daniel, poking her head around his office door.

'Where have you been!' He stood up putting his hands to his head with relief. 'I've been worried sick about you, darling. What on earth's this?'

'It's a shooting-stick. All gentlemen 'ave 'em. Yer open it up an' sit on it.'

He examined the label, looking baffled. 'Thank you.

This is what you've been doing all day? Shopping at Dunn's?'

She had to tell him the truth. 'Daniel, somefink's 'appened!'

At once he put his arm around her as though she needed help to the chair. 'There, there. You weren't nearly run down or something awful?' He rang for tea. 'The speed those motors tear along the Causeway—'

'I met an old friend an' 'e bought me a drink.'

Daniel laughed. 'Really! Then he has made himself liable for a one hundred pound fine or six months in jail. He must be an admirer.'

'Obviously.'

Daniel had gone back to his papers. Now he looked up with a frown. 'It's not that frightful Hugo Handley, is it? I don't know what you see in him.'

'I don't see nuffink in 'im.'

'If you say so. I get the impression that he sees something in *you*.'

'That's not my fault. Daniel, won't yer come upstairs wiv me?'

He glanced at his wristwatch – all men wore wristwatches these days, as if they were officers in the trenches at least in spirit. 'It's half-past three in the afternoon, why should we want to go upstairs?'

'There's somefink I got ter show yer.'

He told his secretary to hold his calls and followed Gloria upstairs, mystified, into her bedroom. She shut the door decisively behind him and he looked around the flowery wallpaper he disliked, the lush scalloped headboard of her bed like a seashell in pink velvet, her frilly pale pink pillows. He stood by the bench-seat in the window which meant nothing to him, looking down at the apple tree in the garden.

'Well, Gloria? What is this new item of decoration you have bought?'

She slipped off her shoulder-straps and let her dress and petticoats slide to the floor, giving a wiggle of her hips at the appropriate moment to help them on their way. The material made an electric hiss on her bare skin. She was wearing one of the new brassières and Daniel stared at its unfamiliarity. She had never undressed in front of him before. He watched as she sat back on the window-seat, one elbow on her silken knee, brassy sunlight in her hair and the last of the apple blossom behind her.

'Are yer going ter make me do it all?' she asked.

Daniel took off his jacket. 'Always happy to oblige,' he said, falling on her with self-conscious animal noises, trying to give her what he thought she wanted.

He slept afterwards – he always did – but this time she did not. Gloria knew that she had failed him, she had not kept her promise. She could not show him what she really felt, because at heart she did not love him. Poor Daniel! He did not realise what he was missing.

Chapter Twenty-seven

A girl's got ter get wot she wants in the world, thought
Gloria, *even if the world don't like it!*

. There was only one man, in all her life, that Gloria had
loved.

The more she saw Jamie, the less guilty she felt. When
she was with Jamie everything was all right. She felt so
alive, that was all: young again. Nothing 'happened',
neither of them wanted it to at first. What they had, they
knew, was love; not desire or sentiment or habit, or even
kindness: they were in love, they had always been. Each
had led their own full life hidden from the other, but what
they felt when they were together was different and
precious, worth any price, and neither of them wanted to
spoil that. And yet she loved the danger: she might hurt
Daniel.

She couldn't help doing silly things just to hold Jamie's
hands, anywhere close to the Tabard, by the river, or
running risks to meet him for an hour in the London Bridge
Station canteen over a cheese sandwich. Once for an
excuse she arranged to have her hair done in the
hairdresser's next to the station baths, and arrived early.

She could tell from his eyes that Jamie had been thinking about what might happen to them: his firm's contract to renovate the Tabard would soon be complete. 'Though the only way to renovate that old dump properly,' he joked, wiping crumbs from the table with the flat of his hand, 'would be to knock it down.'

Away from her, Gloria knew, Jamie was an astonishing personality, and she had watched him storming up and down the yard, shouting up to the men on the roof how things should be properly done, helping out with any task going, lifting beams of timber into place, as at ease with a theodolite as with a hammer in his hands; and that soft lilty voice of his, with a kind of deep burr running beneath it, was as at home whispering lover's nothings in her ear as yelling curses at his men. He was rough and hard with them when he didn't get his way, those practical boots caked to the knee with clay, his fists shoved in the pockets of his shooting-jacket showing his knuckles through the tweed. Yet he could turn it off as soon as his back was turned on them, with a smile and a wink of his eye for her. He always noticed Gloria arriving, and looked at her in the way she wanted.

His wife, Gloria thought sadly, was a lucky woman to have the devotion of such a man.

Gloria's life could have been with him. Now it could never be. She had to hide what she felt from Daniel, and Jamie must lie to his own wife, Letty, too.

'All's for the best, mavourneen,' he told her tenderly, running his finger along the strong line of Gloria's jaw, then touched her high, determined cheekbones with his callused thumb. 'We've been successful apart, my love. Perhaps we wouldn't be together.'

'Why d'yer say that?'

'Always be fighting, we would, an' 'twould fill me with sadness, to watch ye slip away. I learned loyalty from me father, see, Gloria, an' I'd hurt ye if I left, an' hurt ye if I stayed.'

'That's rich,' Gloria said, dabbing her eye with the back of her glove, 'the only man I love I can't keep.'

One day she stood on the pavement opposite the inn, watching without a word. She was supposed to be on her way somewhere else. The workmen finished packing up the last of the scaffold-pipes into an open lorry, then drove off in a cloud of blue smoke. No sign of Jamie: only the silence of the early morning. Then he came out from the yard and waved, crossed the road and touched her hand. She thought the inn's terracotta roof tiles looked unnaturally new and orange, and told him so, but he assured her the sun and soot would soon wear them in. 'In a year no one will know I've been here,' he joked.

'Yer done a beautiful job,' she agreed.

But *she* would know.

The old green van he used came clattering round and he jumped aboard, hardly looking at her, only with their secret wink, hardly more than a flutter of their eyelashes; they couldn't show their feelings in a way anyone else would know. Gloria stayed watching the inn, half mad with frustration. She saw Jamie in everything, the tilted chimneys that had been in danger of falling were now, she knew, shored up by galvanised steel girders concealed in the weather-worn brick, and Jamie had made a hundred other tiny changes. To her mind *he* would always be here, and part of them would always be drinking that bottle of port in the sun by the window, here at the Tabard Inn where he had been born: Tilly O'Neill's place, where she had died screaming in childbirth. He must have taken on the job deliberately at a loss, but a proper job he had made of the Tabard. He was keeping alive a memory of the woman he had never met, his mother.

Mr Wittle – she could imagine his crafty blue eyes glinting totally without understanding – must have thought he'd found a prize fool in Jamie.

Gloria turned away with a sigh, sparing hardly a glance for the old chemist's shop where she had met Daniel. The laboratory had been moved to more modern premises years ago and the place was being rented by a hop merchant.

Although he talked little about his work and less about his money, she had soon realised that Jamie wasn't afraid to be a fool. He could afford to lose now and then. His firm was taking over as main contractor on the Lombard Street resurfacing works – she had begun noticing building sites with eagle eyes these days, and there were lots more he never talked about. That was another different thing about the way they were when they were together – all they were interested in was each other, not business or the rest of their lives, only the here and now between them was real. She knew what must happen.

Gloria thought she was going into it with her eyes open,

and as a place they could meet she suggested the old loft above the stables in Bermondsey, converted into a flat for Jenny Rouse long ago and now long deserted. The bare wooden stairs were very steep and he could not wait until they reached the top, pulling her back on to him half-way, covering her face with kisses just as he used to, and then she slipped down, giving herself to the moment: he made her so aware of what she was doing that she almost screamed, as if she had really never acknowledged herself before, feeling only his fingers and the flats of his hands, his sinewy arms and legs and the heat around his cock.

'Ow, yer given me splinters in me bum,' she told him off afterwards, but then hugged him tight. 'Yer fergiven.'

Soon it seemed so natural for them, sleeping together in bed in the afternoons, for the precious hour or two that was the climax of all the risks they were taking, the deceiving of all the friends and family who were closest to them and cared most about them. 'Ye are my vampire,' Jamie whispered softly to her face beneath his, 'with ye I find myself sleeping in the daylight, an' ye take my life's blood.'

'Yer give it,' she said.

'Aye, willingly I'll give ye all of me.'

'Then take me.'

'No,' he chided her, 'give yeself.'

They lay together, lips pressed tight, hardly breathing, then panted in unison. Gloria never could give anything without giving it all. 'Ye look different when I'm inside ye,' Jamie marvelled, caressing her brassy curls framed by the cool winter sunlight. 'Gloria, 'tis so lovely an' sad. I'm the only one who sees ye as ye really are.'

* * *

But when she was not with Jamie, which felt like it was nearly all the time, Gloria *did* feel guilty, and the more she saw of her loyal husband, the guiltier she felt. Winter was bound to keep her at home with Daniel more, and for several months she saw Jamie not at all. In a way it was a relief: she buried herself in her work with a harder edge, taking decisions, motivating people, manipulating them, rushing on as her career demanded, she could not stop even if she wanted to – most bankers thought that a woman couldn't run a company, Gloria Fox Limited would never have raised loans in the City but for Daniel's half-share – and if a firm wasn't expanding, the banking community presumed it to be in decline. She must post higher profits each year, yet always in the midst of this frantic activity was the quiet, secret place at the back of her mind for Jamie, and even Daniel.

During the few moments of relaxation in her working day she began to realise the full extent of her power over them, and her responsibility towards them.

For the first time in her life she was making the rules in a man's world. By dividing, she realised, she had conquered. Instead of being manipulated by the ruling sex, she had alternatives. Daniel could not hurt her – the most of her he owned was half her company, and anything Jamie did, he would do for love.

She went into Daniel's office. Faye, his pale, wispy secretary, was rattling away on the old Royal typewriter in her room next to the stairs. Gloria came up behind him and draped her arms over his neck, knowing he would yawn.

Daniel would probably talk to her about the doubling of income tax, or supertax, or the surcharge on unearned income from their shares in the company, which as her husband he was liable for. But his mind was far away, and he did not respond to her at all. 'I wish yer'd cheer up,' she said, lifting the industry report out of his hands. It was in a foreign language. 'Wot's this?'

He shook himself back to the present. 'You really want to know?'

'Would I ask yer if I didn't?'

He shrugged. 'A research chemist in Paris has succeeded in synthesising and stabilising perfumes. He is reportedly developing a commercial formula with Gabrielle Chanel, the clothes designer.'

'Boy's jerseys? Wot does she know about perfume?'

'The point about a synthetic perfume is that it would no longer be dependent on flower scents, which fade so rapidly on the flesh, but could be made to last as long as the designer wished.'

'Doesn't sound profitable.'

'The research is expensive but the cost of ingredients is probably negligible, and one would be able to charge very much more for such a unique product.'

'Not ready for mass production, is it?'

'No, not yet.'

'Keep an eye on it, won't yer. I didn't even know yer spoke French.'

'That doesn't surprise me. There's rather a lot about me you don't know, I expect.' She regarded him seriously. Still he hadn't yawned, or looked her in the eye. She made to go but Daniel grabbed her wrist, holding her as lightly as he could. 'I know you're seeing him,' he said without lifting his head.

Gloria's throat closed and she felt a sensation almost of terror. It was such a basic fear, being found out. Amazingly, her voice came without a tremor. ''Oo are we talking about?'

'Hugo Handley, of course.'

Gloria drew a deep breath, trying to hide her relief.

'I know you can probably account for your movements. You're no fool,' Daniel said evenly. 'He has no respect for me, Gloria, and I thought you and I had an arrangement at least of mutual respect.'

'We do.'

'Why *him*, for goodness' sake? I thought you had better taste than that. He's such a swine, the sort of man other men see through in a single glance,' Daniel said bitterly, 'but women always fall for that type with his genial, roué, man-of-the-world looks. He's been deliberately trying to break us up with those gifts of flowers, his life-and-soul-of-the-party act, humiliating me—'

''Ave yer quite finished?'

'No. Because he'll never stop. He despises me because you are the only woman I have ever wanted, the only woman I have ever cared for. And you deliberately set us against one another.'

'D'yer really care about me?' she asked throatily.

'Can't you see!'

'There's nothing between me and 'Ugo 'Andley. I promise yer that.'

Daniel bowed his head in acquiescence. If she said so, he believed her. Gloria pressed her fingers to her mouth, knowing how little she deserved his faith in her. 'Yer a lovely man, Daniel,' she acknowledged. It trembled on the tip of her tongue to confess to him about Jamie, but she could not face losing the only love she had known, not even for Daniel. ''Ugo's finished.'

Trembling with relief that Daniel had fixed on the wrong man, she picked up his telephone and listened, absent-mindedly rubbing lipstick from her fingertips, then spoke when the operator came on. 'Get me Avenue two-nine-six-one, please, luv.'

Daniel covered the mouthpiece. 'What are you doing?'

'Somefink I should've sorted right at the start. I'm going ter tell 'Ugo 'Andley I'm cancelling all 'is contracts. E-vap-o-rate.'

'But that'll drive him out of business!' Daniel hesitated. 'You can't be so hard.'

'Believe me,' Gloria said, white-faced but without a flicker of expression.

Though Jamie, two years older than her at thirty-six, was well within the call-up limit for married men younger than forty-one, he was again turned down because of his childhood scarlet fever. 'Yer'll 'ave ter wear thick glasses in yer old age,' Gloria nudged him, so glad to see him again that she felt like being silly. She ran her fingernail down his nose and he opened one deep brown eye. 'Take yer boots off,' she said, wanting him to be comfortable, 'put 'em up on the sofa.' They weren't making love today but she felt as close to him as ever, making tea for him, unlacing his knotted boots. Only one thing about him had changed from long ago: he walked silently these days, no longer needing to draw attention to himself, and had crept up on her despite the leaves scattered on the pavement: he was as quiet in those boots as most men in rubber-soled shoes. 'Hallo, stranger.' He'd spent most of the summer building homes on the Metropolitan Railway's Grange estate among the beechwoods of Metro-land, then overseeing the construction of a Railway viaduct out by the Edgware Way, which, she decided, taking the teacups over to him, was probably just as well. She had broken with Hugo purely to save her relationship with Jamie, and she had frightened herself by being prepared to go so far. She told herself she had no regrets, Hugo had no doubt richly deserved his come-uppance. But next time, she might have to choose between Daniel and Jamie, and the thought had terrified her.

Plumping herself down on the sofa, she propped Jamie's feet on her lap.

'What's the matter?' he asked, opening his other eye. 'Trouble, is it?'

'Only that Daniel trusts me. I feel like a traitor but I can't be anything else.'

He pulled his boots back on. 'Aye, 'tis the shame of it,' he said miserably, 'Letty trusts me too.'

She looked out of the window. 'I wish there was no pain and nuffink was wrong in the world, but sometimes it seems like everyfink is, an' we can't do nuffink right whatever we do.'

'I can't not see ye again now I'm with ye,' Jamie said. 'I'd curl up an' die without ye. Without the hope of ye.'

She squeezed his hand affectionately. 'There we go again. Talking like we're seventeen years old.'

'We're right,' he said simply. ''Tis not sex we have, 'tis love.' But her grip was tightening now and he stared at her. 'What is it, mavourneen? What's wrong?' Her eyes widened and he scrambled to the window, his hand on her shoulder. 'By Jesus!' he exclaimed.

'Is it one of ours?'

They could hear the buzzing drone of the engines now, the airship above them looking as big as a cloud drifting among the other clouds in the October sky. Gloria craned her head to see. 'Get away from the glass!' Jamie dragged her back, wrapped his arms round her shoulders. There was a bang from somewhere in the direction of London Bridge Station, sounding as harmless as a firework going off.

''Tis a super-Zeppelin,' Jamie murmured in her hair. 'The lads said there was a raid last night, three got through but maybe a dozen more were spied over the Channel. This fellow's a lost sheep, 'tis all.' They jerked as another thudding explosion came, heavier this time and closer, then several more marching slowly away from them across the red rooftops towards the Newington Causeway and Camberwell. Little puffs of very black smoke came up, trailing white dust.

'Doesn't look much,' she said.

'White mortar, wall-plaster an' brickdust. People's homes.'

She gripped him tight. 'Daniel's working at 'ome over that way!'

Jamie understood what she was feeling. 'Ye better go an' look after him, Gloria. Ye never would forgive yeself if he was hurt and ye were not there.'

She grabbed her coat and flew down the stairs. Trinity Church Square wasn't far through the backstreets; lots of people were out staring at the sky, still carrying the implements of whatever they had been doing, women with brooms or mugs of tea, a man with dangling braces looking up with a single mouth-shaped bite taken from his sandwich, kids running around making noises like the anti-aircraft pompom guns, but the queue outside the picture theatre was already getting back together, complaining about the Hun but working out where their places in the line had been. But one old gentleman stood looking up at the clouds, his face mottled with rage. 'Bloody cheek,' Gloria heard him saying over and over. 'Bloody cheek!'

An anonymous-looking building that everyone now realised was an ASC stores was burning, but nobody knew whether the fire had been started by a bomb. A policeman redirected traffic as the fire engine arrived, then tied a dog that had got loose to a lamp-post. Trinity Church Square looked the same as ever. Gloria hurried along the pavement. Her maid was outside flirting with the accounts clerk. 'Go inside, yer idjits!' Gloria shouted furiously. She rushed inside ahead of them. Daniel looked up mildly from his desk.

'What's the matter?'

She put her hands over her heart. 'Sometimes, Daniel,' she threatened him, 'I could kick yer fer being so calm!'

He grinned. 'Yes,' he said, 'I know.' He did not look guilty – but Faye his secretary did.

What on earth could Daniel see in that thin creature, hardly an ounce of curving flesh on her, and that silly tight-waisted skirt? Faye's skin was so pale that she looked almost transparent, and in fact Gloria had hardly noticed her before. Now, outraged, she noticed every single thing about her, the way that young girl – twenty-one, twenty-two – listened attentively when Daniel spoke, nodding obediently as she jotted down notes and memoranda, looking at him sheep-eyed with admiration as though he was handing down words of wisdom instead of stock-level plans and forecasts. When she gave him papers to sign, Faye stood with one hand on his desk, her hip almost touching his shoulder. If Daniel hadn't got the message, he soon would. Gloria got rid of her and transferred Mrs Woolheft from invoices in her place.

So she did still care about Daniel.

'What was that about?' he said, baffled, but there was no answer from Gloria. 'I shall never understand the female gender!' he laughed, because he was innocent, throwing up his hands.

Gloria turned her considerable powers of determination to the business of not losing him, because next time, he might not be innocent.

She knew how far she had to fall. Without her husband, she assured herself, all her success was meaningless, because she would not have achieved anything without Daniel. He had done nothing to deserve the way she was betraying him by seeing Jamie – yet she could not stop doing that.

At almost thirty-five she could pass for twenty-five, but Gloria wanted even more.

She took a taxicab to Lady Jemima Summers's residence at Abbey Place in St John's Wood. The pebble-dash house in the morning sunlight was larger than she had expected for two semi-retired people, but Sir Henry Summers ran his consultancy from here since selling his partnership in Wigmore Street – his crouched figure, in flannel shirt and beige trousers, was knelt by a flower-bed busily planting bulbs with a trowel. He recognised Gloria and put down his pipe, observing her with sharp, thoughtful eyes. Perhaps he thought she had come for professional advice, another childless woman. He pushed his hands on his knees and got up with a grunt, a lock of nicotine-stained white hair falling over his forehead. But Gloria was saved by Jemima opening the front door herself and coming down the steps. 'Gloria is an old friend of mine,' she insisted to her husband, waving him away, 'and I'm keeping her all to myself. Get your smelly pipe off the grass before it burns in and leaves a mark. I don't know why we bother with a gardener the way you play about.'

'Please excuse Jemima,' Henry sighed, 'she's always been the same, and I don't think she'll ever change now.'

Jemima, wearing her hair scraped back into a tight silver bun that made her features seem cold and prominent, took Gloria's elbow and swept her inside. 'The garden keeps

him happy and out from under my feet,' she explained.
'Henry works only two afternoons a week these days, but
he's not reached his threescore and ten yet and that's young
for a doctor, they're only just getting into their stride by the
time they're wrinkled all over, and I warned him he'd be
wrong to sell up the practice. But he's too clever for his own
good, always was, that's why I married him.'

'Do I make yer nervous?' Gloria said.

'You're right,' Jemima said without a smile, 'I talk too
much.' She paused by a photograph of her two sons, Alex
and Gerald. Gloria knew that Gerald had been a young
Harley Street dentist with a brilliant future, but there had
been a family tragedy before the war when Alex died of
blood poisoning after a routine tooth extraction performed
by Gerald. Suddenly everything that everyone had liked
about witty, urbane Gerald was held against him, and
everyone remembered how they had always said he was the
black sheep of the family. Septicaemia was not uncommon,
but because they were brothers the popular newspapers
had a field day: Alex Summers lost his life, but Gerald had
lost his living. Jemima said nothing, leading Gloria quietly
forward through the sunlit rooms. They met from time to
time at Gloria's parties but had formed an understanding
rather than a friendship.

'I wondered when you'd come,' Jemima said.

Gloria looked around her. If the garden was his, then
obviously the inside of the house was Jemima's domain,
with dark wooden floors and cool tall ceilings, simple
furniture and beautiful rugs, modern paintings and sprays
of cut flowers. 'It's lovely,' Gloria said as they came to a

conservatory set across the back of the house, which caught the best of the morning sun. 'An' it's lovely wot yer done wiv it. 'Ow long 'ave yer lived 'ere?'

'Since I married Henry in 1873 – this year is our sapphire anniversary.' Jemima did not bother to wait for polite felicitations, sitting in a comfortable cane chair and nodding Gloria into the other. 'I was a redhead in those days. He was a medical student and you know how impoverished they are, totally useless, but his father's second marriage – he'd been made a widower a second time – had been to a woman of means, and so the house had come to Henry some two years before on his father's death. Tragically, Henry's elder brother had been killed in China, or our story might have been very different. I would have hated to be poor.' Jemima looked at Gloria steadily. 'A girl has to make her chance.'

'An' then 'ang on to it, right or wrong,' Gloria said. 'Yer did well.'

'Absolutely. Henry fell for my hair as much as me, I think.' She rang a bell. 'Elevenses? I usually have coffee at this time. Two cups, three saucers!' she ordered the maid, who bobbed and disappeared.

'Yer were brought up wiv class though,' Gloria said now that they were alone again. 'I fink that's the key to Daniel too.'

'To understanding what about Daniel?'

''Is family was rich an' fell on 'ard times. Daniel was brought up in a little chemist's shop – but his father grew up in a manor-'ouse in the country, wiv servants an' I-don't-know-wot. Daniel's never forgotten that.'

'The situation of his childhood was hardly his fault.'

'But it left him with a sense of . . . loss. Maybe all of us feel that a little bit, some more than others. That fings used ter be better than wot they are now. I was thinking about 'im in the middle of the night, Jemima, and there it was. Daniel's neither 'appy nor unhappy, 'e neither believes nor disbelieves any more. 'E's just comfortable in 'is marriage, doesn't even look at other women, just drifts along getting old. 'E's a lost man.'

'Does Daniel think this?'

'No. But 'e shows it.'

The coffee tray came and they stopped talking. Jemima waved the maid away and busied herself with the ritual of milk. As soon as she filled the third saucer a gorgeous smoky cat appeared between the plant-stems. Ignoring Gloria, she whipped her tail, deigned to accept a lick or two of milk, then curled herself up in a patch of sun.

'An' partly it's my fault too,' Gloria said, ''cause of 'oo I am. Everyone knows 'e married beneath 'im. An' everyone knows 'e depends on me now.'

'Is this your diagnosis of your husband or of your marriage?'

'I fink that's the way yer 'usband speaks ter people, ain't it?' Gloria mocked lightly. She got back to business. 'Yer know I'm speaking the truth about 'im, Jemima, 'cause yer feel it too. Yer was a child at that 'ouse—'

'Yes, Holywell Manor.'

'Yer 'ad everyfink yer wanted, didn't yer? Money an' property an' servants an' everyone in the area lookin' up ter yer. Then it all went, an' all yer was left wiv was yer posh voices an' knowing wot fish-fork ter use.'

'I see Daniel's been talking to you.'

'That's just it, 'e 'asn't. I've known this fer years – as much as Daniel could tell me, anyways – but I didn't see 'ow important it was. 'E wouldn't put it so bitter, neither, but bitter's wot 'e is. 'Owever successful 'e is, 'e'll always feel 'e's a failure.'

They sipped their coffee.

'You do care for him very deeply, despite your manner.'

''E's my 'usband.'

'We're only human, Gloria, our power to create good is very limited. And when we try we usually make things worse.'

'There's something yer should know about me,' Gloria said calmly. She put down her cup.

'What's that?'

'I never give up.'

'So I was right about you after all.' Jemima's face softened. 'You really are the girl I glimpsed in the Pilgrim's Room on your wedding day. Later, at your parties and all that nonsense, I thought you were shallow and – forgive me – a bit of brass. But I was wrong. "In Southwark at the Tabard as I lay, ready to wend on my pilgrimage to Canterbury—"'

Gloria took over without a break, '"—At night was come ter that 'ostelry nine an' twenty in a company, sundry folk, fallen on fellowship, an' pilgrims all." I never forgot wot yer said, see.'

'It was nearly half a century ago, in the Pilgrim's Room,

476

that we children realised we had lost everything.' Jemima shuddered. 'You and I still have our understanding, yes? Pax?' Her cup rattled in its saucer and she put it down with a clatter on the tiled floor. 'How have you done this to me, Gloria . . . ?'

'Tell me if I'm right about Daniel,' Gloria said.

'I'll never forget the shock of that night in 1870. I was seventeen and the last of our family when we, the seven Fox children, including Daniel's father, gathered in the Pilgrim's Room at the Tabard. Martin, Frank who went to Canada, Harold, George off to Australia, Jerome, poor Reuben. And I, the girl. We were never together again. There was almost nothing left of our father's inheritance, you see . . . Holywell was mortgaged to the hilt and repossessed, only a few mementoes of our previous lives remained – books, a few coins, a butterfly collection, happy memories. I think none of us could forget that shock of losing . . . everything. How *could* our father have done that to us, Gloria? It was our birthright. Didn't he love us at all? Our *birthright*.'

The emotional cut in her voice, and the expression of loss in her eyes, made Jemima naked to Gloria.

'Now I know wot ter do fer Daniel an' me,' Gloria said.

'But you see, there's nothing you can do. It's the past.'

''Ow about a day out in the country?'

Lady Jemima could not have looked more surprised. 'You mean, go back to Holywell? Seriously? Surely that's not possible – I'm not even sure it exists any more.'

'There's only one way ter find out,' said Gloria, producing the Bradshaw's railway guide from her handbag. 'We'll catch the Underground from Edgware Road to

London Bridge Station, and from there it's only...' She looked at Jemima for guidance, bringing her in on the project.

Lady Jemima overcame her hesitation and seized the book, but then recited the stations from memory, the little girl who in the middle years of the last century had learned them by rote: 'Spa Road, Deptford, Greenwich, Maze Hill, Combe Forest!' Now in her old age she gave a delighted clap of her hands. 'Isn't it wonderful how the names from one's childhood are remembered with a kind of magic?'

Sitting in the plush first-class compartment of the London and Greenwich Railway, looking at the rooftops passing below them as the train rattled towards the Deptford marshes, Gloria hoped the place would still be there. The locomotive had not stopped at Spa Road but passed straight through, and the conductor told them the old station had been closed down a couple of years ago. Jemima had fallen silent.

They sat looking forward through the gleaming windows, the Thames looping towards them from their left, the hills of the southern heights swooping down on their right as they approached Greenwich. It was two minutes to one as the train pulled in, and Jemima, trying to hide her dismay with cheerfulness, pointed out the sights. The brass ball was raised on the spire of the hilltop Royal Observatory in Greenwich Park, and as the train puffed out the gleaming sphere dropped, signalling one o'clock precisely to the river's shipping.

'Combe Forest!' the conductor brayed, and they hired a motor-taxi to carry them uphill. Jemima told the driver to take the old road, which was so steep that they saw one car crawling up in reverse.

'I remember fields here,' Jemima frowned, but now all the gentler slopes were covered with half-timbered semi-detached suburbs in the style of Metro-land, built by the Railway, with names like Holmdene and Oakwood. Little of the forest remained, yet the hillside was so wrinkled with dips and bumps that the effect looked pretty and countrified to Gloria's eyes, each knoll and cleft preserving its green spray of trees. 'Oh, look!' she pointed. A hollow had been made into a park with a pond and ducks on it, children were feeding them bread, and one little boy pretended to push his sister in the water. Wearing the same colour coats, they ran along beside the car, then peeled away with aeroplane noises.

'These look pretty nice places,' Gloria decided, but the older woman was silent. 'Look, there's schools an' every-fink,' Gloria said. They passed a redbrick building, the Nemeton Grammar School, near the Vaudey parish church which looked incongruously old, being set at an odd angle not parallel to the road. 'Lots of people'd love ter live round 'ere, I bet.'

'But this isn't how it was,' Jemima told her.

'I s'ppose it never is.'

'I should never have come back.' Jemima couldn't help pointing at everything that was already gone without trace – her memories of the way things had been would die with her. Except that Gloria was listening closely, and wouldn't forget what she was hearing. 'I remember a shack there, by the Mickfield, where an old man and his donkey lived. Everything was dust in the summer. The farmer used to string dead crows along that fence . . .' The Georgian village of Vaudey filled the top of the valley with a tangle of quaint streets and bow-windowed shops, stopping dead at its upper boundary as though a knife had been drawn along the rim of the bare Blackheath plateau above, or a strong wind constantly blew beyond that point. The taxi driver reached outside and heaved on his handbrake.

'Do you know Holywell Manor?' Jemima said.

He grumbled, blowing out his walrus whiskers, twisting the heavy steering wheel with an effort, letting the vehicle freewheel downhill for a way to achieve momentum, then made a shuddering turn between stone gateposts, without gates. 'Used ter be boarded up,' the driver groused in his rich Kentish accent, 'bloody kids!' He yanked on the hand-throttle and the motor clattered at full power up a weedy drive set between huge oak trees, by far the largest Gloria had ever seen. She whistled.

'It's going to be a terrible disappointment,' fretted Lady Jemima as the taxi struggled to the top of the short, steep knoll. In front of them stood a large, crumbling house with a dry fountain in front of it.

'Turn off the engine,' Gloria ordered, getting down, and the silence rushed in. She held down her hat, the hem of her dress whipping around her knees. A burst of the wind set oak-leaves roaring like the sea in the treetops below. Last year's leaves rattled in drifts, brown and shrivelled, in circles around the stone pool that the fountain was supposed to fill. A flock of birds took off around the chimneys.

'Rooks,' said Jemima. 'There's a rookery—'

'Sssh,' Gloria said.

A windowframe banged open, banged closed. The windows retaining their leaded glass were brilliant harlequin patchworks reflecting blue sky, green fields. Jemima took Gloria's elbow and pointed with her outstretched finger. Behind them was an enormous view of the City, the river a wrinkled green serpent winding between the tiny church-spires into a haze of cloud-shadows, the ring of low hills encircling the great bowl of London like cupped hands.

I'm not a stranger here, Gloria thought, *I know this place. This is my place.*

'I feel at home here,' she laughed. 'I don't know how to describe it, but I do! This is our place.'

'But it wasn't like this at all,' Jemima said.

'Oh,' said Gloria, 'I know wot ter do about that. I got just the man in mind.'

Chapter Twenty-eight

''Tis madness, of course,' Jamie said, 'but then, 'tis thy madness I love.'

Gloria patted the soft spring grass. 'Sit down beside me an' stop yer Irish jabberin'. Listen ter the wind.' She was wearing a hipless low-necked dress with its hem half-way up her legs, loops of pearls swinging casually from her neck, and Jamie had no doubt he was witnessing the leading edge of fashion. He sat, placing his brown leather boots beside her slim ankles in their white silk stockings, the side of her knee almost touching his. Taking out a pasty he broke it, giving her half. 'Lovely,' she sighed, 'still warm from the country baker's.'

''Tis warm because it has been in me pocket all the morning long, mavourneen.'

'Yer smell funny,' she said. 'Sort of mouldy-dusty.'

'Old, rotten oakwood.'

'Oh, it's not that bad.'

He glanced over his shoulder at the house. ''Tis that bad.'

Gloria was silent for a moment. Holywell was her secret. It would be her gift to Daniel: his family's house would be the home of their family. Because when it was just as it should be, it was Gloria's intention to have her child here. She made herself smile lightly.

'Remember,' she told Jamie, 'I don't want nuffink fake in there – only me!' she joked, nudging his ribs. 'Any of them lovely old beams yer absolutely got ter replace, I want it done proper an' all knobbly an' just the way it was, wiv a wot-yer-call-it.'

'Adze.' He turned back and sighed at the look in her eyes. 'I think I've lost ye to this place,' he said. ''Tis a good way to lose a fortune, too.'

'I got a fortune ter lose. I want wot can't be bought.'

'Ye are not fake,' he said. 'Gloria, ye are not.'

They sat, eating, with the southern sun warm on the back of their heads, surrounded by the scent of growing things. Gloria had lived this dream for a year – the purchase procedure from the London County Council, who had considered the place as a teacher training college but shelved that plan when the war broke out, had been a torture. Twice the council changed its mind, first at the end of the war when soldiers were returning home in a state worse than anyone had imagined, then again after the local elections. But Gloria had not wavered in her determination to buy what was, as she pointed out, nothing but a boarded-up ruin half falling down with decay, and in the end County Hall had been forced to agree.

Now Holywell, the home of the Fox family for so many years, was Gloria's. What was left of it, anyway. Thomas Snapper, her solicitor, proudly told her that he had traced these lands back to the Domesday Book, though in those days the fertile valley was called by something Latin, Valle Dei, and put down as being worth so many pigs and shillings.

Gloria brushed the pastry from her hands, watching the white flakes whirl down the slope falling away steeply below them. These spine-like knolls of steep grass and trees were a curious feature of the area, reminding her of the ones in Greenwich Park, which had a similar view, and now that she knew what to look for she saw lumps and bumps all along these northern slopes – probably cut over thousands of years, the surveyor had informed her, by rainwater running down from the heathland above to the Blackwall marshes below. He had looked over his half-glasses as if to suggest that maybe it would be the best fate for the house too. But Gloria wasn't having any nonsense about it being easier to knock down and start again from scratch. She wanted the real thing, and she knew who could give it to her, both trustworthy and discreet.

'It's not as though I needed the money,' Jamie said.

'Yer don't understand,' she told him as they walked back to the house. 'When the Fox children were forced ter leave 'ere, they took their love wiv them. Fer fifty years nobody gave a damn about the place; speculators bought it ter make a 'otel, then a golf-course, then it was going ter be knocked down fer one of them 'ousing estates, then it fell ter wrack an' ruin an' Gawd knows wot until nobody could do nuffink wiv it. All that time it 'ung on, Jamie. All that time it waited, teacher training college my arse, until the right person came along an' it was almost too late. Until all it needed was love, it was good fer nuffink else. An' 'ere,' she said fiercely, 'I am.'

'I know what ye're saying, Gloria.'

They crossed by the dry fountain and went up into the house. Workmen were stripping out trenches in the walls to install electric wiring, shiny lead plumbing, even toilets upstairs. In one front room, in an extraordinary piece of archaic workmanship that Gloria had insisted on, carpenters on their knees were malleting wooden pegs into massive floorboards, of oak just like the originals, formed from one of the oak trees that had been blown down in a storm. She had placed an acorn in the uprooted soil with her own fingers. Gloria was buying back with money all the advantages she had not been born with, throwing herself into the task of saving Holywell with her customary energy. All for Daniel.

'He's a lucky man,' Jamie said.

They went upstairs and opened one of the windows, its diamond-leaded glass so rippled by age that they had hardly seen through it: the view amazed her every time, tiny shimmering cars trailing dustily along the lane to the Blackwall Tunnel, a toy cargo ship warping into the green rectangle of the huge Royal Victoria Dock, no larger than someone's bath at this distance. Here at Holywell she was deep in the country, with treetops carrying birdsong in them and the scent of mown grass below, yet still she was part of London.

'I'm making a new beginning,' she said, 'I can do it.'

'I understand.' He touched her waist but she turned away and rested her elbows on the windowsill, looking out.

'No, Jamie, yer don't. Wharncliffe Gardens was never mine. Neither was Willy Glizzard's place, God rot 'im in 'ell, or Arnold's mansion, or Lily Alhambra's little 'ouse at the Zoar, God rest 'er an' bless 'er in 'eaven. They all 'ad somefink but they were never me. Now I've found my place, Jamie. A 'ome, not a wilderness. A new beginning where everyfink's special.'

'I do understand,' he said. He didn't caress her or attempt to touch her. 'I think I understand exactly what ye are up to, Gloria.'

'Do yer?'

He cleared his throat. 'After these years of marriage ye believe Daniel may be sterile, don't ye?'

'Apparently it's not me. It's 'Enry Summers's job ter know such fings, an' 'e's expensive enough, Gawd knows. I couldn't tell Daniel,' she murmured, then shrugged.

'Ye cannot give him a baby of his own, so ye are giving him back the dwelling where he was a happy child. His father's house. Ye are a remarkable woman to be of such a sensitivity, Gloria.'

It was all right for Jamie, she knew, he had two children of his own, a boy and a girl.

He never talked of his wife, Letitia, thank goodness, and from her snooty name Gloria imagined her – quite without foundation, trying to justify her relationship – to be a right cow, but she knew his children were called Seamus and Tilly. Gloria had never shaken off the feeling that only he and she knew the full significance of that choice: Seamus his father of course, but Tilly after his real mother. So probably Jamie had not admitted his illegitimacy even to his wife. Then that mystery must run very deep with him. She looked at him unsentimentally.

'We never forget where we come from,' she said, 'none of us.'

'Then mayhap I should be rebuilding Wharncliffe Gardens for ye.'

'No.' She ran her hand along the wood. 'I can't explain. This is the place fer me.'

There came a gruff shout from downstairs, some crisis or other. 'With ye in a minute,' Jamie called. He glanced at his watch. 'Ye better get back to thy office, Gloria, afore ye're missed, or Daniel'll be thinking ye've found yeself another fancy-man on the side!'

'That'd be a turn-up.' She had not made love with Jamie here while he was working to rebuild her house, and she would not. 'Jamie,' she called him back. 'We'll keep each other's secrets, won't we?'

He kissed her hand. 'Always.'

'Yer full of blarney,' she said with fondness.

'Ye do not comprehend,' he said simply, 'how much ye hurt me, Gloria. Don't mock me, don't use me. Be thy real self with me, because we will never be married, an' I will never be all thine, which is what I desire more than all the houses in the world. Thy smile in my eyes. I wish ye contentment here with him in this house ye have bought to make thy husband a full man. But I know what I feel.' He let go her hand and looked back from the bedroom door. 'Always, Gloria,' he promised. 'Always.'

Gloria prowled for the last time around the deserted house.

The workmen were gone but the completed rooms were cold, waiting for life, and her footsteps sounded very loud, almost like an intruder's. She had been as faithful as she could be.

Going outside, she closed the door behind her using the big iron key, then slipped it in the pocket of her fur and blew on her cold fingers. This was more than a cold snap, winter had arrived, and her breath trailed her like smoke as she went down the steps. Her cinnabar-red Lanchester, now out of mothballs, was parked waiting for her in the drive, and she saw that the lawns were already white with frost as evening fell. The fountain tinkled like ice as she passed it, the splashing water now fed by a recirculating electric pump, kept running lest it freeze. The overcoated chauffeur folded his Racing Times and held open her door with gloved hands, then tucked the tartan travelling rug over her knees. 'Ma'am?'

'London Bridge Station,' she ordered.

The journey took longer than she had planned for, Vaudey Hill being so treacherous with ice that the car could not make it up to the main road across Blackheath, so they had to slither downhill and turn left, cutting past the hills of Greenwich to the Deptford flatlands. There were accidents all over the place in the dark and black ice, a policeman on duty at every junction; now the London smoke-fog was coming down too, and the fog-flares were being lit. Gloria saw a man with a torch and paid him sixpence to walk in front of the car, reaching London Bridge Station an hour later than she had expected. She got out in the forecourt approach. 'I'll take a taxi 'ome when I finish 'ere,' she instructed her driver. 'There's no point yer keeping out in this weather.'

'Thank you, ma'am.'

Gloria lost herself in the anonymous crowd, watching her car pull out into the fog, and when it was gone she walked where it had disappeared. She swung her scarf around her face; everyone was coughing as the smoke particles got into their lungs, pushing past her into the station. She found herself in the empty high street. Long Southwark was a wall of November fog: she saw no lights at all, only darkness, as she fumbled her way along the pavement to the Tabard.

Jamie was waiting in the tap-room. He had been waiting for hours and he'd had a drink or two ahead of the little glass of port in front of him, but he said nothing about her being late. 'Drinkin' wivout me,' she scolded affectionately, warming her hands at the open fire.

''Twas Guinness, not for getting drunk on. 'Tis brain-food.'

'Gimme a kiss then.'

'Sometimes I wonder which room 'twas here,' he said, 'where I was born.'

'Yer didn't 'ave no trouble booking us somewhere?' She unwound her scarf and shook out her hair with a sigh of relief, plumped down beside him on the bench.

'Of course not, mavourneen. The Tabard is not the Ritz. Ye don't have to arrive with a suitcase, nor stay 'til morning.' He looked sadly into his glass. Vintage port: their drink. 'I suspect this place has a long tradition in these matters.'

'Of people passing through.'

'Like us.' He clicked his fingers for a glass and the waitress came to him slouching and simpering at the same time. 'Mr Wittle is particularly renowned for his roast beef, I believe.'

'Two plates,' Gloria ordered, and the girl primped away. Jamie filled Gloria's glass. 'We're not passing through,' she insisted.

''Tis sure we're no longer as young as we were, mavourneen.'

She chinked her glass to his: cheers. 'Yer a bundle of laughs tonight, yer are.' She drank and twirled her glass until he refilled it. 'Yer done a beautiful job at Holywell, Jamie.'

'Aye, but 'tis ended.'

'Don't be sad. Cheque's in the post.'

'Oh, don't be silly. I'd have done it for nothing.'

'I know.'

'Because I know ye'll be happy there. 'Tis all I want, Gloria. Thy happiness.'

'Blimey, look at me glass,' she said. 'There's nuffink in it!'

He chuckled and refilled it to the brim this time.

'Now I'm 'appy,' she said. 'Chin up.'

'Gloria, will I see ye?'

A thin, cunning-looking man in a loose apron arrived at their table, giving the air of looking behind him, washing his hands with nervous politeness. He looked as if he needed feeding up, Gloria thought; he should have been eating the meal instead of serving it. Old Mr Wittle had died and she guessed this must be his son, as thin as his father had been fat, but equally the hearty *bon viveur*: after wishing them good evening he flourished the long knife from his belt up and down a steel, cascading sparks, then carved great strokes of crunchy, golden-fat beef from the silver server on to their platters. Vegetables were an emerald-green afterthought. He bowed and backed out without a word. Gloria realised this was the boy she had seen sweeping the yard and being clouted round the head by his father many years ago, grown into a man. She covered Jamie's hand.

'Always,' she promised, and he chuckled again: their word.

'Oh, my love,' he said, twisting his fingers amongst hers, 'what poor creatures we are.'

She raised her glass. 'We're rich, an' we're lucky, an' we're in love. Wot more d'yer want?'

'Everything.'

'Yer'll 'ave ter wait 'til after supper fer that,' she said slyly.

'No,' he said, 'I meant everything. All of ye.'

'All yer see is all there is, chum.'

'Gloria, ye know that is not true. Ye are selling yeself short, as always.'

She tapped his plate with her knife. 'Eat up now,' she said.

He began to eat with increasing speed. 'This place deserves its reputation,' he said, discovering his hunger, and she ate with relief. 'We'll see one another again,' she said. 'Often.'

He sat back and wiped his lips. 'I've moved to Stanmore now,' he said, 'so that we can be nearer to Letty at the National Orthopaedic hospital in Brockley Hill.'

'It's nothing too serious, I 'ope?'

He shrugged before going on quickly. 'This coming summer I have so much work on in Metro-land, the Cedars Estate starting, Sandy Lodge.'

'The leafy housing estates of beechy Bucks. I've seen the Metropolitan Railway's advertisements.'

'Aye, an' now the Prime Minister has been given a country residence at Great Missenden, Buckinghamshire's the coming place. No one wants to live in London any more. It's just a place to work.'

'I've had enough of this port,' she said.

'D'ye remember that night by the canal? D'ye remember running down the steps, an' we were kissing in the dark that was so dark we couldn't see, only feel?'

'I'll never forget.'

The stairs were in the corner. Jamie took her hand.

On Christmas morning, Gloria threw open the door of Daniel's bedroom and knelt on his bed. She licked his ear until he groaned.

'Gloria?'

''Oo else?'

He fumbled for the clock but she intercepted his hand and held it in her lap. 'Whasser time?' he muttered.

'Time ter get up, darling,' she said sweetly.

He half sat up, then his eyes flickered. 'It's Christmas morning,' he muttered. 'We don't have to do anything today. Have a heart, Gloria.' He flopped back on the pillows.

'We have to give the children their Christmas present, don't we,' she cooed, lifting the eiderdown and tunnelling her fingers beneath the sheets towards his toes. Daniel writhed before she even touched him, desperately ticklish. 'Oh! oh!' he cried, half awake now, then opened both eyes as she crossed to the window. 'Children? What children? What have you got us into now, Gloria?' He winced as she threw open the curtain and the pale glare of frost filled his bedroom. 'My God,' he said, 'you're fully dressed.'

She lifted the sash and inhaled the fresh air. 'Yer can drive, can't yer?'

'Yes, of course I can, it's not as though one needs a licence or anything.'

'That's settled, then. Get yer 'at an' coat on, I'll put some bread out fer the birds while I'm waiting.'

She had got this planned, he realised suspiciously as he came downstairs, shrugging a herringbone overcoat over his suit. 'What children, what present?' he demanded again as Gloria opened the front door on the freezing, still morning. She didn't reply so he had to follow her down the steps, lifting his legs fastidiously, favouring his shiny black patent shoes on the sooty slush. It had tried to snow in the night, had melted, and was now almost frozen again, he saw with despair. He hopped, but only succeeded in smearing the splashes with his fingers, then used the end of his scarf. She took mercy on him, came back and kissed the corner of his eye.

'My present ter yer,' she said.

'A kiss!'

'Sure,' she said. 'Now get in the blooming car an' drive.'

The roads were deserted, which was just as well. Daniel found second gear and stuck to it. 'Go left,' she said, pointing him along the old Roman road towards Blackheath because it was straightest. As the car climbed, the slush turned to snow on the heathland: it wasn't a white Christmas in the warm bowl of London, but it was on these surrounding hills. The tyres ran silently over the smooth muffling snow, nothing else moving. A few of the large houses bordering the moor had Christmas trees in their gardens, but the lights were not yet on, except in houses with children. 'Are you going to tell me where we're going?' Daniel demanded. He sounded so angry that Gloria was pleased, sure he had no idea of her surprise. 'Put yer 'and out of the window,' she ordered him. Daniel pulled down the glass, grumbling. 'Rotate yer 'and,' she said, 'that's 'ow yer indicate yer turning left. I seen 'em do it.'

'There's no one to see us!' he growled as the car turned between the bow windows of the village street. He pulled on the brakes. 'But this is Vaudey.'

'Freewheel downhill a way, then go right between the gates.'

He did as he was told, then opened the throttle and drove up between the bare trees to Holywell Manor.

Staring, he stopped the engine. Gloria watched his face, treasuring each moment. The only sound was the water tinkling in the fountain. Each window reflected the scene around them.

'Gloria!' he said. 'What – is this—?'

'Welcome 'ome,' she told him, handing him the quaint iron key. 'Gloria's gift. Merry Christmas, Daniel Fox.'

He jumped out of the car and ran towards the house, trailing footsteps and puffs of white breath, then stopped and came back to the car, opened her door and took Gloria in his arms. 'Come on,' he said. 'You and me, together.'

The house was warm inside, she had made sure of that, as warm as though the family had never left it.

Daniel couldn't be cold and calm about this. He was a little boy, he dashed with increasing speed from room to room. She waited for him in the bedroom, watching as he ran his tracks across the virgin snow of the grounds below, the walled garden leading through to the old say, or dairy, where the Fox children had played. Seeing her, he waved, and she knew she had got through to him at last. Shutting the glass, Gloria was sitting on the bed as he came in. He trod snow across the carpet. He'd ruined his shoes and he didn't care, and that made her smile even more. His face was shining from his exertions and she took his cheeks between her hands. Daniel Fox, the eldest son of the eldest son, the firstborn, was home in his house at last.

'Sssh,' she said. 'Sssh, Daniel.'

'How did you know?' He kissed her without affectation, no animal noises now. 'You know me better than I know myself.'

'There's more,' she said. She patted her tummy. 'I'm going ter 'ave our baby 'ere.'

PART VI

Angel

Chapter Twenty-nine

Gloria's housewarming party had to wait for almost a year. Just at the time she felt weakest, with the baby growing inside her, the Gloria Fox Company lost trade in the recession. Everything had gone wrong for the country since the men coming home threw huge numbers of women out of work, until it seemed that there was only one thing worse than winning a war. Things must be terrible in Germany but even in victorious Britain unemployment and prices were shooting up, old soldiers were reduced to selling matches on street-corners again, but you always saw that, and as always the next generation of children were playing war-heroes in the thousands of uniforms over-ordered by the War Office and sold off through the street markets, exactly as Gloria remembered after the Boer War twenty years ago. Mums went glumly back to the way things had been back then, but this time something had changed. Their daughters said they hated the idea of being maids. These girls had tasted freedom – you had only to talk to them, listen to their strident voices in the dancehalls on Saturday nights. Flapper-girls with tunics above the knee and below the collarbone thought they were as good as anyone, and they knew they could do better: their fathers had won the war and they had won the vote. Daniel researched. Pianos had given way to cheque books as status symbols. Gloria rolled her eyes. He could have found that out by going into any pub, but she felt too ill to tell him. Another strange thing was happening, he said: as the economy weakened and people had less money, the demand for cosmetics rose. Gloria could have told him that too: competitors were now swarming on the cheap'n'cheerful cosmetics bandwagon, tough immigrant women making their way just as Gloria had, Jews and Poles and Russians from the Pale with romantic foreign names, and stylish Frenchwomen with elegant faces and hearts of iron. She fought them, and won more often than she lost, it was not a time to be soft. But it was not a good time to have a baby.

Gloria tried hard to put her baby first. For the first time in her life she had to think, all the time, of someone more than herself. Someone with power over her, too: if Gloria worked too long or travelled too far or partied too hard, the baby let her know in ways she didn't forget. Once the sickness passed the fainting spells began. 'This,' Gloria puffed, 'is the hardest blooming fing I've ever done.' Daniel nodded, not understanding. She lowered herself slowly, groaning, into a chair. 'I got veins in me legs like someone's been scrawling all over 'em.'

He looked at her with professional interest. 'I might be able to develop something to cover those up.'

'Would yer?' Gloria gripped his wrist appealingly. 'It's

pep-talk time fer the north-east region Gloria Girls, an' then new season's colours fer the shopgirls in the afternoon.' The girls would wear a bright, cheerful yellow this summer, with fake pearl buttons: the style with which the product was sold, Gloria believed, was as important as the product itself, but it was one which suited hipless, bustless girls only. 'Wot we 'ave ter go through fer yer,' she sighed to Daniel. Corsets were definitely out and last year's voluptuous girls dieted and flattened their chests with tight bras, feeding their hips into powerful elasticated knickers that made a loud slapping sound when the tension was released. 'See,' Gloria explained, because Daniel never did understand how selling worked, 'I'm supposed ter look young an' beautiful today, in command an' control an' all that.' She held out her hand from the chair. 'So 'elp me up.'

'Don't overdo it, Gloria. Let me drive you home, Annie can take over here. Thirty-seven is not young to be carrying your first baby.'

'I feel like forty-seven, an' I'm never going ter 'ave another one, this is *it*. An' don't keep on about me age.'

'Well, I am ten years older.'

'Yer allowed ter be, yer a man.'

'You're going to do it all,' he said, admiringly, but he did insist on driving her home to Holywell, and being pregnant was the only time Gloria was unable to resist him.

Their house was beginning to feel like a home. There was furniture to be seen now when they came into the hall. Their fortune was the misfortune of others: Death Duty was evicting many great families from their ancestral homes and often their houses were auctioned separately from the contents, the collections either gulped wholesale by American magnates or dispersed to the winds never to return. Sometimes Gloria dragged Daniel along to these classy auctions, though often they were too busy, but the scattered pieces often turned up in market-town salerooms or the secondhand shops that now called themselves antique shops. Shopping, she loved imagining where the pieces had come from, though she knew she would probably never know the real truth, but soon that didn't seem to matter: a lovely walnut dresser saved from a dusty shop window, or the seven-pronged silver candlestick found under sacking in the back of a Vaudey village garage, filled her with joy. Her purchases acquired an identity and made a home because she cared about them: Holywell would be the home of Gloria's child. He or she would come to know all this.

On Sunday afternoon Gloria took a deckchair into the garden, feeling bulgy and slow, polishing the silver sticks with a cloth and a little Silvo for something to do. She moved her chair into the shade of an oak because direct sun was bad for a pregnant woman's skin, hugging dreams of her baby's life to come to herself: these sounds of home, the breeze washing in the treetops, Vaudey parish church clock striking four, the distant knock of Daniel playing croquet with one or another overseas agent, both men wearing plus-fours . . . Daniel saw her watching and waved. He and the Belgian came over to the garden table and drank their tea standing up, wanting to get back to their game. 'Don't yer fink this is pretty?' Gloria asked, flourishing the duster over the candlesticks. 'I thought it was a candelabrum, me Mum 'ad one fer Sunday best left us by Grandma Elsie, but the man 'oo sold me this called it a girandole.'

'Looks like a candlestick to me,' Daniel said.

'Please excuse me, but this is in the shape of a Menorah,' the Belgian Jew corrected them. 'A Jewish symbol meaning . . . many, many things. The Kingdom, the Glory, the Power. I thought everyone knew this.' He looked at their Gentile faces. 'No, do not concern yourselves. That is obviously a girandole, not a real religious object.'

'That's good then,' Daniel said, practising swings with his mallet. 'Come on, Albert, best of three.' He pronounced the name Albair.

'I thought—' Gloria murmured, 'I remembered seeing this shape somewhere else.'

'That was most excellent tea, madame.' The Belgian agent bowed politely and the men returned to their game.

Gloria slipped the coin out of her neckline, sat turning it in the palm of her hand. The pattern on the back, she decided, did look a bit like a Menorah. 'Ow,' she said as the baby moved. Always the baby. It seemed like the nine months would never end.

Tricia was born during the night – it felt to Gloria like all night – on 14 August 1920. Daniel sat in the waiting room at the Greenwich Hospital. It was a male tradition to go and devour a whitebait dinner at the Union while the hard work was done, but he didn't like fish, so he sat there among the most boring magazines he had ever looked at in his life. In all of them, it seemed, he saw an advertisement of Gloria's smile – just her provocatively smiling lips, showing off the new range of shades. Gloria Fox lipsticks for the Smile that Smiles. The slogan had caught on at once. Extraordinary, the power of these marketing ploys, he thought ... somehow even he expected her to be smiling like that when the nurse called him in to the delivery suite that quiet Sunday morning. Gloria was not smiling. She looked like she had been in a war, but her spirit was undimmed. ''Ere she is,' she croaked, holding the bundle up. 'First thing she did was latch on ter me bosom.'

'Just like her father,' Daniel grinned, forgetting the nurses in the room. 'Let me see my daughter.' He took the tiny weight and marvelled at her. They had agreed on the name beforehand. 'Look at her, the little bugger. Hallo, Tricia!'

'Yer can tell 'e didn't give birth ter 'er,' Gloria winked. 'Now get out, all of yer, an' let me rest. Trish can stay.'

'Oh my God!' Daniel slapped his forehead. 'A girl! What about the reservation I made at Eton?'

Yet Gloria could not get over her sadness. Everything was marvellous; Tricia was marvellous, plenty of milk, plenty of sucking, her baby slept half the night then had another suck to relieve Gloria's full breasts and slept the other half of the night, the house was marvellous, and Gloria had achieved everything she wanted from life. Gloria nodded as she fed. She was richer than she had ever dreamed, and her fortune kept piling up. Still, during the night hours, she felt there was something lacking. During the days and evenings Gloria hid those thoughts behind her smiling smile and her party manner, but there the feeling was.

When she was alone with Tricia it was with her all the time, sometimes so strong that she turned as though there was someone behind her. Greeting a guest at her housewarming party, suddenly Gloria turned with a start, but there was no one standing there, only smiling faces like her own, and the aroma of expensive perfumes: these opinion-forming people, industry insiders, gossiping columnists, hopeful starlets hunting at her parties, would not have been seen dead smelling of Gloria Fox's class of merchandise.

Lady Jemima Summers cut through the throng – she had been top of the guest list, of course. 'Congratulations, Gloria, you have achieved the impossible. You have succeeded in making Daniel a happy man.'

''E's at peace 'ere. Well, wot d'yer fink of it? Not bad fer a bit of brass?'

'Don't do yourself down. You must invite me here all the time, because I simply adore what you have achieved. I'm so terribly envious.' Suddenly she gripped Gloria's arm tight, her eyes sparkling with emotion. 'Gloria. I really am.'

'Yer welcome any time, Jemima, yer know that. We're friends.' As soon as she said the word Gloria realised how true it was now. Her best friend was a woman thirty years older than herself: Jemima Summers with her strong silver hair, upper-class voice and commanding manner, but kindly underneath – easily old enough to be her mother.

Gloria looked over the uncaring salon-styled heads and youthful faces of the Bright Young Things bobbing around her. By the heraldic stone fireplace Daniel was earnestly making points to an American distributor from Jersey City, and Peter Fox, his tall cousin who had recently joined the firm, was backing him up. Gloria allowed herself to be drawn to the window by Jemima's hand. 'We are your family and your friends, Gloria.' Tricia's crib had been placed in a niche and Jemima smiled through the lace at the sleeping baby. 'She has such lovely black hair. You are so very lucky.'

'If she was awake yer could see she's got me smile.'

'She'll be a girl who knows her own mind then.'

'I just 'ope she 'as 'er mother's luck,' Gloria said. 'Because that's wot I am, an' that's all. Just lucky, ter 'ave all this.'

'Lucky is as lucky makes,' Jemima said, with a glance. 'That was a saying of my grandmother's, I've never forgotten it. My father made his own luck, of course. Destroyed himself with drink.' She sighed. 'Oh, Gloria, I feel so very privileged to be invited back here after all these years!'

'Feel free ter look round.'

'We youngsters used to call this gallery Lady Bess's Walk,' Jemima confided. 'It's from the Elizabethan period.'

'When's that exactly?'

'About four hundred years ago. The days of Bess Fox, she was supposed to be very clever and, you know, a witch. Frightfully interesting. She rebuilt a lot of the old fortified manor, it's her you have to thank for these lovely big windows.'

'I tried ter keep the original glass, mostly. I didn't know it was that old.'

'This room used to terrify us children. She hanged herself

in here, supposedly. She was found with her hands still around the rope as though she had changed her mind too late . . . holding herself up until her strength failed her. You can imagine what fun we had.'

'Bloody hell,' Gloria said, 'we mustn't talk like this in front of the baby.'

'I'm sorry. There's probably more to this place than we can ever know. But then, that's life, isn't it?'

'Jemima, are we friends enough fer me ter ask yer a question?'

'Only one way to find out.'

'Are yer jealous of me?'

'For actually achieving everything I could only dream of? The simple truth is, yes.' Again Jemima squeezed Gloria's hand, robbing her words of offence, and they stood closer than ever.

'Do yer fink I deserve it,' Gloria said in a low voice, 'all this?'

'Yes. All that you have given Daniel.' The baby curled her sleeping fist around Jemima's finger.

'I still feel like a visitor 'ere,' Gloria confessed, 'like, all this, yer know, it's bin given ter me, but it could be taken away any minute. Just gone.'

'You talk as though you felt guilty about something.'

'Don't we all? I think people are born that way.' Gloria picked up her child as she woke, unbuttoned the top of her dress with prosaic fingers. 'No, Jemima. No regrets.'

That night Gloria lay awake. She had lied.

Of course she had regrets. Her life was full of regrets,

things she wished with all her heart were different, done or undone . . . things that she was honest enough to face. She wished she'd had simply the courage, seventeen years old, with her life before her and everything possible, to run after Jamie along the Edgware Road, catch him, keep him whatever the price. That guilt always hung over her, and at times like now, in the darkest hours, it seemed that everything was just a shadow without love, and that nothing else she had ever done mattered because of her failure then. Gloria waited for the dawn to come.

Though they now had offices in the City, at breakfast time she told Daniel that she would work at home today. He gave her a cornflakes-and-milk kiss – everything seemed to taste of milk with a baby in the house – and kissed baby too. 'Bye bye, angel.' Daniel slicked back his gingery, thinning hair with his palm and crammed his hat on his head. 'Cheerio, Mummy!'

'Don't work too 'ard,' Gloria wished him automatically. 'B'bye, Daddy, see yer tonight. Got yer season ticket an' yer 'anky?'

He patted his top pocket. 'Are you sure you're all right?'

He was such a sweet. 'Sure.'

Gloria sat down again when he was gone. Daniel had never commented on his daughter's dark hair – rapidly growing thicker and darker – and by now he was probably so used to her that all her little differences were as familiar as though they were his own. No one knew, no one would ever know. Babies' noses all looked the same, and all babies were born with blue eyes, but by now Tricia's were brown as Daniel's – the baby could actually have been

Daniel's. Jamie and Daniel didn't look so very different,
both had strong noses and brown eyes, but Jamie had black
Irish hair and lots of it.

Gloria called Mrs Franks, the nanny, and told her to get
Tricia ready to go out. 'Make sure she does her nappy if you
can, I don't want to have to change that more often than I
have to on the back seat of the car.' She told the chauffeur
to be ready at ten, then returned upstairs where her maid,
Florence, had drawn her bath as usual. While Gloria was
soaking she called for her belted Angora dress in soft
aquamarine wool to be laid ready on her bed. As she
dressed she decided on the dark blue knotted wool coat,
preferring to wear darker colours these days – when she
was young she'd worn pale pastels with impunity, but now
that her hair was artificially lightened to hide the first grey
hairs, pale shades made her complexion look washed out.
Pulling on woollen gloves, she went downstairs and held
out her arms for her baby, then swept out to the car waiting
in the drive. The cold air smelt of smoke. Mrs Franks
had already supplied the chauffeur with the baby-bag.
'Marylebone,' Gloria instructed, and the car turned out
of the drive past a gardener sweeping leaves with a
home-made twig broom, piling the brown mould on a
smouldering bonfire.

In Marylebone Gloria directed her driver into Lisson
Grove. The station, the railway yards hadn't changed, but
there was traffic everywhere now and it seemed to go at an
enormous speed; she saw no children playing on the main
road. Wharncliffe Gardens was darker than she remembered, its butter-yellow brick stained an ancient chocolate

brown by smoke. The tangle of loo pipes and gutter-drains was streaked with rust, even the balcony railings were tawdry, you wouldn't want your washing to touch them. The chauffeur opened the door and Gloria put her foot out into a puddle, splashing the satin bows of her pointy fashionable shoes. It was her fault, she told herself, for not wearing something more sensible. She had simply not thought. She adjusted her hat then lifted Tricia carefully off the seat. She was wrapped up warm in snug baby clothes and a white shawl, so that her sleeping red face hardly showed. The chauffeur opened the railing-gate for Gloria.

''Ang about 'ere.'

She settled her baby comfortably in the crook of her arm. The climb up the tall concrete stairwell was steeper than she remembered, her footsteps clapping around her like a jeering audience. She used to run up here! Gloria paused on the third floor to catch her breath, then went quickly up the next flight and knocked on her parents' door.

She looked around her at the chilly space, the peeling door, everything ageing and changed. Only she felt the same, inside.

She knocked again, but still there was no answer.

'Mum?' Gloria waited. 'I can tell yer in there, Mum.' But she couldn't. As though Mum really might have forgotten who she was she said, 'Mum, it's me, Gloria. I want ter come in.' Then she admitted what really lay between them. 'Forgive me, Mum. I'm sorry.'

The older woman stood listening on the other side of the door. Less than a foot separated them but she could not cross it. After all these years there was nothing she could say to Gloria, and Mrs Simmonds turned away like a piece of stone.

That girl was knocking too hard, she might break the panels, didn't she have a thought in her head? The old woman was afraid the door would suddenly burst open and Gloria, her firstborn child, named after her and her favourite, young and full of life and with *everything*, but especially youth, would be standing there with that accusing look in her eye. Mrs Simmonds went back to the cooker and stirred a saucepan until there was silence.

'I got someone ter show yer, Mum,' came Gloria's muffled voice, full of cunning.

'Shut up!' hissed the older woman, stirring. The girl had brought the baby of course. Annie had told her mum about it, not that Annie came over much nowadays, gone over to Gloria's side, and she always brought her own two nippers as though Gran – and how Mrs Simmonds despised being called Gran! – would want to see them, and would remember how to hold them when they were so little or what to say to them when they were older. Mrs Simmonds had had her children because they were what happened, not because she wanted them. Only young Bill still lived at home, had got his delivery driver's job back at the Emporium. Dad had gone up in the world, mind, personal chauffeur to Mr Leibig, driving a Rolls-Royce. At least Mr Leibig had been born to money, and he was a man. You couldn't trust a woman who did well, it went against the order of things. Gloria had dragged Annie down too.

Mrs Simmonds placed her hands over her ears. 'Shut yer knocking,' she wanted to scream, 'yer'll wake yer baby!'

Outside the door, Gloria listened to the silence. Perhaps Mum wasn't in there after all, except that Gloria was sure she was. She called through the door for the last time, 'Sorry, Mum.' No 'Sorry' was returned. Carrying her baby, Gloria went downstairs.

Mrs Simmonds hobbled to the window. There was a long red car waiting below, not a patch on a Rolls-Royce. Gloria walked across the courtyard towards it. Look at that girl! Tarted to the eyebrows, her hair in varnished curls like golden wood, wearing lipstick too, and those silly shoes splashing in the puddles – all that was missing was a poodle on a red leash! Mrs Simmonds shook her head at her reflection for bringing up a daughter who had gone so wrong.

The chauffeur, wearing a pale grey uniform that wasn't a patch on Leibig's imperial purple, swung open the railing-gate. As she went to get in the car Gloria turned and looked up, and for the first time Mrs Simmonds glimpsed the baby properly, but in the same instant she shrank back from the glass in case Gloria saw her and knew she had won.

As the car drove away Mrs Simmonds threw open the window but it was too late. She shut it again and made Dad's tea. She was too old to change.

Gloria sat in the back of the car looking out of the rain-starred window. The chauffeur arranged the rug over her legs. Tricia was waking on the seat beside her, smacking her lips, and would demand milk any minute. The car turned left past the Hôtel Great Central and picked up speed along the New Road. 'Stop!' Gloria said.

She had seen Doris Mabb in the hotel's dustbin area. Face and hair and clothes might change, but not a person's walk.

'Go back!' Gloria ordered. Tricia, frightened by the abrupt stop, was yelling her head off. Gloria picked her up, jogging her, twisting to look through the back window as the car reversed with whining gears. 'Sssh, darlin', sssh.' Doris had gone into an alleyway. 'Look after the baby,' Gloria told the chauffeur. The car stopped and she jumped out. Hearing Gloria's tapping footsteps coming after her, the woman turned with hunched shoulders, her hair over her face.

'Doris Mabb?' Gloria whispered.

'Yer got the wrong name, ma'am.' Doris turned away between the dirty brick walls.

'It's me,' Gloria called. Doris walked, ignoring her. 'It's me, Gloria.' Incredibly, it seemed, Doris had not recognised her, though they'd played every day as children. The loss of her teeth had changed the shape of Doris's face, yet Gloria had a fine dentist, ate no sweets, and looked just as good as she always had, better probably. Doris had aged, not she. Gloria ran after her. 'My name's Gloria Fox now.'

'I know that.' Doris paused, but she didn't look back. 'I read the papers, I know all about yer. Where yer live, 'ow yer dress, the smart people yer rub shoulders wiv. Everyfink about yer.' She heaved a sigh. 'An' mine's Hullabye.'

'I'm sorry. I'd forgotten. It seemed only yesterday we was children together.' Gloria held out her hand. 'Yer got ter let me 'elp yer, Doris.'

'I don't want yer 'elp,' Doris wept. She turned savagely, her face naked with hatred. 'Don't yer understand, Gloria? *Get out of my life.*'

Chapter Thirty

With Gloria's re-purchase and repair of Holywell Manor,
her gift of her home to Daniel and the birth of Tricia Fox,
no woman could have done more for the family she had
married into than she had. Annie warned her that Daniel
wouldn't be grateful, men never were, they were grabbers,
you took their name and they took everything else – but
that was just Annie talking, and Gloria dismissed her
sister's fears. Annie in middle age was learning to be as
rigid and implacable as Mum had become in her last years –
Mrs Simmonds had died in the summer of 1924 from a brain
tumour, and everyone said that explained her bitter
behaviour, but Gloria doubted it. Annie's second marriage
had turned out bleakly discontented, too, and keeping up
appearances had left her sour; her son Edward got on
extremely well with his new father, an imposing barrister,
but Annie succeeded in keeping her grip on her daughter
Lily, now eighteen, thin and pretty as a flower, who had
joined the firm on the bottom rung – in the case of the
Gloria Fox Company that did not entail making the tea but
selling on the doorsteps. For ease within the company
Annie had retained the name everyone had known her by,

Mrs Devine, but Lily had taken her stepfather's surname, Scott-Henderson, and few people outside head office knew she was Annie's daughter.

But Daniel, Gloria told herself, was never a grabber. He simply took everything Gloria gave him. He was in her power, and he knew it, but that was the one thing she could not possibly change for him: herself. She sat by the swimming pool she'd had put in the garden at Holywell, thinking about him but showing no sign of her thoughts behind her severe, pale complexion and dark glasses, timing Tricia's plunging strokes with a stopwatch. 'Yer slowing down, girl!'

'This is my fifth length, Mummy!' splashed Tricia.

'Fourth. Save yer strength fer the end. Come on, girl, yer can do it, wot's wrong wiv yer? Deep breath, head down, swim like a fish . . .' Tricia reached the far end and turned, splashing awkwardly, losing speed. 'Oh fer God's sake,' Gloria said, resting her elbows on her bare knees. She was wearing a black swimsuit and cap, still wet, but the sun was warm now on her thighs and shins and the tops of her shoulders. She smeared on a little cream. 'Was that one quicker?' gasped Tricia from the far end, turning under the diving boards. Gloria had forgotten to click the stopwatch.

'No, not nearly as good. Try 'arder, an' don't yer dare ter put yer toe down in the shallow end!'

'Oh, gosh!' Tricia spluttered. But she kept going under her mother's eagle eye, the clear water sluicing her long black hair down her back. Her skinny ten-year-old figure shimmered very prettily over the mosaic patterns that decorated the pool – the same style of mosaic, in honour of the bits of old Roman bath-floor with sea-gods and porpoises that kept turning up when the pool was dug, as the mosaics which decorated the gleaming sunbathing area where Gloria sat.

No, Daniel was not a grabber. He knew his place, that was all: he had always felt himself born to this life, which Gloria had achieved with such labour by her own efforts. He wore it with a light touch, whereas she clutched at every moment with both hands: her butler carrying a tray of glasses and a crystal pitcher of fresh orange juice across the smooth grass, the rich scents of flowers and carefully tended shrubs, the breeze sighing in the treetops. A white liner was inching up the Thames, and she could see across London clear to Primrose Hill. Daniel was away on business. When he returned they would be affectionate, but now they were apart Gloria doubted that he thought of her much.

And he was away a lot, working for her. With the Hapsburg empire broken in pieces by the war, each European country was a separate market, with peoples and nationalities of diverse tastes and preferences, and setting up the distribution and selling arrangements for each one the Gloria Fox Way took a lot of Daniel's time. By the time Gloria breezed on to the scene with the finishing touches, the round of big hotels and darling-parties and the kissing publicity, her nannies and chauffeurs and little Tricia running around – once a private train for her to run around in – Daniel believed that he had already done all the hard work.

But Gloria was more than his equal now. She was his superior.

To travel ostentatiously conferred class on Gloria at a stroke – it didn't matter now that she didn't speak like a duchess, or that she laughed with her mouth open, or always wore a cheap gold chain from her neck whatever else she was wearing, diamonds, exquisite pearls, she simply didn't care, as long as the cameras clicked. Gloria simply waving from the steps of an aeroplane, or giving interviews in the sumptuous lounge of a Zeppelin, was enough: everything she said was printed, and her opinions were sought on everything, and didn't she just love giving them? The German currency crisis? 'Their new currency just papers over the cracks,' she waded in. 'There's no substitute for good housekeeping.' She knew nothing at all of these matters, unlike Daniel, who always listened aghast, sure she would put her foot in it sooner or later, his face calm but his hands twisting, she knew, like little animals behind his back. She was asked what she thought of the fashion for short, shingled hair. 'Good news fer 'airdressers!' The flashbulbs hardly noticed the smooth grey figure of Daniel in the background, and the sound recordists never caught his voice. One French trade paper did a flattering article entitled 'The Man behind Gloria Fox'. Gloria laughed, but Daniel was not amused. Yet he did not resent her success. He was totally dedicated to 'Gloria Fox' – probably loved the Company, she told herself jokingly, more than he did her. The Company didn't have moods, he probably muttered and grumbled to himself, and the Company always made sense.

What he resented was that his success was due to *her*, personally. Daniel had accent, education and manners, but Gloria was the one people turned to. *He* did the long hours of work. *He* ran the business, *he* steered the committees. But Gloria was the one everyone wanted to see. She was the whole show.

Tricia grabbed the rail. 'Ten!'

'Well done, dear, I'm very proud of you.' Gloria hurried over with the towel. 'Twelve lengths tomorrow.'

'Oh goodness, Mummy, I don't think I could.'

'Try and yer'll find out.'

'No,' Tricia said. Then she laughed and kissed her mother's shoulder. 'I'm going to lie and sunbathe. I wish you'd take that cap off. You manage to make even sunglasses and a bathing-cap look fashionable somehow, it's so intimidating.' With lovely fluid steps Tricia dragged over a mat to lie on, turned her face to the sun, then studied her mother out of the corner of one eye. 'You're frightfully domineering,' she said excitedly. 'Will you really insist I do twelve?'

'No.'

'That means you will.'

'It's up ter yer, Trish.' Gloria poured out the orange juice, holding back the ice with a swizzle-stick.

'No it's not up to me, and you know it isn't. You're such a tyrant.' Tricia was already a pupil at the Nemeton Grammar School, very bright. 'I really will try,' Tricia decided, 'but you mustn't blame me if I drown.'

'As long as yer don't expect me ter get me 'air wet fishing yer out.'

Tricia rolled on her tummy, delighted. 'I suppose you'd just call for Jeeves.' Jeeves was her name for the butler, Morris.

'Don't gulp it down in one, yer'll give yerself stomach-cramp.'

Tricia rested the glass by her mother's foot, then frowned. 'Mummy, how do you get your legs so smooth?'

'Yer starting ter talk like one of me advertisements.'

'But I do admire you terrifically. You are your own best advertisement. Your toes are awfully ugly though.' Gloria snatched them away. 'I suppose everyone's are,' Tricia said loyally, examining her own.

'I wish I 'ad yer skin,' Gloria said.

'You shouldn't stick out in the sun then. I expect you did have, once, didn't you?'

'We wore great 'eavy dresses in those days, yer could 'ardly see us.' Tricia's dresses today were no more than shifts by those standards. How long ago 'Victorian' must sound to Tricia's ears, a different world that must be difficult for her to imagine; yet Gloria could still see it now.

'Your chain's rubbed a red mark on your neck, Mummy.'

'It's probably just the sun, darling.'

'You never take it off, do you? Tricia put up her hair unconcernedly, squeezing the drips from the ends into the pool. 'Your lucky charm.'

'No, I never do.'

Tricia touched the coin with her knuckles. 'What does it mean exactly?'

'A promise, a memory, and a hope.'

'How glorious!'

'A might-have-been, that's all. Its meaning is simply that it was given.'

'Who by?' Tricia's eyelashes fluttered sleepily.

'No one yer know.'

'It must mean whatever you want it to . . . I can't imagine anything more marvellous than this . . . The sun.' Tricia's voice faded away.

Gloria stood and looked down on her sleeping daughter, then adjusted the sunshade so that she would not burn. Slipping her feet into espadrilles, putting her hands on her hips, she walked slowly back across the grass towards the house. Tricia was right. Everything was perfect. But it could have been so much better.

When the pool was put in last year, the digging was done by a cheery gang of Reilly navvies. Jamie had come down only once to check that the work had been done properly, a smiling, jolly figure in a camel-hair coat. He had come sauntering through the French windows into Gloria's study for tea as though he owned the place, catching her with her reading glasses on: Jamie's smile, the look in his eyes, nothing had changed, still friends as though not a moment had passed since they last met alone in a room. They had been knocked together at busy parties, of course, various bustling social dos, bumped into one another at Ascot and an hotel dining-room once, and once even met in the street outside their new City offices so that Gloria had introduced Jamie to Daniel and the two men had shaken hands. But that day when Jamie dropped over to see the pool they were alone. Gloria had taken off her reading glasses and got up from her desk and they had made polite one-lump-or-two conversation, one hand for the saucer, one for the cup, sitting on the sofa, saying everything but what they were thinking. ''Ow is yer wife?'

'As well as can be expected, Gloria.' He'd said it in such a patient way – mocking Gloria because she wasn't really saying anything – that she'd wanted to kiss him.

'And your boy – girl—'

'Aye, both are fine, Gloria. Fine, strapping, healthy.' What she'd really been thinking was of opening her dress and pressing her breasts into his smooth, supple hands: workman's hands no longer, or even a young man's... When Jamie took off his hat his hair was silver, only a few black streaks left in it, but the absolutely extraordinary change – she had never seen this before – was that Jamie now wore his hair in a queue, tightly knotted over the nape of his neck, that made him look very manly and un-conventional; and an unconventional man always looked dangerous. She wanted him immediately and so strongly that her mouth went wet, even though she understood perfectly that he was denying everything she had worked so hard for, these beautiful things that surrounded her, Sèvres vases, flowers, candelabra, hand-woven rugs. Jamie, sil-very and fierce, didn't give a damn for his smart coat or his smart car in the drive, or the polite words they were exchanging. Only her. She filled his velvet brown eyes. She knew it, she saw herself in his gaze. He'd smiled, and she knew he was thinking the same thoughts as she, wanting what she wanted, there was no difference between them.

'Yer looking older,' she had told him.

'An' ye are not.'

'Older and better, Jamie Reilly. At sixty yer'll be a god.'

'But I live in hell without ye.'

'Don't be stupid.'

'Hell improves a man, obviously.'

She swallowed. 'Daniel's coming 'ome soon.'

'''Tis a fine an' beautiful life ye have.' He put down his tea, knocking it over with his foot, kissing her, sucking her lips.

'Jamie,' she whispered.

He stood.

'Jamie, don't yer realise it's bin thirty years since we met? It *is*. It's a lifetime ago.'

'I'm the same man an' ye are the same woman. Ye are,' he said angrily, 'don't deny it.'

'I'm not that girl, Jamie.' She licked her hanky and dabbed the marks her lipstick had left on his mouth and cheeks. 'I can't 'elp changing.'

He had laughed, amazing her. 'But I love ye,' he had said, kissing her forehead.

Then he had been gone before she could stop him.

Gloria stepped through the open French windows in her espadrilles. Slipping into a towelling robe, she pulled off her bathing cap. The interior of the house seemed full of shadows after the sunlight outside so she put her sunglasses up in her hair as she sat down at her desk. Thinking of Jamie always upset her. Driving through Southwark the other day, she had noticed that the island of shops almost opposite the Tabard had been knocked down as part of the road improvements, to make the sharp turn into South-wark Street a smooth curve for motor traffic. The chemist's shop where she had started off with Daniel was gone as though it had never been – smooth tarmac and traffic lights. By chance, the girls transferring files to the new offices had found Martin Fox's original purchase contract for the shop and shown the yellowed papers to Gloria for the fun of it. But she'd thought Daniel might be interested and looked through them when everyone else was out at lunch: the contract was dated February 1871, the year after the meeting of Jemima and the virtually penniless six brothers who scattered to the winds. Martin had purchased the freehold of the shop from the Church Commissioners for £250 in cash, a considerable sum. Gloria had called casually through the door into Daniel's office, 'Where did yer dad get the spondulicks to buy the old shop, d'yer fink?' Daniel had just shrugged, busy. He'd never thought about it, didn't know or care.

Gloria had left him alone, but went through the files for an hour by herself that afternoon, finally turning up a smudged receipt, torn along one side and the ink smeared on the date, January 1871: To Martin Fox, Esq, the cash sum of £250, then an indecipherable signature dashed across the bottom. At the top of the receipt were stamped the faded letters: *Murge & Son, Coin Dealers*.

It was no wonder Daniel didn't know about this, the sale had occurred more than a year before he was born. Nevertheless, Gloria had tapped the old receipt thought-fully with her fingernail. Back then a whole family could live on a pound a week, and £250 was a payment beyond price for a single coin. It must have been a collection, surely. She'd returned the receipt to the folder and had it filed. Whatever the answer was, Daniel was right: it was long dead and buried.

Since their mum had died, Gloria heard, Dad's life had fallen apart. Without a loving woman to look after him and a proper home to come back to after work, he didn't know how to live. Mrs Simmonds had been his prop and his staff, and without her to boss about he had nothing to do. Annie came to Gloria, worried about him. He'd been proud as a peacock of his job as personal chauffeur to Mr Leibig, but the old boy had died ages ago leaving the store to his daughter, and her new-broom husband Ben London had renamed the place London Emporium and swept all the old traditions away. Bert hung on, but a couple of years after Mum died he'd got the sack for cutting a corner once too often – Mr London was not the sort of man to tolerate mistakes by men he trusted. Dad had done hundreds of pounds' worth of damage down the side of the Rolls-Royce, and he'd been two years past retirement age, but he raged at the unfairness with which he swore he'd been treated; it had become an obsession with him. He lived in a one-room flat in Chelsea subsidised by the store, but grouched to anyone who listened to him. 'Men like ter 'ave an 'obby ter occupy their retirement,' Gloria shrugged to Annie in the office, 'an' that's 'is.'

Every Christmas each employee, past and present, of London Emporium received a complimentary turkey, a hamper full of rich dainties, and a bottle of fine wine. Bert

Simmonds also received a determinedly cheerful visit from his daughters and their children whose names he forgot, or even which belonged to whom, and Gloria was sure he did it deliberately. He was rejecting them: here you are, he was saying, this is what you brought me down to, old and cold. Gloria had come to hate these annual pilgrimages, Dad in his little room like a spiteful animal protecting its cave, refusing to be organised or enjoy himself just because his girls wanted him to. 'Still on the chocs, eh, Glo?' he greeted her with a broad grin, hating her for her success, then patted his pot-belly cheerfully, getting at her.

'Wot d'yer mean?' Gloria said briskly. Only one man ever spoke to her like this, and he had to be her dad.

'Fat pig,' Dad said. 'Told yer!' Annie saw the look in Gloria's eye and hastily changed the subject.

'Isn't it awful, Daddy, all the men out of work and the marches.'

'Don't change the subject.' Dad went for her too. 'Wot d'yer know about it, me own daughter a fancy-talker an' married ter a double-barrel name? Yer the enemy, the lot of yer. 'Sides,' he added righteously, 'I got me pension.' Edward and Lily thought all this was priceless, of course, and Tricia was simply amazed.

'I'm afraid to say I actually hate him,' Annie confessed going back in the car, although she didn't normally like talking in front of the children even though her own were grown up, and Tricia looked grown up. 'He's a nasty, vicious old man, and he knows it, and he likes it.'

'No, he doesn't know it.' Gloria shook her head. 'I feel so sorry fer 'im. Young Bill don't go ter see 'im no more, I

mean not really *see* 'im, an' since our Albert moved near
Bristol 'is kids speak broad Somerset, grandad prob'ly
couldn't understand 'em anyway.'

'Poor Daddy,' Annie said, 'five children and he lost them
all while he was still alive.'

'Wot really gets me,' Gloria said gloomily, 'is that I'm
not fat.'

'I know,' Annie said, aware of her own thickening hips,
'but you have the willpower to diet. I wish *I* could. You are
a miracle, Gloria.'

'I still eat me Christmas turkey,' Gloria said. But it was a
quiet Christmas at Holywell that year, festivities considered in bad taste by Society when so many families had
no money going spare – Gloria ostentatiously had shep-
herd's pie served at the Gloria Girls' Christmas bash – and
anyway Daniel was preparing for his annual business trip to
Jersey City. Gloria drove him down to Southampton on
Boxing Day to catch ship. He was finickity as usual, patting
his pockets, sure he'd forgotten his toothbrush. 'Yer could
always buy one on the ship,' Gloria reassured him over the
hum of the motor. 'Got yer 'ankies?'

'Plain or the monogrammed ones?' She laughed and
kissed him because he wasn't joking. He always got in a
nervous state before a trip. When they stopped at a pub for
lunch she nicked his passport to teach him a lesson. He
didn't realise his pocket was empty until they were
bombing merrily down the road again, and he screamed.
Gloria handed it to him. 'I'm good fer yer, aren't I?' she
said. 'I dunno wot yer would've done if yer 'adn't married
me.'

But that started her mind working, and her pleasure evaporated. Waving goodbye to Daniel, smiling her smile, Gloria was already sad. Driving back towards London, rather than take the South Circular through the suburbs, she cut north to Brockley Hill.

The orthopaedic nursing home was set amongst trees, but they were bare at this time of the year, and she saw through them easily to the large house set amid green lawns. People were following the smooth gravel paths, visitors trying to walk slowly, patients in chairs or with sticks, nurses in capes. A footpath cut across the grounds and she scrambled over the stile, her shoes crunching on dry leaves as she moved through the trees, then she had to stop as a twig snagged her hair. Freeing herself, she was now close enough to the home to see Jamie's bottle-green Hirondelle sports car parked, almost hidden among the taller saloons, near the entrance. Of course he'd visit Letitia every day over the Christmas holidays. The dicky-seat was open, so he'd brought his children.

They walked in a group, two men and a girl in dark overcoats. Good God, even his son was older than she remembered Jamie, taller than him, black hair, the same nose, but with a lively blue gaze that caught you straight in the eye. Gloria swallowed, keeping behind a tree. She was looking at her children that might have been.

Jamie, his silver hair knotted back and his overcoat undone because of his exertions, was the one pushing the wheelchair – but it was more a bathchair, half lying down, and the woman lay beneath thick rugs. Her head was held in a padded clamp, so that she remained fixed in whatever position she was put. The path went close by the wood and Gloria shrank to her knees. One wheel was squeaking as it turned.

Gloria's heart went out to the woman she saw.

Jamie had married Letty only when he lost hope of Gloria, and it was obvious why he had chosen her: because she looked like Gloria. Gloria, hiding, was seeing herself, and yet there was little of her own looks now left in that motionless, lifeless face. Her accident had left Letty paralysed shortly after the birth of her children; she had never been able to hold her second child in her arms. Her hair was dull grey, her face wrinkled, her eyes were blue holes.

Jamie halted. The squeaking stopped. He went round and adjusted the rug.

He lifted his wife's hand into his, as lifeless as a puppet's hand in his warm fist. His son took over the pushing and Gloria watched them walk on, their figures shrinking further into the distance until they were gone.

She came out on to the path, shivering.

'Yuss,' Gloria murmured to herself, 'I'm the luckiest person in the world.'

Chapter Thirty-one

Tricia often brought some of her friends down from Vaudey after school and Gloria watched them larking about: skinny, pipe-cleaner girls, shy with the onset of pubescence and anxious about how they looked in their swimsuits, not yet confident of themselves, then losing themselves in their squealing games. Tricia, of course, was top of the pecking order but they were all in awe of Gloria, treating her as though she was frightfully old, fetching out her deckchair from the bathing hut to the poolside, watching in respectful silence when she dived off one of the boards. 'Fer Gawd's sake enjoy yerselves,' Gloria spluttered, coming up, 'yer look like a row of little birds waitin' on a telephone line!'

Tricia jumped in with the school shout and then the lot of them jumped after her, porpoising around Gloria as she swam sedately to the mosaic steps. She climbed out with a flick to tighten her figure-clinging costume over her bottom as everyone did, then turned, the coin sending silver flashes down her front – it was only in this garment that she had to wear the coin outside, on view. She removed her bathing cap and patted her hair carefully into shape, then put on her towelling robe and sat watching the youngsters enjoying themselves. Most of them were well-off middle-class or upper-crust children from Vaudey's fine Georgian quarter; girls from The Oaks development were a step down the social ladder, and the rest lived along the railway at the bottom of the hill and had not been invited. Tricia was quite a snob: maybe she thought Gloria would be embarrassed by younger London-voiced versions of herself – or perhaps she thought her mother would take the side of those children, and Tricia would lose face with the friends who mattered to her. Gloria sat by her own pool made an outsider by more than age. Her daughter wanted to live her own life, of course. Tricia was giving everyone orders, trying to make them swim lengths, and Amanda Carstairs almost disappeared beneath the water rather than admit she could not swim. Finally all the girls got out and huddled at the far end, chattering amongst themselves about the things girls of thirteen chatter about; Gloria could not hear.

Morris made his stately progress across the lawn with a silver tray bearing the martini glasses that Daniel had bought at Bloomingdale's in New York, a pitcher of iced martini and a large bowl of green olives. 'Lady Summers has telephoned, ma'am. She will be a little later than expected.'

'All right.' Since Henry's death in 1929, Jemima had lost some of her sparkle; she had also become rather forgetful. Probably she'd forgotten she had been invited to supper tonight until her grandson, Greg, arrived in the car to remind her. Tonight's open-air party was to celebrate the engagement of Peter Fox's son Julian, now Daniel's private secretary, to a debutante who did something or other in the office, a girl whose name Gloria forgot, but who had a voice like tortured metal. Definitely not a Gloria Girl. Sometimes Gloria wondered whether the firm wasn't losing its way by moving away from its roots and employing these people, if only in administration, but they were accustomed to success and that was a big part of being successful. They became what they believed in, and every year 'Gloria Fox' posted higher profits.

Daniel's Rolls trailed dust up the drive and Gloria shielded her eyes against the slanting evening sun, waving. He came over bringing Peter and Julian Fox in tow, and the girl whose name turned out to be Crystal. Away from the office she considered herself as good as Gloria, quite at her ease. She was dying for a swim and stripped off her dress to reveal a silly-frilly costume. Julian jumped in with her and they swam around, giggling, then smoked cigarettes clinging to the side. They slipped one to Tricia.

'Wot the bloody 'ell d'yer fink yer doing?' Gloria said.

'Oh, Mummy, everyone does it.' Tricia dragged on her cigarette with a sudden savage look, not going to put it down. 'Don't make a fuss.' She meant in front of her pals.

'Pretty please,' Gloria said.

'You're so out of touch,' Tricia said tearfully. 'I'm nearly old enough to do exactly as I want!' She threw her cigarette in the pool and went back to her friends.

'Difficult age,' Daniel murmured.

'It's difficult for 'er,' Gloria said, 'because the others just use 'er. She finks she knows it all but she don't know nuffink.'

'I meant it's difficult for her because she's so much in your shadow,' said Daniel.

'Meaning anyfink wot goes wrong is my fault?'

'No, I didn't mean that at all. There's nothing wrong with being a strong and possessive mother.'

Peter Fox's wife Renée arrived and skidded her car to a stop, tooting the bullhorn, then the doors flew open and her daughters sprinted across the grass, already in their bathing costumes, waving towels, dropping them and disappearing into the water as sleekly as penguins.

'I'm the one 'oo's the stranger 'ere,' Gloria said. 'I'm the one 'oo's face doesn't fit.'

Renée came over swinging the car keys from her finger, kissed Peter then threw herself into a deckchair. She was a beautician with half a dozen beauty parlours of the class that were springing up all over the better suburbs, providing mudpacks, hot towels, aromatherapy. 'I'm absolutely gasping, darling.' Peter poured her a large martini and put it into her hand.

'What a gorgeous sky,' Peter said. 'Turneresque.'

'We always get good sunsets 'ere,' Gloria told him. 'They start early like this an' go on fer hours. Daniel reckons it's the smoke over London.'

She got up as Jemima's car turned into the drive and went across the grass to greet her. Greg Summers helped his grandmother out; he wore a lost, unhappy face. Jemima must be eighty but her eyes were bright, her tongue pin-sharp, the only real clue to her age the heavy clothes she wore on such a warm day, the slowness of her walk. She gripped tightly on Gloria's wrist as they came back to the pool. 'Goodness, you've got the whole Fox clan here. That can't be little Julian.'

'His engagement to Crystal.'

'It only seems yesterday that he was Peter. I mean that Peter was marrying that girl, what's her name.'

'Renée.'

'And now those little babies are old enough to have boyfriends. I swear they grow up faster these days.' She surveyed the drinks trolley Morris had brought. 'I couldn't say no to a touch of brandy, neat. I was born before ice, you see.' Daniel helped her into a chair and the Fox family sat in a pleasant half-circle looking over the children playing in the pool. Morris had turned on the floodlights and the young swimmers floated in streams of silver bubbles, the sunset sky pale red, pale yellow, bright gold above them. Someone went round with a taper, lighting the candle-flares against the mosquitoes.

Gloria opened her towelling wrap and slapped. 'Got one of the little buggers,' she said. Jemima stared at her.

'What is that you're wearing?'

'Oh, she always has that on,' Daniel yawned, reaching out to touch the coin. 'Even in bed.'

'It's just somefink,' Gloria said, covering it with her wrap. Morris and other hands were laying out a table with smoked salmon, steaks, French cheeses. Daniel and the others went over before the youngsters, led by Tricia, scoffed the lot. Gloria is so self-indulgent with that girl, said his glance to the others. 'Hey, Tricia, leave some for us . . .'

When they were alone Jemima moved across and sat beside Gloria. 'It's not just something,' she said in a low voice. 'Daniel doesn't know about it, does he?'

'I dunno wot yer talkin' about.'

'He didn't give you this?'

'No, 'e didn't.'

'May I ask where you got it?'

Gloria shook her head. 'Yer wouldn't understand.'

'Perhaps I would,' Jemima whispered furtively, throwing a glance over her shoulder. The others were still piling food on their plates. 'May I, my dear?' She held the coin in her hand, studying it on the end of its cheap chain. 'The Emperor Tiberius.' She turned it over. 'And the Menorah.' She pressed it between her two palms as if to keep it warm.

'Don't keep me in suspenders,' Gloria said.

'Coins like this were part of the Fox family for a long time, passed down the generations. They're unlike anything else; family tradition calls them the Talents.' There was almost a cunning light in Jemima's eye. 'Also by tradition there were once twenty-nine. Probably they are very old; no one has ever seen them all together. Scattered to the winds. By the time my father died, only seven were left at Holywell. Seven Talents for seven children. No one knows where they come from. *They* were what we divided among us that night in the Pilgrim's Room at the Tabard, and took away. Our father's memory. No, more. Our *family's* memory.'

'I don't fink my family 'ad a memory.'

The others returned to their seats around the two women, putting their plates on their laps, wineglasses by their chairs. Gloria went to the table alone but Jemima followed, putting her face close.

'Yet here you are, Gloria, wearing a Talent.'

'Maybe it's where I get me talent from,' Gloria winked.

Jemima took her seriously. 'Do you believe so?'

'It's just a good luck charm. It meant somefink ter someone I once knew.'

Jemima looked at her wisely, then turned the coin over and over in her withered hands. 'I don't know why, but they *do* exert a certain fascination. When I was young I wondered at their secret.' She dropped it reluctantly. 'I'm so old, and when we're old we know there is no secret, Gloria. I'm afraid I must disappoint you. They're fakes.'

'Not fake ter me.' Gloria munched a stick of celery. Jemima looked at her enviously. Probably she had no teeth left of her own.

'They're not genuine Roman coins, you see, they have no value, no denomination. Forgeries, old ones, but only curiosities. They're worth nothing but their few pence-worth of silver.'

Gloria wondered about Martin Fox's receipt for two hundred and fifty pounds sterling, but kept her peace. Obviously Jemima did not know everything.

'It's not a forgery ter me.'

'Oh, I knew they're worthless, Gloria, because I'd had them professionally valued, but I'm a woman too. That night I asked my brothers to let me keep them, as if by keeping *them* together we would remember our family together, the place we had come from. Reuben refused, keeping his worthless trinket because *I* believed in it. Martin kept his too. George, emigrating to Australia, tossed his coin to me quite casually, a practical sort who wanted no memories of the old country. Likewise my brother Frank, on his way to Canada. Loss, all loss. When we are children the world is ours.'

'So yer got three of the things stashed away.'

'For me the obsession to collect is to remember, to preserve. They're yours when I die, Gloria, because I think you'll understand. They're *us*. My life has been very humdrum, and poor Henry was such an atheist, but I have always wished . . . *wished* I was able to believe. But your Talent is everything to you, is it not?'

'Wot's yer point?'

'You are one of us after all, Gloria.'

They watched the semi-circle of the Fox family eating near the pool, silhouetted by the floodlights. The children were splashing in the water, Tricia standing on Amanda's shoulders, and Julian Fox was kissing Crystal behind the diving-boards, thinking no one could see them. The sunset hung over them all. Suddenly the family and these things carrying them forward seemed more important to Gloria than her own life, and she clenched her hand around the Talent hanging round her neck.

'One of us,' Jemima murmured. 'You really were all the time.'

Chapter Thirty-two

'Yer aren't grown up,' Gloria said. 'Tricia, my love, yer still a child. Yer just doing this ter get away from yer mummy, aren't yer?'

But Tricia thought she was equal to her mother's determination. 'I love him.'

'That's not enough. Not fer a marriage.'

'You should know,' Tricia said spitefully. 'This is *my* life, not yours, and I'm not going to make your mistakes, Mummy, and wait until I'm old until I have my children, so I'm nearly sixty by the time they fall in love and then I can't remember what they feel. Because then I'd be cruel, like you.'

'I'm not cruel, I'm not old, and I do remember.'

'Pigs have wings. Evelyn's kissed me, you know.'

Gloria couldn't hide her alarm. 'Wot d'yer mean, kissed?'

'I suppose Daddy did used to kiss you? Or was it always separate bedrooms with your generation?'

'Yer don't know wot love is,' Gloria groaned. Tricia was a lovely young woman with her self-assurance and her velvet-brown eyes, her cheekbones wearing her mother's flush of willpower. High on her left cheek she had a black beauty spot. Tricia crossed her long legs on the sofa, showing rather a sweep of thigh, and she wore mannish padded shoulders.

'Yer didn't really let 'im touch yer, did yer, girl?' Gloria asked.

'And I enjoyed it.' Tricia flicked her knee with her fingernails. Gloria had always asked her daughter to speak her mind and have no secrets from her, but this was going a bit far: Tricia was using embarrassment to overwhelm her mother's resistance. 'He held me in his arms and he covered me with kisses. Surely you must know what I mean.'

Gloria knew exactly.

'Ha!' Tricia said. 'I didn't think so. Because you've never been properly in love, it's always been a business with you, you've always used people. You still want to keep me all to yourself, your own little girl with the opportunities you never had, and dream yourself young again through running my life. Why do you always have to fancy my young men? You simply don't like Evelyn yourself, that's all, so you think I shouldn't like him.'

Gloria denied it, but it was true. 'Don't yer fink I know better than yer about anyfink? Yer could do much better than 'im. But I suppose he is a good looker,' she admitted.

'It's *my* life,' Tricia said. 'He's in the Guards, he's frightfully handsome, all the girls say so, and he's going to do his bit for his country. His posting could come through any day. Suppose he's killed? There's no *time* for doubts, Mummy.'

Daniel came in reading the newspaper. 'She wants ter be a war bride,' Gloria snorted, throwing up her hands.

'Ah, yes.' Daniel looked over the top of his glasses, and Gloria realised that Tricia had got to him first. 'Well, Gloria, he seems a sound fellow: Eton, good cricketer. His father is a baronet, string of racehorses in Ireland.'

'Wot's that got ter do wiv the price of fish?' Gloria demanded. 'It's just bed, listen ter the way she talks.'

'He's on fire,' Tricia said, 'and so am I.'

'I'm sure he's not that sort,' Daniel said. 'I suppose we ought to pull the black-outs?' He went around the room amiably pulling the heavy drapes closed, clicking on the standard-lamps as he passed.

'Evelyn Sutton is an upper-class twit,' Gloria said, 'I don't care if he's a captain in the British Army, thin red line an' pass the port ter yer left an' all that. Yer too good fer 'im.'

'Now I'm *determined*. I'm going to marry him whether you want me to or not.' Tricia crossed her arms. 'You don't have to come to the wedding if you don't want to. Daddy can come.' She snivelled into her handkerchief. 'I just wanted your blessing.'

'Goodness, Gloria,' Daniel said.

'The biggest blessing yer could 'ave would be ter say no, my girl.'

'I'll be in the front sitting room,' Daniel said, folding his paper and closing the door. He hated rows.

Tricia returned her handkerchief neatly to her handbag, dry-eyed.

'Let's start this conversation again,' Gloria suggested. She remembered back to something Tricia might understand, old Jemima's word for when people might hurt one another too much: 'Pax.'

They stared at one another by the glow of the lamps.

'There's only three things you need to know,' Tricia told her mother. 'I love him, I'm going to marry him, and I'm pregnant.'

Later Gloria went into Daniel's bedroom. When he didn't put down the paper she sat on the stool. 'It's a disaster,' she told him. 'In the end I 'ad ter tell Trish ter go ahead an' do wot she wants, since she already 'as.'

'These war marriages often end up drifting along quite contentedly, you know.'

'I wanted more fer my girl.' Gloria was shaking her head as she returned to her own room. Captain Sutton had been much more attractive than she let on to Tricia – she had even felt her own body respond to the sight of him, though she was just about old enough to be his grandmother. She knew exactly what her daughter saw in him because he reminded her of Hugo Handley when he was young – tall, a fine clothes-horse, sexy and in love with himself. 'An' so it goes,' murmured Gloria as she closed her eyes to sleep, 'wot a bleedin' merry-go-round it is.'

Tricia and Captain Sutton were married at St John's parish church in Vaudey. Gloria cried. Everyone was in one uniform or another, invisible aeroplanes towed vapour trails high above them across the late summer sky – and Tricia even had the cheek to wear white. Gloria stopped her as she was getting in the car.

'Trish, I want yer ter 'ave this.' She pressed the Talent into her hand.

'But you always wear it,' Tricia said.

'That's long ago now. Remember me.'

Tricia frowned, then pulled away from Evelyn who was tugging at her elbow.

'What does it mean, Mummy?'

'A promise.'

Tricia remembered. '"A promise, a memory, and a hope."'

Gloria kissed her. 'Yer always one of us.'

The car drove away, and the wind blew in the trees.

In September Evelyn's posting to Egypt came through. Tricia lived alone for a while at his London flat rather than admit to her mother how unhappy she was; it seemed nobody cared whether she lived or died. Eventually she packed her suitcase and came back to Holywell before Christmas, standing on the doorstep. She burst into tears.

'Welcome 'ome,' Gloria said, embracing her. 'Come back ter yer old mum. Cor, yer fatter than a pudding.'

'I'm frightened,' Tricia said.

'Don't be, darling. Tell 'er, Daniel.'

'Here's home,' Daniel said.

'Our 'ome, yer 'ome, Trish, our baby's 'ome.' Gloria put her arm around Tricia's shoulders. 'Come on upstairs, luv. I kept yer room fer yer, an' the bed warmed.'

'You must be curious,' Tricia said, sitting up against the pillows when Gloria brought her hot milk in bed that night. 'He hasn't written once.'

'I'm sure Evelyn's all right, darling. It's probably just the post. He struck me as quite a survivor.'

'It's not that. Cynthia gets his letters.'

''Oo's Cynthia?'

'I thought she was my pal, but it turns out that she's an old flame of his.'

'Oh. That's very bad news.'

'Rather.'

Gloria drew a breath. 'Wot yer going ter do, then?'

'Kill him, I suppose.'

'That's a good idea.'

'I mean it,' Tricia said. 'Legal separation. I never want to see him again.' She cuddled herself. '*My* baby.'

The Greenwich hospital was too busy with casualties for routine births, and their general practitioner, Dr Palin, was busy dealing with injuries from flying glass – a single stray bomb falling in Vaudey High Street on New Year's Eve like a violent promise of the year to come. The midwife who arrived at Holywell to attend Tricia, who was grunting and swearing her way through labour, had been called out of retirement. She was a cheerful soul with a face like ripe plums, slapping a cold flannel into Gloria's hand to give her something soothing to do for Tricia's forehead, then settled into the corner with a cigarette for herself. 'That's something that's changed,' she commented. 'The girls know such disgusting language these days.'

Tricia's daughter was born three hours into the new year. Gloria held up her granddaughter.

'Wendy,' Tricia said.

Gloria smiled. 'Wendy.'

'Babies!' swore the midwife, 'no end ter them.'

'She's bossy and full of life,' Tricia would tell her mother as Wendy sucked her breast, 'just like you. Oops, other side.'

'Other end,' Gloria said. Conversation about babies was always much the same. 'Don't she never stop?'

'Don't you remember me?' giggled Tricia. She was soft as a blancmange when the baby was about.

'That's the sort of fing one tries ter forget, frankly, luv. It seems such a long time ago, thank Gawd.'

'But she *is* like you,' Tricia said. 'A bit, anyway.'

Gloria liked that sort of compliment. 'She 'asn't got my eyes, though. They're brown as yers are.'

'Ouch!' Tricia flipped her breast back in her bra. 'No biting the tit that feeds you. It's the bottle for you from now on, little one.'

Gloria, the sun glinting on her glasses, later watched from her study window as Tricia walked the pram in the garden, Wendy sitting up holding on to the sides, looking forward. 'But I'm not bossy,' Gloria muttered to herself, 'no more than I have ter be, anyway.' She rubbed the mark the glasses had left on her nose, hating wearing them: most people didn't realise she did. 'I want ter bring Trish into "Gloria Fox",' she told Daniel.

'Tricia is obsessed with two things,' Daniel said mildly, 'her baby and her divorce. I don't think she has time for your obsession as well.'

'She only has ter wait three years, an' there's nuffink much fer 'er ter do.'

'Unfortunately serving his country in Egypt does not count as desertion under the 1937 Marriage Bill,' Daniel said precisely. He was getting very precise, it must be his pharmaceutical training returning to haunt him – his seventieth birthday fell this year. He rubbed the palm of his hand smoothly over the freckled top of his head.

'Those legal hotshots at Snapper and Wells cornered 'im when 'e was on leave. Private detectives nabbed 'im *in flagrante delicto* wiv Cynthia, the whore. Letters, everyfink. 'E was only too pleased ter sign a legal separation in return for no mud.'

'You really took this personally, didn't you?'

'She's my daughter. She needs lookin' after. Three years an' she's free.'

'She won't join the Company, you know.'

'We'll see,' Gloria said, turning back to the window, 'about that.'

She was right, as usual. Tricia said yes at once, and Daniel was amazed. 'It's simple common sense,' Tricia told him, looking at Wendy run around the fountain with a mother's watchful eye. 'You see, Daddy, it's only two days a week and the money's wonderful. I'm doing it for Wendy's sake. I couldn't let Mummy keep on paying for her clothes. This way I get a nanny paid for and two days off in town.' She raised her voice. 'Slow down, dear, you'll get dizzy – oh—'

With amusement Daniel watched her brush down Wendy's grazed knees. Gloria had got her way again.

The day Tricia's decree of divorce became absolute Gloria

held the inevitable party. The black-out drapes had been taken down and lights blazed from the windows of Holywell in celebration. Daniel wasn't there and Gloria was in full flood, drenched in jewellery and a lilac couturier dress, her lips carmine red and her hair a brilliant blonde: everyone *must* enjoy themselves and she wouldn't take no for an answer. A champagne glass and ebony cigarette holder in her left hand, the veteran hostess, her right hand free for shaking, attracting attention, squeezing arms and the cheeks of her especial friends. Except that there were no friends here, only trade acquaintances. And here was the remarkable thing. Here in the midst of all this, swept along, with hundreds of people around her, Gloria was lonely. She was as lonely as a little girl. Tricia was standing in the shadow of one of the tapestries, looking sad.

'Yer wearing a face as long as yer foot,' Gloria said. 'Yer mustn't let 'em see. Think of 'oo yer are. Circulate an' fer Gawd's sake smile.'

Tricia plastered a smile on her face. 'You're right, of course. It's just it doesn't feel as though it should be a celebration.'

'If we didn't keep smiling we'd be crying all the time. Yer well rid of 'im.'

'But Evelyn was rather dishy, after all. He had fantastic orgasms, it was a terrific compliment. And he was my husband.'

'Make yer own life,' Gloria said, grinning and raising her glass to someone passing by, the film star Kaye Francis, who was under contract to Gloria Fox for next year.

'You're right, of course,' Tricia said. 'You always are.

I've decided to revert to my maiden name. I won't be Tricia Sutton working for Gloria Fox.'

'Tricia Fox. Yer own name.' Gloria kissed her. 'The Company will be yers one day, yer know.'

Tricia shivered. 'I wish you wouldn't talk like that, Mummy. It sounds so proud.'

'I am proud, darlin'. Proud of yer.'

Gloria made her way through the crowd. Wendy, her five-year-old's face turned up adoringly, was dancing with Kaye who was playing down to her. 'She's exhausted me!' laughed the film star. Gloria took her granddaughter's hot hand. 'I like orange juice,' Wendy said, leading her to the table. The man who was helping himself from the Waterford jug, his white hair bound back in a queue, sensed the little figure beside him and looked down.

'An' who would ye be?'

'I am Miss Wendy Fox,' Wendy said, putting back her dark strands that had stuck to her forehead, 'and I live here. Who are you?'

'Hallo, Jamie,' Gloria said, holding out her hand. He still wore his wedding ring, and the lines in his face were deeper. 'Told yer. Looking great at sixty.'

'A touch more than that, mavourneen.' He poured a glass of orange for Wendy. 'Are ye well, Gloria?'

'Look at me an' despair.' He sipped his juice; they were not really talking.

'I see ye a fair deal around the place, that yellow limousine ye have, Gloria. The lads are doing a deal of rebuilding work in the City. Ye always look perfect.' He shook his head. 'I don't know how ye do it.'

'Oh, I keep a picture of myself in the loft, like Dorian Gray,' Gloria said, 'an' she gets older while I get younger.' She staggered slightly. 'Come on, Jamie, don't take me seriously!'

'Yer like me, staying young through yer children an' their children.'

''Ow is it wiv yer, really, Jamie?'

''Tis fine.'

'Letty's still the same?'

'How can she ever change?'

Gloria searched for something to say. 'I didn't even know yer were coming, me social secretary must've invited yer. Yer must be someone.'

'Always,' Jamie said. He saw straight through her jewellery to her bare neck.

The next morning Gloria sat at her dressing table putting on her face, the curtains closed because her room faced east, letting through no harsh light, only a soothing glow. She wore only a pink satin robe over her nightdress. Her fingers dabbed and smeared with the ease of long practice among the pots of creams and unguents that lay scattered in front of her on the glass top. Her maid was supposed to be warming the curling tongs. 'Not too 'ot,' Gloria called.

'It was the telephone, ma'am.'

'Wot?'

'The phone was ringing and I answered it, please, ma'am. It's Mr Fox on the line for you.'

'Bring it ter me,' Gloria said, 'an' don't forget those tongs.'

'No, ma'am.' The girl bobbed and carried the telephone from the bedside table on its long flex. Gloria put back her uncombed hair and listened.

Daniel was phoning from Jersey City, and he was slurred as though he'd been drinking. 'Good Gawd, Daniel,' she demanded, 'wot time is it there?' It must be after midnight. 'New Jersey hoshpidalidy,' came his voice.

'Jersey City bourbon, more like!' Gloria said. 'I thought yer were supposed ter be on yer way ter Venezuela by now?'

'Plane leaves id an hour, Glo. Gloria. I'm phoning from der airpord.'

'Well, for Gawd's sake get them ter pour yer on the plane. Are yer sure yer all right?'

'I'm coming down wid a cold, dat's all.'

'Yer'd better ask ter see a doctor.'

'Dere's always a dogdor on a plane,' came his voice. 'Id's a stadisdical cerdaindy.'

'Well, get 'im ter give yer somefink fer yer sinuses.'

'What? Don'd be angry wid me.'

'Sinuses, yer old fool!'

Daniel made a great effort to speak normally. 'I don't want your pity. Who do you think you are, who the hell do you think you are?'

Gloria pushed away the girl who was trying to curl her hair.

'Daniel, listen ter me. I fink yer very ill. Book into a hotel room an' get them ter send a doctor up ter yer. That's an order.'

Daniel didn't answer. He must have known something

was very wrong with him, but he couldn't admit it to her.

'I've never looked at another woman,' came his voice clearly. 'Only at you. You're woman all through, Gloria.' His voice struggled. 'More than I ever knew how to handle.' There was no more. The line clicked.

Gloria put the phone down. ''E's 'ad a premonition,' she said. ''E couldn't bring 'imself ter say goodbye.'

Daniel was out of touch all day; that was the worst thing. She stayed at home as though bad news couldn't come to find her here at Holywell. The telegraph boy brought two telegrams. One of them was from the Gloria Fox distributor in Venezuela, the other came through the Foreign Office from the British Embassy in Caracas.

Gloria called Tricia in.

'It's awful,' she said. 'I can't decide which ter open first.'

Daniel was dead. He had suffered a massive stroke on the plane and was dead on arrival.

Chapter Thirty-three

'This car is sunflower yellow,' Wendy said, swinging her legs off the seat. She spied the pull-down seat in the partition and sat on that, facing Gloria. She had her grandmother to herself and she was going to make the most of it.

Gloria put away her papers, regarding that level stare. 'Yes, it is. They 'ave big fields of sunflowers in France, yer see—'

'Have you really seen them or was it just books?'

'I flew over 'em in an airship once. There was hours of nuffink but sunflowers driftin' below.'

Wendy was impressed. 'You've done everything, haven't you, Gran?'

'It must seem like it to a girl as young as yer.'

Tricia had called through her bedroom door that she wasn't feeling well, so to give her a rest – it was the school holidays – as well as avoid the 'flu, Gloria was taking Wendy into the office for a change, riding in the back of the yellow limousine towards London. No harm in starting 'em off young, Gloria had thought. But Wendy was a vivid little creature, wearing her best dress in honour of her day out, endlessly curious. 'I should've taken yer ter Brighton beach,' Gloria grunted, 'yer like prying under stones so much.'

'You went there with Grandad, didn't you. I've seen the photos.'

'Yer Grandad and I went ter Brighton, my girl, fer more years than I care ter remember.'

'Why? Did you turn over stones?'

'No, that's one thing yer grandad an' I never did.' It was awful talking down about Daniel like this, *yer grandad*. Six months ago he had been alive and still mixing martinis. His embalmed body had been shipped back from Venezuela in a coffin; there had been a church service; now he was buried beneath six feet of good Vaudey soil in the churchyard of St John's. She had never even seen his body, only known it was there.

'Is my grandad happy now?'

'Yes, 'e's in 'eaven.'

'Even though he hasn't got you with him?'

Gloria stared at the traffic. She couldn't really get over the fact that Daniel wouldn't be at the office. Their partnership had lasted more than forty years; he was fixed in her brain. Every time the phone rang in the first few weeks, she thought it was him. The whole business of death was simply dreadful, it had never really touched her before – not since the death of her youngest brother ... for a ghastly moment Gloria could see the little boy clearly, stick-thin, even hear Jack's piping voice, 'Yer bin kissing!'

'Are you going to cry, Gran?'

'Not me, girl! Why should I?'

'I was looking at your face and it all screwed up like this.' Wendy demonstrated. 'Just for a second.'

'Don't make yourself ugly, yer might stay like it for ever.'

'I was trying to make you laugh. I expect people laugh in heaven all the time.'

'Well, I don't know about that.'

'They don't look very happy in the paintings,' agreed Wendy. 'There. You're not showing anything at all now. That's my gran. Everyone's frightened of you, aren't they?'

'Are yer?'

'No,' Wendy said sensibly, 'but I'm a child.'

They watched the traffic for a while, alone with their thoughts. 'Yer Mummy's not frightened of me,' Gloria prompted.

'Yes, she is.'

Gloria tried to explain. 'It's just that it's not easy. I 'ave ter fight an' fight all the time, see, an' I bring it 'ome sometimes, but I don't mean ter. Wot I do is very difficult.'

'What's that?'

'My job.'

'I think you enjoy it,' Wendy said unsympathetically. 'I suppose the traffic jams are the worst bit. It's all these buses.'

'Fer me work an' 'ome are the same fing, that's all. People want wot I got but I fight ter keep 'old of it, right?'

'What for?'

'Well, fer yer. One day, Wendy. In a long time, after yer Mummy, wot I've fought for will be yers. That's wot a family is about. An' yer'll 'old on to it, an' fight fer it, an' then fight ter build it, in yer turn.'

Goodness, Gloria realised, *we've just driven over the place where Fox's Pharmacy was!*

'Do I have to marry someone like old Grandad? I'd rather never get married,' Wendy confided, leaning forward over her knees, her eyes sparkling.

'He wasn't always old,' Gloria said.

'Boys are horrible,' said Wendy. 'I haven't got a daddy, you know. We're divorced.'

The car swept them across London Bridge and Gloria looked involuntarily to the right. Beyond Tower Bridge she glimpsed the derelict mess of St Katherine's dock, the rusty cranes around Prince Henry's Yard where Hugo Handley had shot himself. She could imagine him in his Aquascutum cloak as clearly as though he was standing beside the car, stroking his moustache with that look in his eye, and then his lips moved. *Do you really know yourself so little, Gloria? Do you not see how you affect people?*

'We're not going into the office today,' Gloria said. ''Ere, come an' sit beside me. I'll show yer some secrets wot nobody else knows.' She uncovered the speaking-tube. 'Go right.'

Her journey was bound to be a disappointment, of course, because you could never go back. Creeping along the backstreets of Billingsgate, an old woman peering from the window of a sunflower-yellow Rolls-Royce only made herself more distant from her past: Rodway's Coffee House, where Tragedy Tib had gulled her into buying two breakfasts, was long gone, she could not even identify the spot. Wendy yawned. Gloria directed the car to Piccadilly, through the intricate dance of taxis and buses, not a horse in sight; she was amazed that Savile Row was nothing but smart tailors' shops now, and a frowning Metropolitan Police headquarters rose where Willy Glizzard once kept his girls.

'There's a chip-shop!' begged Wendy as the car manoeuvred through the backstreets. She ate cheerily from the newspaper, glancing at her grandmother from time to time. Marylebone Station looked old and the glass was dirty, with a British Railways sign propped outside. Along Lisson Grove to the canal. Gloria stood on the bridge, looking down at the towpath where Jamie had kissed her.

She turned angrily as the newspaper rustled. 'That's enough of those chips,' she scolded furiously, 'yer'll turn into a fat pig!'

Wendy looked startled, then frightened.

'Oh, I'm sorry, luv.' Gloria bent down and embraced her. 'It's just that it's all gone.' She pointed. 'That's Wharncliffe Gardens.'

'It's a slum.'

'But it wasn't,' Gloria muttered. 'It *wasn't* like that.'

Wendy screwed up the paper and chucked it over the bridge. 'I don't like it here.' She tugged her grandmother's hand. 'Let's get back to the car.' She sat in silence.

'I didn't mean ter speak ter yer that way,' Gloria said. 'I don't know wot came over me, I'm sorry. I seem ter 'ave done a right royal job of frightening two generations now!' She smiled, asking forgiveness, but Wendy sulked. 'Yer can 'ave all the chips yer want, luv, 'course yer can, 'ow about that?'

Wendy mumbled in a very quiet voice: 'And Mummy's

frightened because she doesn't feel well.'

'That's nuffink ter be worried about, yer just call the doctor.'

'She did,' Wendy said. 'That's why she's frightened.'

'It's cancer,' Tricia said. 'Now you know.' She had been sitting in the shadows, but she stood up and threw the curtains wide. 'My beauty spot,' she said, twisting her face into a slant of sun so that Gloria saw the mole on her high cheekbone. 'Not quite so beautiful.'

'But yer too young ter 'ave cancer. Only old people get cancer.'

'Don't say that. Don't touch me.' Tricia wrapped her arms around herself. 'Don't commiserate. I can't stand it.'

'I'll get the best doctors. No reflection on yer, Dr Palin.'

'None taken,' murmured the doctor from the armchair at the foot of the bed, where Tricia usually threw her clothes.

'Take a deep breath, Mummy. A few weeks ago I banged it and it bled. I thought it was just a mole. But it kept bleeding, and it began to do this.' Again that twist of her face. 'Spread.'

'Melanoma,' said the doctor.

'Tell her,' Tricia said, not hiding the black stain.

'Miss Fox asked to be informed exactly,' said Doctor Palin apologetically. 'Some doctors call her condition grassfire melanoma, because it spreads so quickly. There is only one outcome.'

'Everyone dies,' Tricia said jerkily. 'But some die younger than others.'

'There's no doubt?' Gloria asked.

Palin crossed his legs.

'It'll take over my whole face,' Tricia said, 'but I'll be dead by then.'

Gloria tried to hold her but Tricia twisted away.

'Where's Wendy?' Gloria said. Tricia shrugged: with her nanny. 'Does Wendy know about this, Trish?'

Tricia screamed: 'Of course she doesn't know! She's much too young to understand this. What do you think I am?'

'We're going ter fight it,' Gloria said. 'Yer should never give up, never give up 'ope. Together we—'

'Six weeks,' Tricia said.

Doctor Palin stirred, crossing his legs the other way. At most.

'And it's going to hurt,' Tricia said.

'I can give her morphine.'

''Ang on a minute,' Gloria said, 'that's addictive, ain't it?'

'I'm afraid you don't quite understand. Towards the end I shall probably be giving her massive doses of heroin to help mask the pain . . .'

Gloria seized Tricia and hugged her with all her strength, whether she wanted it or not. Tricia struggled then collapsed against her mother. Both women wept.

'I'll come back later,' Doctor Palin said.

'I'm going to die,' Tricia whispered in Gloria's ear. 'You gave me life. It's over for me now.'

Gloria walked in her garden. The leaves were gone from the oaks. The swimming pool was empty, a crack ran across the fake Roman mosaic where the ground had subsided beneath and let the water out. Dry sea-gods and dolphins were poised between drifts of leaves. She turned and went back across the lawn towards the house. The windows held nothing but the sky.

She went inside, leaned back on the door. She wore her scarf and her overcoat, her hands deep in her pockets. 'Wendy?' she called across the hall.

Gloria looked in the playroom, the television room, the lounge, her study. The drinks cabinet was open. She closed it with hardly a sound.

Gloria went upstairs. The entrance to Tricia's bedroom was around two sides of the stairwell. Gloria went round, her footsteps muffled on the fine rugs.

She didn't knock.

The door opened under her hand.

She saw an empty bottle of whisky and an empty bottle of pills set neatly side by side on the bedside table, both with the caps replaced. Keep medicines out of reach of children. Tricia lay under the coverlet of the bed. She had taken her shoes off and her bare feet stuck out of the end, getting cold. Her eyes were wide open.

Wendy had crawled in beside her.

'I found her,' Wendy said. 'She's only sleeping.'

Gloria held out her hands and Wendy ran to her.

Epilogue

Wendy drove like the wind. Gloria sat beside her with her feet planted firmly on an imaginary brake, wishing she had her stick. But Wendy had been very bossy on that subject. 'You won't need that where you're going.' She'd helped Gloria down the steps of Holywell herself, the lights of London spread out from horizon to horizon below them, a map of orange streetlamps, some of the taller buildings picked out by red warning lights because of the aeroplanes, Gloria supposed. Where had all the smoke gone? The air was so clear. The parks were dark holes, and she could tell where St Paul's and Westminster were, partly because she knew the view so well, but also by their floodlit glow. The whole scene flickered and twinkled magically. But at the foot of the steps waited that little white car. 'Gran,' Wendy said warningly.

'I wasn't going ter say a fing.'

'It's a Mini.'

'Do yer ride in it, or on it?'

Wendy held open the door, not taking no for an answer. 'You promised.' She had been invited to a party, and tapped the invitation with a fingernail. 'It says "and friend".'

'That means young an' 'andsome,' Gloria said.

'Oh,' Wendy flicked her fingers, 'there'll be plenty of guys there.' She'd made up her mind. 'Don't put on your venerable old woman act, I know you too well. Don't worry, there won't be anything too wild.'

'Wot a shame! No Elvis?'

Wendy looked horrified. 'Oh, Gran! He's right back there with Cliff Richard.'

'The parties I've been ter. I danced with Rudolf Valentino.'

'Yes, I know. And Fred Astaire.' Wendy covered her smile politely.

Gloria gave in. 'Yer party too much. I wish yer'd get married.'

'That's old hat,' Wendy said firmly.

'I dunno 'ow yer tell wot sex they are anyway, wot wiv all that long 'air.'

Wendy laughed, knowing she had won. 'This from a woman who markets a new range of colours called John, Paul, George & Ringo!'

'They're not new shades,' Gloria sniffed, 'it's the same old stuff tarted up in new packets. The parties I could tell you about. In the 'twenties we—'

'But you can't bring that awful stick,' Wendy said. 'Absolutely not.'

Gloria sat in the little car. She was dressed to the nines and felt ridiculous turning up in Belgravia like this. 'Relax,' Wendy assured her. 'Everyone's seen in a Mini, it's gear.'

By the streetlights flashing overhead Gloria looked at Wendy, who was wearing fashionable gosh! eyelashes with Pearl Mist mascara and lipstick, a Mary Quant hairstyle. The Talent she had taken from her mother's hand swung like a cheap bangle between her breasts. Her skirt was so short it showed her knickers when she changed gear.

'It's the boys I feel sorry for,' Gloria commented. 'There's no mystery left.'

'Who needs it?' Wendy said, taking a sharp left and slipping into a tiny parking space. 'Wendy Fox,' she gave her name to the orang-utang on the door. 'It's hot in here,' said the orang-utang in a muffled voice, 'this thing's got fleas.'

'You see him at all the parties,' Wendy said, drawing Gloria inside. She wriggled her hips to the music, knowing everyone. Gloria found her way to a seat by the wall and sat, relieved that she was not the only person over thirty here, there were a few mums and dads pretending to be young. The youngsters held the dancefloor, mop-top haircuts and jackets without lapels. Several came over and talked, shouting over the music. As their number grew Gloria began to enjoy herself. She was famous. Somebody brought her Coca-Cola in a can but she insisted on a glass. Soon she was holding court to a semi-circle of youthful admirers, and she was in full flood, the life and soul of the party.

Sadness filled Gloria. She didn't know their names, but these young people would be alive at the end of the century, and she would be dead. Her time was past. She was as cruelly aware of her age as though a spotlight had fallen on her.

Gloria smiled her smile. She laughed and joked as though she was brimming with happiness, but she was dying to go home. One young man she had never met seemed to know her, but she couldn't think who he was, which amused him. He wore his long black hair back in a queue.

'That's James,' obliged the woman sitting next to Gloria. 'It's his party.'

Gloria could not make out what had happened to her, it felt as though time was slipping, her memories of the past mixed up with the present. 'Wot? That's never Jamie Reilly.'

'I do assure you, it is! He's making quite a name for himself in the fashion business, and sometimes borrows his grandfather's house to throw these parties. The old man doesn't care about anything since his wife died, they say.'

Gloria looked sharply at Wendy, who flashed her bangles as she danced.

A stooped, kindly figure appeared amid the crowd. His hair was white. When he saw Gloria he almost stopped, then held out his hands.

Gloria walked to him.

'Everyone knew,' Jamie Reilly said, holding her fingers, 'except ye an' me. 'Twas a conspiracy of the young people to bring ye here. There are no secrets from children.'

But no one was thinking about them now, the dancers jostled around them, as bound up in themselves as Jamie and Gloria. 'We lost our lives,' Jamie said. 'We lost our lives.' He chuckled, and she saw nothing had changed in his eyes.

Gloria pushed her hands into his. 'Wivout yer.'

'D'ye have the courage this time, mavourneen?'

'That's up ter yer, Jamie.'

He gripped her tight. 'Never letting ye go.'

The music changed and they danced.

'Years ago I saw thy neck was bare of the only thing that matters between us,' Jamie whispered fiercely, and she felt how angry he was, still full of pain. 'I knew ye were saying 'twas finished between ye an' me. I've abided by that. But it came from my mother to me, an' is my priceless gift to ye, Gloria. 'Twas not thine to give away to thy daughter, Tricia.'

'Are yer angry?'

'Aye, still.' He nodded at Wendy. 'That ye should allow what I feel for ye to be passed on between whosoever pleases, like a relic. It was mine, and thine. But what did it mean to ye? Not much, it seems.'

'Love. That's all it is, Jamie.'

'Sure,' he said dismissively, 'she's a fine an' pretty girl.'

'Yer don't understand. It's more than my gift to 'er. It was yers too, Jamie.'

'Ye're right,' he said, 'I don't understand.'

'She is yer grand-daughter.'

Jamie stopped.

Gloria kissed his lips. 'Always,' she said.